LOST BIRDS

ALSO BY ANNE HILLERMAN

The Way of the Bear

The Sacred Bridge

Stargazer

The Tale Teller

Cave of Bones

Song of the Lion

Rock with Wings

Spider Woman's Daughter

Tony Hillerman's Landscape: On the Road with Chee and Leaphorn

Gardens of Santa Fe

Santa Fe Flavors: Best Restaurants and Recipes

Ride the Wind: USA to Africa

LOST BIRDS

A Leaphorn, Chee & Manuelito Novel

ANNE HILLERMAN

HARPER

An Imprint of HarperCollinsPublishers

LOST BIRDS. Copyright © 2024 by Anne Hillerman. All rights reserved. Printed in the United States of America. No part of this book may be used or reproduced in any manner whatsoever without written permission except in the case of brief quotations embodied in critical articles and reviews. For information, address HarperCollins Publishers, 195 Broadway, New York, NY 10007.

HarperCollins books may be purchased for educational, business, or sales promotional use. For information, please email the Special Markets Department at SPsales@harpercollins.com.

FIRST EDITION

Library of Congress Cataloging-in-Publication Data has been applied for.

ISBN 978-0-06-334478-5

24 25 26 27 28 LBC 5 4 3 2 1

To Dave Tedlock

LOST BIRDS

1

Joe Leaphorn awoke a little past 7:00 a.m. to a steady, irritating noise. He rolled over, pressed the pillow against his ears, and tried to ignore it.

A moment later, he realized the unceasing beat came from his home phone, a phone that, thanks to cell phones, hardly ever rang. He wondered if it had also awakened his housemate Louisa, who he hoped was dreaming in the other bedroom.

Unable to dismiss the irritation, he sat up, reached for his bathrobe, and trotted to the kitchen, where the phone hung on the wall. He answered the call, feeling stiff, tired, and grumpy. What an unfortunate way to start a Saturday.

The male voice on the other end of the line sounded nervous.

"Lieutenant Leaphorn, this is Cecil Bowlegs. Remember me? I'm glad I was finally able to get in touch with you."

Among his growing list of pet peeves, Leaphorn had an asterisk on any question that started with "remember."

The man on the phone didn't wait for Leaphorn to say, "No, I don't remember you."

"I understand that you are a private investigator. That's why I'm contacting you now. I need some help."

"First tell me how I know you." Leaphorn wondered how his number, the number he never gave out except to friends and fellow officers, had gotten into this Cecil person's hands.

"We met a long time ago, sir, when I was just a boy. You worked a case that involved my older brother, George Bowlegs. Years ago, when George ran away, you were kind to me. You gave me your card, and you wrote this number on the back." He paused. "I tried the station number first, and they told me you had retired, but that you sometimes helped people with investigations."

"Why are you calling now, though? It's too early. Make it quick."

"My wife is missing. She been missing for almost three weeks. We've looked for her, got the police involved. They seem to have given up on our case." He rattled off her age, height, weight, and the fact that she had a blue eagle tattoo on her left wrist. "I called you because I don't know what else to do. Because you found my brother, I thought . . ."

Leaphorn heard the man on the phone exhale. He was full of questions, but knew it was better to wait until Cecil had said his piece.

"Sir, back then, you made sure I was safe. I need to make sure my wife is safe, or . . ." The words, which had come in a rush, slowed to a stop.

Leaphorn felt instantly wide awake. "You said your name is Bowlegs?"

"Yes, sir. Cecil Bowlegs. I hope you'll help me."

"This was Zuni, right? Shalako?" Leaphorn remembered the frigid weather and the warmth of the people who lived in the pueblo. He recalled the night-long chanting and drumming, the appearances of the dancers in the sacred costumes, and the soul-stirring ceremony.

"Well, Zuni is where you discovered George's body. My dad and I lived closer to Ramah. When he died, you helped me get a fresh start. You cared about me and my brother. I never forgot your kindness or how smart you were."

With the prompts, Leaphorn clearly recalled the tragic case, one of the first in his long career. He remembered finding the murdered boy as vividly as if it had happened yesterday. He had looked evil in the eye, and neither evil nor Leaphorn had blinked.

"Why did you wait three weeks to call me at the crack of dawn on a Saturday?"

"The three weeks? That's a long story. But I called you so early today because I've got to get to work, and I figured you'd be home now."

Leaphorn remembered Cecil as a shy, quiet child, a boy small for his age. His heart opened. "OK. Let's make an appointment, and you can tell me about your wife. I'll see if there's something I can do for you."

"So you'll take the case?"

"Yes."

"Thank you. Can I meet you somewhere this afternoon?"

"You'll have to come to Window Rock."

"I can do that after work. I'm the custodian here at Eagle Roost School, so maybe around three or—"

He was cut off by the intense noise of an explosion. The blast was loud, and it took several moments for Leaphorn to regain his composure and for the ringing in his ears to calm down.

"Cecil? Cecil? You OK?"

Silence answered.

"Cecil!"

If Cecil had called Leaphorn's cell phone, Leaphorn could have quickly redialed, but without much to go on, Leaphorn had to use the few clues the man had given him. Cecil hadn't said where he was when he made the call, but Leaphorn knew that Eagle Roost School was on the reservation, so he called the Navajo Police in Window Rock, his old home station, and left a message. Then he hurried down the hall to his office to look for his contact with the New Mexico State Police in Gallup. Giddi, their rescue cat, had been sleeping in the office chair, but she stood when Leaphorn entered and removed his cell phone from the charger. The cat, as cats are prone to do, decided that Leaphorn's unexpected arrival meant it must be time to eat. She started meowing and ramped up the sound when he ignored her.

Leaphorn hadn't talked to Captain Roger Martinez for a long time, but found his number. He hoped Martinez still worked with NMSP and, more to the point, that he would be on the job this Saturday morning.

Luck was with him. Martinez answered. Leaphorn bypassed chitchat and got to the point.

"An explosion?" Martinez sounded a bit older, but still plenty sharp. "Tell me more."

"That's what it sounded like. Bowlegs said he works at Eagle Roost. The school is on the Navajo Nation, but just barely. I figure that's where he could have been when he made the call. That's New Mexico, so it's your jurisdiction."

"That's right. I'll have someone check on it. Don't hang up." The phone went dead for a few moments, then Martinez was back. "How the hell are you, anyway, Joe? How's the PI business?"

Leaphorn hated small talk, especially over the phone, but he knew it helped grow relationships. "All good. How 'bout you?"

"No use complaining. Or bragging."

Leaphorn short-circuited the rest of what could have been a rambling conversation. "I've gotta run. I'm on a deadline on another case. Good luck with the explosion. Would you let me know about Bowlegs?"

"Sure. So you're working on Saturday, just like the old days." Martinez chuckled. "Call us if you hear anything else from Bowlegs, OK? And thanks for the tip."

Leaphorn headed to the kitchen with the cat at his heels. He told himself that after he'd made the coffee, fed Giddi, and given his nerves time to settle, he would set worry about Cecil Bowlegs aside and get to work. He had accepted a complicated case he should have said no to—an adopted woman's quest for her biological family, relatives she believed could be Navajo.

He started the coffeepot, his morning ritual, and added cream and sugar to Louisa's empty cup, a mug emblazoned with the Northern Arizona Lumberjack logo, while he waited for the magic morning elixir to brew. The logo reminded him that as eager as she was to get back to her research, Louisa missed teaching and the warm interaction she'd had with the students on the Flagstaff campus. He poured the fresh coffee, took it down the hall, and knocked on her door.

"Come in, come in. I'm awake, and I've been smelling that coffee." Louisa was sitting up in bed in her green nightgown. "I had a restless night. Travel always does that to me. Too many time zones. How about you?"

"I'm OK." He sat her mug on her nightstand. "I hope that phone call didn't wake you."

"What call?" She smiled at him. "I heard you chattering in there. I thought you must be talking in your sleep."

"Do I do that?"

"You do."

He felt the worry on his face.

"But don't fret about it. You're always talking in Navajo, and I'm not good enough yet to decipher what you're mumbling." She sipped the coffee and put the mug down so the logo faced her. "What was the call about?"

He shrugged. "Someone wanted to hire me as PI." He could tell she wanted more, but he didn't feel like talking.

"Wanted to hire you, eh? And you told him you had retired so you could travel more with me, right?"

"No. We got disconnected. Stay tuned."

She grabbed her coffee again. "This is good. Is it the Kona we brought from Hawaii?"

"Yes." He smiled at her.

The trip he and Louisa had taken combined sightseeing with a series of interviews for her research on parallels in beliefs about spirituality among different indigenous people. They had arrived back in New Mexico well after midnight the night before. Flying from Oahu to Albuquerque took about nine and a half hours. Added to that was the time needed to walk through the terminal to the baggage claim, get the shuttle to Louisa's car, and leave the airport for Interstate 40. Then came the three-hour drive from Albuquerque, the closest major airport to their home in Window Rock, Arizona.

Their home. He thought about that pronoun again. The idea comforted him. He was happy to be home, back in the high desert where his roots had grown deep. He counted his blessings. Most widowers his age lacked the energizing touch of female companionship unless the woman was a daughter or a sister. He had neither, but Louisa's warm presence kept him sane and made him happy.

He worked for an hour, and then they shared a breakfast of Louisa's special oatmeal. He washed dishes and retreated down the hall to his office to get back to a case he had set aside during his vacation. He'd promised the client a report, and the clock was ticking. Bowlegs had done him a favor by hustling him out of bed.

He pulled up the case file on his computer and then extracted the associated photos and other documentation that wasn't digital from his desk drawer. He spread the photos and papers on the desktop in front of him. Stella Brown had contacted him after she had exhausted all the obvious steps for finding her biological family. His client looked like an artist's rendition of the classic Navajo woman—silky hair as dark as a raven's wing, large, clear russet eyes, skin the color of light milk chocolate, and a tall, slim frame. She told him her third-grade teacher had called her "our special little Indian." She had always known that her parents had adopted her and that a lawyer had handled the arrangements. They said she was their chosen daughter, and that they loved her from the moment they saw her.

"My dad was in construction and traveled a lot for work. My mom was a teacher. I went to ten schools before I graduated from high school. Life was an adventure then." Leaphorn remembered the pride in her voice as she'd explained her early life. Stella had lived in Albuquerque for a few years and then, moving when her father got new jobs, in various communities in New Mexico and Arizona.

"Did you know any of your parents' relatives?" Leaphorn remembered asking her. He understood that adults sometimes shared information about their sons and daughters with each other, stories they might not reveal to the children themselves.

"No. I talked to my parents about that, and they both said they came from small families and that their own parents were dead. Now that you're asking, I guess that was another odd thing about my situation."

Her parents had divorced a few years after her graduation from high school, and she and her father lost track of each other. Her mother told her he had died about ten years before in Phoenix. When her mother passed away last year in Farmington, Stella had found a little box among her possessions. Inside was an envelope with "For Stella" in her mother's swooping handwriting on the front. She opened it to find a letter from her mother, saying how much she and her father loved her, an old photograph, and a small silver and turquoise bracelet. She had carefully shown Leaphorn the bracelet and given him a copy of the picture when they met a month before.

The snapshot showed a Navajo couple, a young man in blue jeans and a battered cowboy hat standing next to a shorter woman wearing the traditional Navajo long skirt and velvet blouse. She looked to be about sixteen or twenty at most, and held something wrapped in a blanket. From the man's posture and the way the woman's arms cradled the bundle, Leaphorn assumed there was a baby in the blanket.

He studied the picture again as he considered the case.

"Was there anything written on the back of that picture?"

"Just numbers. No note." She exhaled. "The numbers were the year I was born."

"Was there anything else in the envelope?"

"Nothing." She stopped and composed herself. "I don't know for sure that this is a photograph of me, or my biological parents." He remembered her frown when she said it.

When she didn't seem to have anything more to add to the story, Leaphorn had asked about DNA. "Have you considered submitting a sample to a couple of ancestry search websites? I'm no expert on DNA, but I know people who have found relatives that way."

"That's a last resort. I want to see what you come up with first." She emphasized the *you*. "Yes, I've thought about it, but I'm not ready to deal with third cousins or long-lost phony half sisters or whatever. And I know the Navajo creation story. DNA contradicts that, you know, saying that Navajos came from Asia. All I want is to find out about my Navajo relatives and, you know, feel like there's someplace I belong and that I'm not an island on my own."

He nodded. He knew that the Navajo Nation had recently opened an oncology center in Tuba City with genetic testing for cancer as one of its services. And even though he was not a man who took tradition literally, he respected those who, like Christian fundamentalists, viewed the Hajíínéí, the Navajo origin story, as poetic truth.

"OK. No DNA for now, but it would save me time and you money. I encourage you to keep that option open."

She gave him a hint of a smile. "I'll consider it if you recommend it and if and when your research comes up short. I hope it won't. How long do you think it will take you to find my relatives?"

"I don't know."

She leaned toward him. "Please work quickly. If I have any relatives around my mother's age, they aren't getting any younger, you understand? And I leave for a huge job in Thailand at the end of the month, and I won't be back in the States for two years."

Leaphorn understood her urgency, but he also understood the need for building rapport with people who might know the secret of Stella's birth. And that wouldn't happen quickly. "I cannot promise you anything at this point except that I'll give you a progress report in two weeks."

By then, or even before that, Leaphorn expected to learn something about Stella's origins, or acknowledge that her quest was hopeless without DNA. He had spent a bit of time on this case before he and Louisa went to Hawaii, confident that he would find the woman's adoption records, but he had discovered only frustration. Now he had only a day to do more research before his self-imposed deadline.

He was pondering what came next in his quest when Louisa rapped on his office door.

"Joe, there's someone here to talk to you. A detective from the New Mexico State Police."

The officer on the front porch showed him her official department identification: Sergeant Mona Short. She was as tall as he was, with shoulder-length light brown hair gathered into a ponytail. She looked fit, appropriately serious in her black uniform, and nervous.

She apologized for bothering him. "I understand you had a call from Cecil Bowlegs this morning. The captain thought that because I'm working on a case that also might involve Bowlegs, I ought to come out here and meet you."

He said nothing, waiting for her to elaborate. The detective only grew more nervous. She was younger than he'd been when he first made detective, Leaphorn realized. Younger and thrown off-balance by having to work with someone old enough to be her grandfather.

Short cleared her throat. "Sir, Captain Martinez gave me your address and told me to follow up on this case in person. Otherwise, I would have just called you. I mean, later in the day rather than intrude."

"It's not a problem, Detective. Please come on in." He held the door for her and began to motion her toward the couch, then remembered that his housemate was working on her notes from Hawaii at the kitchen table nearby. "Let's talk in my office so we won't disturb Louisa."

"Of course."

Short followed him down the hall, where he waved her to the chair across from his desk.

"Sir, I'd like to hear about the conversation you had with Cecil Bowlegs. Please tell me everything, no matter how insignificant it seems."

"And then you'll answer my questions, won't you?" Not waiting for her response, he repeated everything that Bowlegs had said. The conversation had been short, so the replay didn't take long.

"I was wondering about Bowlegs's tone of voice on that call to you." Leaphorn remembered. "He sounded nervous. He spoke fast."

"Faster than usual?"

A good question, he thought. "I don't know. I haven't spoken to him since he was a boy."

He saw the surprise on the detective's face. "I met him decades ago on a case that involved his brother. He was about eight years old then."

"You mentioned that Cecil was concerned about this missing wife. Can you please tell me more about that part of the conversation?"

"There's nothing more to tell." But Leaphorn reiterated what he had said earlier, including Bowlegs's frustration at the lack of progress on the case. "Who's in charge of missing person investigations for the New Mexico State Police?"

She gave the name of a person he'd never met. "Our office here in Gallup is very involved with the epidemic of missing indigenous women and men, working closely with Navajo law enforcement and everyone else who can help. There is a Bethany Benally Bowlegs on our list. Unusual name for a Navajo. The officer handling that case could give you an update on the progress. Or I could ask him and call you when I get back to the office."

Leaphorn nodded. "With such an unusual last name for this part of the world, I believe that must be her. Is there anything else you'd like to ask me?"

"No, sir. I appreciate your time." Short straightened in the chair, preparing to stand and leave.

Instead, Leaphorn motioned her to stay put. "Detective, I have a few questions for you. But first, I could use some more coffee. Would you like a cup?"

She shook her head. "No thank you, sir. I've had more than enough this morning, but a glass of water would be great if you don't mind."

He got her water, filled his cup with what was left in the coffeepot, and placed it in the microwave, glad to have a few quick seconds to think about the day's developments. It had surprised him to learn that Bowlegs was on her radar.

Short set her phone down when he returned and sipped the water while he settled into the chair across from her.

"What happened to Bowlegs?" Leaphorn asked. "Is he alive?"

"I don't know." She pressed her lips together. "If Captain Martinez knows by now, he didn't share that."

"I found it exceptionally odd that a man I hadn't had contact with for more than forty years would seek me out and ask for my help. Whatever prompted him to be worried about his missing wife must have been seriously concerning. And your arrival here is an odd surprise, too. Tell me, why is Cecil Bowlegs of enough interest to the captain that he sends you in person?"

She leaned toward him. "The captain thinks there could be a connection between the explosion, Bowlegs, the missing woman, and another case we're working. He explained that you were a retired lieutenant and had worked as a police detective for, well, a long time. He said you were a legend, sir, and he said it might be easier to persuade you to share information with me if we met face-to-face."

"You and the captain had Cecil Bowlegs on the radar before this."

"Yes sir, that's right. His wife is a person of interest in another investigation. We were ready to question her when she disappeared. I haven't dealt with many cases like this, and I'd appreciate whatever help you can offer me."

Leaphorn sipped the coffee and thought about what Short had said.

He appreciated her humility in respectfully asking for his help, and he admired Captain Martinez. Beyond that, the case interested him.

"You know, Sergeant, Martinez and I go back a ways. He thought of involving me because I called him about the explosion. The fact that he sent you here has nothing to do with your competence. He knows I've worked on lots of complicated cases, that's all."

Detective Short reacted to the comment by relaxing a bit, giving at least the illusion that she felt more at ease. Leaphorn wasn't one hundred percent sure he believed what he had just said, but he had no solid evidence to the contrary, just his long years of working with people to diffuse awkward situations.

"So here's another question for you, Detective. What was the explosion I heard over the phone?"

"I don't know, sir. All I can tell you is that a Navajo officer was a first responder, and a fire unit is probably there now. An NMSP explosive expert is headed out, too. Any more questions for me?"

He shook his head. "Thank you for the information and for your frankness."

She gave him a card with her cell number. He walked with her to the door, said goodbye, and then sat down to think.

A few moments later Louisa came into the living room and joined him on the couch.

"Joe, you don't look happy."

"I'm not. I don't like the way this day has started. Too much confusion."

"Well, here are two more pleasant things to consider. Remember how you struggled to speak English after the head injury? Now you're more fluent than ever."

He nodded.

"The second happy thought is that my son is coming to visit this week."

"Really?" Leaphorn had rarely heard her mention the man, and when he'd asked about Kory, she had frowned and answered in generalities, so he'd put the questioning aside.

Louisa smiled. "Finally. I haven't seen him since he was in Gallup about five years ago on business. I met Kory there, and we hiked the Church Rock Trail. We both loved that! He has some business in Flagstaff this time, some engineering consultation, and he plans to drive here afterward. He emailed me a month ago that this might happen, but I didn't take it seriously."

"I'm glad he's coming." Leaphorn knew it was close to a three-hour drive on the interstate to Window Rock from Flagstaff.

"It's been a long time. Too long. And this is a good time for a visit. He shouldn't have to worry about the weather." Early spring could bring wet snow as well as wind to their part of the Navajo Nation.

"That's right. Nothing but clear and warmer days in the forecast. Does he know what day he'll be here?"

"He might, but he hasn't told me. Communication was never Kory's strong suit. That's one of the irritations between us." Louisa readjusted her back on the couch and changed the subject. "So, what happened to bring the State Police to our door?"

Leaphorn gave her the story. "What do you think? Should I volunteer to work with Sergeant Mona Short?"

"I think that detective would be wise to use your expertise here, but it will be a distraction from that adoption case you're working on. I know you're already pressuring yourself to find some answers for the woman who hired you—you don't need more aggravation. And not only that. The other situation involves an explosion as well as a missing woman and a suspicious husband. It could be dangerous. I worry about you, Joe."

"You're a natural worrier."

She smiled. "I know it. I'm worried about what happened to Mr. Bowlegs. Is he Navajo?"

Leaphorn nodded.

"Funny, that's a Seminole name. Did you ever hear of Chief Billy Bowlegs?"

He shook his head and waited for her to tell him the story.

"Billy Bowlegs was a leader of the Seminoles in the mid-nineteenth century. The army couldn't stop his warriors' sporadic attacks against Florida settlers, so the government offered him ten thousand dollars—a fortune in the 1850s—to move to Indian Territory, in what's now Oklahoma. Bowlegs became a leader there, too. He even served as a captain in the Union Army during the Civil War. He fought on the Union side, even though he owned about twenty enslaved people himself."

"You're full of information."

She gave him a gentle look. "What is it that you don't want to talk about?"

He refilled his cup and replaced the pot. "Well, on that first call I got this morning, when Cecil Bowlegs said his name, I didn't remember it, and I didn't remember him. It took me a while to conjure it up. I finally figured out who he was when he gave me another hint and mentioned Zuni. It bothers me. That happens more and more often."

"That happens to me, too." Louisa put her hand on top of his. "It goes with the territory."

"Yeah. Old age is a different country, that's for sure." He finished his coffee and rose, taking note of the time.

"Gotta go. I told Largo I'd meet him at the Navajo Inn. You know, our standing coffee date. We'll be quick this morning. I have to get back to the adoption case."

"They ought to reserve a table for you two every Saturday. Tell him hey for me."

2

Captain Howard Largo had recently retired from the Navajo Police. After spending some months enjoying afternoon naps and fixing things that needed fixing, he had grown bored and restless. Leaphorn had assigned himself the job of helping Largo determine what came next.

Unlike his friend, Leaphorn had bypassed that itchy stage of retirement because he almost immediately began receiving requests to look into cases and situations as a private investigator. Luck, or perhaps the residue of his late wife's belief in the Christian God, had served him well. The work sustained him through his grief.

He noticed that Largo had claimed their usual table, but coffee hadn't yet arrived. Good, Leaphorn thought. He hated to be late. The server, a young Navajo woman wearing silver and coral earrings, gave him a moment to settle in and then brought menus and the coffeepot. Her name tag read Debi Jo.

"Gentlemen, we have a special for breakfast. Shall I tell you about it?"

Leaphorn waved her question away. "Just coffee for me."

Largo shook his head. "I'll try the two-egg breakfast. With bacon. White toast."

"And you want the bacon crisp and the eggs over medium."

"Right. How do you know?"

The young woman smiled. "I waited on you last Saturday, and you ordered the same thing."

Leaphorn looked up at her. "What did I have?"

"Black coffee and a Western omelet with whole wheat."

"Do you remember everyone's order?"

Debi Jo didn't miss a beat. "Yes, sir. It sure helps with the job. I'll bring you the coffees and some water."

Largo chuckled after she left. "I forgot to order coffee, and she remembered it for me. And we both always ask for water."

Their conversation flowed smoothly. Leaphorn mentioned that Louisa's son was coming to see her.

"I didn't know she had a son."

"I haven't met him. She doesn't talk about him much. He's in some kind of high-tech business. Lives in California. She's excited about the visit." After Debi Jo brought Largo's food and more coffee, Leaphorn launched into the story of Cecil Bowlegs's call that morning.

Largo listened with greater-than-average attention and then put his fork down. "You heard something blowing up, and that's it for the dude?"

"Well, for the conversation at least. He never called back."

"Did you call the school?"

"No. It was early Saturday morning. I didn't think anyone would be there."

"Eagle Roost? Is that near Sheep Springs?"

"It's between Shiprock and Gallup. On the New Mexico part of the reservation."

They talked about the increasing number of school shootings. Largo had heard that a student tried to bring a rifle to the Crownpoint high school. The young man claimed he wanted to show it to a friend, and the weapon wasn't loaded. The parents and school officials reacted appropriately and then checked it off to youthful inexperience, but the incident had raised concern in the police department.

The conversation turned to Largo's restlessness. He'd spent some time with a nephew, one of his sisters' sons, helping with home repair projects. He hadn't enjoyed it very much.

"This retirement stuff is not what I expected. I don't miss the meetings, the budget stuff, but I need something else now."

"If I come up with a case where I need some help, what would you say?"

Largo shrugged. "Ask me then, and I'll let you know." His hands restlessly rearranged his coffee cup on the table, the salt and pepper shakers, his plate and silverware.

Debi Jo brought the bill, thanked them, and encouraged them to come back. Largo reached for his wallet.

"I'll get this." Leaphorn drained the last of his coffee and put a twenty on the table. "I did all the talking this morning."

"I don't have much to say these days."

Leaphorn's next stop, the Navajo Nation Police headquarters, always stirred memories of his long career as a detective. He noticed more police units leaving the lot than usual, and wondered what was going on.

Rebecca Taylor, a young woman whom Leaphorn had befriended, was at the front desk and looked up when he approached.

"Yá'át'ééh."

"Ya'at'ééh. Lieutenant, where's your surfer shirt?"

"I almost got one with palm trees, but it made me look fat." The way news spread on the Navajo Nation never ceased to amaze him. The recent trip he'd made with Louisa to Hawaii as part of her ongoing interest in commonalities between indigenous religions had fueled the buzz mill.

Rebecca nodded. "What can I help you with today, sir?"

"I've been asked to help find a missing woman. Her husband told me the police hadn't had come up with anything."

"I can check."

Leaphorn spelled out the name, and she focused on her computer. "Here it is."

He watched sleek red fingernails tap the keys.

"Hold on a minute." She stopped typing and walked across the room to the printer. "Here's a copy of the report and a flyer with photos of Bethany Benally Bowlegs. She's the only missing woman in our files with that last name, so I figure she's the one. You can sit over there if you'd like while you read it. Or just take it with you."

Leaphorn looked at what she'd given him. Mrs. Benally Bowlegs was attractive and probably younger than her husband. He noticed a ring on her left hand. The number listed on the poster to call with information was the Window Rock police headquarters. Smart. Unfortunately, some families put their personal numbers on the posters, which led to more heartache when they were called with false leads or approached by phony psychics who could help if they paid in advance.

The report showed that the substation had no sightings of the woman and, other than the husband and a clan brother, no inquiries about her. The follow-up showed no reports of unclaimed bodies that matched her description, and no reports of a Mrs. Bowlegs being arrested.

He rose to leave and thanked her.

"My pleasure, sir. How's Louisa?"

"Fine." He paused. "Do you know her?"

She nodded. "A lot of us came to know her when you got shot a few years ago. We'd call to see how you were doing, you know? Your recovery. She seems really solid."

"She is." Leaphorn studied the poster, uncomfortable with the personal turn the conversation was taking. "Do you know who handled the case when this woman was reported missing?"

"I can find out." She clicked a few keys on her computer. "Sergeant Stanley had the case. Eagle Roost is his territory. That's Sergeant Fredrick Stanley."

Leaphorn pulled out his little notebook and jotted it down. The name wasn't familiar to him, but that was no surprise. Personnel change came with the territory.

"Anything else I can help you with?"

"I'll call the station number, but give me Sergeant Stanley's cell number, too." Leaphorn had learned that telling often worked better than asking.

She tapped some keys and then read the number to him. "Is it OK to give him yours?"

"Sure."

"Lieutenant, I can print a few more of those missing person posters for you if you'd like to put them up somewhere."

"I'll just take this one."

He walked down the hall toward the exit, getting a few odd looks from people he didn't recognize and fewer nods from people who remembered him from the old days or who had worked with him more recently on one of his private cases. He left the building, zipped his coat, walked to his truck, and called Sergeant Stanley, first at the station and then on his cell.

Stanley sounded busy and slightly annoyed. Leaphorn explained who he was and asked about Mrs. Bowlegs.

"Bethany Benally Bowlegs. No new information on her. So, Bowlegs is hiring some help, is he?"

Leaphorn told Stanley about the call and its ending.

"We got a call about an explosion at the school earlier this morning. The fire crew is out there now. Cecil must have been close if you heard it that loudly. He hasn't checked in about Bethany today. He and RP call for updates several times a week. I hope he wasn't hurt in the blast."

"Who is RP?"

"Cecil's sort of brother-in-law. RP is a clan brother of Mrs. Bowlegs."

"It sounds like you know Cecil. Is that right?"

"He's an acquaintance. I'll stop by later today just to make sure he's OK. His place is on my way home."

"So, do you know Mrs. Bowlegs?"

"Everyone out here knows everyone. Beth Bowlegs works at the school, teaches music, and sings with a band. Nice lady. It bugs me that her husband thinks I'd get a lead and not share it with them."

"If you see him, tell Bowlegs that I asked you what happened to him. Ask him to call me."

Stanley's voice had an edge of irritation. "I'm going to be really busy with this explosion. I noticed the fire chief heading out a while ago. Gotta go."

"Thanks. Good luck."

Leaphorn moved Bowlegs to his mind's storage closet and thought about the work for Stella Brown that awaited him when he arrived home. Stella had a laser focus on the task of finding her Navajo relatives. He understood and wanted to do his part in either making her quest successful or putting her questions to rest. Too bad she didn't have much for him to go on.

He'd give it his best, he told himself. That was all she could expect.

3

Officer Bernadette Manuelito glanced out the window of her unit at the gray day. The clouds clung to the Chuska Mountains like a scarf, and the air was heavy with the welcome promise of moisture. It had been a dry winter heading into a drier spring. In her experience, drought made people restless and worried. She was restless, too.

Captain Texas Adakai had recently accepted the assignment as acting head of the Shiprock Navajo Police substation until a permanent replacement for Captain Largo could be named. The officers and civilians who worked at the substation missed Captain Largo, their longtime leader, a smart, kind man who understood crime, those who went astray, and those with the job of keeping safe the families of the Navajo world.

Adakai, who had served in the marines, was much younger and, Bernie quickly realized, full of ambition. He had grown up off the reservation with a mother from Turkey and a Navajo father who had been stationed at an army radar base there. Inspired by his dad, Adakai had joined military service, too. Although they never said it directly, the staff and officers of the Shiprock substation believed that the new captain had some things to learn in order to translate his military experience into the day-to-day operations at Shiprock.

To his credit, Adakai had given Bernie's husband, Lieutenant Jim Chee, a big assignment that kept him busy and allowed him to use his skills in dealing with people—in this case, other officers. Bernie missed the smart, fair ways of Captain Largo, though, and had some feelers out for other jobs in law enforcement. But for the time being, she appreciated the security of a job she knew well. Dealing with her mother's slow but steady decline and getting herself back into a state of harmony after the recent loss of her pregnancy was all she wanted to handle.

Sandra's voice on the patrol car's radio broke her reverie. The dispatcher had news for her. "We got a call about a pack of dogs attacking sheep not far from Teec Nos Pos. Are you still around there?"

"Yes. I was just going to stop at the trading post for a Coke."

"Good. The captain wants you to check it out." Sandra gave her the name and location of the woman who had made the complaint. Bernie knew the area; the home wasn't far.

"Can I tell him you're on your way?"

Bernie looked at the clock in the unit. "I should be there in twenty minutes, depending on the road."

She found the stop, a double-wide trailer with a sheep pen and some outbuildings, more quickly than she thought she would. She couldn't see the sheep until she got out of her unit. Two lay bloody and unmoving. Three huddled against the fence, trembling. A woman about her age sat on the ground with an injured ewe. She looked up as Bernie approached.

Bernie introduced herself.

The woman, Celeste Emerson, did the same. They shared a clan on the maternal grandfather's side. "Thanks for coming out so quickly. I'm so glad to see you."

"What happened?"

"Wild dogs dug under the fence last night." Celeste pointed toward the fresh dirt with her chin. "My mother's two dogs tried to fight them. Now both of her dogs are gone. I don't know if they are dead or out there, injured, somewhere, or just lost and terrified."

"I'm so sorry." Bernie noticed the rifle on the ground next to the woman. "Did you get off a shot?"

"I was too late. By the time I got the rifle out, our dogs were chasing them away." It was a common story: abandoned dogs forming packs and killing livestock. It was nearly impossible for the police or animal control to track the dogs to the former owners who had abandoned them.

Bernie squatted down to look at the sheep Celeste attended. The animal's injures were extensive but probably not life-threatening.

"I've been trying to stop the bleeding, but . . ." Celeste choked up.

"I have a first aid kit in my unit. I'll get it." It was for human first aid, but it had gloves and gauze that might help with wound compression and keep the sheep alive.

Bernie hurried back from the vehicle, opened the case, and slipped on the gloves, listening to Celeste as she did so.

"I've never worked on an animal injured like this." The woman gave Bernie a probing look. "Have you?"

"No. But the other choice is to let the poor dibé die."

While Bernie applied pressure to stop the bleeding, Celeste comforted the ewe.

"It's sad to see something as senseless as this attack."

"It's terrible," Bernie agreed. "I grew up with dibé, raised lambs, helped with the shearing, all of that. Attacks like this really bother me."

She had always loved sheep. As a child, Bernie had helped Mama with her flock, the dibé of her girlhood, some of which she'd bottle-fed as lambs and watched grow into fine fleece producers. Sheep were crucial to their lives back when Mama was still shearing, carding, spinning, and then using that gorgeous wool for her rugs. Mama's sheep were part of the family.

Celeste shifted, seeking a new position on the cold ground. "Are you and your mother weavers?"

"Not me, unfortunately. I lack the patience for it. Mama used to weave, but she can't sit at the loom anymore and her hands are too stiff." Mama hadn't been able to make her beautiful rugs for years, her skill stolen by arthritis.

"What about you and your mother?"

"I wish I had some of that skill but I don't have the talent. My mom used to weave, but she can't do it anymore because of health problems. And she's got macular degeneration. But she loves these sheep, and so do I."

Celeste stroked the injured ewe. "I came to the Navajo Nation after my divorce. I think taking care of the sheep, the quiet out here and most of all my shimá—all that has helped me more than therapy. This landscape makes me feel grounded. And our clan sisters have been great. They stayed in touch with her and with me, while I was gone. And now they act like I've been here always."

"Where did you live before?"

"Oklahoma City. I had a job with an oil company. I used to think I'd like to move somewhere near the ocean next, but . . ." She squeezed her eyes shut for a moment. "I was born here; my umbilical cord is buried under one of these piñon trees. I think I'm ready to call this place home again. How about you?"

Bernie looked up from the animal. "I'm lucky. I've lived near Shiprock almost all my life except for my college days."

Celeste spoke to the sheep in rusty, broken Navajo and then in English while Bernie continued to push against the worst of the bleeding places on the sheep's flank. Celeste went into the house and returned with some old towels to help with the compression. The animal struggled and then quieted, as though it understood that the women were trying to help it.

Bernie figured that she and Celeste were about the same age, which meant they could have gone to Shiprock High School together, but she couldn't place the woman. "Did you grow up here?"

"No, but my mother and I always spent summers here with my shimásání. I loved it." Celeste looked at the sheep and then out toward the Carrizo mountains. "It seemed that there weren't so many loose dogs back then."

"I think that's right." Bernie noticed that the pressure had slowed the bleeding. "I'll show you how to do this. There's another pair of gloves in the kit. Put them on."

"I don't need them. My hands are already bloody."

Once Celeste had a handle on the problem, Bernie rose. "I need to get pictures of the dead sheep and of this injured one for my report." Bernie removed the gloves to get her phone and saw that the sheep had bled on her uniform pants.

Celeste noticed it, too. "I'm sorry about that mess."

Bernie took the photos she needed, and when she got back to the injured animal, the bleeding had stopped because of the pressure and the ewe was struggling to get up. Celeste still faced the challenge of closing the gash with sutures, but the ewe's chances of survival looked more promising. She could see the relief on Celeste's face.

"Celeste, can you ask your mother how to seal the wound, you know, to keep it from getting infected?"

She shook her head. "I can try. Mother knows all about how to care for sheep, but she's recovering from a stroke. It limits her speech, so it takes her a while to say what she means so I can understand her. If you can stay another minute or two, I'll ask her."

"OK. Don't be too long." Bernie realized, again, that she was lucky Mama had her voice, even though her daughters might not like what she said.

Celeste left Bernie alone with the injured sheep, the dead ones, and the traumatized survivors of the little flock. Coyote predation, Bernie realized, was an act of nature. But feral dogs? That was a human-caused problem.

She looked again at the two dead sheep. At least the coyote would have used the kill to feed itself and the pack. The dogs seemed to have caused all the damage for sport.

Celeste was back, and she had a round tin, like the kind cookies come in, and a large bottle.

"My mother told me where the medicine was to keep out infection. And showed me how to stitch up the wound. She has some thick thread in here, and some large needles." Celeste tapped the container. "Can you help me?"

Bernie held the sheep while Celeste did the stitching. Then Bernie stood. She started to brush the dirt from her pants but stopped when she noticed the mess on her hands.

"I'd like to wash before I go."

"Mother has a bucket and soap inside the house. And she says ahéhéé, and she'd like to meet you. Just go on in. Mom has a bit of trouble hearing, so please speak loudly to her."

Bernie went inside. The house was small and neat and felt wonderfully warm. She saw the water and soap and some paper towels and put them to good use.

Then she greeted the woman from the wash bucket.

"Yá'át'ééh, shimasaní." Bernie introduced herself and then continued to speak in Navajo. "I came to help your daughter, and now I am needing your water to wash before I leave."

"Yá'át'ééh." The voice, worn as smooth as a river rock, came from the other room. Celeste's mother may have struggled with English, but her Diné words flowed easily. "Warm up in here. Thank you for coming to help us. Can you do me a favor before you go?"

Bernie struggled with Navajo politeness versus her sense of duty as a cop. She had a long list of stops to make that morning but how could she say no to this grandmother?

"I'll try. Do you want me to come to the bedroom?"

"Yes."

The room was small, outfitted with twin beds, one neatly made. Celeste's mother lay in the other with two pillows propping her head. Bernie hoped the help would be as simple as walking with the woman to the bathroom or bringing a cup of water.

"Sit here with me so I can see you." She patted the edge of the bed with her hand. "My eyes aren't much good now."

Bernie obliged and waited.

"Hold my hand."

Her fingers were long and slim, the nails natural but nicely trimmed, the skin the color of mahogany and warm to the touch.

"What can I do for you, shimásání?"

"Please talk to my daughter. Tell her that she needs to live her own life. Tell her I am content to be old now."

The woman chuckled. "Maybe she will listen to advice that comes from a policewoman. More than when it comes from her mother."

"I can tell your daughter loves and admires you. She just wants to help you."

"She helps me most by being happy herself. That lightens my heart. Tell her. That's all I have to say." She patted Bernie's arm.

Back outside, the morning seemed a bit warmer. Bernie relayed the message.

"My shimá tells me that several times a day. I tell her I'm honored to help her, as she helped me when I was young. Reciprocity." Celeste smiled. "My clan sister and her husband are coming to help with those dead ones and to look for our lost dogs. We need to get the fence fixed, too."

Bernie nodded. "What do you know about the animals that hurt the sheep?"

"One of them is black, maybe eighty pounds, with a big chunk of its ear gone. The other two are tan and smaller, sort of like thin German shepherds. One of my relatives said they've been causing problems for months. That's why I got the rifle, but I'm not that good with it." Celeste looked at the injured ewe. "I couldn't get a shot off because I was afraid that I'd hit one of the sheep, or even our dogs."

"If you're going to continue living out here, you ought to practice. A weapon will come in handy if those dogs come back or if a coyote gets in with the sheep."

"Good advice."

"Take care of yourself and that poor animal, OK?"

"I will. Stop by if you're out this way again."

As she headed back to her unit, Bernie heard the radio calling and trotted toward it. Sandra, as usual, got to the point.

"Are you done there?"

"Yes."

"Two things. The FBI wants to talk to you about something. Agent Johnson said it's not crucial but she'd like to chat with you today. She left her cell number." The dispatcher rattled it off, but Bernie already had it memorized.

"Thanks." She waited for item number two.

"Lieutenant Leaphorn wants you to call him. Again, he said there's no hurry."

"Did he sound OK?"

Sandra hesitated. "Not exactly. He sounded like there was something on his mind."

Because Agent Johnson said it wasn't crucial, Bernie called Leaphorn first. She always tried the landline before the lieutenant's cell phone.

Louisa answered cheerfully. "Hey there. Good to hear your voice. How's life?"

"OK. How about with you?"

"I can't tell yet. I'm still struggling with jet lag, but Hawaii was great." Louisa chatted a moment about her trip. "You've been there, right?"

Bernie didn't want to chat but she smiled at the memory. "For our honeymoon. I'll never forget how beautiful it was. We enjoyed it, but we were both glad to get home. It sounds funny, but we missed work. Speaking of work, I'm returning the lieutenant's call."

"I was there for work, as well as for fun. The Hawaiian Native experience with colonialization parallels what happened here in the rest of the US and Canada, except it was much later. I didn't realize how much I missed doing those interviews. Joe sat in on a couple of the conversations that I thought might be of interest to him. He even asked some questions. Of course, he wanted to know about missing and murdered indigenous women and if it's a problem there."

"Is it?"

"Yes. Almost everywhere, and throughout history, women have been exploited and subjugated. Women with fewer resources take more than their share of abuse. Native Hawaiians . . ." Louisa paused. "Don't get me started. But you didn't call to get a lecture from me. You wanna talk to Joe."

"Is the lieutenant there?"

"No, but I'll ask him to call you."

"Thanks."

Bernie tried his cell phone, although he always muted it when he was working. Luck rode with her; Leaphorn came on the line. He got right to the point.

"I could use your help on something."

"Go ahead."

"I need to track the adoption of a Navajo baby by a non-Navajo couple back around 1977." He outlined the situation and his request and told her what little he had learned about Stella Brown's case. "I assume that somewhere there ought to be records of the Navajo mothers or families who relinquished their babies for adoption. But I've run into dead ends."

"You know, sir, Chee handled some cases where the reunions didn't go well. He knows much more about these situations than I do. He can help you better than I could."

4

Joe Leaphorn kept his private business to himself and admired those who did the same. He sympathized with both Cecil Bowlegs and Stella Brown. He thought it was ironic that despite his personal philosophy, he was in a business that required his clients to share their troubles with him in detail so he could offer his help.

He was dealing with two missing person cases, he realized. He had a lot of work ahead of him. In both instances, he wished the folks he was working for had contacted him sooner.

Louisa sat at the kitchen table with her notebooks and the interviews she'd recorded in Hawaii. He nodded to her. "I'm making some coffee. Want some?"

"No, thanks. But I'd like to talk about my son's visit."

He frowned. "Can it wait? I need to focus on that adoption case I mentioned to you."

"Yes. But not forever. Kory just texted that he'll be here tomorrow." Louisa closed the book of notes she was studying and smiled at him. "You've been busy this morning. Adoption is a complicated issue, but you're good at complicated."

Leaphorn turned on the coffeepot. "I'm not sure how good I am at complicated these days. My brain works slower than it used to. It takes me longer to remember a birthday, or to balance my checkbook."

"I know that I'm not as good at complicated as I used to be either," Louisa said. "I'm facing a challenge just organizing this indigenous

Hawaiian material. But work like this is good for our brains. Getting older is a lesson in patience, isn't it?"

Leaphorn took two cups from the cabinet and set them next to the machine. "Let me know when the coffee is ready, and we'll talk about your son."

"Thanks. What I need your thoughts on shouldn't take long."

He went to his home office, sat at his desk, and did a quick, unfulfilling search for background information on Stella Brown. He was finishing that when his phone rang.

"Lieutenant, this is R. P. Benally. The sergeant at Eagle Roost said you were going to help us look for Beth." The voice sounded young and excited.

"That's right. The sergeant mentioned that you know Cecil Bowlegs and his wife. He's your friend, isn't he?"

"Yeah, sorta. My brother-in-law, too."

"I'm a private investigator. Cecil called me early this morning and asked if he could hire me to find his wife. I told him I would take the case, but I haven't been able to reach Cecil, and I'm worried about him."

"Cecil finally took my advice?" The man on the phone laughed. "Is this a joke?"

"No." If it's a joke, it's a bad one, Leaphorn thought.

"I told Cecil we should do that, get us some help finding Beth after she didn't come home that first weekend. It's weird. She won't respond to phone calls, texts, nothing. And nothing seemed to be moving with the official search, you know? No leads. It was like that woman just vanished. Poof. I'm glad you can help us, and just so you know, I'll pay you myself. Cecil, he's a good man, but he's got some money problems." RP spoke a bit more softly. "Why are you worried about Cecil?"

Leaphorn told him.

RP was silent for a long moment. "The explosion at the school?"

"That's what I've been told."

"It's bad, man. I hear that there's a lotta smoke and a building is on fire. Cecil works there at the school, and sometimes he goes in on Saturdays."

As long as he had RP's attention, Leaphorn thought, he would make the most of it. "I'd like to talk to you about your clan sister. Do you have a few minutes now?"

"Nope, sorry. But my lunch break is in half an hour. If you can come out here then, I'll talk to you. We have to find her. I'll show you a picture that will help."

Leaphorn hesitated. He needed to focus on the adoption case. The client was coming to meet with him tomorrow.

RP said, "I'm working double shifts, so I really can't do it any other time."

"Can you call me over your break?"

"Bro, I could, but this is really personal. If I'm telling you private things about my clan sister, I want to look you in the eye and make sure you get it."

Leaphorn couldn't fault him for that. "Where do you work?"

"DIT."

"What's that? Never heard of it."

"You're behind the times. Navajo Nation Information Technology Department." RP gave him the address.

"OK. I'll see you in half an hour." Leaphorn paused. "How will I find you?"

RP laughed. "Just ask for me at the front desk. You're a retired cop, right? I'll spot you a mile away."

Leaphorn had a few minutes before the meeting, and the smell of coffee enticed him back to the kitchen. Louisa was waiting.

He explained his errand as he poured coffee. "Want some now?"

"OK. Half a cup."

He filled the empty cup he'd grabbed for Louisa to use. "So, what's on your mind?"

"My son says he's worried about me. That's the reason he's coming."

"Why is he worried?"

"He thinks I have taken leave of my senses because I've retired from teaching, and because of our trip to Hawaii."

Leaphorn smiled. "None of that is really his business. I know you'll straighten him out."

"We haven't seen each other for a while, and the last time wasn't pleasant." She twisted her coffee cup to put the NAU logo in her line of sight. "You've dealt with difficult people. I thought you might have some advice for me."

"Well, in general I've found it's better to listen than to talk, to let the other person get what it is off his chest, and then to ask questions rather than getting defensive."

"Yeah. That's right. But easier said than done."

Louisa was a woman of strong opinions, and she didn't hesitate to share what she thought. Like many bilagáanas he knew, she talked a lot. He'd grown used to it over the years they'd been friends and housemates.

"My son has had some struggles in life, but, well, who hasn't? I made peace with the fact that I had done the best I could as a working single mother long ago. But I think Kory still feels like I loved my job more than I loved him."

Leaphorn sipped his coffee. "Are you glad he's coming?"

"Yes." She smiled. "But I wonder who will show up here. Will it be the sweet, smart son I cherished, or the guy who's angry at the world?"

"You know he's your son, either way. Just remember that you love him and work toward forgiveness. What else can you do? You have to forgive yourself for not being perfect. None of us are. And you might have to forgive him for not treating you well or being appreciative of what you've done for him." He took a breath. He wasn't used to talking so much or to giving her advice. "Is there anything you'd like me to do while he's here?"

"Two things. I'd like you to meet him. And, I guess, give us time alone together."

"You've got it."

As Leaphorn drove out to talk to RP about the missing Bethany Bowlegs, he wondered what he would do if Louisa went missing. He knew he would act sooner than Bowlegs had.

RP WORE HIS HAIR IN one long braid that hung between his shoulder blades. He came to the front desk when Leaphorn asked for him, and led the way to the room that served as a space for breaks and storage.

The room had two tables with folding chairs, and RP nodded toward the closest empty one.

"I'll be right with you." He went to a small refrigerator and removed a lunch bag. "How about a drink from the machine?"

"Not for me, but go ahead."

While RP selected a soda, Leaphorn thought of how to make the most of their time.

RP took a seat in the chair across the table from Leaphorn. "Would you like half of my sandwich?"

"No thanks."

RP unwrapped a peanut butter and honey sandwich. It looked sticky, Leaphorn thought. Then RP removed a bag of chips and an apple from the lunch bag and opened the can of Dr Pepper he'd bought.

Leaphorn began. "I appreciate you meeting me here. What can you share with me that might help me find Bethany Benally Bowlegs?"

"Well, Beth was a restless soul. Cecil loved her, and she loved him back in her own way. When she'd go off on her adventures in the summer or during school breaks, she'd stay in touch with me and him with a phone call or text or something. Except for this last time. When we tried to contact her, no luck, no response. She asked me to keep some stuff for her, so I knew she was planning on coming back here. But, well, she hasn't."

"When was the last time you saw her?"

"We got together to celebrate the anniversary of her job as a music teacher. I think that was last month. Cecil called me a few days later to say she hadn't come home."

Leaphorn raised an eyebrow. "Almost a month?"

"Well, at least three weeks. Cecil took a long time to start looking. He thought she'd come back, and he was really mad at her for disappearing on him again."

"Again?"

RP nodded. "Like I told you, she was a free spirit. She liked having adventures and traveling."

"I have to ask you a hard question, and you need to tell me the truth. Do you think Cecil ever abused her?"

RP shook his head. "No sir. I was at their place a couple of times when she'd get on him about his gambling. He just walked away and worked on their car or something until she cooled down. He never said anything bad about her to me, except that he worried when she went on her adventures. Cecil understood his wife pretty well most days, I guess, but he got tired of being single and married at the same time. That's why he waited so long to get in touch with you. I wanted him to do it sooner, but he was embarrassed. He didn't want to find her if she was just making some space between them. Understand?"

"I do. What kind of adventures did she go on?"

"Well, music was her big love. She sings with the Hop Toads and she sings on her own, you know, a solo act. She has a voice on her."

Leaphorn had never heard of the Hop Toads, but he didn't mention that to RP. "Did Beth have a stage name?"

RP smiled. "Songbird. We called her our restless songbird. Her voice is bigger than she is."

When RP went back to eating his lunch, Leaphorn thought a moment, and then he asked a question. "So, have you heard anything today from Cecil?"

"No. I tried to reach him after I called you. Nothing. Then I reached a few folks Cecil knows." RP shook his head. "They hadn't talked to him either. They said the explosion was intense."

"I haven't heard from him since he called this morning." Leaphorn shook his head. "He hasn't called back. I hope we don't have two missing Bowlegs."

"Cecil's a survivor. I hope he's OK." But RP frowned at the news. "Tell me how you'll start looking for Bethany."

Leaphorn laid out the plan he would have shared with Cecil Bowlegs. "I'd like to follow up on where she traveled with the band. Did Beth talk about the places she performed?"

"Not much, and nothing specific. She mentioned some rodeos in the summer, you know. Bars, clubs. You should talk to Big Rex. He's the guy who runs the Hop Toads. He could tell you more about that."

"I'd like the names of the band members, too, and whatever contact information you have for them."

RP opened the bag of chips and offered Leaphorn some. "Well, like I said, there's Big Rex. Junior on bass and Agnes plays the drums, but I don't know their last names."

"Do you have any phone numbers?"

"Nope, but Cecil might. He can help you better than I can."

"What about Beth's other family members? Have you or Cecil checked with them?" Leaphorn knew from experience that sometimes missing people found havens with relatives.

RP ate the last chip and balled up the bag. "It's funny when I think of it. Beth and I aren't close to the rest of the relatives, except she talks to her sister in Arizona all the time. We help out the rest of the clan when we can, but we just don't seem to have much in common with them. I can give you names and numbers, but I'd have to look them up at home."

Leaphorn understood. "What about friends?"

"That's different. She has tons of them. Women from work, people she's known over the years, students she taught music to or worked with in the school chorus."

They sat in silence for a moment, watching the wind outside the lunchroom windows stir the new leaves of a New Mexico locust tree. "I'm worried about that woman. She's a good soul. And now I'm worried about Cecil, too."

"Let me know if Cecil calls you, OK?"

"I will."

The young man looked at Leaphorn. "Can you find Beth?"

"I'll start with my contacts at the Navajo police and get a handle on what they've learned, then follow up with the band members."

"The band is a good idea, but Cecil and Big Rex, the main dude who organizes the gigs, never got along. Big Rex called me when Bethany had been gone a week and asked what I knew. He said he'd ask her to check in with us if he saw her. She used to be tight with those guys."

"Used to be?" Leaphorn caught the verb change. "What happened?"

"She got additional duties at the school, something to do with keeping track of money. This was besides everything else already on her plate, so she had to leave the band for a while. Then she quit her jobs at school. I hope she's OK, just doing her own thing. But she's never been out of touch with Cecil and me this long. Something different is happening there. I just hope it's nothing bad."

RP went back to his food and Leaphorn thought about what he'd learned and if it was connected to Cecil's disappearance. He noticed the young man's unsettled look. "Is something else bothering you?"

RP studied the ceiling for a moment. "Cecil has been acting weird, too. Not just about Beth, but like someone's out to get him or something. He's spooked. When I try to talk to him about it, he shuts up. He's not right."

Leaphorn waited for RP to say more, but the younger man stood and quietly gathered the debris from his lunch. "I've got to get back to work."

The detective rose, too. "Please call me if you think of something else that might help me find Beth."

The younger man nodded. "You know, I looked for her, too. Nothing but a brick wall. It's like she just evaporated, or was abducted by aliens."

"I'd like to see that photo you mentioned before we run out of time," Leaphorn said.

RP pulled out his phone and called up a snapshot. He laid the phone on the table. The woman in the picture was thin and had a toothy, lopsided grin, a thick mane of hair, and full lips turned up in a faint trace of a smile. He noticed a bit of resemblance to RP.

"Let me text you that photo," RP said. "I have your mobile number right here."

As Leaphorn walked to his truck, he thought of the many families of missing people he'd worked with over the years. The problem had grown worse recently. He attributed some of it to the expansion of the internet, which made it easier for naive or desperate people to be lured into dangerous situations.

He reviewed what he had learned from RP as he headed for home and came up with the standard suspicions:

- Despite what RP said, Bowlegs was an abusive husband, and his wife left to protect herself.

- Bethany Bowlegs was pursuing her own creative outlet. They hadn't found her because she didn't want to be found.

- She had succumbed to drugs or alcohol addiction.

- She had picked up with a new partner.

- She was living with a mental illness that prompted her to disappear.

- She was not only missing, but dead.

Focusing on the disappearance of Bethany Bowlegs reminded Leaphorn of the other Navajo women he'd learned about as part of his work on the Navajo Nation's Missing and Murdered People task force. He needed to ask Darleen Manuelito, Bernie's sister, to make time to create some new designs for the missing person posters. Ever since Darleen enrolled full-time at Diné College, he'd had trouble getting her attention for the poster assignments.

When he pulled his truck into the driveway at home, Leaphorn noticed a car there, a new black Ford Echo with New Mexico plates. Probably one of Louisa's friends stopping by to visit, he thought, or maybe her son had arrived early.

He decided he would call Darleen from the driveway. He pulled out his phone and noticed a missed call from her sister, Bernie, one of his favorite Navajo police officers. Bernie hadn't left a message, so he called Darleen.

He heard something uneasy in her voice when she answered the phone.

"Hi, Darleen. I wanted to talk to you about doing some art and design work. Is this a good time?"

"Not exactly. I'm here with Mama, and I've got to get the house cleaned up before I can study for my class."

"It sounds like you're busy. I could find another artist to help with the posters."

"Oh, no. I'm sorry I missed the deadline on that other job. There's just so much going on right now. I love doing those designs. It keeps my art brain alive, you know?"

Leaphorn didn't know much about art brains, but he knew that it was important for people to do what they loved.

Over the phone Leaphorn heard the chatter of television and an older voice saying something in Navajo as if in reply. "Hold on," Darleen said.

Leaphorn listened to a younger voice speaking Navajo and a response from the older voice. As he waited for the conversation to stop, he studied his own house from his truck and caught a glimpse of Louisa's visitor through the living room window. The guest was a slim man, perhaps in his early forties. Leaphorn had never met Louisa's son, but he guessed that was about to change. He hoped the encounter would be a pleasant one.

Then Darleen was back. "I've got to help Mama with something."

"You sound kind of scattered. Call me when you're free. I've got some more work for you."

"Thanks. I promise to make the deadline this time."

"We made it last time, but just barely." Leaphorn thought about how much to say. "You have talent, and we were able to get the poster out in time." The project had been stressful, but the product was beautiful.

"I'll get back to you when I can. Don't give up on me, OK?"

After that, he returned Bernie's call and learned she was out of cell coverage. He took the little notebook out of his pocket and wrote some observations on the Bowlegs case, a pair of fresh ideas that called for follow-up. Then he climbed out of his truck and walked past the generic-looking sedan, noticing the mirrored sunglasses on the dashboard, and the small sticker on the bumper that indicated a rental. The guest must be Louisa's son.

He took a deep breath and went inside to meet the man who, after half a decade, had decided the time had come to visit his mom.

5

Cecil Bowlegs' head finally stopped ringing and he almost felt safe enough to climb out of bushes in the sandy bottom of the arroyo. His whole body ached from the explosion. But a quick survey of vital body parts found everything intact, and except for cuts and scrapes acquired on his hands and face from the scramble down the hillside, he was in fair shape physically. The discomfort of poking branches and the cold ground against his back and legs annoyed him. If his heart returned to its normal rhythm and stopped racing, he might be able to think straight.

Filling his lungs with the frigid early-morning air, he tried to figure out what to do next. He strained to capture the sound of an approaching vehicle over the pulsing of blood in his ears, but heard only the distant vibration of tires on the asphalt. He exhaled. Maybe whoever had tried to kill him thought he was dead. Or maybe they were waiting on the road to nab him.

Cecil carefully pushed himself to sitting and looked out over the cold, dry landscape for potential danger. He saw rocks and dirt, piñon trees, some sprouting evening primrose and sagebrush awaiting the kiss of spring. The sun had melted the last of the snow that had blessed them earlier that month. What could have been mud was frozen solid.

The smoke from the explosion hung in the air, and Cecil knew that if anything was left of the school building, it must have been seriously damaged. He wondered if it would be considered a crime scene, or just the site of a terribly unfortunate accident.

He knew the man who was after him wanted money—a problem he couldn't solve at the moment—and had threatened to hurt him if he didn't pay up. But he had never expected this. He understood now that the man he owed would stop at nothing. He would have made the explosion look like an accident, maybe even one Cecil had caused.

Bethany had warned him. She'd told him to stay out of the casinos, and each time, he'd promised in good faith. But after she disappeared, he told himself his luck would change. All he needed were some good cards, the right horses, a decent point spread on the games, some winning lotto picks, the best slot machine, a lucky touch at the craps table. But since she'd left, nothing, nothing had gone his way.

Perhaps his luck had changed, he told himself. Be glad you aren't dead.

A burst of movement caught his attention. He lowered himself back into the brush and watched as a chestnut horse approached, on its back a young Navajo man in faded jeans, a plaid shirt, and a black cowboy hat. He didn't recognize man or horse.

The horse stopped, and the man straightened his legs in the stirrups and looked around. If this was a neighbor Cecil hadn't met, he might be willing to give Cecil a hand, lend him a phone to make a call. But if the man who rode that horse with so much confidence was one of the people who wanted him dead, he had to stay quiet and still.

Cecil held his breath and tried to control his shivering as the horse walked past. Neither the animal nor the rider noticed him hiding in the sagebrush.

He couldn't exactly remember how far he'd run from the explosion, but he was no marathoning teenager. He couldn't have gone more than a mile or so before he slipped, rolled, and decided to stay down. Things could be worse, he thought. He didn't have his phone, but his keys and wallet were still in his pocket.

Serious thinking wasn't Cecil's long suit, but he realized that if he was dead, the man he owed wouldn't get his money. The explosion might have been a way to show him the guy meant business, but something had gone wrong—if he'd been inside the building, he would have died for sure. He probably had at least a few hours until the person realized that his body was not in the rubble.

Cecil knew he had to plan his next move, but his cache of ideas had run empty.

His legs started to ache from the cold, and he flexed them as best he could from his hiding place. Then he cautiously hobbled to standing. The cops and firefighters must be at the school by now, and some curious parents milling around, too, all focused on the smoldering mess.

He began the long limp home. He knew he couldn't stay at his house for long. They'd find him and hurt him again until he paid up. When he finally made it to his place, he could use that old landline to call his friend. He kept going, struggling along the shortcut he always used on the walk to work and back. Despite the pain and the brain fog, he finally got home, let himself in, headed for the bathroom, then collapsed against the couch cushions. He wouldn't be safe, but he needed to rest for an hour or so. Relax and think of what Beth would do.

He tried to unwind, but his brain kept spinning, and the roar of the blast had ground itself into his memory. His ears were still ringing, and when he closed his eyes, he felt churning worry. He didn't know what came next or if he'd survive it. But the Holy People, God, the universe—whatever was out there—had not let him die, so he could find Beth. He had connected with Joe Leaphorn, and Leaphorn said he would help. Would anyone except himself, and possibly now Leaphorn, assume the explosion was not an accident?

Fatigue began moving over him, wrapping him gently in blessed sleep. Somewhere in the distance he heard an old-fashioned phone, ringing against the background of ringing in his ears. He told himself it was a dream, and let it go.

6

Louisa Bourbonette remembered that this man who'd arrived in the black car, this man who was her son Kory, was a tea drinker, so she put on the kettle for hot water. She was bursting with questions: Why are you here? How come you've arrived a day earlier than you said? How long can you stay? And the important, unspoken question: Why did you cut off my love for so many years?

But she decided not to ask him anything, to keep even the whiff of judgment out of his reach. Perhaps he would volunteer the information. She opened the front door with a smile.

He greeted her with a quick hug. "You look good, Mom, happy. Are you?"

"Yes. Joe and I just got back from a trip to Hawaii. I did some interviews, but we had a nice stretch of time to relax, too."

"Interviews, huh? I figure you're old enough to retire. You're taking on a new job?"

"Actually, I'm returning to work I did maybe a decade ago, a project on the deep similarities between indigenous religions. The interviews are mostly with old Native Hawaiian people who are willing to talk about their spiritual practices."

"Well, great! That sounds practical and lucrative."

She heard his sarcasm. The comment reminded her of the arguments they'd had about money. "It's interesting work I truly enjoy."

"Is it dangerous?"

She smiled at the question. "No. Why would you ask that?"

"People might not like prying old ladies, you know."

"Well, people who don't want to cooperate just don't talk to me. Usually, it's elders I meet with for these interviews, but often their children or a grandchild might sit in on the conversation, or get a copy of the tape afterward." This was the first time he'd seemed interested in her work, and she saw that as a positive sign.

The teapot whistled. "Kory, would you like some tea?"

He hesitated. "Sure. I'm glad you remembered. Do you have Navajo tea?"

"I do. I'm surprised you know about it."

"Mom, there are lots of things about me that would surprise you."

"I'd like to hear about them." She took the canister of Navajo tea from the shelf and scooped the loose leaves into a tea ball, poured the steaming water into a teapot, and put the lid back on. "I've missed talking to you."

"I booked a room at the Window Rock Lodge for a couple of nights, so we'll have time, I guess. I heard that you retired from teaching up in Flagstaff."

"'Retired' is too definite. I'm taking a break. Getting back to the research I missed when I was teaching. So, tell me what's new in your life? I can't remember the last time we were together like this."

He frowned. "I can. It was five years ago in Gallup. You told me you were staying out here to teach at that college in Flagstaff, and I told you that you were nuts."

The conversation, so fractious and unpleasant she'd blocked out the details, came back to her. Kory had been drinking, and their discussion had moved from a civil exchange of information about her job at Northern Arizona University to a rant that stirred up issues going back all the way back to Kory's turbulent early years. It reopened unhealed wounds for both of them. Afterward she had called Kory, hoping to make peace. He never answered or returned her calls, but she kept at it. And now here he was.

"I'm glad to see you." She managed a smile. "I don't see any point in reopening that discussion."

"Water under the bridge for me, too. And now you're going back to something you left behind, right?"

"My research? I guess you could say that I'm returning to something I loved." She filled their mugs with steaming tea. "What about you?"

"I'm getting ready to die, Mother. I wanted to come say goodbye. I've got cancer, and I'm going crazy." He said it with the same intonation that he might have used telling her that he was off to the grocery.

Earlier she had speculated on the reason for his visit. Perhaps he was starting a new job or about to leave the country. Perhaps he needed a loan. Lots of possibilities, including the idea that he wanted to make peace with her. Death from cancer—or anything else—hadn't made her list.

She focused on him again. He was thinner and looked older than she would have expected for a man just approaching forty. His skin looked waxen, and his eyes had a dull sheen to them.

"Tell me everything."

"The oncologist says it's a rare type they don't have much experience with. The treatment slowed it down a bit, and I'm not in much pain yet. Thought we'd come see you while I'm just tired and fuzzy-brained. I'm still working as a consultant for that engineering firm. I told you about them, didn't I?"

He hadn't, of course, because they didn't talk, but she let it go, moving the conversation back to cancer.

"Are you getting chemo? Radiation? Surgery?"

"No, no, and no. Been there, done that. Got the scars." He chuckled when he said it, but his eyes were cold. "And before you ask, probably between six months and a year. That's the educated guess."

The revelation left her speechless. Her throat tightened, and her eyes filled with tears. She reached for his hand. "Oh, Kory. I'm so sorry to hear this. You know I love you, and I wish there was something I could do to change things."

Kory's voice was unnervingly calm. "The diagnosis means pain that will continue to grow, eventually becoming more severe and less manageable until I die. I like the idea of ending things myself first. When they talk about the side effects of cancer treatment, they tend to leave out depression."

Louisa collected her emotions. "You know, I had cancer myself a few years ago. Treatments are better now than when I had it. Science is full of hope, and that's as valuable as anything the doctors can offer you. Maybe even more valuable. Is there anything I can do for you?"

"Let's just drink our tea before it gets cold, Mother. Give my news a chance to soak in. Then I have something else to tell you."

When she lifted the cup, her hand trembled, and some of the tea splashed onto the wooden countertop. She sipped the warm liquid. There was something soothing about the tea, a calmness in its warmth. Everyone dies, she thought, but it isn't in the natural scope of things for a mother to outlive her child. It indeed had taken a monumental change to bring her beloved, estranged son back into her life, something as monumental as looking at his own death growing closer.

As she waited for Kory to tell her whatever would come next, she remembered Joe's recent cynicism about the relationship between parent and child. He'd mentioned his client, who wanted to find her birth parents. "I'm willing to help her, of course," he'd said, "but sometimes people are better off not knowing what's out there in the world of family. I hope she doesn't learn something that adds to her distress, but I told her that's a possibility."

Louisa looked at her son's hand, at the wedding ring on his finger. When had he gotten married, and why hadn't he told her? "What else do you need to say?"

"Well . . ." Kory fell silent, and Louisa heard the front door open and then the crisp sound of boot heels on the wooden floors.

Leaphorn glanced into the kitchen.

"Hey," Kory said loudly. "I figure you're Joe Leaphorn. I'm Louisa's son Kory, but you know that already."

"Hello." Leaphorn stopped and stood there like a polite host, silently waiting for Kory to take the lead.

"My mother and I are having a serious, private discussion. Do you mind?"

"Not at all." Leaphorn nodded to Louisa. She felt her face grow hot with embarrassment at her son's rudeness as she watched Leaphorn walk down the hall. Then she heard the door to his office close.

7

The image of the dead sheep stayed with Bernadette Manuelito as she drove to her next assignment. Although she missed the sheep Mama had raised for decades, it was a blessing that the flock had gone to a clan sister when her mother stopped weaving. Sheep involved work that Mama couldn't handle anymore.

She headed out toward the Teec Nos Pos trading post. She liked driving because it gave her time to think. She moved the sheep out of her mind and focused on something joyful. Mama's birthday was coming up. She thought about that and how best to celebrate. She'd considered a party, but Darleen suggested that they surprise Mama with a trip to Chinle to see Mr. Natachi, her old neighbor. The drive from Toadlena would take them through the beautiful landscape of Red Rock, Lukachukai, and Tsaile. They could treat the two elders to a picnic lunch at Canyon de Chelly. She was making a mental list of what treats to serve when Sandra's voice came through the radio.

"There's been an explosion, and the captain wants you back here on the double."

"Of course." She remembered the incident Leaphorn had mentioned. "What happened?"

"I don't know much except that it was this morning in Eagle Roost."

"Eagle Roost?" That part of the Navajo Nation was at the southern end of the Shiprock district and had its own police officer.

"Yeah. Eagle Roost. Evidently, it's bad. It was at the school. Thank goodness this is a Saturday, right?" Sandra lowered her voice. "From his attitude, I'd say the captain doesn't think this was an accident."

"I see." An explosion that wasn't an accident could be a bomb, Bernie thought. "Was anyone hurt?"

"I don't know. The captain needs you here for a briefing ASAP." She heard Sandra's long exhale over the phone. "And there's something else. I hate to say this, but your mother called."

Bernie's heart sank. Mama seldom called her at work, but when she did, it usually meant bad news.

"What did she say?"

"She said to tell you to come home for lunch. I told her you were out working but that I'd give you the message. She sounded confused and . . . wait a minute."

Bernie and her sister Darleen shared care of Mama, and until recently Darleen had been her main caretaker. But now that Darleen had returned to school, Mama's slightly younger neighbor Mrs. Darkwater, Bernie and Chee, and Darleen's boyfriend, Slim, had all begun to help with Mama's care. Not only was her memory failing, she also lived with physical challenges that they worried about. It was a blessing that Mrs. Darkwater came to visit every day.

Sandra was back in a moment. "The captain wants to talk to you right now."

Captain Adakai came on the radio. "Manuelito, do you know Eagle Roost School?"

"Sort of. I was there a few years ago for career day. They have students from kindergarten through high school."

"There's been an explosion there, and Sergeant Stanley, our officer out that way, is overwhelmed. Get there ASAP and help preserve evidence until the feds arrive. Put what you learned in that explosives class to good use."

Bernie had requested and received training in bomb scene investigation and explosives removal after she was a first responder at a car bomb incident and had felt out of her depth. This time, if she had to deal with the aftereffects of a bomb, she'd be more prepared for whatever came her way.

"An explosion? A bomb?" The idea that someone would set off a bomb at a school chilled her.

"Maybe. No one knows much of anything yet. Agent Johnson asked for you because of the car bomb incident you handled." Sage Johnson was the FBI's Farmington person and had a small staff.

"Any casualties?"

"I don't know. One more thing."

"Yes, sir?"

"Stay safe out there, OK?"

"You bet." She pulled her unit onto the shoulder for a U-turn and switched on her lightbar. "Thanks for the opportunity. I'm on the way to Eagle Roost now."

Bernie drove south on NM 491, a paved four-lane highway that rolled past Shiprock itself and then near the dark rocky cores of other extinct volcanos that rose from the tan earthen bed into the towering blue sky. The openness of the landscape always pleased her, although she knew the Navajo stories of witchcraft that came with the unusual lava and basalt geology. The trip to Eagle Roost was one she didn't often make.

As she headed toward the school she wondered what she'd find there. As a distraction, she searched the horizon for clouds, even though it was too early for spring rain. Then she used her cell phone to call Mrs. Darkwater, who promised to check on Mama and give her sister Darleen the message that Bernie was on a new assignment.

"Just between us," Mrs. Darkwater said, "ever since that sister of yours started school again, your mother seems kinda blue—more troubled, you know? I'm glad that Darleen's boyfriend comes by. That's a good thing. I think your mother likes him."

Darleen's boyfriend, Slim, was a levelheaded man, a teacher who seemed to understand Darleen's creative energy and expressive personality. He had encouraged her to begin training as a nurse. And to Bernie's deep gratitude, he treated Mama with respect and kindness.

"Thanks for all you do for our mother. I really appreciate it."

"How's the life going for you, honey?" Mrs. Darkwater asked. "Your sister told me that you were trying to have a baby but it didn't work out. I'm sorry."

"Thank you. I'm feeling better." Bernie didn't feel comfortable discussing the miscarriage on the phone even though her doctor had suggested talking about it as a way to move on. "I can't talk now. I'm heading down to Eagle Roost."

"Stay safe."

As she drove, Bernie thought again about the failed pregnancy. Chee's kindness and Darleen's sympathy had helped her regain some equilibrium. She hadn't mentioned it to Mama. She knew miscarriage happened in about twenty-five percent of pregnancies. She'd stopped asking why she and Chee had been part of that sad statistic. They had decided they'd try again to become parents when she was ready.

Bernie recalled what she knew of Eagle Roost. A conversation she'd had with Lieutenant Leaphorn when she was just a rookie cop came to mind. He had chided her for discounting some detail on a case and mentioned that one of his first assignments had taken him to an area of the reservation near the Eagle Roost area, at the margins between Zuni Pueblo and Navajo land. The job had progressed from the hunt for a missing Navajo boy to searching for the reasons behind two tragic murders. A seemingly random comment had ultimately helped him figure out who had killed a Zuni boy and his Navajo friend, he told her. Always listen with both ears.

But dark thoughts of dead children would not prepare her for whatever chaos she might find at the school. She pushed them aside, took a few soothing breaths, and let the richness of the New Mexico landscape calm her. She knew she'd need to have her wits about her for what lay ahead.

8

Joe Leaphorn prided himself on his ability to solve problems, but whatever was going on with Louisa and her long-lost son was not his to solve. From his office, he heard their voices, muffled at first and then louder with a sharp overlay of emotion.

He forced himself to focus on the job at hand: checking available resources to help Stella Brown reconnect with her Navajo family if, in fact, she actually was Navajo. She'd given him a copy of her birth certificate that listed her name, date of birth, place of birth—the hospital in Farmington, New Mexico—and adoptive parents, Rita and Stan Brown. Their address at the time of the adoption was also in Farmington. He was surprised that her adoptive mother's maiden name wasn't included.

Based on the birth certificate, Stella had turned fifty-five this year. Her biological mother would have to be at least seventy by now, and much older if Stella had been a late-life child. That meant the grandmothers, if still alive, were probably in their nineties.

Leaphorn knew Navajo grandparents that old and even older who were amazingly sharp and physically active. If Stella was lucky enough to be related to an elder like that, she would learn a lot about her birth family. But he understood her urgency to complete the search. The odds for a reunion with someone who knew her mother were growing slimmer with each passing day.

His research confirmed what she'd told him about closed adoption back in the 1970s. This kind of adoption, sometimes known as confidential or secret adoption, meant that when a child was accepted by another family, the record of the child's biological parents was permanently sealed. Often, the name of the biological father was left unrecorded—even on the original birth certificate. The Browns had finalized Stella's adoption just before the US Congress passed the Indian Child Welfare Act, or ICWA, which limited the adoption of Indigenous American children by those outside their tribal communities.

He leaned back in his chair and considered the history that led to the law and, more recently, its survival, thanks to a US Supreme Court decision. The decision of the US Congress to impose "American" education on tribal members to enforce what it called the "civilization process" led the federal government and Christian missionaries to establish Indian boarding schools. As Leaphorn saw it, the true goal was to forcibly assimilate Indian children into mainstream society and eradicate their cultures. The story of the suffering students experienced has been told and retold.

These schools eventually fell out of favor—due in part to the strong resistance by Native communities—and the boarding school–era ended. But another policy aimed at assimilating Native Americans emerged. The Indian Adoption Project supported placing Indigenous children in need of foster homes or adoption with non-Native parents—even if communities objected and extended families were willing to take the child.

He remembered how, eventually, protests created change and Congress passed the Indian Child Welfare Act, or ICWA. It wasn't perfect, but the ICWA had enabled Navajo children to stay with their extended families.

If Stella had been adopted after the act was in effect, she would probably know her biological family. But she hadn't benefited from the ICWA, and now it was up to Leaphorn to fill in the blanks. Time to get back to work. He turned on his computer.

Before taking the case, Leaphorn had done a quick background check on his new client and found nothing suspicious. She seemed to be who she said she was: a newly retired teacher with a degree from the University of New Mexico. Married, divorced. No children of her own.

No siblings. Perhaps that was part of the reason she was interested in finding her Navajo family.

Because he didn't know much about adoption, and especially the processes in place decades ago, Leaphorn did some online research. Talking to Stella stirred his own heart and memories of the past. She'd mentioned that her adoptive mother had been on the faculty at Arizona State University, the school where he'd earned his degree many years ago.

He had survived the culture shock of moving to Phoenix thanks to attending ASU. Not only was he the first in his family to go to college, but he was also the only one to leave the Navajo Nation by choice for a reason other than joining the military.

He could have gone to college closer to home, but his deep curiosity about America beyond the reservation and funding provided through the GI Bill drove him to the big city. It hadn't been easy, but he'd received his degree. While at ASU he met the woman who had guided his life for several decades, his dear Emma. When they came back to the reservation, he went to work for the Navajo police. Thanks to his parents' and clans' deep rooting in Diné culture, he had been able to balance traditional lifeways with his growing comfort in mainstream American society. He'd learned to straddle both worlds.

In sharp contrast, Stella Brown had grown up in the white world without Leaphorn's cultural grounding. Her adoptive parents had offered no details about her biological mother and father. And now they were dead, and whatever they knew about Stella's birth parents and the particulars of her adoption had died with them.

"I wish I'd been curious about this when they were still with me." Leaphorn remembered the deep sadness in Stella's eyes when she said those words. "Now, I'm mourning them, the questions I never thought to ask, and, well, my own lost self."

He reread his notes from Stella and then made some calls to a contact at the Navajo Nation Social Services office. Royce Will answered on the first ring and Leaphorn identified himself.

"Hey Joe, I recognized your voice. You finally interested in signing up for that foster granddad program? I know a boy you would really love."

"Not today." Leaphorn explained the reason for his call. "A question for you. Is there a Navajo or Indigenous database to help people who have been adopted find their birth parents?"

"Not exactly. We've been getting a lot of interest in these records lately, ever since the Texas challenge to the ICWA made the news. Do you know about that?"

"The Supreme Court's decision to uphold the Indian Child Welfare Act? Of course."

Will murmured his agreement. "The state of Texas and some white families who want to adopt or foster Native children contended that the law illegally discriminated against them because they aren't Native. They said it put the interests of the tribes above the needs of Native children. They argued that race-based discrimination was built into the ICWA."

"I remember that," Leaphorn said. "The lawyers on the other side said that the law acknowledges the tribes as sovereign governmental entities, and that race wasn't the issue. The US Supreme Court agreed with them, almost unanimously."

"Well, the case stirred up a lot of interest in Native adoptions, and our agency started getting a truckload of inquiries from people who had been adopted out of the tribe as infants and young children."

"That's why I'm calling."

"Well, sorry to say that tracing these adoptions is difficult. Records at the time weren't computerized. We were just moving into the age of technology. You remember the seventies."

Leaphorn smiled. "Back when everyone had a landline, a tape player, a wristwatch, and a calculator. Seems like yesterday."

"I'll try to help your client. The more information you guys can share with me to narrow this down, the better chance of success we'll have. I can't let you paw through the files based only on the date on her birth certificate."

Leaphorn agreed. "What if we start today?"

"I'll be here until five. Glad to help you."

After that he called Stella, left a message, then sent her a text for good measure. She texted back that she could meet him in the social service office in an hour. He agreed.

While he was on the phone, the voices from the other room had grown louder, then quieter. He had heard the front door slam and went to check on Louisa.

She was standing in the living room with her hands on her hips, staring at the door. Unfortunately, he recognized the pose. It meant trouble.

"What happened?"

She turned toward him, and he read the anger in her face.

Leaphorn waited.

"OK. I guess it's my fault. I should have kept my mouth shut and let him finish. But I just couldn't listen to any more lies."

Questions filled his brain, but he kept them to himself. Instead, he said, "I'm here if you want to talk about it."

"Do you think you can help me figure out how the kid I loved and raised turned into a selfish, crazy jerk?"

"Louisa, I know you, and I know you did your best. He's an adult. He's been shaping his own life for years."

"Well, he stinks at it, and it breaks my heart to see him giving up, throwing his future away, however long it might be." She took a step toward Leaphorn. "He's been diagnosed with terminal cancer, a rare type that the oncologists don't know exactly how to treat. They want to do more, but he's depressed, discouraged, and has decided to just give up."

Leaphorn put his arms around her in an awkward hug. Her tears made him uncomfortable, but he didn't pull away.

After a quick moment she moved, embarrassed. "If you aren't too busy, would you sit down with me? I could use your help to think this through."

"Now?"

"No, I need to collect my thoughts first."

"Later, then." He nodded. "I'll be in my office. I've got an appointment in an hour at social services with that woman who's looking for her family."

"After that. This will keep." Louisa sighed. "So much for a storybook reunion."

AS LEAPHORN WAS DRIVING TO the appointment, he got a text message from one of Royce Will's staff members, explaining that Will was running late, tied up with another case. So it went, Leaphorn thought. He could use the time to learn more from Stella.

His client was standing alone in the social services building entry hall, and she looked more rested than the last time he'd seen her. The wrinkles around her eyes were fainter. She gave him a quick smile of greeting. "Thanks for setting this up. I'm excited."

"Royce Will, the man who will be helping us, is running late. Let's sit and talk a minute."

They found a quiet corner.

When Stella had come to him with her request, she'd told him what she had already done on her own. She explained that she had posted her photo of the people she'd thought might be her birth parents on social media and shared as much information as she safely could. She had used several sites designed to help adopted children find their birth families.

Leaphorn told her she had made his job easier.

"But I may not have any luck discovering the people you're looking for. And if I do, well, these stories don't always have happy endings."

He remembered her reaction. "I understand." She held her hands on her lap, squeezing the fingers of her right hand with her left. "I'm willing to take a chance."

He was glad that they had a few minutes now before the meeting with Royce Will to remind her again about low expectations.

She brushed away the pessimism. "I know that he may not be able to help us directly, but maybe he will at least know where we can look next."

"Stella, why does this matter so much to you after all these years?"

She studied the ceiling for a moment. "Ever since my mother died, I've felt adrift. I need to try to solve my own mystery. I need to do my best to discover my own origin story. If the search is fruitless, at least I know I gave it my best shot."

Leaphorn understood. "Have you wondered about your birth parents your whole life?"

"No." She looked thoughtful. "I didn't think about it much until my mom died. Maybe my birth parents are dead, too. Maybe Dad was in prison and Mom was an alcoholic, or even worse." She shrugged. "I'm an adult. I've seen how life can work. I just want to know the truth, even if it hurts."

When they had first met, Stella promised to show him photos of herself as a baby. She had some on her phone and showed them to him while they waited.

"These are lovely. I'm surprised you didn't bring some that show you with your parents."

She smiled. "I know this sounds odd, but Mom and Dad hated to have their photos taken. Mom said she never liked the way she looked. And Dad? Well, he was one of those guys who had a lot of suspicion about people watching him, the government collecting data, you know? Our house was full of photographs. Whenever we went on vacation, Mom was always taking snapshots of me and the scenery. But if another tourist or someone offered to take a picture of the three of us together, my parents always declined."

Royce Will walked toward them. Leaphorn introduced Stella Brown, and they followed him to his office. He sat across from them with his computer monitor turned so they could see it.

Will smiled at them. "Before we get started, I want to tell you a little about closed adoptions in general. Closed means the records are sealed to protect the privacy of the biological parents. Their identities and the child's original name, if one was given, and actual birthplace stay secret. All of this is specifically intended to make it harder for anyone to learn the baby's true origin.

"Mr. Leaphorn gave me the information you shared with him. I plugged that in. Unfortunately, I didn't get any results. There's no official registry that I can find of your birth or the adoption."

Stella frowned. "Are you kidding? I have a birth certificate. I've used it as official identification for passports, for my social security card, and whenever else it's been required. No one has questioned it."

As she talked, she opened her leather messenger bag and pulled out a large envelope.

"Here's my birth certificate. This is the original document, not a copy." She handed the envelope to Will, and he opened it, slipped out the folded page, and spread it flat on his desktop.

"What other information do you have about your birth or your adoption?"

Stella told him about the parents who had raised her. She gave him the date on which she'd been adopted, and the names of the places in her earliest memories.

Will typed, and they waited.

"I'm sorry. Nothing comes up. Are you sure about that adoption day?"

"Absolutely. We always celebrated on August 23. That day mattered even more than my birthday. My mother said that was the day we became a family."

Will rubbed his chin as he examined the birth certificate closely. He glanced across the desk at Stella.

"I gather this is the only birth certificate you have."

"Of course. Is something wrong?" The heel of Stella's right foot was tapping on the floor. "Do you think there was some problem with my adoption?"

Leaphorn frowned. "May I take a look?"

Will slid the paper toward him over the smooth wooden desktop. Leaphorn studied it a moment and then gave it back to Will.

Will looked at it again and then set it down. "This document is unusual. I've noticed some things about it that don't make sense. This form is very different from the standard documentation I'm used to and so is some of the information it contains, or doesn't contain."

"Like what?" Stella's voice shook with anxiety.

"Well, for instance, it tells me evidently your adoption was finalized less than a month after you were born. I've never seen the process move that quickly in the many years I've been looking at birth certificates, especially back when computerization was primitive. It raises a red flag about the legality of the procedure."

He tapped his finger gently on the bottom third of the document. "Usually, these certificates have the adopting mother's name before she was married. Yours lacks that. It does include the required notary seal and signature here at the bottom, but without the embossing these certificates usually have."

Stella looked at the paper. When she looked up, Leaphorn saw new wrinkles on her forehead.

"Was one or both of your adoptive parents a lawyer?" Will asked.

"No. Not at all. My dad was a high school graduate and proud of it. My mom went to college and taught school somewhere before. I . . ." Her voice cracked. "I didn't expect this process to be easy, but I thought it was doable. Now it seems like a big mess. Like a question that needs to go back in the box."

Will handed the certificate back to her. "Good luck, Ms. Brown." He turned to Leaphorn. "If I need a PI someday, maybe you'll give me the friend and family rate."

"You bet. That's double the regular fee."

Stella put the birth certificate back in the envelope and then in the leather bag. She rose and headed for the door. Leaphorn read the disappointment in her slumped shoulders.

He followed. "I'm here to help you. I'm on your team," he said, trying to sound reassuring. "That's why you came to me, remember? We're in this together."

"So, you'll help me see this through to the end." The set of her jaw reflected Stella's determination.

Leaphorn nodded.

They walked side by side in silence to their cars. Then she turned to face him.

"Do you think my parents faked my birth certificate?"

"I trust Will when he says there's some issue with the records. We'll get it sorted out." He wanted to tell her there was nothing to worry about, but he wasn't good at lying. "I know you loved them, and from what you've told me, I'm sure they loved you. They didn't fake that."

"I used to think love was all that mattered."

After Stella drove away, Leaphorn sat in his truck, thinking. Then he walked into Royce Will's office and asked half a dozen more questions. Although he wasn't pleased with the answers, he appreciated the man's openness. It offered him a way to proceed once a few details fell into place. To move the process forward more quickly, he called Jim Chee before heading home.

9

Leaphorn knew that Jim Chee had been in law enforcement long enough to understand how things worked, and how to work around things that didn't work. Chee could usually figure the way to jump from point A to point C if people and systems declined to cooperate. He could roll with the tide or push things along to get what he needed.

So when Chee felt his phone vibrate and saw it was Leaphorn, he relished the opportunity to step out of a workshop on new regulations for regional law enforcement—an unfortunate waste of a perfectly good Saturday that came with his promotion to lieutenant—and into the hall to take the call.

Leaphorn got right to business. "I need a favor."

"What can I do for you?"

"I need a background check on a couple of dead people." Leaphorn gave Chee the names of Stella's parents. "Something's wrong with their adopted daughter's birth certificate, and they didn't want their photographs taken. It makes me suspicious." Leaphorn explained in more detail.

"Did she come to you because she thinks she's a lost bird?"

"Right." *Lost birds.* That was the name for children who had been removed from their homes in Navajo land or on other reservations by the government or stolen by private adoption bureaus. The name came from the translation of the name of the Lakota girl Zintkála Nuni, "Lost Bird" in English. As an infant, she was found alive on the battlefield following the 1890 massacre at Wounded Knee and adopted by a white army general.

Chee read back the names and spelling. "What else do you know about the Browns?"

"They lived in Albuquerque at least for a few years. Her dad was in construction. Her mother was a teacher, even taught at the University of New Mexico. Her mother died three years ago in Farmington. Her dad passed away before that."

"What does she know about her birth family?"

"Nothing. A grade-school teacher called her 'our little Indian,' and the Browns told her she was Navajo. She has a snapshot of a Navajo couple standing near the Elephant Feet buttes with what might be a baby wrapped in a blanket. That's out by Tonalea."

"Tonalea, eh? I knew a fine hatáálii out that way." Chee mentioned the name. "I'll see what I can find out for you, but I won't be able to get to it until later today."

"That's fine." Leaphorn changed the subject. "How do you like the new job?"

"It's OK."

"And the new boss?"

"We're still sorting things out. I'm not sure he's the right captain for Bernie. Of course, no one can replace Captain Largo." Chee paused, and Leaphorn wondered if he had more to say about the new man in charge, but he changed the subject.

"By the way, welcome home, Lieutenant. Did you and Louisa enjoy Hawaii?"

"It's lovely, but too much green for me, and being on an island isn't my thing. I'm glad to be back."

"I enjoyed it on our honeymoon, but of course I had Bernie to distract me." Chee laughed.

"How's she doing?"

"She's busy. There was some sort of explosion at a school. You'll remember that she had that explosives training, so she's helping with that. From what she said, it happened at Eagle Roost."

"What else do you know about it?" Leaphorn asked.

"Not much, except that it got people's attention. We got the most 911 calls in history for that area."

"Was anyone hurt?" Leaphorn thought about the aborted call from Cecil Bowlegs.

"I don't know. There could be sports practices, meetings, you know, all that stuff that happens at schools on Saturday mornings when classes are out. Evidently, it's a mess."

"That's the other reason I'm calling," Leaphorn said. "I was talking to a client who works at Eagle Roost School when I heard something blow up. Now I can't reach the guy, and I'm worried about him. The officer there hasn't called me back."

"Who did you reach, sir?"

"Sergeant Fredrick Stanley."

"Bernie must be dealing with him. Should I have her call you?"

The line went quiet, and Leaphorn gathered his thoughts. When he spoke again, his tone was lighter. "Based on what you just told me, I doubt talking to me is at the top of Stanley's list. And I'm sure Bernie has her hands full. I'll follow up."

Leaphorn phoned the Eagle Roost substation again and left a message that he had information that might be relevant to the bombing. There was a call from Louisa, but he didn't call her back. He'd be home soon.

As he drove and waited for the next idea to percolate up about Stella or Cecil Bowlegs, he thought about Louisa. Did she really want to talk to him about her son? Family issues were certainly not his strong point, but in his years with Louisa as friend and housemate, he'd learned something important. Sometimes all he had to do was listen, ask a question or two, and that helped her solve problems, or so she said. He wished Stella Brown's issues could be that easily handled.

He considered the fake birth certificate stating that Stella had been born at a hospital. Most Navajos her age were born at home. If hers had actually been a hospital birth, perhaps her birth mother was still living in Farmington, NM, or maybe in nearby Aztec or Bloomfield. Was there a problem with the pregnancy that had required her birth mother to be hospitalized? He'd also heard of cases where the mother was under eighteen—too young to put the baby up for adoption without the consent of her parents. That might lead to a falsified birth certificate. He filed the ideas in a to-be-explored slot and turned his truck toward home.

When he pulled onto their road, he hoped to see Kory's black rental sedan, but the man hadn't returned. Odd that he would come to see his mother after so many years of absence, and then leave in less than an hour.

Leaphorn parked and entered the house through the kitchen door, curious to talk to Louisa about her son. He could hear her and a second woman whose voice was unfamiliar chatting in the living room. He called out a hello and strolled over to them.

Sitting in Louisa's favorite chair was a young woman with short blond hair and deep blue eyes. She looked like she could be thirty, or maybe only twenty-five, though he had learned not to make assumptions.

Louisa acknowledged him from her spot on the couch across from the visitor and made the introductions. "Joe, this is Erlinda. Kory's wife."

The young woman glanced at him, then lowered her eyes. "Please call me Lin."

He could see that Erlinda had been crying. The situation made him uneasy. He felt like an intruder in his own house, but he found some words. "Welcome to our home. Nice to meet you."

Louisa spoke gently. "Lin and I were talking girl talk. Would you give us a few minutes?"

"Of course." The relief came through in his voice. "I have lots of work to do."

He found Giddi stretched out in a sunny spot on the windowsill and offered the cat a rub behind the ears. Then he sat at his desk, started his computer, and, to his surprise, found an email from Will Royce with copies of requests to the Navajo Nation and the states of Arizona and New Mexico for Stella Brown's adoption records and the original birth certificate. He skimmed it. The language reflected a dense combination of legalese and bureaucratic jargon. He forwarded the message to Stella and switched to a game of solitaire.

He turned toward the window. Giddi eyed him suspiciously from where she had been napping, stretched, then made a graceful leap into the oversize upholstered armchair by his desk. She gave Leaphorn a look of disdain, stretched again, turned, pranced over his computer keyboard and left some random letters on the screen, then settled down with the look of a feline in charge of the situation and ready to resume a nap.

Leaphorn realized he had had a long morning. Now a nap could be in his immediate future. He looked at his cell phone and turned off the ringer. It was convenient, he concluded, not to be a working cop like Bernie and Chee. Whatever had happened to Cecil Bowlegs would be resolved eventually. A sweet twenty minutes of downtime on that comfy office couch Louisa had encouraged him to buy would help Joe Leaphorn think more clearly.

JIM CHEE FOUND IT DIFFICULT to focus on the workshop, although the presenter had more personality than some of the instructors he'd been subjected to. When he'd accepted the promotion to lieutenant, he, the soon-to-be-retired Largo, and the chief had agreed that they'd use Chee's experience as a Navajo speaker, a person exceptionally well versed in the culture and a man with strong ties to the Hopi nation, to the department's advantage. And Chee's dislike of administrative tasks would be duly noted.

He hadn't thought to ask for an exemption from the job of representing the station at seemingly endless meetings both within the Navajo Police Department itself and with the agencies it collaborated with in the jurisdictional soup that made up the Four Corners area—the unique spot on the Navajo Nation where New Mexico, Arizona, Colorado, and Utah shared a border. Today's session at the Navajo Police headquarters in Window Rock featured a kaleidoscope of topics strung together by new regulations that the organizer wanted to share with the attendees.

The first hour focused on revised guidelines for getting and using federal money in drug interdiction. An important topic, but the information the presenter was discussing had been covered in the handout he'd distributed and reinforced in the online slide presentation the man was reading aloud to the officers in the room. The program wasn't worth getting up early and driving two hours for, but Chee told himself to cheer up. At least he wasn't in danger of being shot, stabbed, or kicked in the groin.

The room's dim light made it easier to think about other things. He did some research on the medicine man he'd known in Tonalea, but had no luck tracking down where to find the hatáálii out that way. He texted the man's name to Leaphorn. His old mentor would have better luck asking about that face-to-face. Then Chee focused on Leaphorn's request and the issue of the adoption of Navajo children by non-Navajo parents. He'd agreed to try to find information on the couple, but his first searches on his laptop while pretending to pay attention to the speaker had come up empty.

He dove deeper and saw the Browns' names in a story about a fund-raiser for a co-op preschool in Albuquerque. From there, he found driver's licenses, tax payments, and the usual public records. But he found nothing on either Stan or Rita Brown dated before Stella had entered first grade in Albuquerque. It was, he thought, as though the Browns had reinvented themselves as Stella's parents.

He wasn't sure that Lieutenant Leaphorn ever used the text function on his cell phone—he'd been pleased when his old mentor bent to that technology at all—but he gave it a try:

Chee here. I'd like a photo of your client and her adoptive parents. Have some?

To his surprise and delight the Lieutenant responded.

No, but one interesting old shot the Browns gave her. Want it?

Sure.

Chee's phone buzzed, and there it was, in black and white. It showed a geological formation Chee recognized—one of the Elephant Feet—with what looked like a Navajo mother and father standing next to the towering sandstone oddities. The woman seemed to be holding an infant in a blanket, but he couldn't tell for sure. Capturing the unusual stone from top to bottom must have been the photographer's goal; beside it the humans, in soft focus, seemed like a side note.

The artistic quality of the picture surprised Chee. Interesting perspective, he thought, and an accurate vision of the role of humans in this vast, harsh, and beautiful landscape.

The fact that Leaphorn's client's mother had saved this photograph told him it must be important. If this baby was the woman who had hired Leaphorn, could the two adults pictured be her Navajo birth parents?

Even though he couldn't remember seeing the picture before, something about the photo seemed familiar. Chee left his phone open on the table with the photo looking up at him, and returned his focus to the meeting.

The workshop topic changed. Now the assembled officers would learn about an update to an agreement approved a few years ago that required the BIA and the FBI to cooperate on Indian country investigations and to develop written guidelines outlining roles and responsibilities for investigators from the BIA, FBI, and tribal law enforcement agencies. The agreement required all BIA, FBI, and tribal law enforcement officers to receive training regarding investigative approaches that took tribal culture into consideration. It defined the responsibility of FBI, BIA, and tribal investigators to make sure that missing person cases were entered into the National Crime Information Center, National Incident-Based Reporting System (NIBRS), and other appropriate federal criminal databases.

This presenter, a Sioux who worked with the FBI, had passion for the subject and noted that DNA from the missing person should always be submitted to the National Missing Person DNA Database when appropriate and available.

Chee listened to the part of the presentation that dealt with communication problems between the agencies and ways to solve them, but when the speaker focused on the value of the NIBRS and how it had been "implemented to improve the overall quality of crime data collected by law enforcement," his thoughts drifted.

He focused again on the old photo. What did it remind him of? Why was it familiar? From the deep recesses of his mind, he recalled a similar photo, this one of a Navajo woman, a man, two young children, and a couple of horses, all in front of what he called a window at Mystery Valley, an area adjoining Monument Valley filled with geological splendor. He remembered that it had been in a book, part of a series of environmental portraits taken on the Navajo Nation at iconic scenic spots. He had seen the book for sale at the book store at El Morro National Monument and at the El Malpais store, too.

If he let his memory ferret out the information, he knew he could come up with the name of the book, and that would lead to the photographer. Maybe the person who took the pictures was still alive. Maybe he or she had kept a record of the people featured. Even if the Elephant Feet photo was not in the book, the style and setting in the picture from Leaphorn reflected the same artistic sensibility. A lot of maybes, Chee realized, but if he could find that book, it would give him a place to start.

When the meeting ended, he walked to the tribal library in the building that also housed the Navajo Museum. He asked the librarian on duty about the book he remembered. She was younger than Chee, about Darleen's age, but he could tell she took her job very seriously.

"Sorry, I'm afraid I'm not aware of anything like that, but I can research it for you if you'd like me to."

"I would like that. This might give you a clue." He showed her the photo Leaphorn had sent. "This is an image like those in the book, or at least similar to them."

She gave it a close look. "It's beautiful. Too bad there's no signature at the bottom. That would help." Then she stood. "I have an idea. Wait here, please."

She trotted off and in a few moments returned with a man in his sixties.

"This is our director, Mr. George Haskie."

"Yá'át'ééh." Chee introduced himself and Haskie did the same. Haskie and Bernie had a clan in common.

"Eleanor told me you were interested in historic photos. How may I help you?"

Chee showed Haskie the picture on his phone. "This reminds me of a book I saw that features a collection of photographs of iconic places, spiritual places, with people in the pictures but not as the focus. Some of the pictures were taken long ago, and some were more recent."

Haskie smiled. "That sounds familiar." Chee could almost feel Haskie's effort to remember the volume. Then the older man nodded.

"I believe we have that book. I can track it down for you. It was a limited edition, so it ought to be shelved in our special collections area.

Come with me. If we have it, you'll need to look at it here. It isn't online, and the book doesn't circulate."

"Circulate?"

"Oh, sorry. That means it can't leave the library. It's not that we don't trust our readers, but things happen, and some of these books are irreplaceable."

Chee followed Haskie past the rows of bookshelves to an area of glass-fronted cases at the rear of the building. The director stopped in front of one of the cases, studied the spines of the books protected there, and then pulled out a key ring with three small keys. He studied them and then selected one to unlock the bookcase.

Chee watched him struggle, but the key didn't work. He tried a second key, and then a third, with the same failure.

The director started to stammer. "I'm sorry. I haven't accessed this case for a while, and I just realized where the correct key is. Our archivist was doing some work with some of these volumes that concern the Long Walk and the establishment of the first reservation that led to the Navajo Nation. She has the key we need, but unfortunately she doesn't work on Saturdays, and I'm afraid her office is locked. She will be in Monday morning, and I know she will be able to help you then."

Chee took a few moments to consider his options. "Do you know a man named Joe Leaphorn?"

"Indeed I do. An elderly gentleman. He worked with our museum on an investigation. Why do you ask?"

"He's the one who's interested in tracking down the photo I showed you. I'll explain to him what we discovered today, and he can make arrangements to see the book. I'd do it myself, but I'm based in Shiprock."

Haskie nodded. "I remember that Lieutenant Leaphorn lives in this area. Please let him know that the book, and the key to open the case, will be available whenever he finds a convenient time next week. He can ask for me or the archivist." He gave Chee her name.

Because he was in Window Rock, Chee decided to stop by and talk to Leaphorn in person. He tried the cell, got no answer, and called the landline. When Louisa answered, she squashed the idea.

"No, sorry. A visit today won't work. I'm in the middle of something.

Have a good trip back and tell Bernie hello for me." And before he could ask her to tell Leaphorn about the book, Louisa was gone; only the clear rejection of his idea remained.

He could have called the lieutenant's cell phone again, but he decided to leave well enough alone. When he got back to Shiprock and the office, he'd email the information about the book. The library was closed now anyway.

Chee had made the drive from Window Rock to Shiprock scores of times. Today, because it was not only Saturday but also, in theory, Chee's day off, he drove over Narbona Pass. He recalled the days when he had been able to see Mount Taylor, Tsoodzil, their beautiful Turquoise Mountain, from the summit in the distance with clarity. He stopped to look today, but the sacred mountain hid in the hazy air, a blend of wood smoke, dust, and other emissions. From the top of the pass, at an elevation of sixty-one hundred feet, he saw a vast stretch of the Navajo Nation and west central New Mexico. Here and there among the browns and grays he caught a glimpse of early spring's soft hint of green, a time for new beginnings.

At Sheep Springs the road merged with the main paved four lane, a route he had driven when it was still known as the Devil's Highway because of its designation as 666, numbers some Christians believed were a sign of the devil. Now it was NM 491, safer with wide paved lanes and shoulders. The New Mexico state legislature had named the portion of the highway that ran in New Mexico as the John Pinto Highway in honor of a long-serving Navajo leader, a marine and World War II code talker who had represented Four Corners County in the New Mexico Senate for several decades.

Chee enjoyed the ride. He didn't hear more about the explosion at Eagle Roost until he got back to the station.

10

Bernadette Manuelito knew that one of her strengths was that she learned from experience. After she was the first responder on the scene of a car explosion that killed a young man in the parking lot outside a packed basketball game, she'd asked Captain Largo for more training. Sure enough, he sent her to programs for dealing with emergencies such as bomb threats, explosions, armed shooters in schools or churches and more. She took refresher classes online when she could. She hoped she could remember all that she had learned when she reached Eagle Roost.

She had to admit that she was excited to be heading to the blast site, with the opportunity it would offer to use that training. She loved a challenge, and this assignment promised that, as well as a chance to further hone her skills as an investigator.

The officer at Eagle Roost had been vague about the incident except to tell her that, because it was early Saturday morning, the campus had no scheduled events around the time of the explosion. She picked up chatter about it on her police radio while she drove to the school. As of now, there was no report of casualties either on the grounds or in the building that blew up.

She made good time in the light traffic and found the school without difficulty. The place would have been hard to miss, given the cloud of dark smoke still rising from the explosion. She joined the few cars and trucks headed in the same direction.

Half a dozen vehicles were parked along the road beyond the closed gates that led to the school grounds, with a handful of drivers standing outside looking through the smoke at what must have been a classroom building. On the other side of the gate, she saw another Navajo police unit, a fire truck, and an ambulance.

A middle-aged white man in jeans, a light-blue jacket, and a ball cap with Eagle Roost printed on the bill stood at the entrance to the school property. He opened the gate when he saw her patrol car, and then signaled to her to lower her window.

"I'm Charles Morgan, the principal here."

Bernie introduced herself.

"If you need anything, I'll be around." Morgan looked past her at the other vehicles. "Up here, probably, dealing with the sightseers and worried parents."

Berne asked the foremost question. "Was anyone hurt in the blast?"

Morgan was watching the fire crews. "Not that I know of. And no one has figured out what happened to cause the explosion. Not yet."

Bernie saw smoke rising from a building that had lost some of its roof and a wall. Beyond it was a gymnasium and a field for track and football. On the other side of the damaged structure, she saw an older building with parking spaces in the front and three portable buildings.

"You're the boss here, Mr. Morgan. What do you think happened?"

He shook his head. "I don't know what to think. This construction of our special education center—where the explosion was—is new. It passed all the inspections. I'm worried that it might have been something intentional. I just hope this was an accident, not, you know . . ."

"Was the building used for anything except classes?"

"Not much. Our special ed and music classes were in there, and a small office, too. We plan to use the garage for our new auto mechanics program when we get the funding. For now, it's storage. As bad as this is, it would have been an unmitigated disaster if the kids had been here, you know? I'm glad it didn't happen yesterday morning just as everyone was getting here." He tapped the roof of her patrol car with his palm. "I'm talking too much. Thanks for coming."

She drove ahead, leaving her unit near the other Navajo police cars at the far edge of the debris from the building. She spotted an officer in a uniform like hers and walked over to him. Sergeant Fredrick Stanley introduced himself the traditional way and she did the same.

"Manuelito, glad you're here. I understand that you're some kind of expert on stuff like this."

She shrugged off the praise. "I got some training. I'd like your take on this mess."

"I was at the substation and heard a rumbling noise that sounded like distant thunder. A few minutes later we started to get a batch of 911 calls about something blowing up out here, an explosion that sounded serious, like a bomb going off. As soon as I went out to my unit, I smelled and saw the smoke. At first we thought it might be a trailer out this way, but it was worse."

The smoke was heavy, but drifting away from her and Stanley, out toward the other campus buildings. The explosion had collapsed part of the building and blasted debris in every direction. The ground sparkled with fragments of glass that captured the sun. Metal, wood, and other wreckage from the blast littered the dirt and the sidewalk.

"By the time I drove up, I could see the flames through what was left of the roof. I turned on the siren and waited there at the entrance. A few people came by to see what had happened, and I made them park outside the school fence so they wouldn't block the road. The principal was down by the building, but he saw my unit and opened the gate for me. The fire crew was already getting set up and had on their Tyvek suits by the time I got here."

Bernie studied the scene a few moments, appreciating Morgan's statement that, as bad as this was, it could have been worse. "I need to talk to the fire crew chief."

"I'll introduce you. We're lucky the guy in charge is a veteran fire-fighter. He worked in Denver before he moved out here."

They walked down to the fire truck, where the smoke was intense. Two firefighters were spraying the remaining flames with water. The third man, an older fellow, was typing on a computer tablet keyboard.

"Hey, Chief, this is Officer Manuelito with the Navajo Police. She's been trained for situations like this. She needs to talk to you."

The chief looked up from the screen. "Tom Bronacky. Pleased to meet you and glad to have your help."

"When will It be safe for me to look at the damage?"

"Maybe an hour. I'll let you know for sure."

Bernie offered a nod of acknowledgment. "I have a few questions in the meantime."

"Go ahead."

"What did you find when you got here?"

"Principal Morgan had the gate open, so we drove right to the scene. We turned off the gas first thing. We're focusing on saving what we can of the building and keeping the fire from spreading to the rest of the campus or the trees. It's lucky that these classrooms were detached and a bit isolated from the others.

"It looks like the blast originated inside the main building, the one that it mostly destroyed. Nothing else was damaged, but this structure— the main classroom area, the office space, the attached garage, and the janitor's closet—all of it is history."

"Do you know what caused the explosion?"

He shook his head.

"What's your best guess?"

"I believe the explosion was based in the janitor's closet, but I can't say what blew up or why. Sergeant Stanley and I spoke as soon as I got here, and then we did a quick reconnaissance. We didn't spot anything obviously unusual, no signs of accelerants. Right, Fred?"

Stanley nodded. "I searched as close to the fire as I could, then I went back to the entrance gate to tell Morgan to secure the scene, you know, keep the neighbors out. There were already a handful of lookie-loos on the road. Morgan probably has his hands full up there."

Bronacky took up the narrative. "When I got here, I asked the principal if there was something especially volatile or unstable in the building. He said there was nothing he knew of, but that the custodian might have had some chemicals, cleaning supplies, stuff like that." He took a breath.

"Morgan mentioned that the custodian sometimes works on Saturdays. We haven't seen him this morning, and we haven't found a body. We'll do a final search when it's safer for our crew."

Bernie nodded. "I hope he's OK. I need to scout around and see what I can learn."

"As soon as the fire is out." Bronacky watched the crew for a moment. "I need to get back to work. Be careful, you two. Stay safe."

Bernie began walking back to her unit to radio in her location and an update. Stanley trotted along beside her. The wind had shifted, making the morning colder and bringing the smoke toward them. She waited until they had reached her vehicle to start a conversation with Stanley.

"Who arrived here first?"

"The principal, then the fire guys, then me. The FBI will send their investigators, too."

Bernie zipped her jacket against the morning chill. Spring in the Four Corners meant unsettled weeks that were a hybrid of winter and summer weather filled with almost constant change, including wind that could propel a fire.

"When did Principal Morgan arrive?"

The sergeant hesitated. "You'll have to ask him. He lives close to here. I wouldn't be surprised if the noise from the blast got him out of bed."

"Did you talk to him?"

"Yeah. He told me he didn't see a vehicle driving away or a person running from the scene. That would have made it easier to pin down what happened."

"Good." Bernie looked at the smoldering rubble of what was left of the building. In addition to the chief, four firefighters were at work quelling the flames. She heard a chime, and Stanley reached in his pocket for his phone and turned to her. "It's NMSP. I called them before I knew you were coming. Their explosive expert should be on the way."

Bernie knew the New Mexico State Police had resources that helped local law enforcement, including the Navajo Nation, when necessary. She gave Stanley credit for asking for help with the incident.

"Tell whoever comes from NMSP that I'm here and to keep me in the loop. I'm going back to the gate to talk to Principal Morgan."

As she approached the principal, Bernie noticed that the number of watchers had grown by three more cars and a pickup. Someone in a blue parka was taking pictures of the destruction with a cell phone. She saw Morgan chatting with a woman, but he broke away from the conversation and headed to Bernie.

She read the question in his face. "Any news from the fire chief?"

"No. He just told me they're making good progress on the fire, but it's not out yet. What did you see when you got here?"

"The fire. Lots of smoke. The classroom complex I helped build destroyed . . . or at least seriously damaged. I saw disappointment and tragedy for the students who used that building and their teachers."

Morgan turned his glance to the smoky sky. "I'm worried about the janitor. Sometimes he does the extra cleaning on weekends. I don't know when he starts work or if he was in there today. I've tried calling the guy, and he doesn't answer."

"The fire team hasn't done the final search for victims yet because of the intensity of the flames," Bernie said, "but they will as soon as it's safe for them. The New Mexico State Police are sending an explosive expert to help figure out what happened."

"Even though the rest of the campus was not involved, I'm wondering if I need to cancel school on Monday."

"You should. Things will be a mess down there, and cleanup will take a while. And if this wasn't accidental and there's a fatality, the FBI will be involved. Any murder or suspicious death in Indian country, and that includes the Navajo Nation, is the FBI's job. You'll need to leave the structural damage and all the debris in place until they're done."

"The FBI? Really? Way out here in the sticks?"

"Yes, unless the fire chief or the expert from the state police can make the determination that it was not intentional. The FBI is deeply concerned about school bombings."

"That makes sense," he said, "but I hate for our students to miss class. Adding the FBI sounds like a lot more uproar."

Bernie glanced at him, curious. "What else has been going on out here? Have you had bomb threats?"

"No, nothing like that. But ever since I arrived two years ago, the campus has been under construction, trucks coming and going, noise, distractions galore. We just finished work on the building that was destroyed, so finally the children and teachers here had almost had enough space. I'd hoped to start working on outdoor improvements next, but it looks like the special ed center will need major repairs." He sighed. "It's a challenge."

"Anything else?"

"Well, one of our favorite teachers quit abruptly a few weeks ago. That upset the students. And now this."

Bernie noticed another SUV heading down the road toward the school entrance gate. "You're drawing a crowd here."

"Some of these folks are curious neighbors, but most of them are bringing their kids to the gym for basketball practice and they don't know what happened. Could I let them through to get to the gym? It's not close to the special education building."

"Of course not!" His naïveté surprised her. "No one except law enforcement and firefighters can be on campus until the team can assure you that everything is safe."

"So that means no practice today, probably no school Monday. Is that right, Officer?"

Bernie nodded. "At least that long. You can tell the people waiting for practice that the school is closed until further notice. Want my help?"

He looked tired and sad. "No, thanks. I'll do that. They're my families."

"Why don't you ask the parents out there to call the other parents with kids who were expected to practice today and let them know it's canceled? You'll have enough to deal with."

"Good thinking." He glanced at the first truck. "Marian can explain the situation. She's good with people."

Bernie saw the change in his posture and knew he was about to walk from the gate to find Marian. "Before you go, tell me about the custodian who might have been working out there."

"Cecil Bowlegs is his name."

"I've heard that Bowlegs name before." Bernie searched her memory and recalled a poster her sister Darleen had done for the Missing and Murdered Indigenous People project. They had talked about how Bowlegs was an unusual surname in Navajo land. "A woman with the same last name was missing, right?"

"Yes, that's right. Cecil's wife. Bethany. She's the teacher I mentioned who quit and disappeared. She still hasn't been found. Ever since she left Eagle Roost, Bowlegs has been upset and distracted. The quality of his work has declined. I wonder if he might have done something that caused this disaster."

"Do you know the man well?"

"Well enough to notice that he's not himself. Uneasiness hangs heavy on him. Poor soul. He's a decent man, a good worker, but he was troubled even before Bethany vanished."

"How so?"

"I got to know his wife pretty well when she worked for me. She was worried about his gambling losses. That money issue put real stress on both of them. Sometimes I overheard them arguing on the phone."

He paused. "I feel uncomfortable talking to you about this, but between us, she made more money than he did. At one point, he had so much casino debt he had to sell his car. Luckily, he lives close enough for him to walk to work if he needs to."

"Have you tried to call him since I've been here?"

"No." Morgan pulled a phone from his jacket pocket and looked at it. "Do you want to ask him about the explosion?"

"I do, but you place the call. He knows your number, so he's more likely to answer than if it's a stranger like me. After you say hello, please hand the phone to me."

And, Bernie realized, if Bowlegs wasn't home, the fire team should be alerted to the fact that they might find a body when they were able to search the ruined building.

Morgan dialed and seemed to be listening intently. Then he tapped the screen a few times, put the phone in his pocket, and frowned. "No answer. I sent him a text to call me instead of leaving a voicemail. No mailbox set up for him."

Bernie stood with Morgan, watching the fire crew work.

"Tell me more about Cecil."

She learned that Bowlegs had worked at the school for five years, cleaning the building and handling other custodial jobs and simple maintenance. He volunteered to help with other duties, especially those involving athletics. When the principal admonished him for neglecting his job, Bowlegs grew confrontational and declined to discuss the issue.

"Why didn't you fire him?"

"I'd given him a verbal warning, you know. Firing a public employee is complicated, and rightly so. Not only that, I felt sorry for the man. Bethany wasn't an ideal woman, but she and the job were about all he had." Morgan paused. "I sensed some dissatisfaction on her side, and I know from my own divorce, that kind of attitude is hard to deal with. I think she ran off to pursue her music career. It would be easier for Bowlegs if another man had been involved."

"I thought she was a teacher."

"Well, she started as a teacher's aid, then helped with an after-school music program, got certified, and segued into teaching three classes a semester. About a year ago she went to work for me as an assistant, and I set up a little office for her in the special ed building. She already taught her music program there. To make room for her, we stored a bunch of supplies and old textbooks in the garage. And the tools we thought we'd need for the auto mechanic's program."

"It sounds like the school was crowded even before this."

"That's right." Morgan studied the smoldering building for a moment. "With the loss of this building, things will be tighter. And it's not like there's extra money to cover new construction. These families work hard out here, and they sacrifice for their children. The school is the center of our small community. It's a huge loss. Breaks my heart."

The fire chief walked up the hill toward them. Bronacky looked tired, Bernie thought, tired and worried.

"I think we've got things under control over there. We were really lucky nothing else exploded and that the fire didn't spread to other structures or into the trees. I'm surprised at how quickly that building burned."

"Me, too," Morgan said.

"I remember that the school had a nice grant to build it, so I would have expected it to be more fire-resistant, new construction and all, but it burned fast." He turned to Bernie. "You and Sergeant Stanley can take a look now if you want. Please be careful."

"Is there anything in there we should pay special attention to?"

"Oh, everything, I guess." He shook his head. "This is the first school explosion I've dealt with, so I appreciate whatever insights you might have. It looks like someone might have been sleeping in that building on a cot or something, unless they use that for the kids." Bronacky looked at the principal. "Does anyone spend the night in there?"

"No." He paused. "The music teacher was having some problems at home, and her office was in there, so she might have spent the night. I think they mostly use the cot for naps for the special ed kids. I remember seeing a little one snoozing there last week. I feel bad for those kids, and the music kids, too. I imagine all their supplies and whatever work the teacher had saved for them are ruined."

"It's too early to say this officially, but I'm sure the building and contents are a total loss. There's not even enough left of the room to tell if the students there were kindergartners or high schoolers."

"Do you think the explosion may have come from the janitor's closet?" Morgan asked. "You know, set off by improperly stored chemicals or something?"

"Maybe the blast did start in there. I can't speak to the chemicals."

Bernie said, "Where was that closet?"

"In the back of the building, near the garage." Bronacky moved his hand toward the damage in front of them. "That was the center of the destruction."

Bernie saw a black-and-white New Mexico State Police unit pull up to the gate. Morgan opened it and greeted the officers, and they watched the SUV drive through. It parked near the other police units. Bernie recognized the driver, a crime scene investigator who had helped train her in explosives. Sergeant Mark Donovan was a bright young officer whom she respected. She left Morgan and walked toward where Donovan had parked.

He greeted her with a quick hello. "Glad to see you here, Manuelito. While we suit up, you can tell me what you know so far."

Bernie introduced Sergeant Stanley. "Do we need to wait for the FBI explosives team?"

"No. I know they're on the way," Donovan said. "They can play catch-up. From the looks of this mess, the job will take a while. What's the story?"

"Sergeant Stanley and I both talked to Principal Morgan and the fire chief about what they saw when they arrived. The site was in flames until a few minutes ago."

"What was the building used for?"

"Special education and music classes, and office space. Also there's a garage and a janitor's closet. That's where the fire chief believes the explosion happened."

Donovan looked at her. "I remember you from the training. You're a quick study. I'm glad you're here."

"Thanks. I'm glad you're here, too."

"I'll put on my Tyvek, and we'll look at the building as soon as we're ready." He studied Sergeant Stanley. "Do you want to join us?"

"Not unless I have to. The smoke and fumes are bad for my asthma."

"That's OK, Sergeant," Bernie said. "We can handle it."

Stanley glanced at the school gate. "I'll go up and give Morgan a hand. I've read that sometimes in cases of arson the perpetrator likes to survey the damage. I'll ask the principal about people in the crowd up there. He'll know if there's a wild card in the mix. I want to take photos of everyone and every vehicle."

Bernie went back to her unit, where she quickly slipped the protective coveralls over her jacket and uniform pants. She and Donovan walked to the smoldering building and surveyed the wreckage. They started with a slow study of the outside of the building, stepping gingerly over the shattered glass and metal fragments. They took pictures of things that might have been linked to the explosion and left markers in places they thought the FBI might wonder about as significant clues. They touched nothing.

"Send the photos you take to me, the FBI, and whatever other agency gets involved," Donovan said. "Logically, we'll work together, team up, solve the problem, and leave egos aside."

"That would be nice." She laughed. "I have a good relationship with Sage Johnson, the FBI agent in Farmington. When we've worked together a couple of times before this, she built a cross-agency team."

"That sounds good."

"Johnson is sharp, and she likes working with Navajos. She told me that she wants to stay."

Donovan bent down to look at an oddly shaped piece of metal and photographed it. "Hard to believe she'll really stay. Most people that competent move on to more money, more status, more opportunity. Maybe she's in love."

"I think she likes the scenery."

"How about you? I heard you might be looking for something different."

The statement caught Bernie off guard. "Where did you hear that?"

He laughed. "I've got my sources."

"Well, you can tell the rumor mill I'm dealing with some family stuff that makes staying close to home best for now."

"You know NMSP is always in the market for a sharp woman officer."

They finished their survey of the exterior of the site, finding nothing that looked like possible arson. Donovan noticed a cell phone partially buried beneath the rubble. He marked it for the FBI. Then they went into the building.

Bernie watched her step as she took photos of the destruction. There were papers everywhere, most of them damaged by the fire or the water used to contain the flames or both. Splintered desks, ruined books, collapsed shelving, and more debris crowded the space. The glass from the shattered windows covered the floor like brilliant snow. She took dozens of pictures, moving efficiently through what was left of the building. She didn't know enough about explosions to determine exactly what had happened here, but she understood that the destruction was extensive.

The classroom shared a wall with the garage, and that wall remained intact. She doubted that the garage itself had suffered any damage, except perhaps from the smoke and firefighter's water. They walked back outside to survey the damage again. The metal garage door remained sound, but the small window had shattered from the force of the blast.

Donovan studied the exterior of the garage for a moment. "There's less damage to this part of the structure."

"That's what is looks like." Bernie agreed. "But I want to take a look inside."

11

Jim Chee thought about the photo as he drove. He hadn't spent a lot of time in Tonalea, the Navajo chapter near the Elephant Feet sandstone, but he knew an officer who lived out there. He started to call him from his unit, then realized he didn't know exactly what to ask.

He stopped for gas at the convenience store near the turnoff for Bernie's mother's house. He missed Bernie's sweet presence and knew she'd call when she could. When he climbed out of his unit, he saw Mrs. Darkwater at the gas pumps and felt a rush of gratitude. Her help with Mama had made it possible for Darleen to enroll in college again and for Bernie to keep working full time.

Mrs. D recognized him, too, of course. "You should tell that wife of yours not to worry so much about her mother. That lady and I look after each other."

Chee nodded. "My wife is a skilled worrier."

"She's a warrior?"

"That's right. And she appreciates everything you do for her mother and for her sister. I do, too."

Mrs. Darkwater grinned. "Those two are so different. Your wife is so serious, you know, she likes everything in order. Her sister is like a butterfly, going from one thing to the next and the next. Now, she's back at school. At her age." The woman removed the pump nozzle from her car and replaced the gas cap as she spoke. "And she has that boyfriend."

Chee couldn't decipher her tone of voice. Was she accepting of Slim,

Darleen's steady male companion, or did he hear a note of criticism? He finished washing the windshield of his unit and started to work on Mrs. Darkwater's dusty windshield, listening as she talked on. She seemed to be in no hurry to leave.

"The boyfriend says he can stay with your wife's mother when I have to have my operation."

"Operation?"

"He seems to be a nice young man, polite and respectful to us old ladies."

Chee said it again. "Operation?"

"The doctor says everything will be fine. Don't worry, and I won't worry. We'll give that job to your wife. She's good at that, too. A worrying warrior." She tapped her windshield with a stubby fingernail. "Hey, you missed a spot." Chee took care of it, and she climbed into her car and drove away.

He pulled away from the gas pump, too, and radioed the station. "I'll be there in about half an hour unless the captain needs me sooner. I'm watching for speeders and working on my report from the meeting."

"Everything's quiet as far as I know." Sandra chuckled. "So quiet I'm getting nervous."

Chee parked his white SUV with the green-and-gold Navajo Nation shield on the shoulder near the intersection with Highway 491 and the road to Toadlena, and got to work on his report. He knew that the sight of the police car was enough to slow speeders and even give those texting while driving a reason to desist for a few minutes. Writing didn't come naturally to Chee, but he paid attention to the notes he took and used them and excerpts from the handouts to create a concise summary of the meeting at Window Rock.

When he heard his phone *ping*, he assumed it was a text from Bernie, but instead it was his sister-in-law, Darleen.

Hello out there. Bernie is ignoring me. Can you have her call me?

He responded: What's up?

Mama wants to tattle on me.

Poor Bernie, he thought, but he texted, I'll tell her.

He had finished writing his report and was checking it for typos a final time when his phone buzzed with a call. He hoped it was Bernie, but this time it was Leaphorn. As usual, the Legendary Lieutenant got to the point.

"Louisa mentioned that you'd called. Do you have some news for me?"

Chee explained about the photo and his visit to the library. "Did your lost bird say anything about that picture that might help?"

"Just what I told you."

Leaphorn hadn't talked to him about it, in fact, but Chee didn't contradict him. "Could you go over it again?"

"Sure. She found the picture in a box with her birth certificate and a very small silver and turquoise bracelet. That's it."

"Was there anything on the back of the picture?"

"Just the date I gave you, remember? Nineteen seventy-seven, the year before the Indian Child Welfare Act was passed. What have you got?"

Chee explained his hunch that the picture was part of a larger project. "The librarian said it wasn't available electronically," he said, "but the Window Rock library has a book of photographs that might give us some clues. They keep it in a locked case as part of special collections, and the woman who has the key wasn't there. I couldn't check it out, but I wanted to see if Stella's photo was in it and if it had a list of names of his subjects. Anyway, the librarian said you could take a look on Monday."

"Did you speak with the director?" Leaphorn asked.

"Yes."

"Haskie, right?"

"Yes sir."

"You have Haskie's number?"

Chee found a business card in his pocket. "I have his office number and his cell phone."

"Great. I'll take them. Do you have any other news for me?"

"No sir. Just a question. Louisa sounded stressed when she answered the phone. Is she doing all right these days?"

"I hope so." Chee heard the Legendary Lieutenant exhale. "Hard to figure out what's going on with her. But women have never been my strong suit."

Chee waited for Leaphorn to say more, but instead he hung up.

Chee drove back to Shiprock, where the new guy, Roper Black, awaited him. He had recommended Roper for the job. It was good to have another trained officer on board to ease the load, and especially a person who spoke both Navajo and technology. He'd promised the captain he'd introduce Roper at the chapter houses and elsewhere. While they were out, they'd visit a few families who, he knew from experience, tended to call for help more often.

Bernie would have been the one to do this had she not been sent to Eagle Roost. Officer Bigman could have done the orientation, but he had the day off. And, besides, Chee knew the players and had credibility with them.

As he headed toward the substation, Chee thought again about Leaphorn's request for information. The fact that he'd been asked to help with a background check on Stan and Rita Brown told him that Leaphorn knew, or at least suspected, that something was amiss with the adoption. He had found no record of the couple until Stella began attending elementary school. That told Chee that, at the very least, the Brown family was extremely private and camera shy. In his experience, people like that sometimes had something to hide, including their true identities.

He mulled over the situation as he drove. Usually, people tried to disappear because they were wanted for something or running from someone. Fraudsters and felons escaping from the people they'd ripped off, or from the law or other bad guys. Children or spouses slipping away from abusive relationships. People with huge debts hiding their real identities. Women and men in danger of retaliation for telling the truth relocated in the witness protection program.

Chee had discovered during his days at St. Michael's High School that when a person entered a convent or a monastery they buried their old persona and took on a new name to match the transition. Disappearance and transition.

His imagination went into overdrive. What if the Browns had both been part of a religious order, or even a cult? Could they have somehow found each other and restructured their lives together with a new identity and an adopted baby?

He got to the station, did some preliminary searches for Stan and Rita Brown, and came up with nothing except a few hits related to Stella. Stan had passed away without an obituary or funeral notice that Chee could find. Rita Brown's obituary lacked her birth date and any trace of family genealogy. Their death certificates listed date, time, location, and cause of death—a heart attack in one case and kidney failure in the other. No help there.

Chee spent the rest of the day driving in his unit with Roper, wondering about the mysterious Brown couple, and hoping he would hear from Bernie.

12

Bernie and Donovan had trotted away from the rubble and smoke to take a break when Bronacky joined them.

"How are you two doing? Find anything?" He asked as though he really wanted an answer.

"I haven't seen any evidence that yells bomb or Molotov cocktail or school terrorism. I figure that's a good thing." Bernie looked at Officer Donovan. "What about you?"

"Ditto. I'm tired, and I'd like to go home and see my son's Little League game." Donovan rolled his neck from side to side. "What a way to spend a Saturday!"

Bronacky shared an exhausted smile. "I'm glad to hear that you don't think this was intentional. It's a sad loss for our community, but so far, I'm guessing it must be some kind of weird accident. It was lucky that the fire didn't spread to the garage."

"I hope you're right about this being an accident. Maybe a malfunctioning gas line and something with a spark to ignite an explosion?" Bernie took a welcome deep breath of the fresh air. Even wearing a mask, she'd felt the smoke from the building burning her lungs. "The FBI will make the final call, of course."

"After this break, Bernie and I will check out the garage and take a second look at the classroom space," said Donovan. "By then, Agent Johnson from the FBI will probably be here to double-check."

"Yeah, we're about to get out of here, too, for some lunch at the station. I'm gonna help the crew pack up. Some volunteers are bringing food for you guys and Morgan and the FBI when they show up. Your lunch should be here any minute."

"That sounds good." Donovan spoke with enthusiasm. "It's already been a long day."

"Food would be great. Let's eat before we tackle the garage." Bernie had only had coffee for breakfast because she had to squeeze in her run. Her plan had been to stop in Shiprock for a quick bite to eat in her unit, but then she got the call to drive out to Eagle Roost. She hadn't realized she was hungry until Bronacky mentioned that lunch was on the way.

The fire truck left, and Chief Bronacky followed in his red car. A few minutes later, a pickup truck turned onto the road to the school. As it drew closer, Bernie recognized the official-looking shield logo on the door—an eagle in the background, with a ladder, firefighter helmet, and hatchet in the foreground and the words "Eagle Roost Fire Department" circling the images.

Principal Morgan opened the gate, and the truck drove through and parked next to Bernie's unit. She went to greet the two volunteers as they got out—a man in his fifties who introduced himself as Joseph, and a high school student, Nadia, carrying a cooler.

"Chief Bronacky mentioned that some FBI investigators were coming, so we made plenty for everyone," Joseph said. "We have bottled water, Cokes, root beer, and some energy drinks. Roast beef, turkey, and a few sandwiches with just cheese."

"Thanks so much. Nice ice chest. I like the way it's built so someone can sit on the top."

Nadia smiled at the compliment. "My mom let me use it. She said to tell everyone thanks for trying to save our school."

"Sure. It's part of the job."

"The chief said we could ask you if you would show us the building that exploded," Nadia said. "He gave us the big lecture about safety and said it was up to the investigators."

Bernie thought about it. "I don't think so. The cause of the blast is under investigation. We can't take a chance on contaminating the scene or on either of you getting hurt."

Joseph moved the cooler into the shade behind Bernie's unit. "Let's eat, and we'll get back to the station."

Bernie raised the lid and took out a cold Coke, her first of the day, imagining its sweetness. She turned to the volunteers. "Are either of you interested in becoming a firefighter?"

"I've been a firefighter," Joseph said. "I worked up in Taos for about ten years, until I quit and moved out here to raise a few cows." The man had some gray at the temples. "I volunteer in dispatch with Eagle Roost and I have a granddaughter in school here. That's the reason I wanted to help with the delivery for you and the crew here. I wanted to see the damage."

Nadia pushed her shoulder-length black hair away from her face, and Bernie noticed that the turquoise in the rings on her right hand was the same shade as the stones in her earrings. "I want to be an EMT. Once I graduate from high school, I'm taking emergency medical training. I'm already studying online, and it's way cool. I might get into fire control, too. When I heard the explosion, I knew that it was close to or at my school. I'm worried about it, and I wanted to look at what happened for myself. I promise not to pick up anything or walk anywhere except where you tell me."

The girl was outspoken for a Navajo teenager talking to a law enforcement officer. Bernie gave her credit for that. She looked at the smoldering building. "OK. I'll walk with you a little closer to the structure, only because you guys are volunteers with the fire department. Follow me. Watch where you step, and don't touch anything. Got it?"

They both agreed.

Bernie led the way, making sure they didn't get too near the damaged building. Nadia followed at her heels, asking question after question about the explosion, how cooperative agencies divided the work, and what kind of evidence they needed to figure out this situation. Bernie briefly explained the steps involved. Part of her guiding philosophy of life was that you could never be too kind to other first responders or the volunteers helping them.

They stood a few moments, looking at the wreckage. Most of the smoke had cleared with the breeze, although a few areas of the structure were still smoldering slightly.

Nadia turned away. "I love my school. My most favorite teacher worked in that building, and she taught me how to read music and how to sing. I used to practice for the chorus here. And now it's all ruined."

Joseph looked at the mess with his hands in his coat pockets. Unlike the young woman, he seemed unmoved, a reaction Bernie didn't find surprising, considering his background.

"When you worked for Taos FD, did you deal with explosions?"

"I handled a few there, and one or two here when I was on the crew. I dealt with a house that was destroyed when a hot water heater blew. Luckily, no one was home. The worst was a blast that killed a worker—a natural gas leak and a cigarette."

He rubbed his nose; the stench was strong. "Officer, did anyone see anything that makes you think this was not accidental?"

"I can't talk about that. As I said earlier, the situation is under investigation."

Bernie noticed Nadia wiping away tears.

"This is hard to take, isn't it?"

The girl nodded. "My little brother went to his music lessons in that classroom, too. Only a crazy person would do something so awful. Why would someone do something so terrible? I don't get it."

Bernie looked at the ruined building. "No one here knows why this happened. That's what we want to find out."

Joseph put his hand on Nadia's arm. "We love our school. This place is our place. I'm on a committee to raise money for the football team, and I'd say Morgan has done a good job of getting grants and donations for us. He's an outsider, but he's done OK. Now, he has a lot more to deal with."

Bernie nodded as she looked at the rubble.

"Whoever did this might be crazy," Joseph said, "but he's crazy smart. If this was intentional, it took planning. We live in a strange time, you know? Kids blow things up all weekend in video games. It's not a stretch to imagine some person with too much time on his hands wanting to try a bomb in real life, is it, Officer?"

"I didn't call it a bomb." Bernie knew she'd been careful to use the word *explosion*. "The cause is under investigation."

"In that case I bet you cops will look into the custodian here. He's an odd duck. Doesn't socialize much. I've heard that he doesn't like the principal, but he really loves this school and his job. He's a big help at track meets, fundraisers, all that additional stuff schools do to build community and just stay afloat."

Nadia nodded. "You mean Mr. Bowlegs, right? He's always nice to me and to my little brother."

"How do you know Bowlegs and the principal didn't get along?"

Joseph laughed. "You know the way things go in small towns. People love to talk about their neighbors. Bowleg's wife got an extra job as Morgan's assistant. Sometimes she and he would be here together, late. Just the two of them. I'd see them when I came for PTA meetings. I never noticed anything inappropriate, just so you know."

Nadia moved farther away from the wreckage. "If anyone had been in the classroom, they would have been killed, right?"

Bernie nodded. "That could have happened."

"But the kids were home because this is the weekend." Nadia sounded more mature than Bernie would have expected. "Even if this was a bomb, whoever did it didn't want to kill kids or their teachers. If it was an accident, we're lucky it happened today instead of yesterday."

"I agree," Joseph said. He turned to Bernie. "This girl is smart."

Nadia looked embarrassed by the compliment.

"A lot of people love this school, too, like Nadia's mother and her friends." Joseph shook his head. "It's been here their whole lives. This place is where they learned, where they got in trouble, fell in love, part of our history. We know it might not be the best school in New Mexico or even on the Navajo Nation, but it was ours. And now it's been hurt. This makes me, makes all of us probably, feel threatened. Threatened and very sad that our community came under attack."

Bernie walked back with them to their truck, thinking that it was part of her responsibility to keep them and the site safe.

"Do you like being a cop?" Nadia asked the question shyly. "Maybe that's the direction for me. A cop or an EMT."

Bernie smiled at her. "It's an interesting career, and we could use more Navajo women in law enforcement." She pulled out a business card and handed it to the girl. "Here's my cell number. If you'd like to talk about what it's like to be a cop, call me and I'd be glad to chat with you. I know a lot of EMTs, and I could put you in touch with someone to discuss that, too."

The volunteers started to drive away but Joseph backed up, and Nadia rolled down the window and yelled to Bernie. "I left the cooler by your police car. Can you give it to Principal Morgan when you're done, please?"

"Of course, no problem."

Bernie and Donovan each ate a sandwich and offered one to the principal and Sergeant Stanley. The cooler had plenty of food for the FBI team when they arrived. Donovan wanted to finish his survey of the classroom for clues about the cause of the explosion, so Bernie agreed to tackle the garage.

The garage had only one small window, and because the firefighters had wisely turned off the power, it was dark inside. The big metal door that would have rolled open to let fresh air and light into the space remained intact and tightly closed. Bernie left open both the smaller door to the outside and the door that connected the garage to the brighter damaged classroom space.

She noticed the late-model Hyundai Elantra parked inside right away, since it took up a large part of the space. The flames hadn't spread this far, so the floor was dry, but, like the rest of the building, the room stank of smoke.

She used the strong flashlight from her unit to inspect the room. It looked messy, but compared to the rest of the building, it had held up well. As the principal had told her, in addition to the new auto repair program, the garage served as storage for a large collection of miscellaneous folding chairs. Utility tables leaned against one wall, and cabinets with supplies for special education and music classes occupied another. She assumed that the impact of the explosion had forced most of the cabinet doors open, and crayons, markers, kazoos, and more littered the floor. She stepped over mechanics' tools and a fire extinguisher. She took a few pictures to verify the chaos and the structure's minimal damage.

She turned to go, but as she walked past the car, something in the front seat caught her eye, a shape that could have been a person. Steeling herself for the worst, she swung the beam of her flashlight into the vehicle's interior.

The light reflected on a human face, eyes staring blindly, mouth hanging open. Bernie forced herself to keep looking. Death had claimed a Navajo woman, slumped behind the steering wheel. Even though the fire hadn't reached the car, smoke could be equally deadly. Was that what had happened here?

Pushing away her questions, Bernie opened the car door with her gloved hand.

The dome light picked up a dark patch of dried blood on the woman's scalp, and she could now see the long, black hair resting against the instrument panel. From the smell alone, she knew there was no reason to touch the corpse. The woman had clearly died days before the explosion.

On the passenger seat next to the body, Bernie noticed a neatly folded Navajo blanket.

She took a step back from the vehicle, put her hand on the medicine pouch she always wore for protection, and yelled toward the classroom for Donovan.

She knew the investigation had just gotten a whole lot more complicated.

13

Leaphorn called Haskie's library work phone from his home office and left a message. He and the library director were longtime associates, so even though it was a weekend, he felt confident in using the man's cell number.

Haskie not only answered but sounded happy to have the call. They exchanged pleasantries, and then Leaphorn asked for the favor.

"I'd like to help you," Haskie said, "but one of my staff people has the only key to the locked case. She went to Phoenix for the weekend, but I can help you on Monday. We haven't had the case open for a long time. Not to sound discouraging, but I wouldn't be surprised if her key doesn't work anymore either."

Leaphorn chuckled. "Well, I'm good with locks. I've got some tools that do the same job as keys. And we wouldn't even have to wait until Monday."

"Really?" Haskie laughed. "You're a man of many talents."

"And the tools don't leave any damage. Only you and I would know, and I'm great at keeping secrets."

"You old fox. Come on in. I'm at my office today until five thirty when the library closes. I can stay a bit later so it's just you and me in special collections. You'd like that, right?"

"Sounds like a plan." Leaphorn mentioned the book. "I might like to take that home with me. Could I do that?"

"Well, we can talk about that once we find it."

"Ahéhéé. I appreciate this."

Why, he wondered, did finding out if she was Navajo matter so much to Stella now? He had asked her that question in different words almost every time they spoke. And each time, her answer was a variation on the same theme: knowing why wouldn't help him solve the problem.

If he'd known the birth certificate Stella brought to Window Rock was a fake, Leaphorn would never have agreed to such a limited time frame for helping her find her Navajo roots—if they even existed. Either her adoptive mom and dad, or her biological mother, or maybe even the father, had something to hide. The birth certificate had been falsified skillfully enough for Stella to use it as proper identification. If she hadn't been so curious, the lie would have stayed.

He wondered where her original birth certificate was, or if it had been destroyed many years ago. He pulled up her file on his computer and began mapping the names of the towns she remembered living in from her girlhood. She'd said that her family had lived in Albuquerque for her kindergarten and first-grade years and then moved away. Her father had died in Phoenix and her mother passed on in Farmington. Stella told him she didn't remember all the places they'd lived when she was little. She'd hoped that the boxes of material she'd acquired after her mother died would offer some useful clues, but Stella had come up short.

Leaphorn's careful review of all of Stella's dates and places took concentration, and he forgot about Louisa and the woman she called her daughter-in-law until he heard the front door open and close.

A few moments later Louisa knocked at his office.

"Got a minute?" He heard exhaustion in her voice.

"Come on in." He saved his work on the computer and minimized the screen.

Louisa sat in the big chair and gently put Giddi, who had been enjoying the sun's warmth on the broad window seat, onto her lap. Louisa patted the cat absentmindedly. He could almost hear her gathering her thoughts, figuring out how to say what she needed to tell him. He turned his chair to face her.

"I would like to discuss what Kory told me," she said, "and tell you about Erlinda, but I don't even know where to start. It's overwhelming."

Leaphorn felt more comfortable dealing with drunks or giving in-struction to rookie officers than he did talking to Louisa about feelings, but he sat calmly, hoping she wouldn't start to cry. One thing that he appreciated about this woman was that she used her words wisely. Sure, she sometimes said more than he needed to hear, but he'd grown used to that. She had a direct way of letting him know if she wanted his advice or just wanted him to help her understand the issue.

She surprised him by starting with a question. "What did you think of Kory?"

"I didn't talk to him, except to say hello."

"I know, but you're a quick judge of people."

Leaphorn waited to hear if she had more to say. She did.

"Do you want to know what I think of my son? I think he acted like a jerk. He was rude to you and then rude to me. He got horrible news about the cancer, sure. I can cut him some slack, but I don't know how to help him." She leaned toward him. "Go ahead, ask me some questions."

"Why did he come to see you?"

"Well, that's complicated. At first, he seemed interested in my life, you know? He asked if I was still teaching, how long I'd lived in Window Rock, why I didn't move closer to NAU, and how you and I met. Some of the questions were about things I had told him in my emails, but he doesn't respond to them very often. And then he just says 'Message received.'

"As we were talking, well, it felt more like an interrogation than a conversation. I asked him what his plans were, and that didn't go well at all. He started to swear and said his life had been a mess for a long time even without cancer, and that now another part of the disaster was that he'd been stupid enough to marry the wrong person."

She swallowed. "I was stunned by that, by his fury, and by his self-pity. I didn't know what to say, and it made him more annoyed that I was silent. He got up and started pacing. I tried to backtrack and ask him when he'd gotten married, and if there was anything I could do to help. Then a young woman rang the doorbell. Erlinda, the one I was talking to when you came in, remember? She said, 'Hi, I'm Kory's wife,' and of course I invited her in."

He nodded.

"Well, Kory lost it. He was enraged, far beyond angry. He yelled at me that I should have asked him before opening the door for his wife. Then he swore at Erlinda, and called her terrible names. He slammed out the front door and drove off. Left his glasses behind.

"Both of us were speechless. She started to cry, and we hugged each other. Then I got mad and I'm still really upset. I don't understand that behavior." Louisa coughed, then coughed again.

"I'll bring you some water." Leaphorn went to the kitchen. When he came back with the glass, Louisa was on her feet, looking out the window.

He handed the drink to her. "The good news is, you have a daughter-in-law now."

She smiled. "And more than that. Lin learned she was pregnant last week. She talked Kory into coming here so we could meet and she could give me her good news."

"Where did she go?"

"Back to the hotel. She called Kory, and he picked her up. He didn't even come in to say goodbye to me. So, here's my question: What did I do wrong?"

"Nothing." He answered without hesitation. "Your son is an adult and he's responsible for his life. I know you and I know you always do your best at whatever you take on."

"I guess my best wasn't good enough."

Leaphorn took a second to compose his thoughts. "That name-calling and Kory's anger concern me. Do you think Erlinda feels safe?"

"The Kory I loved would never hurt his wife. He'd never hurt anybody. But the Kory I talked to today was out of control."

He noticed that she'd sidestepped the question. "Do you know how to reach Erlinda?"

When she said nothing, Leaphorn let the silence sit between them. It grew heavier, then Louisa nodded. "She made sure I had her phone number, and I gave her mine. Maybe you're right about this, Joe. I could tell she was scared. I guess I'm in denial."

"I'd like you to text her, to ease my mind, to make sure she's safe."

Louisa pulled out her phone, clicked a few buttons, and shoved it toward him, with Erlinda's latest text message on the screen. He watched Louisa type: Checking to make sure you and K got to the hotel. You guys OK?

After waiting a few empty minutes for a response that didn't come, Louisa slipped the phone back into a pocket. She frowned. "You told me to remember that Kory is an adult. Well, so is his wife. If she's unhappy or feels threatened, she could leave."

Leaphorn had learned from sad experience that leaving wasn't always possible for people threatened with domestic violence, and he knew Louisa understood that, too. He checked the time.

"If we don't hear from her within twenty minutes, I'm going to call her, so please let me know if you get a text. I'll use my own phone." He asked Louisa for the number and she gave it to him.

"I realize that Kory has a temper," Louisa said, "but he'd never harm anyone, and I'm not saying that just because I'm his mother. You're overreacting. I'll let you know if I hear from Lin."

Leaphorn let the comment go. He hoped she was right.

He went back to working on tracking the Brown residences and transferring the names of the towns where Stella remembered living to a map, marking each with a red dot. Then he'd check public records there for any sign of the Browns. He thought fondly of the map he'd had as a cop and how he'd mounted it in his office so he could use pushpins with different-colored heads to categorize crimes and their locations. Now computer programs kept track of all that automatically. He could access all kinds of data once he managed to remember each different username and the accompanying passwords, each with so many letters, numbers, and ampersands.

When he had finished his plotting, he stepped back to take a look. At first glance, Stella's hometowns didn't seem to have much in common except that they all were small burgs. Why, he wondered, had her parents moved to these places? And moved away to another small town, and then another? So many moves at a crucial time in her development from child to adult.

Leaphorn took some tape from his desk drawer and fastened the map to the back of his office door, where he could study it whenever he looked up from his computer. Perhaps an idea would come to him. Perhaps Chee's contacts would learn something about the Browns that might connect to Stella's Navajo mom, or give him the information he needed to tell his client that there was no Navajo mother in her background.

The day had gone so quickly that he'd barely given Cecil Bowlegs a second thought until the phone rang. To his surprise, it was Detective Mona Short, the officer who had stopped by his house earlier that day.

"Lieutenant, I thought you might like an update on the explosion you heard over the phone."

"Go ahead."

She quickly got to the point.

"There was a second discovery at Eagle Roost a couple of hours ago, also on the school grounds. We are keeping this part confidential. As part of the investigation into the explosion, our guy Donovan and a Navajo investigator discovered a body. The body is female. We checked the VIN and ran the plates, and the car where they found it was registered to Bethany Bowlegs. And the body seems to be about her age."

"Any sign of Cecil Bowlegs?"

"No sir."

"Was the car damaged in the explosion?" That, he thought, would explain the death.

"No." She stopped and Leaphorn let the information register.

"Sir, there are two more things I need to tell you. No ID on the body, so they'll try for fingerprints and dental records.

"Second, if you're willing, I'd appreciate it if you'd work with me as a consultant, you know, like Chief Martinez suggested."

Leaphorn made some notes before he spoke. "I'll do what I can without violating my client's confidentiality. I've heard nothing from Cecil since that call. Do you know who else is on the scene at Eagle Roost?"

"Two Navajo Nation officers besides our guy, Sergeant Mark Donovan, who specializes in explosions. There's Sergeant Fredrick

Stanley, who runs the Navajo Eagle Roost substation, and the Navajo cop with training in explosives who discovered the body."

"Is the Navajo explosives person Bernadette Manuelito?"

Short paused. "I think so. Donovan said he helped train her."

"She's a good officer. Smart. Solid. How much damage did the explosion do?"

"Donovan thinks the garage might be structurally sound, but the rest of the building is a total loss. The first responders didn't find any other victims. This could have been a lot worse."

Leaphorn had a final question before he ended the call. "What can I do to help?"

"I'd appreciate it if you could help us locate Cecil Bowlegs. Because the car was registered to his wife, he might know something about the body. And because he's the custodian there, he should be able to tell us if there was something in the classroom that could have led to the explosion. The investigators are still looking for the cause. We want to interview him as soon as we can."

"I understand."

Leaphorn also needed to talk to Bowlegs, he thought. After the call ended, he pulled out his little notebook to jot down some observations.

What caused the building to explode?

Why was Beth Bowlegs' car there?

Who is the woman in the car?

Where is Cecil?

Where was Beth?

Is the dead woman in the car connected to the explosion in the building?

What can Bernie tell me?

He called RP, left a message, and then texted him: Pls call Leaphorn He thought about Louisa's unanswered text to Kory's wife. The worry-free time he'd allowed himself was up. He walked out of his office to talk to Louisa and have her call Lin, but the aroma of something warm and savory, something that reminded him he'd missed lunch, distracted him. Louisa was at the stove.

"Whatever you're cooking there, it really smells great."

"Thanks. Chicken soup. It ought to be ready in about half an hour." She turned toward him. "I'm sorry I was snippy with you. You were right to be concerned about Erlinda. Right and big-hearted, too. I called Kory, just to see if they were coming back and wanted to join us for dinner, but no answer. I'd love to get this straightened out. As I see it, few things are worse than complicated family problems."

Having little family of his own, Leaphorn's personal experience was limited, but he'd known enough unhappy families to nod in agreement. "I'm off to the library for a few minutes."

"Good luck. We'll eat when you get home, and I'll let you know if I hear from Kory."

DIRECTOR HASKIE STOOD AT THE library door. He welcomed Leaphorn as the last of the patrons left, and locked the door behind them.

Leaphorn pulled the lockpicking tool, a device known as a rake, and a tension wrench from his pocket. He inserted the rake, the pick that gives lockpicking its name. As the slim piece of metal slid into the keyway, he applied pressure. Sometimes he was able to release the lock quickly. Sometimes it took many tries—he had spent as long as thirty minutes on a job like this. And sometimes the tools failed to work, period. Today, fortune smiled on him. He had the special case open on the fifth try.

Haskie studied the titles and pulled out a slim volume. He held it a moment, then placed it on the large wooden table and flicked on the desk light.

"I have about half an hour of work to finish at my desk. If you need more time, or if you have to take it out of the library, please let me know."

"Thanks."

Haskie lingered. "This book is special. I'm pleased that someone is interested in it."

"You're welcome to sit here with me."

Haskie shook his head and retreated to his office.

Leaphorn lowered himself into the chair. If he was lucky, he wouldn't be in the library long. As he took his phone from his pocket and called up the photo Stella had sent him, he smiled at himself. He remembered the days when he'd resisted getting a cell phone. Now it simplified his life in many ways that he appreciated.

He opened the book. The editor had organized it chronologically, with the older photos first. His plan had been to skim through it for the Elephant Feet picture, but the beauty of the images stunned him into slow motion. He gave himself permission to savor the stunning photographs before he got to the business of searching for the photo Stella had given him.

As Chee had said, the photos in both black-and-white and color captured the iconic scenery of the Navajo world. If the landscapes featured people, they were secondary players, included by the photographer to emphasize the size and scope of the land.

Among the stellar collection of Navajo photographers featured, he had heard of Paul Natonabah and his protégé, Donovan Quintero, who captured images for the *Navajo Times*. The book included other well-known Diné photographers: Priscilla Tacheney, Eugene Tapahe, Donovan Shortey, Will Wilson, Tyana Arviso, and other artists he had never heard of. There were also shots by a few bilagáana photographers he recognized as old friends of the Navajo, to add to the mix. The photos covered several decades and some of the older shots had no names attached, or used only initials, for both the artist and the models.

He found a version of Stella's photo on page sixty-eight and compared it to the one on his phone. The photos were close, but not identical. In Stella's, the people were larger, and their postures slightly different. Still, to Leaphorn's eye, they were clearly the same people. The light, the clothing, the way the subjects arranged themselves, the position of the clouds, all that told him the pictures had been made at close to the same time. He knew photographers often took multiple shots of the same setting so they could find the best one.

The caption in the book read "Elephant Feet, Coconino County,

Arizona, Navajo Nation"; it made no mention of the people, and did not name the photographer. Leaphorn thumbed to the back of the book, hoping for an appendix with names. Nothing.

He turned back to the photo in the book and took a picture of it, noticing some small initials, BH, in the bottom right corner.

He pulled his little notebook from his pocket and jotted down the full name of the book, the publisher, date of publication, the title of the photograph, and the initials, BH, although he knew he wouldn't forget any of it.

Leaphorn took the book to Haskie in his office.

"Thank you. I'm done." He showed Haskie his photo of the picture in the book. "Is this photo part of the library's collection?"

"I don't recognize it. Sorry. We have a huge collection. You're welcome to look through our photos, but that will take you a while. I hope the book was of help."

Leaphorn set the book on Haskie's desk. "It certainly lifted my spirits to see the amazing photographs of our beautiful Dinétah."

The puzzle of the unidentified image stayed with Leaphorn as he headed to his truck. It was close to dark when he got home. It reassured him to see Louisa at her improvised workspace at the dining room table with her laptop, recordings, and notebook arranged before her. And, as a bonus, whatever she had in the kitchen smelled even more delicious.

She looked up when he approached her and closed her laptop.

"Before you ask, I heard from Kory. He called about his glasses and I told him they were here. He shouldn't be driving without them, but as you said, he and Lin are adults. They are on their own path, aren't they? And I need to be on mine. He can pick up the glasses if he wants them. I'm moving on."

He rested his hands on her shoulders and felt how tension had hardened her muscles. "If you're ready, let's move on to dinner."

"Just another five minutes. Did you get what you needed at the library?"

"Not exactly." He explained.

She opened her computer. "Let me see that photo you're trying to track down."

He called it up on his phone, and she made a copy. He admired Louisa's computer skills. She clicked at the keyboard for a few moments and then leaned back in her chair.

"Look at this."

He pulled up a chair next to her so he could see the screen illuminated with more fine old pictures of the Navajo world. Some looked like Stella's, and none of them included names of the people pictured or the photographers.

"Let's eat. Thanks for your help."

He'd reached a dead end, but at least it had brought some beauty.

14

The tone of the Eagle Roost investigation grew more somber with the discovery of the body. Bernie and Donovan left the garage, and Donovan called his boss. Bernie waited for the FBI agents she had seen pull up to the school gate in the Tahoe. She had worked with Sage Johnson before and knew she was a good investigator. A muscular blond man, introduced to Bernie and Donovan as Agent Blaine Fisher, accompanied Johnson.

As the agents changed into protective clothing, Bernie told them what she and Donovan knew about the school explosion and the body. It wasn't much. She and Donovan still wore their Tyvek, but she hoped no one would ask her to go back into the garage.

"We'll do the car first. Good timing, I guess." Johnson pursed her lips and exhaled. "We will need to interview the fire crew, too, but we will find them at the station. They've had a long day already."

"You'll want to talk to Sergeant Fredrick Stanley, too," Bernie said

"Stanley?"

"He's the Navajo cop at the gate doing crowd control." She indicated him with a jut of her chin. "And the man in the black sweatpants at the gate with him is Charles Morgan, the principal."

Johnson said, "I saw them up there keeping people out of the crime scene. They waved us through."

"Morgan arrived at the scene first and called 911."

Fisher spoke. "I'm ready to take a look."

Johnson nodded. "Go ahead. I want to talk to Bernie and Donovan for a moment."

Fisher left, and Johnson motioned toward Bernie and Donovan. "Which of you found the body?"

"I did." Bernie summarized her time in the garage.

Johnson looked at her notes. "I have to ask. Did either of you touch the body or anything in the car?"

"No." Donovan seemed surprised at the question. "We're professionals. We left it all undisturbed."

"What did you think?"

Donovan shrugged.

Bernie gathered her thoughts. "I was horrified when I first saw a body in the car. Horrified and puzzled, too. For a split second, I thought the dead person might be the suspect who'd planted explosives in the building. Maybe she waited too long after the building blew up and then for some reason couldn't get out.

"But then I saw the dried blood. That's not a self-inflicted wound. The woman was murdered. I've been around enough death to know that she died long before the explosion."

Johnson didn't react to Bernie's conclusion but turned back to the other officer. "Donovan, you got anything to add about that?"

"No. I agree with Bernie."

Johnson asked what they had found in the investigation.

"We marked debris that might mean something," Bernie said, "but there wasn't much. No detonator, no accelerator, no timers. We found an old ruined cell phone, but nothing obviously suspicious."

Donovan turned to Johnson. "Agent, what do you know about the car registration?"

Johnson gave them the details. "Principal Morgan has been trying to reach the janitor with no luck. Same's true for his wife. There's nothing to do now but get to work."

Bernie led them closer to the garage. She frowned as she thought about the body. One thing Officer Bernadette Manuelito seriously disliked about working in law enforcement was the unavoidable association with the dead that her job on occasion involved. The rest of it—the long hours, relatively low pay, internal politics, and ever-present danger—bothered her less. She loved the opportunity to be of deep service to her Diné relatives, and relished the challenge of doing something different each day.

As they approached the dead person, Bernie hung back, letting the federal agents and Donovan take the lead. The body in the car brought an eerie reminder of the case she had handled at Shiprock High School. She had been the only law enforcement person in the area at the gymnasium when the car bomb exploded. She'd discovered the dead man in the driver's seat and had to break the news to his family. The tragic death still haunted her.

As if reading her mind, Johnson called to her. "I am leaving investigation of the body to Agent Fisher. You and Donovan can take another look or not, but I'd need you both to search for evidence. Take your time. Be meticulous. Anything catches your eye that might have to do with the murdered woman or the explosion, take photos and let Fisher know."

"I'll start on the right side of the garage," Donovan said. "You OK with the left?"

"Sure."

Agents Johnson and Fisher dealt with the car. Investigator Fisher had opened the door closest to the woman and was photographing the body in place with a professional, no-nonsense, strictly business attitude. As though, Bernie thought, the person who had once lived in that flesh meant no more than the car itself and the other wreckage from the explosion. That attitude, Fisher's ability to look at a dead human with the same detachment with which he viewed the damaged car, was what kept investigators sane.

Bernie admired his coolness, but she didn't want to be that guy. She had a lot of time to think about her future after she'd been rejected as crime scene investigator with the Navajo police, and she'd become philosophical about it.

Donovan kept up a steady prattle with Agent Fisher while Bernie did her job. She wondered, not for the first time, why white people always felt compelled to talk.

"Why is that rug next to the body?" Donovan asked. "Any ideas?"

"No. Not a one." Fisher frowned. "We need to find out if the body has anything to do with the explosion. It's hard to believe it's just a coincidence."

"I'm wondering why someone would put a body in an old car and leave it in a school garage." Donovan straightened up from his investigation of the garage floor and stretched. "Why would someone destroy a special ed classroom? The motivation puzzles me. What do you think, Bernie?"

Bernie noticed that the weaver had used the beautiful gray, brown, tan, and black yarns typically found in the rugs from the same area where Mama lived and worked—Toadlena and Two Grey Hills. From what she could see, the blanket in the car exemplified that highly technical creative style.

"I had a great mentor who told me to be suspicious of coincidence. He said never assume anything you find at a crime scene doesn't matter. I guess that goes for the weaving there on the passenger seat."

An hour later, she and Donovan were finished and Johnson had done a quick review of the space damaged by the explosion, paying special attention to the things Bernie had discovered and Donovan had questioned. Donovan and Bernie both came up short on obvious clues to the murder. They saw no blood splatters and nothing in the garage that looked like it had been used to cause the victim's head wound.

They left Fisher examining the car, and returned to the food and drinks to talk further.

Bernie asked Johnson the overriding question. "What's the story on the dead person?"

"Well, here's what Fisher told me. He confirms that the person is probably in her mid-thirties. She's been dead at least twenty-four hours, and he believes one factor in her death was that severe head wound. He identified at least four different sets of fingerprints on the steering wheel and door handle." Johnson sipped from a water bottle. "We'll go over the car thoroughly for hair and skin samples. The Omega van is on the way to take the body to the medical investigator. We will know more after the autopsy."

Donovan nodded. "I marked a few things inside the main building that could be evidence of a bomb, but basically what I saw was nothing beyond a mess of debris, glass, metal, and plastic. I'll send my report. I'd like to go."

"Go ahead. And thanks."

The women watched him head back to his unit and saw him pause at the gate for a moment to chat with Principal Morgan.

Bernie had another question.

"Did Agent Fisher find evidence of a second person in the car?"

"It's too soon to say for sure, but that's a possibility. The dead woman is about your height, Manuelito. But the seat was pushed far back. There's no way she could have reached the gas or the brake pedal to drive that car into the garage herself."

Johnson glanced toward what was left of the classroom building. "Before you ask, in terms of the explosion, we didn't discover anything that looked like it could logically have been a detonator, just a lot of scraps of metal and plastic, the same as you and Donovan. The explosives experts will be here from Albuquerque soon to do the wrap-up. We're more concerned about cases like this because of the rash of school violence. And while it's tempting to dismiss this as some kind of mechanical problem with gas lines or whatever, perpetrators in cases like this are increasingly sophisticated. I don't want to speculate further until I get a definitive report from our crew."

Bernie understood. "Before I leave, I'd like to talk to Principal Morgan again. He seemed shell-shocked when I first tried a couple questions. Maybe he's processed this a little and can give us some better information. I wonder if he could identify the body."

Johnson shook her head. "He's distraught, overwhelmed. We need to do a lot more work before we can allow anyone who isn't law enforcement in here."

"Of course. I'll leave the cooler here for Fisher. If you'll put it in my unit when you're done, I'll give it to the principal to return to Nadia."

Bernie grabbed a soda and a sandwich for Morgan and another for herself and was ready to walk to the gate when Fisher arrived, looking serious. He reached for a second bottle of water but let the food sit.

Johnson stared at him. "So?"

"Give me a minute, OK?"

Bernie headed off to talk to Morgan. She realized that she was both relieved to leave the work ahead to Agent Johnson and disappointed that she wouldn't be involved in solving the mystery of the dead woman.

CECIL BOWLEGS HEARD A TRUCK on the road to his house and positioned himself in his hiding place so he could watch it approach. He recognized the vehicle as RP's because of the busted headlight and moved out onto the road so his friend would see him. When RP stopped, Cecil opened the door, tossed his bag onto the floor, and fastened the seat belt.

"What now, Legs?"

"I've got a buddy at Zuni. I can wait there until—"

"Until they find you. You gotta get this straightened out, bro."

"I know. Thanks for coming. I'm in a bad place, man." Cecil had called RP from the house landline and explained the situation. Luckily, his friend knew the territory and understood his cryptic directions for the pickup. Cecil assumed that whoever caused the explosion knew where he lived, so a place on the road seemed safer. He told himself he couldn't be too careful now. He looked out the window at the piñon and juniper forest, searching for a distraction. He remembered one of his teachers calling it a pygmy forest because the trees grew so slowly—a century-old piñon tree might only be ten feet tall. Waiting and thinking, he watched the green shapes silhouetted in the fading late-afternoon light.

Even though his boyhood had been hard, he'd never been as scared as he was when the building exploded. As far as he knew, until today no one had wanted to kill him or scare him to death.

He chuckled. "You know how they say smoking will kill you? Well, going outside for that cigarette saved my life."

"That's funny."

Cecil listened to the rumble of the truck's tires on the dirt road as he tried to make sense of what had happened. His thoughts revolved around two things: the amount of money he'd lost at the casinos, and how much better his life had been with Beth around. Neither circuit offered a practical solution for survival.

"Bro, you got anything to eat in here?"

RP made a hissing noise. "You want dinner *and* a free ride? There might be some chips or something in the glove box."

Cecil opened it. He removed RP's duct tape and flashlight and rested them in his lap, but found only crumpled receipts, the required insurance and registration papers, a supply of napkins, a couple of ballpoint pens, and a tire gauge. He put it all back and closed the glove box.

Now that he was on the move and in RP's confident hands, Cecil let himself relax a few beats. The truck's single working headlight did a decent job of finding the potholes. He stretched his shoulders against the seat back. "I might doze off." He closed his eyes, but as soon as he started to drift away, the trauma of the explosion flooded his brain.

"Before you check out, tell me who wants you dead."

"I don't know."

"That's BS. Seriously, man." RP raised his voice. "This is heavy, Legs. The building you worked in must be toast. I heard it explode from a mile away and saw the smoke. Who did you damage? Who's got a grudge? You've been thinking about this."

"Damn straight. I'm trying to figure it out."

"What happened back there, man?"

"I went outside for a smoke before I started to work, you know, and I made a call to someone who I thought could help us find Beth. And then, kabang. The bastards nearly got me."

"Who?"

"That's the thing. I don't know. I gotta think about this."

"Who did you call?"

"A dude in Window Rock. A Navajo private investigator. He's helping me find Beth. Leave me alone, now, OK?"

RP touched the brakes to slow for a curve. "I'm glad you finally found a private investigator. Is your detective an old guy?"

"Yeah."

"I thought so. He came to see me at lunch and asked some questions about Bethany. He's sharp. He just sits there real quiet and waits until you have something to say."

"I hope he can help us." Cecil closed his eyes. "I can't figure out how a person like her just disappears."

RP drove in silence for a few minutes, then asked another question.

"Are you sure someone wants to kill you? It might have been an accident, man."

"You think I'm stupid? If I'd stayed in there, it's a sure bet I'd be sitting here dead."

RP turned up the truck's heater. Early spring in Navajo land had a lot in common with winter. "If someone really does want you dead, they might decide they need to come for me, too, now that I'm helping you. I'm an accessory to whatever you did to get in their face. Be straight with me here. Who's after you?"

"Leave it, bro. How could they know about you? That's why you didn't come to my house, in case there's a camera on it for surveillance or something." Bowlegs turned on the radio. It was set to country music hits, and he changed it to a sports talk station, hoping RP would stop asking questions. He needed to make a plan for what came next, not rehash old news. They listened to speculation about what college teams might make it to March Madness. The drone of the announcers' familiar voices would have allowed Cecil to drift into sleep if RP had stopped with the questions.

"Does this Zuni guy know you're coming?"

"No, but he owes me. I can take a chance on him." Cecil shrugged. "Why don't you shut up, already. I wanna get some rest."

He knew his Zuni buddy played poker every Saturday, and had invited him to join the game often enough. If he had good luck at poker tonight, he could buy a bus ticket out to Beth's sister in Tucson. Talk to her about his wife and where she might have gone, and get himself far away from the current trouble until he figured out how to handle it. He'd give Leaphorn a heads-up about the plan when he called him.

When he gambled, Cecil Bowlegs had coached himself never to consider what might happen if he lost. It killed his nerves and wrecked his luck. But handling RP's questions had left him unsettled, so he gave up on sleep, sat up straighter, and tried to stay focused on the radio.

"Legs, did that PI you hired find out anything about Bethany?"

"Not yet. Like I said, I had just started talking to him when the building blew." Cecil remembered that he should call Leaphorn back. He'd use his Zuni buddy's phone when he got there.

Cecil realized that the distraction of thinking about his missing wife, talking about something other than his own brush with death, eased his anxiety. "And after what happened at the school, disappearing seems like a good option to me, too." He chuckled. "If Leaphorn finds her, I'll ask her how I can just slip out of here like she did."

"Don't joke about this. My gut tells me that my sister didn't leave on her own and blow us off. I keep thinking about how much she loved that job, loved those kids she worked with, singing with the band, singing on her own. And then, all of sudden, poof."

"It's weird all right." Cecil nodded. "Last time we talked, she said she had some gigs with the band, and then she was going to Flag for a solo. Before, she always came back. We've gone over this a million times, bro." He fell quiet; talking about Beth made him miss her all the more.

The late afternoon morphed into early evening. RP adjusted his back against the truck seat and took a deep breath.

"Were you two getting along OK, Legs? When Leaphorn asked me about that, I told him yes, because Beth never bad-mouthed you much except to grouse about you going to the casinos."

"We get along fine. She only nagged at me about my gambling when I lost."

"And you were losing a lot lately, right?"

Cecil ignored the comment. "I'm probably not the world's best husband, but I love her and she knows that. And she never said she didn't love me. I guess she just loved music, her other life, more."

"I think Big Rex has something to do with all this. Have you talked to that guy?"

"I tried to. Called him. Even showed up at one of their gigs." Cecil remembered the night. Beth wasn't there, and Big Rex reacted to Cecil's question about her by taking a swing at him. The guy would have hurt him, but Cecil was quick on his feet, and the other band members intervened.

"He won't say a word about her. He's a total jerk. I don't know why she liked to sing with them."

"She told me Rex claims he's the best guitar player in the Four Corners." RP adjusted the rearview mirror. "Leaphorn asked me about the band, but I didn't have their information so I just mentioned the website, told him he could track them down that way. You should fill him in, you know, so he can get in touch with them as part of his job."

"OK. I'll do it later."

RP turned off the radio. "Tell me about this Zuni guy you're going to see. I never heard you talk about him."

"Oh, Steve Sueño and I are old poker buddies. I served with him in the army, and we got to be friends because we were the only natives in our barracks at training. As time passed, we stayed in touch."

Actually, Cecil thought, he and Sueño had drifted apart after the army, but the foundation of camaraderie remained, and they both enjoyed a good poker game.

After an hour, when RP finally arrived at Sueño's house, Bowlegs thanked him and gave him $5 for the ride. Bowlegs went inside, and after his friend's initial surprise at seeing him, Sueño wanted to talk about what he'd just seen on the television news.

"It looks like there was a big explosion at Eagle Roost School. Do you know anything about that?"

"Yeah. It was bad." Cecil wondered how many details to include and quickly decided to keep his mouth shut. Sueño continued talking.

"Not only a building, but a car, too. That's heavy duty."

"A car? You're kidding." Cecil thought about it, glad that Sueño was still talking.

"On TV they said a garage was attached to the classroom, and that it was supposed to be used for auto mechanics."

"Yeah, that's right." Cecil tried to remember what car was there and came up short. He hadn't seen a vehicle in the garage last time he looked, but he seldom went into that room. "Hey, I need a bite to eat and then how about some poker? Is your regular game tonight?"

"That's right, my friend. It's on my radar. You gotta come with me. The guys remember the last time you played. They'd like their money back."

Cecil smiled, relieved at the invitation.

"You picked a good night, too. A couple of the regular dudes are gone. It will be nice to have a fresh fish in the game." He laughed. "We need to go. There's some peanut butter and bread on the counter, so make yourself a quick sandwich. It's forty-five minutes to Buddy's place, and they start on time."

"Let's leave now and stop somewhere and get a burger or something."

"Sure."

Sueño stared at the scratches on Cecil's hands. "You don't look so good, man. Are you OK?"

"A hard day, that's all. Remind me where the bathroom is, and I'll clean up."

When he studied himself in the mirror, Cecil agreed with Sueño's assessment. He washed the dirt off his face and hands and smoothed his hair. He felt better, and he looked more like a winner.

Sueño had his coat on and keys in hand.

"I'm ready," Cecil said, "but hey, I lost my phone. Can I use yours?"

Sueño grinned as he thought it over. "It'll cost you dinner. Do it quick, the battery's almost dead."

He tossed the phone to Cecil, who caught it and then reached into his pants pocket for Leaphorn's card. He punched in the number and then typed his text:

Bowlegs here. Sorry about the lost call. I'm OK. Please find Beth for me.

He pressed send, then gave the phone back to Sueño. "I need to stop at the Walmart for a new phone. Can you do that for me?"

"Sure. Let's go. I feel lucky."

"Me, too." Cecil touched his jish for a blessing, and they headed off to Gallup. What better way to celebrate his good fortune at surviving the blast than to put it to use again at cards?

JOE LEAPHORN WAS THINKING OF going to bed. He checked email on the computer for the last time and turned it off, then removed his phone from the charger. There was a fresh text message from a number he didn't recognize. Annoyed, he'd started to delete it when he realized the message came from Bowlegs.

Leaphorn texted back, We need to talk. Call me asap.

Then he called the number from which the text had originated. It rang a dozen times, and then the phone went dead.

Even though it was late, he called Detective Short. She answered, and he read her the text from Bowlegs and the phone number from which it had originated. "I just called, and nobody answered. Nothing on the voicemail to indicate who has the number. I haven't done a reverse check."

"I'll follow up." Short's voice sounded flat, not the happy response he'd expected to his positive news.

"You sound tired, Detective."

"I'm beat. It's been a day and a half. I guess you heard about the body at Eagle Roost."

"I did." Leaphorn sat a bit straighter. "But not many details. What happened?"

"They found a car parked in a garage attached to the building that blew up. Officer Manuelito discovered a body inside it. The FBI team is finishing their site evaluation tonight, so I don't even have the prelim on the incidents. And the body just got sent off to the medical investigator's office in Albuquerque."

"Has the person been identified?"

"No, but I can tell you that it's definitely not your Cecil. The body is a female. No ID on her or in the car to tell us who she was." She paused. "The car was registered to Bethany Benally Bowlegs."

Leaphorn felt his residual sleepiness drop away and recalled his conversation with Cecil. "Her husband said that Bethany had a bird tattooed on her left wrist. Did whoever saw the body mention anything like that?"

Short didn't answer immediately. "I don't think so, but I don't have the preliminary report. I'll contact the investigators about the tattoo."

"Roughly how old is the dead woman?"

"I haven't heard. Officer Manuelito was at the scene, and so was our guy, Sergeant Donovan. They're more up-to-date on details of all this than I am."

Leaphorn understood. "I'll call Bernie. Remember I'm here. I'm a consultant on this case, right?"

"Right. Yes, sir, I appreciate that. Thanks."

When that call ended, he thought about reaching out to Bernie, but decided he could wait until she called him. He assumed that she'd had a long, stressful day. In their years of working together, he'd learned to appreciate the comprehensive way she processed new information. Her agile brain seemed to be wired for details and, much like his own brain, craved getting the facts lined up.

When his phone rang, he expected it to be Bernie, but the screen read "Unknown Caller." Because of the cases he had in progress, he answered it.

"Uh, hello. I had a message that you wanted to talk to me." The deep male voice sounded smooth as velvet.

Leaphorn thought a moment and then remembered.

"You're Alvin Rexworth with the Hop Toads?"

"That's me. You wanna book us for a party?" The roaring of a dozen conversations, the clank of glassware and bottles, and the other high-decibel bar noise behind the voice on the phone challenged Leaphorn's hearing.

"No, I want to ask you some questions about Bethany Bowlegs."

"Beth? Sorry, the songbird's flown the nest. She hasn't sung with us for a month. She might be taking gigs on her own now, man. Can't help you."

"I think you can." Leaphorn noticed that he was shouting. "Do you have an idea of where she might have gone?"

"No clue, man, but I wasn't surprised she left her husband. He's a jerk. Otherwise, I can't tell you much about the lady except she could wail out, sell a tune with a lovely tone. I like her. Ask that dude what happened to the songbird."

Leaphorn had heard the I-don't-know-much line before. Too often. "I only have a few questions. It won't take long. Sounds to me that you'd like to have her back with the band."

"That's right. Hey, I can't talk now. I got to keep my vibe up for the next set. Stop by here when we're done." He gave Leaphorn the name of the venue.

"I can't make it there tonight. What if I give you a call in the morning?"

"Tomorrow? OK, bro, but I won't be up until the afternoon."

"At this number, Mr. Rexworth?"

"Sure. And everyone calls me Big Rex."

15

Cecil Bowlegs understood the ebb and flow of poker. He waited five hands for his luck to change, watching for the key tells of the other men at the table and working hard to keep his own giveaway tics undercover. His patience paid off, and when he finally saw that full house, he knew how to play it. He stayed cool, but he was celebrating on the inside.

Poker had always been his game, and in addition to his time at the casinos, he had tuned up his skills watching the World Series of Poker on TV and playing against real and virtual opponents on the school computers at work, weeknights, and on Saturdays.

Sueño's poker friends expected everyone to play until midnight. A few hands after his big win, Cecil tried to beg off, honestly pleading exhaustion and the drive back to Eagle Roost. But he could tell the other men at the table considered that bad sportsmanship, so he toughed it out. He wanted another invitation to play these suckers.

Before they finished their last hand, he'd put back half of what he'd won. He still had enough for the bus ticket to Arizona, he figured, but just barely. He'd checked the departures from Gallup on his phone and asked Sueño to drop him at the bus station. When the cards told him to fold, he'd used his new phone to check the schedule to Tucson and even book himself a reservation.

He informed Sueño of his plan when they were in the car.

"Legs, come back to Zuni with me," Sueño said. "I'll give you a lift in the morning. You look beat. Your brain isn't working right."

"I'm OK. I'm too worried about Beth to sleep, anyway." He was worried about Beth, that was true. But he'd worried about her ever since she hadn't come home. His worry now centered on his own survival. "You've already been a big help. I don't want to put you out."

"It's no trouble, seriously."

Cecil knew whoever had tried to hurt or even kill him had probably figured out by now that he wasn't dead. They might have known that he'd called RP to pick him up. They might have ferreted out his Zuni connection. He didn't want to put either of these friends in jeopardy. This was his mess, and he'd clean it up himself, maybe with the help of the private investigator he'd found. When he got to the bus station, he'd send Leaphorn a text and let him know the plan.

"Relax, buddy." Cecil forced a smile. "Don't worry about me. You worry too much."

"But what about luggage, man? Aren't you even bringing a toothbrush?"

"I've got some cash." He also had credit cards, but he knew that would make him easier to track. "I'll buy what I need if I end up in Tucson for a while, like I did with the new phone. I'm not planning on staying long, just long enough to find Beth, make sure she's OK, and get her to come back with me. Persuade her to give me another chance."

"When does the bus leave?"

Cecil told him.

"Sleep on it, man. Take a shower. I'll get you there in plenty of time tomorrow. Chill at my place and get your head on straight."

The man's meddling had begun to annoy Cecil. "Just take me there now, OK? I need to be by myself awhile. I need time to think."

Sueño frowned. "OK, dude, your life. But something's off here."

"Yeah, I should have headed to Tucson sooner, that's what's off about it." Cecil had picked up some energy bars when he bought his phone, and he opened one. He broke off a piece for Sueño as a peace offering and saved the rest. "I love her, bro, probably more than she loves me. I thought I'd lost her. I've got to see her as soon as I can. You know how that is."

Sueño shook his head. "I don't understand how staying up all night helps, but OK. I'll take you down there. Good luck. Tell her hello for me if you find her."

The bus station in Gallup, however, turned out to be a bad idea. The bus stopped at a gas station that accommodated big trucks as well as tourists' minivans and included a convenience store, a restaurant, and an abundance of parking spaces. Although the door was unlocked and the lights were on when Sueño drove off, the attendant explained that Cecil couldn't wait inside all night. The bus he needed wouldn't arrive until 7:30 a.m., and they had strict rules against loitering. The other man on the staff would show up to reopen, sell tickets, and answer questions an hour before the westbound bus pulled off Interstate 40 to stop for passengers getting off, buying food, and getting on again.

And, no, the attendant said, he could never make an exception for anyone, anytime. He'd lose his job. The best he could do was to let Cecil stay in the building until he finished cleaning the restrooms and sweeping. So Cecil sat and texted Joe Leaphorn.

Decided to take a bus to Tucson for Beth

Think she's with her sister

Need to get outta here

Someone wants me dead or hurt bad

As he was leaving, the ticket guy told Cecil there was a bar a couple blocks away that stayed open until 2:00 a.m. Then he locked the door.

Cecil strolled over to the bar and listened to country songs by a Navajo band about broken hearts that reminded him all the more of his missing songbird.

He nursed a beer until they shut down for the night, then walked back to the convenience store/bus station and circled around the building to try and stay warm. He walked until his feet ached, his back hurt, and his legs grew too heavy to move. A cop came by once and offered him a spot in a shelter. He was so cold that the offer tempted him for a split second. But he couldn't risk it. He explained his situation—stuck outside waiting until the bus came—and the policeman left him alone.

The station would reopen in a few hours, he told himself, and he could warm up and rest then. In the meantime, he found some flattened cardboard boxes leaning against a dumpster and used the dry cardboard to insulate his body from the cold. He sat with his spine against the side of the building, away from the street traffic. The frozen night turned his breath into a cloud of frost.

At this time of the morning the interstate traffic had lessened, and the surface streets were mostly deserted. Cecil must have fallen asleep, because the sound of the vehicle approaching startled him. He first assumed it was the station's customer service agent coming to work. The car pulling into the lot was a black Escalade, its paint shiny under the streetlight. Odd, he thought, fancy wheels for a person working a job like this. When the man climbed out and went into the building to open for business, he'd stand up and stretch a minute, give the dude time to set up for his shift. Then he could go inside to warm up.

The huge new SUV pulled up next to where he'd been resting. Before he realized he should have been thinking like a man who had nearly died that morning, it was too late.

The door opened and, reflected in the SUV's interior light, Cecil saw two large men and the glint of a gun barrel in the passenger's hand. He clicked to the situation.

The man attached to the gun snarled something undecipherable as he climbed out of the car. Cecil froze. The man yelled the command again and pointed the gun at Bowlegs.

"What did you say?"

"I said stand up." The man held the gun on him as he opened the back-seat door with his left hand. "Get in the car. You are one lucky sucker."

Cecil Bowlegs did as directed. He figured his luck had run out.

The man with the gun sat next to Cecil, as though he considered him a dangerous threat. He wore two white earbuds, shaped like little tubes, and smelled of old sweat. Cecil probably stank too, he thought. He should have taken Sueño's offer of a bed and a shower. Then he'd be clean and rested. But the bad guys could have found him there, too, and that would have put his friend in danger.

The driver was alone in the front seat. Cecil couldn't see his face, but he had a tattoo on his neck that looked like the tip of a lightning bolt.

"Who are you guys?" Cecil's voice grew taut with tension. He felt his heart beating like a hummingbird's, "Why did you pick me up?"

"Shut up. We're not paid to answer questions."

Cecil had never considered himself especially smart, but he was bright enough to keep his mouth closed.

Earbuds spoke to the driver. "Ramon, step on it. We need to deliver the package."

"Package? Oh, you mean the jerk we picked up. Right?"

Earbuds said nothing. The car cruised uphill from the station into a part of town Cecil didn't recognize. He heard a dog bark. The moon's light filtered in through the clouds, and he noticed that someone had used a gun to shoot holes in the stop signs. The car bounced over a few potholes.

As his body warmed, Cecil realized that his brain and its propensity for keeping him alive had started to work again. He searched for a way he could get free. His captor had made him put on a seat belt, but left his hands and feet unbound. He couldn't remember if Earbuds—or Ramon—had locked the car doors, but even if neither had, they would probably lock automatically at a certain speed unless his captors had disabled that feature. Earbuds, besides being armed, was larger than Cecil. And Ramon certainly would intervene if he tried to overpower Earbuds and steal his weapon.

Ramon ignored the stop signs, not even slowing down. Cecil would have done the same, in this eerie interlude between night and morning, with no one on the streets.

Cecil spoke quickly. "Hey. Stop the car. I gotta take a leak."

"Tough."

"Come on, pull over. I mean it."

The man with the gun wrinkled his brow. "Hold it, man."

"I'm trying, but . . ." A reasonable lie popped into Bowleg's head. "I've got bladder cancer."

Earbuds' frown encouraged him to keep talking.

"I have to go all the time now, and the Big C makes my pee extra stinky. This is a nice car. You don't want me to use it as a toilet. It would be a tough thing to explain to your boss."

Keeping the gun on Cecil, Earbuds tapped the driver's shoulder with his left hand. "Pull over."

"What?"

"He's gotta pee."

"No way. Seriously?"

"You bet," Cecil chimed in. "Really bad, too. Right now."

Ramon kept going. "No can do. You know what the boss said."

"Yeah, but he likes to keep this car clean," Earbuds said. "You remember how mad he was when we got it muddy. This would be worse."

"I can't hold it much longer." Cecil groaned to add emphasis.

The Escalade slowed and pulled to a stop at the side of the street. Cecil silently undid his seat belt. Then Earbuds meant to unlock the door, but instead he hit the wrong button, and the window began to roll down, letting in the cold night air. In those seconds of distraction, Cecil unlocked the door on his side, opened it, and slid out onto the ground.

Earbuds cursed, but by the time he fired off a shot, Cecil was crawling along the dirt to the rear tires. Then he was up and running. His luck had returned.

Behind and to the right of where the car had stopped, Cecil spotted an alley, the entrance partially blocked by a large dumpster. He sprinted that way, glad for his head start, and noticed an opening in the wooden fence someone had built to conceal some banged-up garbage cans. He squeezed through, hunkered down in the dark, and waited.

Almost immediately, he heard Earbuds running toward him and the sound of the car backing up toward the ally. The car stopped, the engine running. Next came the sound of a car door opening, the heavy pounding of more footsteps, and muttered swearing. Holding his breath, Cecil listened as the men drew closer. Through the slats in the fence, he saw the glow of a flashlight beam. The light intruded into the garbage can corral where he hid. It bounced off his boots as it probed the space, and his heart hammered fiercely against his ribs. Then the flashlight beam moved, and he heard the men running again, heading away from where he hid.

A few minutes later, their footsteps turned back toward him again.

But they didn't stop until they reached the car. He heard more cursing, and then the car slowly drove away.

Cecil waited until he could no longer hear the rumble of the engine. Then he stood and dusted himself off. He pulled out his phone to check the time. The bus wouldn't leave for another two hours or so. He thought about what to do next. Sunday morning couldn't come soon enough.

16

Leaphorn woke early as usual. Some days, his body complained about the abuse he'd put it through over the years, but today he felt fine. The sunrise came earlier now with spring nearly there in full force. Before long, Louisa would be putting up her hummingbird feeders.

He started the coffee and went to his desk as it brewed. He had a plan for the day that involved something more cheerful than an unidentified dead woman, a missing client, and the aftermath of a school explosion. He would take a drive north and west. He would head toward Tonalea, the village closest to the Elephant Feet in Stella's photo, and see if there were any old-timers around who might remember the photographer or the people in the picture.

The hope that the trip would yield useful information was a long shot. But many Navajo people had long memories. The worst that could happen would be that he had a pleasant drive with time to think about Stella's case. Once he figured that out, if he could, he would move on to consider the mysterious disappearance of Bethany Bowlegs, the discovery of her car with a body in the front seat, and her missing husband—his client and custodian at the school where the FBI was investigating an explosion.

The aroma of fresh coffee called him back to the kitchen. Louisa was up, dressed, and had reorganized her work so they could use the table for breakfast. She cooked and served their usual oatmeal, and they'd finished eating in companionable silence when he broached the issue of her keeping him company on his all-day road trip.

"I don't know." She looked at the handwritten notes, her laptop, and some computer printouts. "I'm really behind here."

"It might clear your head."

"Remind me. How far is it?"

"It's about three hours, one way."

She frowned. "When do you want to go?"

"Soon." He glanced at the clock on the kitchen wall. "Twenty minutes?"

"So that's at least six hours in transit, plus the time you'll need to talk to people about the picture and the blanket. Let me think about it. I'll let you know."

When he was ready to leave, he asked her again. He wasn't surprised that she declined.

"After all the commotion with my son, I'd like some alone time." Her voice was tinged with sadness. "And, well, I want to be here in case he or Erlinda comes by before they leave."

"Have you heard anything else from either of them?" Kory's behavior toward his mother angered Leaphorn, but he kept the emotion out of his voice.

Louisa shook her head. "Not today. Not yet. I got a thumbs-up emoji from Lin's phone last night. I asked her to get in touch if she needed something or felt unsafe, and she hasn't responded."

She turned away from him. "Kory and Erlinda need to resolve this situation together. It's their marriage. I hope they make it, for the baby's sake." And then Louisa went back to work on the recordings from her Hawaii interviews, a sign he knew meant "Discussion closed."

Leaphorn understood that immersing herself in a project was Louisa's way of avoiding painful personal issues. That was what she'd done after she had declined to marry him in Hawaii. At least she had rejected his proposal with a smile.

After the "No, thank you," she'd added, "You don't give up easily, do you?"

"I don't." He smiled back. "And I'll keep asking."

BACK IN HIS OFFICE, LEAPHORN turned his attention to Stella Brown's quest for her Navajo roots. He looked forward to the trip to Tonalea, a small settlement on the northwest side of the Navajo Nation. Although he hadn't been there for a while, he remembered a case that had brought him to Tonalea several times. He'd always stopped at the historic Red Lake Trading Post, once known as one of the best places on the reservation to buy Storm Pattern rugs, the design woven into the blanket in Stella's photo.

As he prepared to leave, Leaphorn took his phone from the charger and tapped it awake. After reading the texts from Bowlegs about taking the bus to Tucson and about people wanting to kill him, he called Mona Short again, gave her the update.

"I'll handle it," she said. "Thanks."

"I'm going to be out of the office today, driving where cell service is marginal."

She laughed. "It's Sunday, sir. You're entitled to a phone-free day."

He drove past the junction for the historic St. Michael's mission and noticed the change in elevation as the highway climbed into the cool ponderosa forest of the Defiance Plateau. Patches of snow remained beneath the trees. The road, US 264, flattened out and then began the long downhill roll west to Ganado, then north to Beautiful Valley, Chinle, and Many Farms, and on to US 160 toward Kayenta. When he had cell phone service, he called Chee to see if he'd learned anything that might help Stella Brown. He placed the call to Chee's old landline. If Bernie was home, he could talk to her too.

Chee answered. "I haven't had a chance yet to focus very much on the adoption stuff you asked about. Bernie's mother had a crisis, and I offered to help."

Leaphorn swallowed his irritation. He understood that a man's wife's request outranked any other favors in the queue. "I'm heading to the Elephant Feet and Tonalea now. I'll see if there are any old ones out there who remember the photographer."

"Good luck with that, sir."

"You mentioned that you had to do something for Bernie's mother. Is the lady OK?"

"Yes." Chee paused. "She has a problem with her stove, but I'm working on it. She's a tough one."

"What have you heard from Bernie?"

"Not much. She's at the station, writing her report about the explosion." The phone went silent for a few moments, then Chee's tone changed. "She's uneasy, having a hard time putting the sight and smell of the body in the car out of her mind."

"I wanted to talk to her about that. You know I'm working with the husband of a missing woman, one of the teachers at Eagle Roost."

"Mr. Bowlegs, right?"

"Yeah."

"Bernie doesn't talk about the dead. You know that." Leaphorn heard Chee's muffled irritation. "Like I said, she's having trouble with this case."

Leaphorn changed the subject. "Thanks for alerting me to that photo book. I checked it out, and it was helpful. Have you found anything on Brown's adoptive parents?"

"Not exactly something. Just enough to say that something is amiss." Chee's voice grew faint and then strong again as the signal strength fluctuated. "I came across small bits of information about her parents, beginning around the time Stella started first grade."

"Interesting." Chee's research paralleled Leaphorn's own discoveries. "Nothing before that?"

"No. No arrest records. No proof that her mother and father were involved in any organizations. They didn't make any political contributions, didn't pay property tax—I guess they rented. And no record in my search of anyone named Stanley or Stanford or Stanislav Brown, or any other male name that might be conceivably shortened to Stan. No record of Rita or of their marriage.

"There seems to be absolutely zero trace of either of them before Stella was about six years old. It's like they were in the witness protection program or something."

Chee paused. "It made me wonder if they had something to hide before the baby came into their lives. Or if they were hiding from someone or something during the first years of Stella's adoption."

"Those are valid questions and Stella doesn't have the answers."

Leaphorn remembered the way Royce Will puzzled over the legitimacy
of Stella's birth certificate.

Leaphorn called Stella Brown, pleased that he still had phone service. She said hello and then posed the inevitable question.

"How are you doing on the search for my Navajo parents?"

"Nothing definitive yet." Leaphorn gave her all the information
he had. "It makes me wonder if there might have been something, ah,
inappropriate, with your adoption. Are you sure about your birth date?"

"I thought so, but now I'm really not sure of anything, Lieutenant.
That's why I wanted your help. What were my parents up to with a
phony birth certificate? If I'd known how fruitless and upsetting this
would be, I would have just stayed ignorant. But now . . ." Her voice
cracked. "But now, well, the genie is out of the bottle, and it's too late to
turn back. I need to know who I am and where I came from."

"I'm hoping to come up with some solid information for you about
the possibility of a Navajo relative today." Leaphorn knew she was leaving soon and that she wanted a face-to-face meeting with someone who
might have known her biological parents if he was unable to find the
parents themselves. And Stella had to leave soon. He softened his voice.
"You could do a DNA test that would at least confirm your heritage.
People have used those sites . . ."

"Stop it." Her impatience sizzled over the phone. "Don't talk about
that. I told you I'm not spitting in a test tube. I'm interested in my
cultural roots, if there are some, not finding a third cousin. Besides the
issue of getting stalked by strangers who might be distant relatives, I
don't trust those tests, and I'm worried about my privacy. I don't want
my DNA out there."

Leaphorn flinched at her hostile tone, but she kept up the rant.

"Just to be even more clear, I resent the historical misuse of Native
people's DNA in medical research. You realize, I'm sure, that there is a
conflict between DNA data and the Navajo creation story, which tells
us this is where we have always been. Here, surrounded by the Sacred
Mountains. Not Asia or Mongolia. Please don't bring it up again."

After he'd ended the call, he put his phone on vibrate and focused

on the winding two-lane paved road. He could see the dark shape of
Agathla Peak rising in the distance, a remnant of an ancient volcano that
had helped shape the landscape some 25 million years ago. He turned
west toward Kayenta at the junction with US Highway 160, picked up
a quick lunch to eat in his truck, and proceeded toward Tsegi and on
to Tonalea.

Black Mesa, known for its coal and as an area of land that had been
home both to the Navajo and their Hopi neighbors, stretched to the
south of the highway. Traffic grew heavier and Leaphorn was glad that
he'd first enjoyed the pleasant scenic drive on this road before so many
vehicles traveled this way.

He pulled out onto the broad shoulder of the highway at Elephant
Feet. It pleased him that, unlike so many things in life, this geologic
feature looked exactly as he remembered it. He climbed out of the truck,
zipped his jacket against the wind, and walked to have a closer look at
these unique buttes. They looked the same as ever. He took a photo for
Louisa and even a selfie. It was a challenge to frame the shot so that the
elephant toes of red Jurassic-era Entrada sandstone showed up. He took
another shot of the white rocks that resembled elephant legs, with an
icing of red rocks at the top.

If the trip turned out to offer no helpful information for Stella
Brown, at least he could verify that the picture she had matched the
actual Elephant Feet on the Navajo Nation. Traffic flowed along US 160
in both directions, but no one else, Navajo or visitor, stopped for a photo.

He noticed some malt liquor cans littered on the ground and picked
them up and tossed them into the bed of his truck, then spent another
moment admiring the solid-looking sandstone, light rock towers against
the vivid blue sky. As sturdy looking as an elephant's legs, and with
flatter stone at the base that anyone with an imagination could picture
as large toes. He watched a single cloud float above the dry landscape.
Rain, if it came at all, would be weeks away.

He headed on another mile or so to the old Red Lake Trading Post.
He'd see what he could learn there. It always made him feel nostalgic
to visit these spots. The few historic trading posts that remained were
relics of the past, speaking to a time when the Navajo lived in greater

isolation from mainstream America. This store, founded around the end of the nineteenth century after The People returned from imprisonment at Bosque Redondo, originally catered to their cravings for commodities they'd discovered during their sad and brave time at the prison camp.

The trading post could be a movie set, he thought. The wooden floor creaked as he entered. He had hoped to find some old locals here to talk to about Stella's situation, but this Sunday morning he was the only customer. A bored-looking teenager sat on a high stool behind the counter, playing at something on her cell phone.

"Hello there."

The girl glanced up, then went back to her phone.

"I'm interested in Storm Pattern rugs. Do you have some?"

She frowned, then turned away from him and stood to remove a key from a nail on a board beneath the window that faced Highway 160. "At the end of that hallway. Bring this back." She handed him the key and looked him up and down. "You're not going to buy anything, are you?"

He considered the answer. "I don't know. Maybe. Maybe not."

She went back to her phone, and he went to see the rugs.

The room he unlocked was lit with a high window that desperately needed washing and a supplemental bare light bulb in a socket in the center of the ceiling. He turned it on by pulling the metal chain. Someone had piled the rugs—perhaps sixty of them, or more—onto two long tables. Each had a paper tag with the dimensions and the price. Some tags, he saw, also included the weaver's name. It looked to him as though the rugs had once been neatly arranged by size, but someone, perhaps potential buyers, had moved a number of rugs and unfolded them. Some were rolled up like giant multicolored cigars, and others were spread flat to reveal their intricate designs. He loved the variety of colors and motifs the weavers had used. Each rug shared the classic geometric features despite the diversity of style.

Some say that Storm Pattern rugs tell the story of The People's emergence from the underworld. Each of the rugs stored here had a perfectly woven border and rectangles to represent the sacred mountains anchoring the four corners. Zigzag lightning bolts dramatically connected the mountains and the rug's center.

Unlike some classic styles of Navajo weaving, Storm Patterns with their iconic designs could be made in any colors and tones muted or vibrant, dyed with plants or commercial dyes. The weaver might include water bugs, snowflakes, or sacred arrows.

Leaphorn spent a few moments savoring the experience, wishing that Louisa, who also loved good weaving, was with him to share their beauty.

As he examined the collection, he came across a rug that reminded him of the one in Stella's picture. It felt smooth in his hands as he pulled it from the pile and unfolded it to reveal a striking stylized gray hogan design against a white background at the center. Red and black formed the rest of the color scheme. It had the same palate he'd seen in Stella's picture. Then he noticed the thin white line, the same border as on the blanket in her treasured photo. He set the rug apart from the rest. He found a few others with that same fine white line, separated them, and moved his pile to the end of a table. He gave the beautiful collection a final look, then turned off the light and locked the door. He went back to the young woman.

"Is there someone around who could give me some background on a few of those rugs?"

She shrugged. "Mr. Hawkman?"

"Is he here?"

She shook her head.

"Anyone else?"

She shook her head again and returned to whatever she found more enthralling than real-life conservation. Leaphorn stood before her until she grew uncomfortable enough to speak.

"Hey, so I'm the only one here. I don't know squat about weaving."

The older he grew, and the longer he was in the investigator-for-hire business, the less tolerance Leaphorn had for incompetence. And the more often he had to put real effort into trying to charm incompetent people to get them to do what he needed.

He resisted saying "You don't know squat about customer service either" and presented her with a way to solve his problem.

"If I had Mr. Hawkman's number, I could set up a time for him to come and talk to me. If you could give it to me, then I wouldn't have to bother you, and I'd leave."

He could see her considering it.

"That's against store policy."

"Does the policy say that you can handle purchases?"

She gave him a quick nod.

"I may buy a rug, but I can't do that until I get more information on the age of the weaving and the weaver. So you'd be following policy to give me Mr. Hawkman's number."

He could see her considering it, but her thought process trudged slowly.

Leaphorn rephrased it. "Like I said, if I can get the information I need, I might want to purchase one of those. I'm going outside to get my phone. That will give you time to think about it. I bet your boss would be pleased if you made a sale. But I can't consider it until I know more about what I'm looking at."

He went outside, filled his lungs with fresh, dry air, and gave his frustration time to dissolve. Somewhere he smelled water and green things considering coming to life now that the deepest cold of winter had past. He removed his phone from the charger and went back inside.

The young woman opened a drawer in the cabinet behind her, pulled out an embossed business card, and handed it to Leaphorn.

He walked back to his truck. He leaned against it as he turned on his phone and called John Hawkman, Red Lake Trading Post owner and manager. The card had a little picture of the post.

Leaphorn had long grown accustomed to people he hadn't met ignoring his calls, checking him out based on the caller ID, and then, if he was fortunate, phoning him back. So he was pleasantly surprised when Hawkman answered on the third ring. From the voice, Leaphorn assumed the man might be as old as he was. Leaphorn identified himself as a retired lieutenant formerly with the Navajo Police Department and now working as a private investigator. He talked about himself more than usual to help build rapport before asking for the favor.

Before he could ask, Hawkman interrupted. "Hey there, glad to meet you. I don't have a chance to talk to gray-haired cops very often.

It's pretty quiet out here. What can I do for you this bright Sunday morning?"

"Well sir, I'm working with a client who wants to find some family roots. I think she might have relatives in the Tonalea area, and that some of them might be weavers. She has a picture of an old rug, but no one's named as the person who made it."

Hawkman interrupted again, as white people tended to do. "That's a shame. That must be why she hired a private investigator. Smart gal, huh? What's her name?"

"Stella Brown, that's what she goes by. I've been doing what I can to help her track down the information she needs to reconnect with her extended family. We're hoping that she might still have relatives out here."

"Oh, I see. You probably know this, but a lot of people do DNA tests to track down family roots. I had mine done and learned that my dimple and my hazel eyes come from Bavaria, on the side of my dad, Bernard Hawkman."

"I've talked to her about DNA tests, but in the meantime, I'm here in Tonalea on a search for the name of someone who might have woven a rug that's in an old photo she has."

"Well, I have a pretty good memory when it comes to things like that. So, what family do you and your client need to find?"

"That's the problem." Leaphorn thought of a better way to explain it. "She doesn't have any names because she never had contact with her birth family. She's adopted and she's not really even sure she's Navajo. That why she hired me."

"Huh. I get it."

Leaphorn hoped so. "I took a look at the collection of rugs in your storeroom and there are some that seem similar to the one in her photograph. If I took pictures of them and sent them to you, could you give me the names of the weavers?"

"No sir. I don't do that stuff." Hawkman laughed. "I'm impressed that a codger like you can handle taking pictures and sending them out."

Leaphorn waited, giving the trading post owner time to think. Finally, the phone came back to life.

"Where are you now?"

"I'm outside the trading post."

"Are you the man with the big truck?"

"It's a king cab." For a split second, Leaphorn wondered how he knew.

"I'm right next door. Give me a minute to put my shoes on, and I'll meet you on the porch. Have a seat in one of those rockers."

Leaphorn realized that the man he was speaking to on the phone must be in the mobile home parked beneath the trees at the end of the dirt lot. He sat. As he watched the man approach, Leaphorn called up Stella's Elephant Feet picture on his phone so he could show it to the trader.

John Hawkman was a bit older than Leaphorn had suspected, but his blue eyes shone brightly. Hawkman took off his glasses and held the phone close to his eyes, then handed it back to Leaphorn.

"Come on in. Let's see if the rug room gives me any ideas about that. Some of these weavers were just girls when I started buying from them. Shoot, now they are grandmas."

The young woman at the cash register sat a bit straighter as they entered. Hawkman said, "Everything OK this morning, Patricia?"

The girl put down her phone. "Yeah."

"Good."

She handed Hawkman the rug room key without being asked. "Are you sore at me because I told him your phone number?"

"No, honey." Hawkman gave her a gentle smile. "I'm no more sore at you than usual."

Leaphorn showed him the small group of rugs, all woven with black, white, red, and gray yarn, that he'd placed together at the end of a table. Hawkman examined each of them. He used his hands as well as his eyes to assess the quality of the weaving.

"Can I take another look at that photo you've got?"

Leaphorn showed him.

"A Storm Pattern, probably from the 1950s. You see the border?" He pointed to an edge of the blanket. "This design is popular in this part of the reservation. You can spot Storms because they usually have a box in the center. They say its a hogan or center of the world."

Leaphorn listened.

"Usually, the weaver adds water bugs or piñon beetles at the center top and bottom. But each rug is a different. That's the joy of them."

One by one, Hawkman unrolled the rugs and spread them out. The grassy, warm, and slightly sour smell of wool made Leaphorn nostalgic. His memory flashed on a scene of his own grandmother at the loom, humming to herself as she worked.

"You've got a good eye. These rugs you pulled out are by the same family of weavers, sisters and their mother, the Alava Singer family. The mother could weave quicker than most, and her work was always first-rate. Alava had magic hands and a fine sense of design. The daughters weren't as productive, but what they did was good solid weaving. Her girls were craftswomen more than artists, but their rugs are lovely too."

"Do you know where Alava Singer lives?"

"She doesn't. COVID, you know, the Big Cough, that got her early on. She was probably close to ninety. One of her clan sisters looks after the place now."

"What about the daughters?"

"One of them moved to Chinle a while back for a job with the tribal government. Probably retired by now. She stopped weaving a long time ago."

"Do you remember her name?"

"Sure do. Suzanna Singer."

"What about the other one, her sister?"

He sighed. "Starla. She was younger, and beautiful. When her mother or sometimes the older sister came in with the rugs, she'd come, too." Leaphorn heard a touch of sadness in Hawkman's voice. "There's a lot of pressure on young people to get out in the world, leave their relatives behind, and make money. Because Mother Singer had special talent, I paid her half again what I'd typically pay for a rug. But even that's not much, considering all the time that goes into their creation."

Hawkman looked at the three rugs again and wrinkled his forehead. "Starla Singer. An enticing young woman. I haven't thought of her for a long time." But something in his tone told Leaphorn that wasn't quite true.

"These weavings do resemble the one in that photo. Your client might like a picture of these rugs because they were made by the same family as the one in her picture. Go ahead."

Leaphorn took several shots. The trader not only knew a lot about weaving in the area, he was also a decent judge of human nature.

Hawkman rerolled the blankets as he spoke. "I had forgotten about these, you know? They are treasures, for sure. I have a couple more, larger than these, in another storeroom. I need to bring them out here anyway. Would you like to see them?"

"Next time I'm here. The little one interests me more because it's close to what was in the photo."

"That sure brings back memories." Hawkman reached into his shirt pocket for a pen and wrote SINGER FAMILY on each of the three tags above the dimensions.

Leaphorn said, "I'll tell the woman I'm working with about the Singer family. You've been a great help."

"Is your client a weaver?"

"Not that she's mentioned."

"Well, if you get a chance, ask her about that, will you? Tell her I'd be glad to see what she does."

Leaphorn nodded, although he doubted that Stella knew how to weave; she hadn't had the shimásání, the grandmother, to teach her.

"Do you know if any Singer family relatives still live around here?"

Hawkman rubbed his chin. "I'm not sure about that, but you could take a look at their old compound. A gal named Janey Singer, a relative, goes out there to check on the place. Nice woman. She might be there now."

Leaphorn asked for directions to the house. "I'll drive out there and see who I can find. Thanks for all your help."

"Let me know if Starla turns up, will you? I always liked her."

Hawkman locked the rug room door, and Leaphorn offered the trader a bit of unsolicited advice. "Your prices on those rugs are too low. A person buying a beginner rug that size at the Crownpoint auction would spend a lot more. And yours are expertly made and high quality."

Hawkman nodded. "You know, a few buyers have told me the same thing. I keep cost low because it's not easy to get here. But you're right. I should raise the prices."

As Leaphorn was leaving, a question occurred to him. "Did the Singer girls have boyfriends or get married out here?"

"Boyfriends?" Hawkman chuckled. "Yes. Their mother came in one time with smoke coming out of her ears over that. Starla had taken off with some fella her shima didn't approve of. I think he was a Ute or something. She came back after a week or so."

Leaphorn picked up a family-size package of cookies, a bag of peanuts, a bottle of cold water, and a candy bar before he left, paying Patricia with the exact change. Then he drove his truck to the junction for Alava Singer's old place and stopped to eat the peanuts, drink some water, and gather his thoughts. He had a cell signal, so he called Louisa, dialing both the house phone and her cell. She didn't answer.

He headed down the long dirt road to the compound where the Singer family had woven their beautiful rugs, hoping that some relative would be there who might know a bit about the couple in the picture, the blanket, and especially a baby born more than fifty years ago.

The property had a traditional hogan, a manufactured home that had seen better days, and a single-wide trailer with an added-on front porch. He saw smoke coming from the chimney on the single-wide. Behind it was a newer building that could have been a garage or workshop, and an assortment of old cars, pickup trucks, and SUVs, some of which looked like working vehicles. A ramada, to offer shade for the weavers in the summer, stood near an abandoned sheep pen.

Leaphorn parked in front of the smaller house and waited a moment. A large yellow dog approached his truck, barking fiercely. Then a wiry gray-haired woman opened the door. She scolded the dog, then walked outside and hollered toward the truck.

"Yá'át'ééh."

Leaphorn rolled down the window and returned the greeting.

The woman introduced herself with her clans. Leaphorn did the same, and they continued to speak in Navajo.

"I came to visit because I saw some beautiful weavings done by the Singer family down at Red Lake Trading Post." Leaphorn described his two favorites. "The man there told me that this was where those ladies used to live. He said maybe there were still some of that family around here. Some relatives."

"He was right. I'm a Singer too. Janey Singer. But I don't have any more of my aunties' work, if that's what you're after."

"Actually, I'd just like to chat with you about those ladies."

He watched the woman's face cloud as she considered his request. She pushed her thick glasses back up to the ridge of her nose. He could see that she was ready to go back inside.

"Have you heard of the men and women who are called lost birds?" He waited to see if Janey responded to the terminology, or if he needed to explain that these were Navajo children who'd been adopted outside the Diné world and grown up without their relatives.

She nodded. "I know about that. Some of them were stolen from the nest out here, too."

"There's a lost bird who may have come from around here. I think this lady could be related to those Singer family weavers because of a photograph of a couple with a baby at the Elephant Feet. In the picture, it looks like the baby is wrapped in a blanket woven in the same style as the Singer family's."

Janey stood with her hands grasped in front of her, listening impassively, her eyes on the ground. Leaphorn couldn't tell if what he said interested her, or if her attention simply reflected Navajo politeness. He continued the story.

"The woman, Stella, regrets that she didn't have a chance to grow up here in Dinétah. She asked me if I could help her find her relatives. She looks like us Navajos, but she was raised by a white family." He didn't like making speeches, but he had more to add.

"You and I may not be able to help her, and she knows that. But she would be reassured to know that you and I had tried to help her find the family, the relatives, she has been without for her whole life. There are many of these lost birds, and if they can come home, they will help make us all stronger. I would like to show you that picture and talk to you about the women who made such beautiful blankets."

Leaphorn gave her time to process his request, and while she was thinking, he sweetened the offer. "I bought some cookies at the trading post. Would you share them with me?"

"What kind?"

"Oatmeal raisin."

Janey nodded. "Come on in. I'm not sure I know much about the ones who wove the rugs, but I know that cookies are good. I'll make some coffee."

Yellow Dog had slunk under the porch, but when Leaphorn reopened the truck door, he moved toward the vehicle and began barking again. Janey Singer addressed the animal sharply in Navajo, and it retreated. Leaphorn took the cookies and headed toward the house, nervous about the dog but relieved that he might have found someone who could help him bring the lost bird home.

The house was neat and packed with memories. She motioned for him to sit on the couch while she stirred the fire in her potbelly stove and added a single piece of wood to warm the blue enamel coffeepot that sat on top. Leaphorn put the cookies on the coffee table, moving a few bottles of vitamins and some pain-relieving lotion to make a bit of room. He felt warm in the house without the stove putting out more heat, but he could see that the woman was thin and not dressed for the cool spring day.

She busied herself with cups and paper towels to use as napkins and found a yellow plate for the cookies. She set a bowl of sugar on the table next to him with a tablespoon. By then, she determined that the coffee was warm enough. She poured him a cup and set it silently on the table. Then she went back and got a cup for herself, to which she added three spoonfuls of sugar.

Finally, she eased herself onto the couch.

He called up the Elephant Feet photo on his phone. "I want to show you the picture my client Stella found. This photograph makes us think that perhaps she is related to people who live on this part of the reservation."

Janey nodded, and he pointed the phone toward her. As she studied the image, Leaphorn thought she might be older than she looked. He had assumed that she was around Stella's age, in her fifties. But now that they were together on the same couch, he could see crow's-feet around her eyes and strands of gray in her black hair. She moved with the careful hesitation he'd noticed in other people of a certain age, a protective way of dealing with aches and pains that he himself was accustomed to.

When Janey looked up from the photo on his phone, her eyes glistened with tears. "I would like to talk to this woman. I know things she should hear."

"What things?"

"Family things. Tell her to come tomorrow."

"How do you know these things?"

Janey smiled, and the joy in her face took years off her age. "My story is for her, not for you. But you can tell her I was there when they took that picture. I was a young schoolgirl, but I remember it clearly. No one mentioned it afterward, so I thought it must be a dream. I didn't think it was real."

Leaphorn thought about the long drive and Stella's short fuse. He didn't want to encourage her to make the trip, only to find disappointment at the end of it. "She will ask me if I'm certain that what you have to say is the truth."

Janey smiled. "Tell that lady that I watched our shimásání make the blanket that is in the picture. It was soft and warm, made for a little one. Perfect for an awéé'. Tell her that sometimes what seems to be the right thing to do looks different over time."

"I will tell her." He felt a wave of anxiety settle in as he thought about the type of story that ended with an infant removed from her family. "If she comes, will she be glad that she talked to you?"

Janey shrugged. "Tell her to come in the morning."

"I will give her your message. She may ask me to come with her."

Janey nodded. "You are welcome if the woman wants you here after we speak alone. Joe Leaphorn, you are a valuable man, but I can only say what I have to say to Stella, to this lost bird."

Before he left, Leaphorn ate a cookie and asked Janey about the Singer sister who had moved to Window Rock. She had no information on the woman. He asked if she knew the hatáálii Chee had mentioned, a person who lived somewhere in the Tonalea area. She smiled at the name of the healer.

"A good man. Oh yes. He did quite a few ceremonies around here."

"I would like to find him. Can you help me?"

Janey obviously heard the question, but she sat impassively for quite a few moments. "Well, he had to go to the hospital in Tuba."

Interesting, Leaphorn thought. Some medicine men resisted modern doctoring and medicine. Others worked with hospitals to help them incorporate Diné tradition with contemporary healing.

She continued her story. "He went there twice. And then, after all that, he had to go back again last month."

It was a long story, full of detail. He listened until she finished. "Is the man back here now?"

She shook her head.

"Do know where I could find him?"

She frowned, a sign that he had asked too many questions. "You can't find him. He died in the hospital."

And with him, Leaphorn thought, his memory of the people for whom he had done ceremonies. Among them, perhaps, Stella Brown's Navajo mother. He knew he had to tell Chee of the loss, and he regretted it. The passing of each of these healers also meant the disappearance of irreplaceable knowledge. Even though Leaphorn didn't adhere to many traditional Navajo beliefs, he respected the work of the Diné Hatáálii Association in keeping this traditional healing alive.

Leaphorn thanked the woman for her time, left the cookies with her, and prepared for the drive back to Window Rock. Before he left, he called Louisa again, and again she failed to answer. The situation left him with a splinter of worry.

Then he called Stella Brown.

"I found a woman who has a story for you. She wants to talk to you in the morning."

Stella was quiet for a while. "Who is she?"

"The woman's name is Janey Singer."

"How did you discover her?"

"The picture you had was the key." Leaphorn told her about the weavings that resembled the blanket in the photo, and how a conversation with the Red Lake Trading Post owner had then led him to the old homestead.

"How is this woman related to me?"

"I don't know how she is, or even if she is. She said she has to give you the story herself, just the two of you. She wants you to meet her in the morning at her house."

"That won't work. It's impossible. I'm leaving the day after tomorrow, and I have a to-do list that stretches . . ." The phone fell quiet for a long moment. "I've been down this road before, you know. People tell me they have information about my birth mother or father, and it turns out to just be smoke and mirrors."

The phone was silent for another moment, and then Stella had a question. "Did you at least get a hint of what she might have to tell me?"

Leaphorn exhaled. "Janey said she was there when the picture was taken. She was just a little girl then, but I could tell she remembered the day clearly."

"Joe, do you trust her?"

"Yes." He considered how to phrase what came next. "I'm not sure you'll like what she has to say, but I think she will honestly tell you what she knows."

"To tell you the truth, even though we've come this far, maybe I don't want to know the whole story. I'm scared to hear what she has to say." She sighed.

"Stella, don't live with fear. Drive out there tomorrow to hear what she has to share. Even if she can't tell you much, or if what she says is not what you wanted to hear, do it. At the very least you can leave for Thailand with the assurance that you gave the search your best effort."

"Will you come with me?"

Leaphorn had expected the question. "Yes. I will drive to the area with you and tell you how to get to her house. But she says her memories are only for you, and I have to respect that. She seems to be a wise, kind woman. I've met a lot of people over the years, and I can tell that she has a story you need to hear. Do you understand?"

"I get it. Thanks." He heard a heavy dose of relief in her voice. "I'll see you tomorrow morning."

17

On his way back home, Leaphorn noticed that Red Lake Trading Post was still open. He went inside and made a purchase he'd been considering. Patricia accepted the money with remarkably little enthusiasm. Then he called Louisa, both numbers, and again got no answer.

He refreshed his memory—had she mentioned doing something today that he had forgotten about? But the only thing he remembered her saying was that she wanted to focus on her work and be available in case Kory wanted to get together before he and Erlinda left town.

Vague worry rode with him back to Window Rock.

When he arrived, he saw Louisa's car in its usual spot in the driveway.

The first thing he noticed when he went inside was that she hadn't started dinner. Very unlike her. And she wasn't working at the table where her notes were spread. "Louisa? Everything OK?" She didn't respond. He checked her bedroom, the bathroom, his office, and even his bedroom.

She was gone.

Maybe she'd left for a walk, he told himself. She did that sometimes to clear her head, and it was a pleasant afternoon. He had advised her to always take her phone with her, just in case of emergency. Maybe she'd simply been out of range when he had tried to reach her. Leaphorn called her cell phone, heard it ringing, and tracked the sound to her purse on the shelf in her closet. Her sneakers were there, too, the shoes she had purchased expressly to support her commitment to long walks.

His worry spiked.

He didn't have a number for her son, but he knew how to reach Erlinda. He called her, again with no answer. As he considered what to do next about Louisa, he checked to see if Louisa or Lin or even Kory had sent a text. Instead, he found the messages from Bowlegs. After he read them, he called Detective Short, glad that he had her private cell number, gave her an update and forwarded Cecil's messages to her.

All the while, of course, he was thinking about Louisa.

Then he got in his truck and drove to the Window Rock Lodge, where he knew Kory had booked a room, hoping against his instinct for trouble that Louisa was with him and Lin, and that everything was all right.

The motel was about a twenty-minute drive from the house, and as he drove, he thought about what to say to Kory if Louisa wasn't there. Would Kory think he was a neurotic old coot? He realized that he didn't care about Kory's opinion of him. He just needed to find Louisa and make sure she was safe.

He parked, berating himself for not paying more attention to Kory's black rental sedan so he would know if it was one of the several small cars in the crowded lot. He walked into the small lobby. Erlinda, also known as Lin, the woman who had been in their living room crying the day before, sat alone on a generic couch, staring out the window.

He called her name once and then again. The second time she looked at him and then flashed with recognition. "Leaphorn. I don't know how you got here, but I'm so glad to see you."

A score of questions flashed through his mind. He settled on the most pressing. "Where's Louisa?"

"Louisa? Isn't she at your house? She called me, and then Kory grabbed my phone and said he had to talk to her in person, and that he was driving over there and he'd be back in a few minutes. So I packed up our things and . . ." She swallowed. "And I've been waiting here for two hours. I called him, and he won't pick up. I called her, and the phone just goes to voice mail."

"Louisa doesn't have her phone. That's why she didn't answer. What did he want to talk to her about?"

She shook her head. "He didn't tell me, but he was furious about something."

"What made him angry?"

"Oh, it's complicated. To start with, cancer." Lin looked at the floor a moment. "Last night, he told me that his mother has never been fair to him. He said she should have helped him more, should never have gotten divorced. Stuff like that. Old baggage."

Leaphorn assumed Kory was in his forties. That seemed like enough time to make peace with the past and move forward. He studied Erlinda more closely. Noticing his gaze, she held her hand up to her face to hide the redness and swelling on the right side near the jawline.

"He hit you, didn't he?"

She shifted on the couch, embarrassed. Leaphorn sat next to her. After a moment Lin looked toward him.

"Louisa called me earlier today. She wanted to make sure I was OK after our talk at your house because I was crying and all that. She asked me how I was feeling, you know, and I said something like all right, I guess. That made Kory all mad. That's when he slapped me."

Leaphorn sensed that she had something else to tell him. He gave her time. "Kory hated it that his mom called me and not him. He thought we were ganging up on him. He yelled at me some more and then left angry. He said he was going to talk to her in person, to make things right. I hope they worked it out."

"They weren't at the house. Do you have idea of where he might have gone with Louisa?"

"No." She studied her shoes for a moment. "Kory likes to hike and he told me his mother does, too. Maybe she took him to one of those places she mentioned. I hope they went for a walk and had a good talk. I hope he calmed down and they made peace."

"Me, too. I need to call him. Give me his number."

Lin pulled out her phone and typed something. "I just texted it."

Leaphorn heard the tone for incoming text.

Lin stood, took a few steps toward the lobby window, and then walked back. "Please call him and find out what's going on. He doesn't want to talk to me, but maybe it's different with you."

Leaphorn called while Erlinda watched expectantly. He got no answer and he knew what he had to do next. "I'm going to look for them and I'll call you if I find Louisa or Kory or both of them. I know some of her favorite places to hike. I need to go now, before it gets dark."

"I want to go with you."

"No. You need to be here so you can call me right away if they come back to the motel. OK?"

She frowned. "OK. But I'm worried. I feel terrible."

She looked pale and sad and older than yesterday, he realized. "Have you had anything to eat or drink today?"

"Not yet." She hesitated. "Kory has our money and the credit cards. But I'm too worried to be hungry."

Leaphorn took out his wallet and gave her the money he had, a pair of five-dollar bills. "There's a vending machine down the hall, and you probably saw the café. Get a little something and eat a little, even though you don't feel like it. It might raise your spirits and it could be a long night."

Before he climbed into his truck, Leaphorn thought about the situation that might await him. He called his old friend Largo and explained, hoping for a bit of good counsel. Instead, he got a lecture.

"So, if Louisa hasn't come home yet, she's probably off somewhere with her son, who, according to what his wife told you, is flaming with anger. She left her purse and her phone, so she was obviously under some sort of stress, and she can't call you."

"That's right. And . . ."

"Let me finish. You plan on going out to find Louisa and make sure she's OK, but you really don't know where to search. They could be anywhere. Have I got that straight?"

Leaphorn grimaced. Largo's summary of the problem made it all the more real. "Yeah, but you know I need to look somewhere. I'm concerned about this. It's not normal. It's not like her."

"Right. You're going to try to find her, and you want me to be available in case she kicks your butt or shoots you for sticking your nose into her business. That way I can retrieve your body."

Leaphorn laughed despite himself. "She might be mad enough to do that, but her gun is in her purse at home. Seriously, I don't know what this guy is capable of."

"You have a gun." Largo sounded serious now, too. "Make sure it's loaded, and take me, too. You could need some backup." His friend had been a cop long enough to appreciate the unease that often came before disaster. Largo and Leaphorn had logged thousands of hours in their units riding solo. Because the Navajo Nation encompasses 16 million acres, or about 25,000 square miles, officers often patrol alone, with reinforcements hours away. Serving as backup is both an honor and an important responsibility.

Leaphorn started the truck's engine as he spoke. "I might be nervous without much reason. Louisa is independent. She's a strong woman. She won't appreciate it if I'm interfering with a big breakthrough conversation with her son."

"You're right to be worried." Largo sounded worried now, too. "Women never leave their phones and purses at home. Where are you?"

Leaphorn told him.

"I know that area. Isolated, but not far from my house. I can be there real quick."

"I'll think about it. Thanks for offering, and keep your phone on, OK? Just in case."

"No problem. Stay in touch. And don't try to be a superhero. Remember, you're not thirty anymore."

Leaphorn drove back to his house, quickly parked, and went in on the chance that Louisa had returned, but nothing had changed since he'd last been there. He grabbed some bottled water, pulled his flashlight out of the glove box, and checked to make sure his gun was loaded.

When he arrived at a hiking destination Louisa favored near Window Rock, he looked for Kory's rental car. A black sedan caught his attention until he saw its Texas plates; he remembered that Kory's rental was from New Mexico.

There was only one vehicle at the second area, another black sedan. This car, like Kory's rental, had New Mexico's classic red-and-yellow license plates. It was empty and locked, but a pair of men's mirrored sunglasses was on the console between the seat, and he remembered Kory wearing similar glasses. He parked his truck behind the car, blocking it in—there was no way this guy was leaving until they talked.

He called Largo again and left a voicemail with the location, asking his friend to join him. He hoped Largo got the message. He'd been in enough situations without backup to last a lifetime. He didn't need another one.

The mud from the earlier snowmelt had softened the ground enough to hold a few tracks. Leaphorn wished Chee was there, with his younger eyes and well-honed skills as a tracker. But the path seemed clear enough, and he followed it. After a few minutes, he realized that he wasn't dressed for hiking, but he continued on, doing the best he could. He was glad he had his windbreaker, at least, and a heavy shirt beneath it. He hoped Louisa had grabbed her coat.

As the trail twisted uphill, the mud gave way to a base of slick, wet rock. Leaphorn stopped to catch his breath. He listened for Kory's and Louisa's voices, but only the breeze and a few birds who thought forty degrees was a harbinger of spring broke the silence.

He had been walking for another twenty minutes or so when he heard something human ahead of him on the trail. He stopped to listen again, wishing his ears worked better.

"Louisa?"

He knew that Louisa sometimes had trouble hearing, too, especially with her hiking hat over her ears. After a few minutes, he heard something again, stopped, and called out.

"Louisa, is that you?" He moved as fast as he could on the steep, narrow trail, speeding up where he felt steadier on his feet, his ears ready for a response.

"Joe? Joe?" This time it was definitely her voice, frantically calling his name.

"Yes. I'm on the trail heading toward you."

"Thank God. We have to help Kory."

After a ten-minute climb, he saw Louisa sitting on a boulder, her nose and cheeks red with exertion. She was wearing the moccasins she used as house slippers, but he was thankful that she had on a jacket and her hat.

She sucked in a breath when she saw him. "Oh, Joe, we have to help him. He threatened to kill me and then his wife. And now he's turned his anger on himself. He has a gun."

"Did he hurt you?"

She ignored the question.

Leaphorn spoke gently. "What did he do to you?"

She sat in stunned silence.

"You're safe with me. Just tell me about Kory so I can find him."

She let the question sail by. "I never thought something like this would happen. He needs help, just like Erlinda said. I tried to help him, tried but . . ."

Leaphorn put his hand on her shoulder. "Where is he?"

"I, I . . ." Louisa pulled her jacket around her more tightly. "We walked up this trail for a mile, neither of us talking much, although I did everything I could think of to get him to confide in me. Then I told him my knees were bothering me and I needed to start back to the car.

"When I said that, he grabbed my arm, and then he screamed that I never made him a priority, that his wife and I only thought of ourselves. The more he yelled, the more his anger accelerated. Finally I kicked him hard in the leg, and when he let go of me, I ran."

"Did he follow you?" Leaphorn looked up the trail but saw only an empty path.

"I don't think so. I heard him sobbing." When she exhaled, Leaphorn imagined her forcing away the memory of the sound.

"Where did he go?"

She shook her head and he saw the tears.

"Louisa, did he talk about suicide?"

"He said he's a dead man anyway because of the cancer. What difference does it make to cut things short? I didn't know what to say except that it would make a difference to me. He wouldn't hear it, he—" A sob cut off her words.

As Leaphorn gave her a quick moment to regain some composure, he

looked and listened for any sign of Kory. The trail was quiet. He pulled
out his phone, grateful for service, called 911, and explained the situation.
Then he turned to Louisa.

"We need to talk to Erlinda. I know she's frantic with worry about
you both." He offered Louisa a hand to get up from the rock. "Let's walk
back to my truck, and you can make the call."

The sun had slipped lower in the sky, but there was enough light to
keep them on the trail. Leaphorn was alert for the sound of Kory returning, or following them, but heard nothing except their own breathing
and footsteps. When they reached the base of the trail, they sat on a
bench with a view of anyone heading toward them.

Leaphorn put his gun in his right hand, and gave the phone to
Louisa. She clicked the phone onto speaker as she called Lin.

"You talk to her first." Louisa held the phone close to him as the
call connected.

Leaphorn explained where they were and what had happened, keeping his voice calm. "Louisa is here with me at the hiking area."

"What about Kory? Is he OK?"

"We're waiting for him, and I've called for help to find him if he
doesn't show up here. Louisa wants you to know that she's safe. Hold
on." Leaphorn nodded to Louisa, and she took a breath. "She wants to
explain."

She stared at the phone and exhaled. "No," she said, "Kory's not OK.
My son, your husband, he's having some sort of mental breakdown. He's
depressed, and agitated, saying crazy things."

"Oh no, I get it. He promised me he was taking his medication, but
he must have stopped. Crazy like what?"

"He told me he wants to kill us both." Louisa swallowed a sob. "He's
out on the hiking trail, it's almost dark, and I'm terrified that something
bad will happen to you or to me or to Joe. And I'm worried about Kory,
too."

Leaphorn motioned for the phone. "Lin, I've called 911, and they are
on the way here to find Kory. A crisis resolution expert is on the team."
And, he knew, plenty of armed SWAT officers, but he didn't say that.

"I'm going to call the Window Rock station again. I'll ask someone to come and pick you up at the motel and take you to a secure shelter where you'll be safe until we know more about Kory's state of mind."

"No, I have to be there when he comes back. He'll be upset, and I can help with that."

"Listen to me. You need to think straight. He's threatened to kill you. You can't help if you're dead and he's in prison."

Lin didn't respond.

Louisa moved close to Leaphorn so the woman could hear her. "Joe knows what he's talking about. He's dealt with these situations before. The Kory who was on the trail with me is not the son I know or the husband you love. He's dangerous. He scared me."

"Lin," Leaphorn said, "tell the hotel manager you need to wait in their business office until the patrol unit arrives. Don't go back to the lobby or your room. We're assuming Kory is still on the trail, but we don't know that for sure."

"You're positive I can't help?" Lin's voice sounded thin and desperate.

"Absolutely. Not now. Later, probably. That's why you have to stay safe."

"What about Louisa? He threatened her, too."

"She's here with me. I'll make sure she's safe."

Leaphorn disconnected and called the Navajo Police, glad he still had some contacts there. After learning that the SWAT team was on the way, he arranged for someone to safely transport Lin from the hotel to the shelter. Before he ended the call, he added, "Because the situation is fluid, Louisa Bourbonette also needs a safe place until this is resolved. Tell the shelter staff she'll be there temporarily, too."

As he hung up, he saw Louisa frown. "Joe, I have to be here to talk to my son, especially if cops are coming. He could panic and, well . . ."

Leaphorn shook his head. "Remember what you told Lin? Give yourself that same advice. He has a gun, right?"

"Yes."

"And he threatened to kill you. It's too dangerous for you here."

"Joe, life is dangerous. I'm his mother."

Leaphorn shook his head.

"You don't understand. I have to talk to him."

"You can talk to him later, I promise."

"No. You aren't a parent!" She was yelling now. "You don't get the bond between a mother and her son. It doesn't matter how old he is or what he does. Kory will always be my child."

Leaphorn sucked in a breath. "When this is over, you can mother him all you want. Trust me. You have to go."

Louisa glared at him. "Forget it. I don't like this plan. I'm staying here. I have to make sure he's OK."

Leaphorn pushed down his impatience. "Kory hurt Lin. I saw the damage he did to her face. It could happen to you, too. The man out there isn't the same son you love."

"He would never hurt me."

"He grabbed your arm and tried to restrain you. You had to kick him to get away, remember."

She said nothing.

Leaphorn put both hands on her shoulders and she shrugged him away.

A truck pulled in, and he recognized it as Largo's. His friend climbed out and trotted over to them, joining them on the trail bench. "What's happening out here?"

Before Leaphorn could answer, Louisa turned toward Largo. "Joe thinks I should abandon my son."

"Not abandon him. Just give him space for now." Leaphorn spoke slowly, as if he were talking to a child. "You need to get out of here so you don't get shot. I need to start looking for Kory so I can mediate the situation before the other officers come. Largo can drive you to the shelter."

Largo exhaled. "No. It's better for you to take her. Louisa, you have to cooperate. You don't want to hear this, but you'll only add to the confusion when search and rescue or whoever the chief sends arrive. I promise to watch for Kory if he comes back before the cops get here, and to talk to them about the situation."

Louisa gave them a stare cold enough to ice the San Juan River. "If you're both convinced that I can't help here, and that my son would harm me, I can drive myself to the shelter. That is, if Joe will tell me the address and hand over the keys to his truck."

The men stood quietly, absorbing the development. Then Leaphorn pulled out his keys and pushed the button to unlock the vehicle. He gave her the address and directions to the location.

She frowned. "Not a very appealing neighborhood."

"But it's safe. There's no sign on the building, and lots of security. When you get there, be sure to tell them you are the woman I called about."

"Give me some credit, Joe. Of course."

"You have to go directly there. Promise?"

"I understand." She took a deep breath and let it out again. "If Kory shows up, it will be safer for you two if you face him together. Try to be kind to him. And, when the other officers get here, tell them he's not a bad man, just a poor soul having a mental breakdown."

Leaphorn heard the raw emotion in her voice. "I promise I will do everything I can to keep him from harm."

"And you'll tell me what happens here?"

He nodded.

"Even if it's bad news, Joe?"

"Yes. I'll call the shelter as soon as I know. And I'll come and bring you home when it's safe."

"OK."

He handed her the keys to his truck and started to walk toward the vehicle with her, but she put her hand on his chest.

"Stop. You and Largo stay here in case he shows up."

They watched her walk to the truck, and heard the engine start. The headlights switched on, and she drove away.

18

After Louisa left, the men looked at each other. No police had arrived yet.

Leaphorn studied the trail. "I want to walk up that way again. A few minutes from here, there's a spot where I can see into the cliffs and also watch the road so I'll know when the cops get here. I noticed some caves, and it could be that Kory is in one of them."

"Hiding in there, with a gun to shoot you."

"You heard what I promised Louisa. I know the man. I might be able to persuade him to come down before SWAT gets here."

Largo shook his head. "I don't like it, but if you're going, I'm going. And as soon as we see the cops, we come back. Deal?"

"OK."

Largo quickly reparked his truck behind the sedan, blocking it in as Leaphorn had done. Then they hiked off, Leaphorn setting the pace, guns at the ready.

"Hey, slow down a little, will you?" Largo sounded breathless. "You want the rescue team to have to carry me off this trail before they even look for your guy?"

"Sorry." Leaphorn stopped. While he waited for his friend to hike up to him and catch his breath, he yelled Kory's name. There was no response.

Largo, naturally a big man, had grown rounder with retirement. "Did I ever tell you my theory of exercise?"

"No. I'm surprised you have a theory." Leaphorn laughed. "I thought you weren't a believer."

"That's true, I don't subscribe to it. I think exercise is something people do because they think they can cheat death out of a few more years. But guess what? Death always catches up with us, and yet those fools keep trying."

Leaphorn knew there was no point in making the arguments Largo had undoubtedly heard before: exercise helps people feel better, think better, even find more happiness. He had picked up the habit years ago, and knew it had served him well.

They reached the overlook, and Leaphorn scanned the cliff face. He saw no movement.

"I want to wander up here another half mile or so. If we still have nothing, we head back to your truck and turn it over to the search-and-rescue folks."

"You go ahead. I'm done." Largo eased himself onto a flat-topped boulder. "I need time to give my legs the bad news that they have to walk back. They like plenty of warning."

"That's fine. I'll holler if I need your help."

Leaphorn walked faster now, prompted by both his frustration and the failing light. At the top of a ridge, he came to the place where the trail forked. He was glad he had persevered. If Kory had gone to the parking lot that way, they would have missed him. Leaphorn hurried back to where Largo waited. He could see that the black sedan was still there, trapped behind his friend's big truck.

"No luck?"

Leaphorn nodded. "A little. I didn't get shot."

"It's almost dark," Largo said. "We need to get out of here. The cops will be here any minute, and you need to tell them what's up."

Leaphorn agreed. He knew his strengths and his limits. Hiking on an unfamiliar trail in failing light had challenged him. He was bone tired, and his joints would be complaining about this mistreatment, but he'd done what he had to do, what he'd promised Louisa.

He and Largo limped to the parking area together, reaching it just as the lights of the Navajo Police responders came into view. Leaphorn explained the situation, and the officers began their careful preparation for an extended search for Kory. Largo knew some of the cops, and wished them luck. Then he turned to his old friend.

"Shall I give you a ride to the shelter so you can get your truck?"

"Sure. I'll call them and ask the director to tell Louisa I'm coming." They walked to Largo's vehicle together while Leaphorn waited for someone at the shelter to answer.

The shelter staffer sounded puzzled. "You're the gentleman I spoke with earlier, aren't you?"

"That's right. I mentioned that Louisa Bourbonette might be staying tonight. She drove herself there earlier this evening."

"I'm sorry. There's no one here by that name."

"You're wrong. I know she's there." He told the woman on the phone when Louisa had left, and how long it should have taken her to arrive.

"Sir, she must have changed her mind. There is no Louisa Bourbonette here. I swear it."

"Double-check. She has to be there." He described her.

"I don't want to argue, but I know she never rang the buzzer. That's the only way people come in. I would have seen her. I've been here ever since you called the first time."

Leaphorn felt his chest tighten. "Are you sure?"

"Positive. We only received one new guest this evening."

"Erlinda?"

"Ah, I'm not supposed to tell you because of guest privacy."

"I'm worried about her, too. She and Louisa were threatened by the same man."

"Sir, I'm sorry, but . . ."

"She's my daughter-in-law." It wasn't quite the truth, but it was as close as he could get.

"Lieutenant, all I can say is that our new guest is resting, and she said to call her Lin."

He thanked the staffer and then dialed Louisa's cell phone on the chance that she'd stopped at home to pick up her purse. But no one answered.

Largo stood with him, looking as worried as Leaphorn felt.

Then, with a sinking feeling, he tried Kory's phone.

"It's Joe Leaphorn, Kory. Is Louisa with you?"

"Indeed she is. I bet you want to talk to her?"

Leaphorn leaned against Largo's truck and exhaled. "I'd like that. Where are you?"

"Oh, we're driving. Actually, I'm driving. Mom is sitting here next to me. And, sorry, she can't talk to you. She's all tied up." He laughed as he said it, and Leaphorn grasped the meaning.

Leaphorn thought about the times he had dealt with people teetering on the edge of a terrible decision. His training in law enforcement and crisis situations kicked in. "Kory, I didn't have a chance to ask if you and Louisa were able to finish that conversation I interrupted. I know you mean a lot to her. I worried that maybe you . . ."

Kory chuckled. "No, you weren't worried about me. That's a crock. You were hoping I'd just disappear and leave my mother all to you."

Leaphorn picked up the bitter hysteria in the man's voice. He switched the phone on speaker so Largo could hear.

"You know, my mother sincerely hoped that one day I'd finally grow up and become the perfect son she'd always wanted. I didn't, so she only pretends she loves me. She's all sweetness now that she knows cancer is stealing my life cell by cell. Well, Mommy and I are settling things between us. No need to fret. I'm telling her all the things she did wrong as we're driving. It's a long list."

Leaphorn pushed aside his deep desire to defend Louisa. "I'm sorry you and I got off on the wrong foot. I'd like to get better acquainted. Where are you?"

"You know where I am. I'm in your truck." Kory burst out laughing, but Leaphorn felt no joy in the sound. "It delighted me that you gave Mom the keys and told her to drive away. She didn't notice that I had disabled the overhead light before I climbed in and hid in the back. I'm glad you have a king cab. After Mommy had driven out of your sight, I grabbed her around the neck and choked her until she pulled over. Now she can't help but listen to me, can she?"

Leaphorn's heart sank, and he watched Largo kick at the dirt. In the background of Kory's call, they heard highway noise, including what sounded like semitrucks. Kory must be on Interstate 40; none of the tribal roads would carry that kind of traffic.

"Mom and I, well, we've had a good run, Joe. May I call you that? Or do you prefer Lieutenant? Or Dad?"

"Joe is fine. Tell me something about yourself."

Leaphorn saw Largo walk toward the Navajo police cars. While he was keeping Kory on the phone, Largo would tell the officers that they didn't need search and rescue and ask for an APB on Leaphorn's stolen truck.

"Well, Daddy Joe, here's the deal. I'm approaching middle age, and I'm still a loser. My wife is afraid of me, and my mother thinks I'm a jerk. Pathetic, don't you agree? Cancer is eating me alive, but that death will take too long. In the meantime I'm just occupying space, breathing oxygen that could be put to better use."

Leaphorn turned up the volume so he could hear Kory more clearly.

"Instead of waiting to sink deeper, I need to, as they say, pull the plug. But that would leave this dear lady feeling responsible, somehow, for not saving me. I've caused my mother enough grief and worry over the years, so I'm taking her with me."

"You don't have to do that. What's the hurry? Let's talk about this some more. There are all kinds of ways Louisa and I can help you. I'm good at generating ideas, and so is your mother."

"Good ploy, but been there, done that. No hope for me now."

Leaphorn looked at the clouds with their streaks of orange, pink, and brilliant red against the fading blue of the sky. He noticed the way the soft sunset light made the sandstone glow.

"Can you see the sunset?" Leaphorn asked. "It's a beauty, right?"

"If you say so, Papa Joe. To me, it's just another day down the tubes. Another dead end."

"Take a minute to look at the view. It always reminds me of the possibilities."

"Weeds, dirt, a few scrawny horses." Kory sounded tired. "I've got to go. I'm looking for a place to park. And Mom and I need to talk a while longer before we say good night."

"Where are you now? Tell me. I can get Louisa when you're done talking to her. You won't have to mess with her anymore."

Kory didn't answer.

"What are you planning to do out there in the dark?"

"Oh, I can't tell you, Daddy Joe. You probably like surprises. I don't want to spoil it."

"May I speak to Louisa?"

"Nope. I'd hold the phone up so you could tell Mommy goodbye, but I have to focus on driving. I bet Mommy never even told you what happened to her marriage, did she?"

"No, she didn't."

"Well, my father decided Mom and I and life in general were too much trouble. I was about eight years old the night when he went out after dark, down to the place where the trains came past our house. He got a black garbage bag, like the ones we used for the huge trash cans, and put it over himself and stretched out across the tracks. It's doubtful that the engineer or anyone noticed him until they felt the impact. A little thud, and Dad was history."

Leaphorn felt a shiver move up his spine.

"My pops wasn't the brightest, but he did that right. Mother freaked out for a long time, of course, but I came to admire him for it. The more I thought of his plan, the more it seemed like a quick way to end the pain. But of course, I'll change it up a little."

Leaphorn realized he was considerably colder than he had been on the hike. Louisa had never explained why, as she put it, her marriage "didn't work out." He hadn't suspected that she had to deal with the aftermath of a gruesome suicide.

"Where are you and Louisa now?"

Kory ignored the question.

"I'd really like to chat with her."

"Sorry, old man. We've reached a dead end."

Leaphorn felt his stomach tighten when he heard that phase again. "Kory, let me help you figure out another solution. Louisa loves you, and so does Lin. And Lin is pregnant. A baby. That's a lot to live for and . . ."

Kory cut him off. "They both say they love me no matter what, and that's why I didn't want to leave Lin behind. Oh well. Mom will have to stand in for her, for all the women I've disappointed. Teachers, friends, coworkers. I've got to go."

Kory hung up.

Leaphorn's attention shifted to the police cars that were standing by, engines running, and his old friend and former boss beside him. He told Largo what Kory had said.

Largo shook his head. "Do you have an idea where they ought to search?"

"Not really." Leaphorn paused. "If I were in a truck, had a gun, and wanted to commit suicide, I'd drive to some out-of-the-way place before I shot myself. Kory used the phrase 'dead end.' Lots of roads like that out here."

"What about Louisa?"

"He threatened to kill her, so I imagine he'll shoot her before he kills himself."

"I gave the officers a description of your stolen truck, and Louisa, and told them that Kory had kidnapped her. I know some of these folks. Good officers. You need to give them the plate number and a description of Kory."

Leaphorn walked to the waiting police units, exhaustion on his spirit like a hundred-pound weight. He gave them the vehicle information, descriptions of Kory and Louisa, Kory's cell phone number, and his own number, too. The officers had alerted the state police and the McKinley County Sheriff to be on the lookout for his truck. He watched as the patrol cars headed off, lights flashing.

Largo put his hand on his friend's shoulder. "You want to look for them, too, right?"

"I have to. I should have been with Louisa. I should have driven—"

"You wanted me to go with her, and I talked you out of that." Largo looked at his truck, still in place behind the abandoned black sedan. "I'm driving. You navigate. We know the dark spots out here. You need to be able to focus in case Kory calls back."

"OK. You're right," Leaphorn said, relieved at his friend's take-charge attitude. Largo started the engine. "I had a couple cases where someone stole a vehicle with a person in it. He let the hostage go. Be sure to keep an eye out along the shoulder."

Leaphorn didn't like to think about Louisa alone, walking along the interstate in the dark, but the idea of her surviving this disaster gave him hope.

Leaphorn understood the Navajo Nation's roads, but here, outside of Gallup, he was less comfortable.

Largo fiddled with the rearview mirrors. "We'll find them."

Leaphorn clicked on his seat belt. "From the background noise, I know they're on the interstate. I told the cops that. Let's take the west-bound toward Arizona looking for exits that lead to dead ends."

"If we see a police car taking that exit, we move to the next stop."

"I agree." Leaphorn suddenly felt the pressure of time bearing down on him. He didn't say what he and his friend already knew. Ranch roads, roads that led to oil and gas sites, roads that wound their way to isolated hogans—so many roads that dead-ended in remote places in rural McKinley County, on the Navajo Nation and in Arizona. Leaphorn wished he could have kept Kory on the phone longer, listening for clues to what part of the vast, empty Four Corners the troubled man knew best. Then he'd have a clearer idea of where he planned a murder-suicide—if Kory himself even knew.

Largo moved the truck to the passing lane and cruised by an eighteen-wheeler. Traffic seemed heavier than usual, but Leaphorn realized that could be a reflection of his state of mind.

They both knew the Navajo reservation well and had a deep ac-quaintance with border areas like Gallup and the stretch of land toward Arizona. Not only had they spent their lives here except for college and the military, but working in law enforcement for the tribe had taken them to places all over the vast and varied region.

Largo's truck had a powerful engine, good clearance, and was at least a decade younger than Leaphorn's. His friend drove well, always in control and properly cautious while far exceeding the speed limit. Still, Leaphorn felt out of place watching dusk fall from the passenger seat.

He looked at his friend, confident hands on the steering wheel, eyes focused on the interstate. "Help me think this through, OK? Too many options. I'm worried that we won't find them in time."

"Try calling Kory again."

He did. No answer.

"Where do Kory and his wife live?"

"California or something." Leaphorn watched as Largo's truck smoothly gained on the Corvette in front of them. "If I had known we'd be driving ninety miles an hour trying to find him, I would have had a longer conversation with the man."

"I didn't even know Louisa had a son until today."

"Well, Louisa didn't know her son was married. And the wife is pregnant."

Largo kept his gaze on the road. "You'd think that guy had something to live for."

"You'd think."

"Does Kory know this country well?"

"No. I don't think so."

"Would he pressure Louisa into giving him directions to the final stopping point?" Largo passed a pickup with a horse trailer.

Leaphorn didn't have to think about it. "She's a great navigator, but she wouldn't help him kill himself. She could give him the wrong information on purpose. Mislead him. I don't think Kory's state of mind will let him drive far. I'm watching for an exit."

After ten long minutes, Leaphorn saw what he wanted.

"Take this one."

Largo flicked on the turn signal and they pulled off the interstate. The exit ramp ended at a dirt road and a stop where they had to turn left or right. Both directions led into the approaching darkness.

They rolled toward the red sign. "Which way?"

Leaphorn saw no vehicles in either direction and no dust rising from the road. Neither way had a sign that read DEAD END.

Leaphorn was silent for a moment. "Get back on the interstate."

The last crimson ribbons of sunset light were fading to grayish pink. The moon wouldn't be up for hours. Largo continued west on I-40.

Leaphorn thought about his dear friend, a woman he loved. He assumed the son she treasured had filled the car with dark thoughts. It stirred his anger and conviction to find her.

Largo made a soft hissing sound. "You heard the saying, 'Like finding a needle in a haystack'? This is our equivalent."

"I've got an idea."

Leaphorn called Detective Short, his best contact at NMSP, and left a quick voicemail explaining the urgency of the situation and asked her to alert the Arizona Highway Patrol and to call him.

Leaphorn's phone chimed, and he grabbed it, then put it down.

Largo said, "Kory?"

"No. Not Short either. A text from my dentist. But it gives me an idea."

He typed into his phone, reading the text to Largo as he composed it.

Hey, let's keep talking. I'd like to get to know you before you sign off.

"Send it." Largo sounded grim. "You've got nothing to lose."

Leaphorn pushed the button and waited. Quicker than he had hoped, his phone responded.

Nice try. Not interested.

Leaphorn texted back

How about something to eat? A last meal?

Another chime.

U R funny. Maybe we can get it to go, and I'll take it to Hell with me.

Leaphorn thought about what to respond before he typed.

Come on. Even guys on death row get a last meal. Where are you now?

A chime. He read Kory's response out loud.

In the middle of nowhere looking for a perfect parking spot. Cheers. Nothing else to say here.

Leaphorn responded quickly.

I'd like to say goodbye to Louisa.

He waited for Kory's response, but his phone stayed dark.

Largo put on his blinker and moved into the right lane. The next exit was less than a mile away. While Leaphorn was thinking of which way to turn after they left I-40, his phone rang. He saw that it was Chee and put the call on speaker.

"Hey, I learned something interesting about the photos, Lieutenant."

"Not now. I need help." He laid out the situation and asked for his ideas.

"Where are you?"

"Heading west on I-40." Leaphorn gave him the mile marker. "Looking for exits with dead ends."

"I didn't get that."

Leaphorn tried again. His palms begin to sweat.

The third time, Chee understood.

"OK, I located a dead . . ." Chee faded out and then came back ". . . more or less. Take that exit and turn west . . . farm . . ." And then came the "lost signal" chime.

They continued to the next exit, saw nothing, and got back on the interstate.

When his phone rang again, it was Mona Short.

"I asked the Arizona troopers to be on the lookout for the vehicle. I'm monitoring calls about it. Nothing yet."

Largo inserted himself in the conversation. "Can you ping a phone in the truck to get its location."

"Give me the number. This might take longer than you'd like. I'll call you or text when I know something."

Leaphorn and Largo drove in worried silence.

They took the next exit. Largo sped along the ramp, and a few moments later took the frontage road. They drove south, skidding around an unexpected curve. Largo kept his truck under control.

Leaphorn held his breath as they approached a DEAD END sign. No vehicle sat on the end of the road.

They looked for evidence that Kory might have driven through the brush to park farther away from the road, but in the glare of Largo's headlights the dry soil showed no disruption. They noticed the smooth, dark steel of the railroad tracks flowing on as far as they could see.

Largo sped along the frontage road, past junctions with two more dirt roads before they spotted another sign for a dead end. This time,

the road was full of potholes and washboard that screamed for maintenance. The truck's lights moving like bobbers, and Largo momentarily
lost traction as they powered through a place where deep sand had
collected in a dry streambed.

After all that, the result was another failure. More time wasted; more
gloom accumulated. They both hated guessing wrong.

Largo drove back onto I-40 west. "It's like we're chasing a tumble-
weed in a windstorm in the dark and the clock is ticking. Did Louisa
ever mention some spot she and Kory liked to go together?"

"I've been thinking about that, trying to. . ." Leaphorn exhaled. "It
just came to me."

He clamped a hand on Largo's arm. "We're headed the wrong direction. Turn around now and go back toward Gallup as fast as you can. I
should have figured this out sooner."

Long before they reached the next official exit, Largo spotted a sign
in the highway median that read AUTHORIZED VEHICLES ONLY and took
it heading east toward Gallup.

"OK. Now what? Tell me."

Leaphorn said, "Kory plans to park on the tracks and let the train
kill him the way it killed his father. He told me about that, but I was too
slow thinking to connect the dots."

"What happened to his dad?'

Leaphorn summarized for Largo. He could still hear Kory's voice in
his head, describing his father's death.

"That's tough." Largo sped up to pass another pickup. "That kind
of death is enough to stick with a child forever."

Leaphorn visualized the blackness of the night, and the terrible
sound of the train colliding with Kory's dad. He remembered Kory's
exact words: "I doubt that anyone even knew he was lying there until
they felt the impact of that collision. A little thud and my dad was
history."

"He wasn't just talking about the suicide; he was talking about the
way his father ended his life." Just remembering it Leaphorn suddenly
felt colder.

Largo said, "Train tracks. Are you sure?"

"No, but it's worth a shot. I remember a place near where they hiked. A spot where the road crossed the tracks near old route 66. No warning lights or gates. That would make it easier to park a truck there and wait for the end."

Largo exhaled. "I'm in. Let's do this. This might be crazy but it's better than more dead ends."

Interstate 40 east was crowded, big trucks outnumbering the cars, pickups, and vans. Largo drove with focus and experience. He continued to push his truck considerably over the speed limit, watching for inattentive drivers.

Leaphorn stared out the window. "Take the next exit and drive on old US 66. It parallels the tracks.

"OK. You sound sure."

"I remember Louisa saying that next to Red Rocks, she and Kory liked this area best. They spent an afternoon hiking around and she said Kory watched the trains. Not many safety gates out here and not much traffic."

"I hope you're right."

"I'm running on instinct, but it feels better than what we were doing before."

They were approaching the exit when Short called. Leaphorn put the call on speaker.

She got right to the point. "We tracked the phone. It's near the Gallup Flea Market site. The last call was from your number, Lieutenant. The police are on the way now. But our location tracker says it hasn't moved since that call."

The call was Kory's goodbye message. If he and Louisa had stopped there, Leaphorn knew his decision to turn around was hopelessly wrong.

"Wanna know what I think, Lieutenant?"

"Sure."

"My opinion is that he tossed it out of the vehicle there and drove on. There's too much light there and too much traffic for what you think he has in mind."

"That's how I see it, too," Leaphorn said. He shared his theory about the trains.

"I'll look into stopping the rail traffic and get back on that."

"OK."

"And I'll call you if we find your truck." Short hung up.

The lights from a cluster of newish motels on the east side of Gallup came into view, and then the Fire Rock casino, with a parking lot full of vehicles, flew by.

Chee called. "Anything new?"

"I had what I think is a good idea." Leaphorn explained. "Can you find the train schedules for this area?"

"Hold on." Chee was back in no time with the information for both east- and westbound trains into or out of Gallup that night. "I'll let the Navajo cops know where you're headed. Sounds like our jurisdiction. Good luck."

"Thanks. You said you discovered something interesting about that old photo from Elephant Feet. Go ahead. I could use some good news."

"Haskie asked the archivist if she could find out anything more about your photo. She noticed that the book's cover page was signed by a man named Bernard Hawkman. Next to his signature, he wrote 'Photographer in training.' She traced the name and learned that he's the one who donated the book to the Navajo Library."

"Hawkman?"

Chee spelled the name and ended the call. Leaphorn filed it in his memory, linked it to the BH on Stella's photo and perhaps to the John Hawkman he knew.

They drove, Largo's vehicle filled with the roar of fast-moving traffic, the rhythmic beat of the truck's tires on the pavement, and the sweaty silence of shared worry.

Largo had been quiet for too long. Leaphorn studied the expression on his friend's face. "What are you thinking about?"

"Nothing good. If Chee's right about this, we could start to see the westbound train in about twenty minutes. What are you thinking?"

Leaphorn didn't answer. He put the idea of Louisa trapped in the truck, feeling the track vibrate as death rumbled closer, out of his mind. He didn't want to imagine her terror as she heard the shrill warning whistle as the crew realized the tracks were blocked with the train rolling toward the vehicle at fifty miles per hour. A single locomotive engine weighed around two hundred tons, and he'd seen two or three of the engines pulling a line of up to a hundred train cars, each weighing perhaps 80,000 pounds. By the time the engineer saw the truck on the tracks in the dead of night, it would take too long for an engine pulling scores of cars to grind to a stop.

"I'm thinking of something else now," Largo said "Ho'aahidziniih." Leaphorn recognized the one-word request for protection. They repeated the word four times. Though he was a skeptic when it came to the world of the spirit, he saw no harm in praying now.

The truck found the exit they needed. Before Leaphorn could point it out, Largo said, "I'm taking this toward old Highway 66."

He drove the vehicle down the ramp and sped onto the two lane. Leaphorn stared out the window, looking for any place Kory might have turned north toward the railroad tracks and hoping not to see the bright light of a locomotive in the distance. North, he thought, the traditional direction of death. He shoved the thought aside.

Away from the glow of the city, the stars were intensely bright. The crescent moon offered them little competition. Louisa loved the night sky. Leaphorn thought of how many times they had gone outside after dinner to look for shooting stars or with hopes of spotting satellites. He didn't want to imagine life without her.

Largo switched the headlights to high beams. "You know, there's a possibility Kory might have changed his mind. Maybe he remembered something that gave him hope. Maybe Louisa softened his heart."

"Thanks for trying, but you know the score as well as I do."

The red cliffs beside them, a sight he'd always enjoyed, now reminded Leaphorn of a prison's intimidating walls.

The truck's headlights led the way. Largo accelerated to the edge of safety without Leaphorn's prompting. They appreciated the lack of traffic. Leaphorn stared at the road ahead, searching for taillights and hoping not to see a train. His eyes searched for the classic yellow-and-black sign that marked the place where a road to a farm or someone's house crossed the tracks.

Largo cleared his throat. "I think we might have made a bad guess. We should have spotted your truck—"

"Give it another minute," Leaphorn interrupted. "We're not at a crossing yet."

The truck's high beams found the railroad crossing sign. The road crossed the tracks here without a barrier. The deep water in the irrigation ditch close to it glistened in the starlight.

Largo closed in on the spot and his headlights reflected off a bumper just ahead of them. Kory had parked the truck directly on the tracks, and Largo turned toward it.

Leaphorn expected him to slow down, but instead he kept his foot on the gas. Just as Leaphorn started saying, "What the . . . " he realized the logic of his friend's seeming madness. He moved the passenger seat as far back as he could to avoid the airbag when it went off, and braced himself for impact.

Leaphorn heard the terrible sound of crunching metal as the heavy-duty front bumper of Largo's pickup collided with the back of his own truck. He watched its tailgate yield to the force of the push. The impact to the front end of Largo's vehicle drove the airbag into his friend's face. Largo yelped with pain, but he kept both his truck and Leaphorn's moving forward. The collision jarred Leaphorn, too, but to his shock the airbag didn't inflate.

Largo didn't let up on the gas pedal until both vehicles had cleared the tracks and moved beyond. His nose was bleeding heavily. Before the vehicle fully stopped, Leaphorn had his seat belt off and the door open. He leaped out, forgetting about his bad knee, fueled by adrenaline and hope. He ran to his truck, a corner of his mind noting the rear end damage, the rest focused on Louisa and her dangerous son.

Leaphorn ran to the driver's side of the truck. Through the window he could see Louisa, as still as death.

"Kory, it's over. Out of the truck."

Leaphorn tugged at the door. It was locked.

"Hold on, Old Joe. I was just saying a little prayer. I've been expecting you."

He saw Kory turn his head toward the door, the moon's glow

reflecting off his face. The man had an odd smile. Next to her son, he could see Louisa in the passenger seat.

"Kory, show me your hands."

Instead, he pushed a button, the action followed by the click of the door lock releasing. Leaphorn yanked the door open and the overhead light showed the gun in Kory's hand pressed against Louisa's head. He read the terror on her face.

Leaphorn kept his weapon on Kory. He heard a train approaching and felt the ground beneath him tremble slightly.

"Well, now we have to do this the hard way. You get to be part of the family drama, right, Daddy Joe?"

Louisa's voice was deathly calm. "Kory. Don't do this. Think about your child."

"No use arguing, Mommy. I'm tired of thinking. Tired of everything. This is for the best."

Then another voice roared in the night's darkness.

"Drop your weapon. Now."

Largo's deep tone carried a captain's authority. When Kory turned his head toward Largo's bloody face, he shifted his hand with the gun from Louisa. Leaphorn surged forward and hit the younger man in the head with the butt of his weapon. Kory collapsed into the steering wheel with a grunt, and the gun he'd been holding fell to the floor.

The train was closer now, barreling toward them through the darkness over the smooth metal tracks, a rush of sound and flood of bright light from its headlamp. Leaphorn turned off the truck's engine.

"Louisa, I'll help you out in a moment."

Largo was next to him now, and together they pulled Kory from the front seat and put him on the ground.

The light seeping onto the sandy earth from the truck found the back of Kory's white T-shirt. The man looked smaller now.

"Joe, I've got some zip ties. In my back pocket." Largo raised his voice to be heard over the noise of the approaching train.

Leaphorn secured Kory's wrists, and then straightened up. "I'll get Louisa."

"Go ahead." Largo's nose was bleeding again, and that, together with the growing roar of the oncoming train, muffled his voice. "I called for an ambulance and an officer."

Louisa was still staring ahead in stunned silence. Leaphorn undid her seat belt, then took out his pocket knife and cut through the tape Kory had used to bind her arms and legs. He gently put his arms around her and helped her out of his truck, noticing how cold she felt. She looked pale, almost ghostlike in the desert moonlight, and older than he had ever seen her. She shook all over when she stood.

When Louisa finally raised her face from his chest, he saw the silver streaks of her tears. She said, "Oh, Joe, thank God you're still alive. I . . ." And then a flood of relief stole her voice.

He held her a long moment, and then she spoke again.

"Kory?"

"He's alive, too." Leaphorn pointed with his chin to Largo and the place on the ground where Kory lay. "Let's climb into Largo's truck and warm up."

Leaphorn felt her body quiver and realized that he was shaking, too. He looked up to see the bright headlight of the locomotive racing toward them, a tsunami of sound and vibration. The wheels roared by in a blur of gray steel. The long line of cars that followed looked gray, too, in the faint moonlight. He squeezed Louisa to him more tightly.

He and Largo did what they had to that night, with a bit of help from Jim Chee and Mona Short. Not bad for a couple of technically challenged old cops and a pickup truck.

But all that really mattered was that Louisa was alive.

19

Bernadette Manuelito was cold, hungry, and, most of all, exhausted. She turned the heater in her unit up full blast as she headed back to Shiprock in the dark. She texted Chee that she was finally on her way home, then called Captain Adakai, fondly known as Triple X for his ample girth, and summarized her day over the phone.

"I'm just about outta here, Manuelito. Go on home. Come in tomorrow and do the report. You OK?"

"Yes sir. Thanks."

"I heard there was a body."

"That's right. A woman."

"Do you know anything else about her?"

"No sir. That's a mystery." Bernie was too tired to say more.

"A Detective Short from the New Mexico State Police wants you to call her. She said it concerns the explosion at Eagle Roost." He paused. "If I were you, I'd put that off until tomorrow, too. Maybe she'll go away."

"Thanks for the tip."

Bernie thought about calling Mama's house, and did it before good sense got in the way.

"Hey Bernie," Darleen's boyfriend Slim answered.

"Hi there. I'm just checking in. Are you guys OK?"

"Oh, mostly, I guess. Mrs. Darkwater came over to give your mother some help. Hold on, she wants to talk to you."

Darleen's phone usually picked up the noise from the TV, which

Mama tended to have on extra loud. Tonight, it only picked up an odd beeping. Bernie couldn't place the sound and felt a jolt of dread. Why was it, she thought, that calling home was always a crisis? She heard Slim's and Mama's voices in the background, and then, instead of Darleen, Mrs. Darkwater came on the phone.

"Nothing to worry about. Your mother will be just fine."

Bernie's worry increased. "What's happening?"

"Oh, the ice really helped, and I gave her some aspirin. Don't worry that the alarm went off. We took it outside. Too noisy."

"Mrs. Darkwater, could you start at the beginning?"

"Oh no, shideezhí. That's too long a story, and I need to get back to your mama. Just call again later, OK?"

"Wait. Just—"

But the phone went dead.

She called Chee. It took him more than the normal number of rings to pick up, which added to her anxiety.

"Hey, there. Do you have a minute to talk?"

"You bet." He sounded breathless. "I just heard an amazing story about Lieutenant Leaphorn and Captain Largo. They are heroes! I'd tell you all about it now, but I'm in the middle of making dinner. Hope you're hungry."

"Starving. And worried."

"What's bothering you?" The tone of his voice changed.

"I tried to reach Darleen and heard an alarm beeping. Then I had a strange brief conversation with Mrs. Darkwater about Mama needing ice and aspirin."

"Well, if ice and aspirin handled it, it doesn't sound too serious. That neighbor practically lives with your sisters and mother. Maybe their goofiness is rubbing off on her." Chee chuckled. "You ought to be calling her auntie."

"No joking. This worries me. I called on Darleen's phone, and she wouldn't even answer it herself. And something's going on with Mama. Maybe she's getting sick or had an accident."

"Darleen might be studying. She's a caregiver for your mother, working hard at school and trying to make time for Slim. A lot on her plate."

"I hope everything is OK out there. I'm driving, and I'm going to lose the cell signal."

"I'll call your mother's landline, and I've got Slim's number, too." She heard a noise in the background, something like the sizzle of meat on the grill. "I'll give you an update on that when I see you. Soon, I hope."

"I appreciate it."

"No prob. If something went wrong, I'm glad that for once your sister could handle it without involving you. Maybe that nurse training she's taking is paying off."

"I'm stopping at the station to get my car. I'll be home as soon as I can after that."

"I hope so. I miss you."

She pulled into the substation and parked next to her Tercel. She went in to drop off the keys to her unit and say good night to Sandra.

"Before you go," Sandra said, "tell me what's happening at Eagle Roost. Any more bodies?"

"Not that I know of." She briefly gave Sandra the highlights. "The FBI is in charge now. Agent Johnson and Agent Fisher turned the explosion investigation over to some new guys, the Evidence Response Team."

After the smooth power of the unit, her smaller Tercel was slow and noisy. She chugged home, the heater kicking out warm air only when she finally turned onto the dirt road that led to their trailer. She parked but left the engine running while she checked her phone messages to see if anything work-related had dribbled in. She'd missed a text from Lieutenant Leaphorn, asking if she had confirmation on the victim. She responded:

Not yet. Mrs. Bowlegs?? Car is registered to her.

I'll call you, Leaphorn texted back.

In the house, the aroma of Chee's simmering dinner greeted her like a warm hug. He looked up from the stove when she entered and wrapped his arms around her, then quickly stepped away.

"I can slow down dinner if you want to take a shower."

She smiled. "That stinky, huh? OK. I get the hint."

"I didn't mean to, ah . . ." Chee stumbled as he searched for the word.

"Oh yeah you did." She punched him teasingly in the bicep.

The warm water worked its magic. Every time she showered, she remembered her years growing up, when running water was an unimagined convenience. She thought of the elderlies who still lived without indoor plumbing and didn't complain about hauling water to their homes or bringing clothes and bedding to the Shiprock laundromat. She admired them, but she also wished their lives were easier.

Chee had set the table for dinner. His beef stew with a touch of red chili powder in the gravy was a great tonic for the day's stress. She considered adding a Coke, her third of the day, but settled for water. They ate in companionable silence until he opened the conversation, telling the story of the way Leaphorn and Largo had rescued Louisa.

Bernie listened closely. "Wow. Those two really figured it out. I feel sad for Louisa."

Chee moved to something more personal. "After you and I talked, I called your mother's house and talked to Slim."

She wondered why Slim, not Mama or Darleen, but waited for the story to unwind.

"Based on what he said, it looks like there's a carbon monoxide problem at your mother's place. He told me the alarm was going off when he got there to see Darleen. Mrs. Darkwater had come over, trying to figure out where the fire was. Slim took all three of them to the Darkwater house and then opened all Mama's windows."

Chee wiped his mouth with a napkin. "Your mother is spending the night at Mrs. Darkwater's place. I'm going out early tomorrow to check on her chimney and the way it's vented. Slim thinks the issue was a camping stove Darleen was burning for extra warmth until she could get the fire in the wood-burning stove going."

Chee went back to eating.

Bernie lost her appetite. "Carbon monoxide?"

"It seems likely. The smoke alarm is also a carbon monoxide alarm, and there was no smoke in the house."

"Mrs. D mentioned ice and aspirin. What was that about?"

"Well, your mother had a fall, probably because she was disoriented from the lack of oxygen. From what Slim told me, she hurt her knee. He said it doesn't seem serious, but we know she is fragile. I'll talk to her about it when I'm over there in the morning."

"I'll go with you."

He grinned. "I was expecting you to say that."

"What about the camping stove? That's totally unsafe. I thought Darleen was smarter than that."

Chee sighed. "OK. I need to tell you something that Slim shared with me about Darleen."

Bernie felt her spirits drop.

He folded his hands in front of him. "I'm sorry I have to say this, but he told me that she's drinking again. I had to worm it out of him. He's protective of her, but he had to let me in on what was going on when I kept asking for her to come to the phone and asking him why she couldn't talk to me. Finally, he admitted that she was in the bathroom, throwing up."

Bernie thought about everything her sister had accomplished. She recalled Darleen's successful stint at the famous Institute of American Indian Arts in Santa Fe, honing her art talent. She had enjoyed her work as an aid to Mr. Natachi, and that led to her decision to go to Diné College to begin nurse's training. Darleen had even saved Mrs. Darkwater's life after the woman fell when she was home alone.

"Why? I thought Darleen was done with drinking." Bernie shook her head. "I guess I overestimated her. I thought she'd grown up, but she still breaks my heart."

"I love your sister. I'm sorry she's disappointing you again."

"Where is Darleen now?" Bernie pushed her plate away, no longer hungry. "Did she sleep at Mrs. D's too?"

"No. That's another problem. Mrs. Darkwater yelled at her for being drunk and blamed her for your mother's accident. Slim said Darleen was furious because Mrs. Darkwater wouldn't let her stay with your mom. She stormed out of the Darkwater house and slept in her car."

Bernie sighed. "Why didn't you tell me this sooner? I would have gone to Mrs. Darkwater's house to help."

"That's exactly why I didn't tell you. Things are under control. Sweetheart, you've been at Eagle Roost all day. You're exhausted."

"So now a stranger is taking care of Mama? She's doing that while I just sit here?" Her voice flared with anger. "Just when I think my mother is safe, something like this happens." They both remembered the time criminals tried to set Mama's house on fire. "You should have told me."

They ate in silence for a few moments, then Chee took a new angle. "You know Mrs. Darkwater and your mother are like relatives. Mama is in good hands. When we go over there in the morning, you can visit with your mother and Mrs. D while I check the wood stove and make sure that's not the problem."

"I know what one of the problems is already." Bernie reached for her phone. "I need to talk to Sister. What a mess."

"Wait. Give her time to sober up. You've had a lot of stress already. The crisis is averted." He put his hand on top of hers. "Your sister is an adult. You and I have talked to her about her drinking so many times. Give it a break for tonight."

Bernie knew Chee was right, but she called Darleen's phone anyway. When her sister didn't answer, she left a four-word message.

"I'm worried. Call me."

20

Cecil Bowlegs had a problem. The westbound bus for Tucson would leave in half an hour. He wanted to be on it. But Ramon and Earbuds must be looking for him. Because they had discovered him at the bus station, it made sense that they would go back there to wait for him. That's what he would do if he were stalking someone. He would hunt like né'éshjaa', the owl, waiting for the prey to arrive and then snatching it up while it was vulnerable.

He asked himself two central questions: Could he enter the convenience store where the bus would stop without the thugs spotting him? And if he did that, could he leave it to get on the westbound bus alive? There was a third question, but he kept it at the edge of his consciousness. If he made it to Tucson, would he be safe there, or would someone else be waiting to harm him?

He was fortunate to have been endowed with a strong sense of direction. Despite his terror when he was abducted by the men in the Escalade, he remembered where the bus station was in relation to where he'd hidden from the kidnappers. He'd used the hours of darkness that followed his escape to move slowly and quietly back toward the station. He saw no vehicles on the street and no one on foot on this miserably cold night.

Now he crouched beneath a tree across the street and half a block away from the bus station, watching for it to open and, of course, watching for the Escalade to come back so the two men could again try to

capture him. He hadn't noticed the vehicle yet, but that didn't mean
they hadn't parked somewhere. He pictured Earbuds and Ramon waiting for him to emerge, beating him up, and threatening more pain if he
didn't pay the debt.

But the night was his friend. Cecil Bowlegs pulled his knees tightly
into his chest, turned up the collar of his jacket, shoved his hands
into his pockets, and tried to rest. He wondered if Joe Leaphorn had
received his messages and knew he would be on the way to Tucson if
his luck held.

Eventually he heard a vehicle—not the smooth engine of the
Escalade, but something in need of a tune-up and a better muffler.
An old van turned into the bus station driveway and parked. A young
woman climbed out, locked the van's doors with a key, and entered the
building. A few moments later, the employee who'd told him he couldn't
wait inside drove off in a small red truck. Finally, Bowlegs thought. It's
the shift change. His cold wait was nearly over.

More lights came on inside the building, even though the sun was
rising. The brightness and the warmth lured him like a siren song, like
the smell of Beth's freshly made fry bread calling him into the kitchen
when he and his songbird were together. It took all his willpower to stay
in the cold darkness. He told himself he would run to the station when
the bus arrived, getting inside as quickly as humanly possible. That
couldn't be much longer, could it?

But it took an eternity before, finally, he heard a deep rumbling
noise and saw a bus pulling into the station driveway. It came to a stop,
and after a moment or two the doors opened. He watched a man wearing
a dark sweatshirt and another man in a parka come down the steps and
head stiffly toward the well-lit building.

Simultaneously, he spotted a green coupe pull up and stop near the
front door of the bus station. In the glow of the streetlights, he could
see the driver walk to the back of the car, pop the trunk, and pull out
a large black suitcase. The driver, a guy in a cowboy hat, set the bag on
the asphalt driveway. Then he went back to the trunk and extracted
what looked like a portable wheelchair, although, from this distance, it

could have been some kind of cart. Then the man opened the passenger door, and Bowlegs watched as he gently helped a woman struggle out of the vehicle.

The combination of events provided a distraction, and also assembled plenty of witnesses in case the black car returned and the dudes inside it tried to do him harm again. Cecil Bowlegs took a deep breath and raced along the side of the building near where he had been hiding, barely slowing to check for traffic before sprinting past the woman and the wheelchair. He opened the door and rushed into the warm, bright space of the bus station.

The woman behind the counter, the one he'd observed earlier, smiled at him. Her name tag read PAT. "Hey. You can relax. The bus won't leave for half an hour."

"I need a ticket."

"The best way to do that is to buy your ticket online." She showed him where to go on his new phone, and he clicked the right clicks, finally got the screen he needed, and made the purchase.

The waiting area had few seats but offered lots of merchandise people could buy to take with them on the bus or in their cars after they got gas at the pumps. A restaurant shared the building, but it wasn't open yet.

Cecil bought coffee and a doughnut and found a place to stand with a view of the highway and the storefront but away from the entrance, in case Earbuds or Ramon showed up. He leaned against the wall and exhaled. Maybe he'd make it. It was too early to call Leaphorn, but he sent the man a text, a quick update that mentioned again that someone had wanted to hurt him last night. He had just started to relax when an officer in a New Mexico State Police uniform came through the door. He knew he didn't have anything to worry about, but it made him nervous when she headed straight toward him.

"Cecil Bowlegs?"

"That's me." What now? he thought.

"Joe Leaphorn told me I would find you here. Detective Mona Short."

"What do you want? I didn't do nothin'."

"I'll explain in a moment, but I need you to come with me now, sir."

"I have to get on the bus to Tucson. This is the only westbound bus today. I told Joe that." He wondered why Leaphorn had involved the police. "If this is because of the explosion, I can't help you now. Can we talk about what happened at the school on the phone or something?"

"Sir, please come with me."

"I can't. I'll help you, but I'm looking for my wife. She's supposed to be there in Arizona, ah, with a sister of hers. I can't miss the bus."

The detective frowned at Bowlegs, but he kept talking.

"I think I finally know where Beth is, and I need to find her. I've been looking for her, you know, and this is my first good lead. And by the way, two guys tried to kill me last night. They might be outside right now in a black SUV."

"I didn't see it," the detective said, "but thanks for telling me. Another reason to get you out of here and back to the station." She moved closer to him. "Sir, we can talk about that at the police station. Let's go."

Bowlegs had a new idea, a sobering one. "Did you find my wife?" The woman in the wheelchair was looking at him. He spoke more softly. "Oh goodness. Did you find Beth?"

He saw Detective Short hesitate a split second. "Maybe."

He knew by the expression on her face that what he'd feared and what he had dreaded since his songbird had disappeared might have become reality.

The attendant called the bus for boarding. Bowlegs tried to move, but his legs failed to cooperate. He had no reason to go to Tucson now, he realized.

"She's dead, isn't she?" The ticket seller was staring at him now. He realized he'd been shouting and lowered his voice to a whisper. "Tell me. She's my wife, damn it. Tell me." And then, despite his best efforts at manly self-control, he started to cry.

Detective Short put her hand gently on his arm. "Cecil, come. We need to talk about this privately. Let's go." She moved her hand to his right elbow and pushed up with a bit of pressure. He wobbled as he stood, and they walked out together to her unit.

By the time they reached the state police headquarters in Gallup, Bowlegs had regained some composure. Detective Short showed him to a private room with a table and a couple of chairs, asked if he wanted coffee, and brought him some with sugar as well as a package of salted crackers held together with peanut butter. She said she had to do some paperwork and wanted to get some things to show him and that she'd be back in a few minutes.

The coffee was good, and the crackers made him realize he hadn't eaten anything except a doughnut since before the poker game. With the food and coffee, he started to feel better. He began to trust that he might make it out of this day alive.

Bowlegs had never been in a police station until Beth went missing. His first dealings with the police had come when Joe Leaphorn arrived to investigate the disappearance of his brother and ultimately became his protector. The second series of encounters clustered around Beth's disappearance, beginning with the phone call he made to report her missing. The police had interviewed him extensively and called frequently to see if he had anything to report. He and RP continued to follow up, to find out what the cops were learning and doing to locate her, but they couldn't get any information except that the police were working on it. They told him and Beth's clan brother to be patient and to keep looking for her themselves. Safely, of course.

Then Joe Leaphorn agreed to help with the search, and it was as if that outreach set off a chain of unfortunate events. And now it seemed that, like his big brother, his songbird had migrated out of his life forever.

The room where Detective Short had left him was warm, and after enlivening him, the coffee and food made him groggy. He put his head down on the table, resting his forehead on his forearms, and closed his eyes.

He must have dozed off, because the detective startled him when she came back. She sat across from him, holding some sheets of paper.

He had a mental list of questions for her, but before he could speak, she surprised him. "Cecil Bowlegs, you're here at the request of the FBI as a person of interest in the Eagle Roost school bombing and a fatality that may or may not be related to the explosion."

"What? Fatality. That means someone's dead. Is it Beth?"

Detective Short said, "I don't really need to tell you, do I? You already know, because you're the one who killed her."

Bowlegs sat in stunned silence.

21

When her phone rang that morning, Bernie expected the caller to be Darleen, but she saw that Joe Leaphorn was on the line. As much as she honored and respected the man, she didn't want to talk about the explosion and a dead woman. She let his call go to voicemail to leave the line open in case Darleen or Mrs. Darkwater needed her. If Leaphorn had a crucial request, she knew the lieutenant would call back.

So when her cell phone rang as she and Chee were leaving for Mama's house, she assumed it was one of those three, and she answered.

"Hi, this is Nadia. Remember me?"

Nadia's face came into Bernie's mind immediately. She'd liked the young woman from Eagle Roost who wanted to be an EMT.

"Sure, I remember you. Hi there."

"You gave me your card, and I thought of something that might help with the investigation at the school." The girl hesitated. "Well, you might not think this is even anything."

"You wouldn't have been brave enough to call me if you thought it didn't matter. Go ahead and tell me. Then I can decide."

"OK, this happened the last time I saw Mrs. Bowlegs. It was Valentine's Day." Nadia sighed. "It was an odd thing. I went to her office to ask her something, and I noticed that there were some flowers, nice flowers, in her wastebasket. I wondered about that, you know, because I worried that maybe she and her husband had a fight or something. She didn't want to talk about it."

"Did Mrs. Bowlegs seem angry?"

Nadia didn't respond immediately. "She looked worried, you know, like there was a big problem on her mind."

Bernie sucked in a breath. "Thanks for your help. You did great with the details."

"I hope you can find Mrs. Bowlegs. We miss her. I hate hearing about missing women. It makes me really sad. And nervous!"

"I know what you mean." Bernie didn't say it just to be polite.

"Officer, if you find out that Mrs. Bowlegs is OK, would you let me know? I'm really, really worried about her."

"Sure, Nadia. I'll let you know."

Bernie collected her thoughts. "Before you hang up, tell me about Mrs. Bowlegs. What is she like?"

"She's a great singer. I loved her music classes, and I sang in the chorus she started for kids after school. She was sad when she told us that she had to stop chorus practice because she had another job helping the principal with the accounting."

"Where did the chorus rehearse?"

"In the special ed room. She did private classes in there, too."

"That building seemed small for all the use it got."

"It was. They said that when the school got the grant for it, it was supposed to be bigger, and there was supposed to be money for the auto mechanics class, but the prices for everything went up. We thought we were getting a room where we could practice and give concerts, you know? And for meetings, and for Mrs. Bowlegs's office, stuff like that. But Principal Morgan said the full grant didn't come, and everything cost more than they expected, so music and special ed had to share. That's where Mrs. Bowlegs' desk was, too, and her files. She didn't have an office, but she kept her music and other things for her classes in there and in the garage."

When the call ended, she turned to Chee. "I just learned something interesting about the Eagle Roost case. I need to make a call, but I can do it from the truck. Let's see what's happening at Mama's house."

"As long as I'm driving, and you agree to give me ten minutes of your attention before the first call." He put his arm around her. "I've hardly seen you in the past two days."

"I know. The school case is winding down, and I won't have much to do with it now that the FBI is involved. Then we'll have more time together."

"I would like that. I'm happy that you're getting work you love now, and I hope it lasts."

"Me, too. I'm not sure about the new captain yet. I miss Captain Largo."

Chee pulled into the grocery store parking lot. "I'm stopping for a package of fresh batteries for your mother's smoke detectors. Need anything?"

"Can you please buy some coffee and some apples for her, too?" Bernie never liked arriving at Mama's house empty-handed.

Chee left to shop, and Bernie called Sage Johnson and reviewed the information Nadia had shared. "Principal Morgan told me that Beth and her husband, Cecil, hadn't been getting along. The discarded Valentine's Day flowers point to that."

Agent Johnson had news for her, too. "The autopsy on the woman in the car determined that she died from a blow to the head as you suspected. She had been dead at least three days. She had a tattoo of a blue eagle on her wrist. The DNA results won't be back for a few days, but it's a good bet that the dead woman in a car registered to Bethany Bowlegs who has a tattoo that matches Mrs. Bowlegs's tattoo is actually Mrs. Bethany Benally Bowlegs. I think our missing woman has been found."

"Was the woman dead when she was put in the car?"

"I'm not sure about that. What I can say for certain is that she did not die in the explosion or from the smoke. The autopsy report specified that the injuries from the skull fracture caused her death." Agent Johnson paused. "Her husband is a person of interest in the investigation, and the New Mexico State Police just picked him up."

Bernie mentioned Leaphorn's contact with Cecil Bowlegs to Agent Johnson. "It seems odd that, if Cecil killed her, he'd hire someone to look for his wife, but it gives him a good backstory."

22

Joe Leaphorn had expected to feel tired and sore after the train adventure, but instead he felt lighter, even joyous, that morning. And he smelled coffee. He put on his bathrobe and trundled out of bed and into the kitchen.

Louisa and Lin were sitting together at the table, but at the sight of him Louisa stood. To his surprise, she walked to him and gave him a long, warm hug.

"I didn't thank you properly last night, Joe. I have never been happier to see anyone in my whole long life."

She seemed to sense his embarrassment, so she stopped talking and poured him a cup of coffee. He joined the two women at the table.

Lin had been doing something on her phone, but she looked up and smiled at him. "Good morning. I just got a text from Kory at the hospital. He sounds better. He asked me to find a program that can help him, and I told him I would. I hope someone offers special mental health services for cancer patients." She frowned. "Of course, he'll have to face charges after last night."

Leaphorn nodded. "You can stay here with Louisa and me as long as you'd like. You can have my room until you and your husband get this sorted out. That couch in my office makes a good bed."

"Thanks, but, like I told Louisa, I'm going to my parents' house while Kory's in treatment and I decide what's next for me and the baby. My dad just had back surgery, so I know my mother can use the help.

I'm talking to my boss later today to find out how I can work remotely for a couple of weeks."

Louisa nodded. "That's smart. It's up to Kory to do what he has to to get his life back together. We're not giving up on him, but after what happened, we both need to take a step back."

Leaphorn enjoyed his coffee and hearing Louisa share the advice he'd given her with Lin. It felt good to realize that she had listened to him. When the women paused in conversation, he stood. "I have to meet a client in Ganado this morning and then we have a drive ahead of us."

STELLA BROWN WENT BACK TO her room at the Ganado Quality Inn after breakfast and a lengthy and wonderful conversation with the hotel manager about the Navajo code talkers. She admired the deep sense of patriotism among the Navajo people, and the talk had distracted her from her anxiety about what would happen today when she met Janey Singer.

It amazed her that after all the injustices the US government had inflicted on the Diné, the warrior tradition had not only persevered but also transformed into a genuine, eager willingness to help protect the very institutions that had oppressed them. The answer, as it had been explained to her, was simple. Patriotism was love of country, not of government. This had been Navajo land from the start of time, and it always would be held sacred.

As she got ready to leave for the day, Stella thought about the reality that, according to what the old detective had said, she might finally meet someone who knew, or had known of, her Navajo mother. Maybe someone in her Navajo lineage had been a code talker or a veteran. Or maybe, she reminded herself, she wasn't really Navajo at all, and the woman she met tomorrow would put an end to that dream, to the idea that this was the place she was meant to be.

Leaphorn had been vague on the details, but Stella trusted him. He could be a grump, but he dealt with her honestly, and she appreciated that even when she didn't like what he had to say. He wanted to lower her expectations in case things didn't work out on their trip to Tonalea. A good strategy, she thought, but her hope still simmered.

Because Stella hadn't been raised as a traditional Navajo, Diné politeness didn't come naturally to her. She gave herself a lecture: Be patient. Listen. Don't interrupt or ask too many questions. Be grateful for whatever comes. Treat Janey Singer and all elders with respect.

Taking out the envelope, she looked at the old photograph and at the little turquoise and silver bracelet again. Then she put them in the purse she planned to take to Tonalea and turned on the television to watch a bit of morning news before Joe Leaphorn came to get her.

The lead story was about an explosion in a special education classroom at a school on the Navajo Nation. The footage showed the blackened shell of the building. The reporter noted that the New Mexico State Police, the FBI, and the Navajo Nation police had all responded to the disaster. No one was releasing any information except that the incident was "under investigation," and no events had been underway at the school when the explosion happened.

Stella didn't know the geography of the Navajo Nation well enough to understand where the school was. She'd have to ask Leaphorn about that. She wondered if the building that blew up was close to where they were going to meet Janey Singer. Leaphorn told her it was a long drive, but she didn't mind. She'd been waiting a long time, and she could wait a little bit longer.

She had tried to get a good night's sleep so she could charm Janey Singer into sharing whatever she could about the woman who was Stella's birth mother—and perhaps about her biological father too. But instead she'd lain awake for hours, creating versions of the meeting with Ms. Singer. She'd been told not to have high hopes, but she kept a flicker of optimism alive that perhaps she'd find out where she really belonged.

Hiring Joe Leaphorn was a step toward taking charge of her own life. Maybe she wasn't Navajo, but her easy comfort on Navajo land surprised her. She loved the dominance of the vast blue sky and the stunningly stark contrast with the red sandstone cliffs. And, especially, she loved being with people who looked more like her than her parents.

Her therapist, the psychologist who had encouraged her to look for her Navajo roots, had helped her understand why she'd always felt like an outsider. People who are adopted often struggle with a sense of their own worth, he'd told her. There's even a name for it: adoption trauma.

Hearing a vehicle pull into the motel parking lot, she gathered her things and was at the door of her room before Leaphorn had a chance to knock. Instead of the truck she'd always seen him in, he was driving a small sedan.

"Hi there. Where's your truck?"

"It needs some repairs, so I borrowed Louisa's car. Looks like you're ready."

"You bet. I'm excited. Do you mind if I drive? My rental is right here."

"Not at all." Leaphorn started to give her directions.

"No worries. I set it up on my navigation last night." She smiled, then turned serious. "I hope you don't mind if we don't talk much on the way out. I'm working on quieting my expectations, you know? A meditation to help me stay grounded."

THE IDEA OF A QUIET trip appealed to Leaphorn, and he settled into the two-and-a-half-hour ride. The road from Ganado to Red Lake was one of Leaphorn's favorites on the Navajo Nation, full of the open spaces and big vistas he loved. It was rare and enjoyable to see it as a passenger. The day was bright, with a promise of spring in the air. In the spots where the snow's moisture had accumulated over the winter, sagebrush and tiny wildflowers showed signs of new life. April, T'aachil, a month that often started as the end of winter and then settled into calm, warm beauty.

Stella drove well, and they rode in companionable silence until they were a few miles from Cow Springs. Then Leaphorn told her of his plan.

"I think I mentioned earlier that the woman I met was adamant that she could only share her story with you—you alone. She said if you wanted me there, after she'd spoken to you privately, you could invite me to join you. I'd be more comfortable waiting for you at the trading post than sitting in the car for however long it takes the story to unfold. It seemed to me that you both would be more at ease without me waiting outside in the car."

"OK, but I don't know much Navajo."

"Her English is good."

"Are you sure you don't mind waiting at the trading post?" Stella frowned. "We should have discussed this before."

"It will take as long as it takes." He glanced out the window at a group of horses looking for spring greens. "I'm content to wait at the trading post. I wouldn't have suggested it otherwise. You can tell me all about it on the drive back. I brought some work to catch up on, so don't worry about me." He noticed a new foal among the herd, a baby carefully watched by one of the mares. "Just remember to come back for me when you're done, OK?"

Stella pulled off the highway and parked near the old trading post. There was a single vehicle outside the building, a fast-looking pale-blue new car. Leaphorn unfastened his seat belt and opened the door. It surprised him when Stella climbed out, too.

"I want to get a box of . . . oh, some tissues. I'm not sure how this will work out. Maybe tears of joy."

"You've done a lot to prepare yourself for whatever she has to say. Even if it's disappointing, you'll do fine."

Leaphorn made sure she knew how to find the Singer place. The look of expectation on her face made him happy that he'd given her all the help he knew how to give. They went inside the trading post together.

The worn wooden floor squeaked as they entered. Patricia wasn't there; instead, the trader himself stood behind the counter. He looked up from organizing a case of earrings and acknowledged Leaphorn and his companion with a touch of the brim of his hat.

Stella studied the old place, full of dust and the spirit of the west, then walked to the counter. "Sir, where can I find some tissues?"

Hawkman looked at her. His eyes opened a bit wider, and his face softened. "They're in the middle of the third row, left side, bottom shelf."

She came back with the Kleenex and two bottles of water from the refrigerator case and set them on the counter. "Would you like a bag, miss?"

"No thanks."

He made no move to ring up the items.

"What do I owe you?"

"Nothing. On the house, because Joe Leaphorn here only hangs with the best folks."

"Wow. I'm touched. Thanks."

Leaphorn nodded to the trader. "I hear you sell hot coffee."

"That's right." Hawkman smiled. "I'm making a fresh batch. Would you and the lady like some?"

"No thanks. I'm hyped enough already." Stella picked up the items Hawkman had given her.

"Coffee sounds good to me," Leaphorn said. "I'll be right back."

He walked out to the car with Stella. "I've got something for you. You might want to show it to Janey Singer."

Reaching for the computer bag he'd brought with him, he unzipped it and pulled out a small rug that he had stowed there next to his laptop. "This was made by someone in Janey's family."

She stared at the weaving. "It's like the one in my picture. May I touch it?" Her voice held the excited wonder of a twelve-year-old's.

"It's yours. A gift to take back home."

Leaphorn handed the weaving to her, and Stella looked surprised for a moment, then hugged it to her heart. Glistening tears slid down her cheeks. "I—I don't know what to say except thank you. Thanks for this, and for everything, no matter what happens next."

Leaphorn watched her head down the highway and turn at the intersection that led to the Singer place. When he couldn't see it anymore, he went back inside.

He found the coffee in a display along one wall, along with big rectangles of Rice Krispie treats and round peanut butter cookies, everything wrapped in clear plastic. They looked homemade, so he picked up one of each. He settled in at a wooden table at the back of the store and sipped his coffee while he worked on his notes for Stella's case. If time allowed, he'd write up the Bowlegs assignment too. Anticipating that it would be several hours before Stella returned with the news from Janey Singer, he prepared to work and wait here in comfort.

He wondered about the person who had driven up in the blue car and assumed whoever it was had Hawkman's full attention. He was considering a second cup of coffee when he heard voices from the rug room. He turned toward the sound and saw the trading post owner walking toward the cash register with a rug in his hands. The two gray-haired bilagáanas with him were smiling broadly.

Hawkman unfurled the rug, holding the two top corners in his hands. "It's easier to admire it in this light," Leaphorn heard him say, then picked up scattered phrases—"Elegant," "very special," "one of a kind," and "I know you'll like it."

He couldn't hear the couple's response, but the man reached for his wallet and extracted a credit card. The rug they selected was among those he'd looked at yesterday and moved to the top of the pile, one of those by the Singer family. The trader's praise for it was not exaggerated.

When the transaction was complete, the woman ran her hands over the soft wool. "Do you expect to get any more rugs from this weaver? I really love her work."

"No, ma'am. The lady has passed."

"Is anyone in the family keeping up with the tradition?"

"Not that I've heard of." He paused. "I showed you all the rugs I have by the Singer family of weavers. If you want to think about buying another one, I could hold on to what's left for a while for you."

"I bet you could." The woman laughed. "You're hardly overrun with customers." Then she spotted Leaphorn and called to him. "Sir, are you here for a rug?"

He didn't need to think about his response. "Yes. As soon as your business is done, Mr. Hawkman and I will talk."

Hawkman shook his head. "I should have raised my prices on these. I always do that when one of my weavers dies. But because I haven't gotten around to that, you got a good deal on this rug. I'm going to take care of that now."

The trader disappeared into the rug room. The couple took the rug out to their car, clicked open the trunk, and stored it inside. Leaphorn could see them talking as he returned his attention to his coffee and his laptop. Then the bell on the building's front door rang again. The woman stayed outside, but the white man had returned.

Leaphorn saw him looking around, and then he stopped at the table where Leaphorn sat.

"Hey, what happened to the guy who runs this place?"

"He's in the rug room." Leaphorn watched the man walk back there and heard bits of conversation. In a few moments, they emerged with the largest Singer rug. Hawkman held it up, and the old white guy examined it. This time he took longer and, without the woman hurrying him along, seemed to study it more carefully. Leaphorn had admired the rug. Even from a distance he could tell it was a fine piece of weaving, the best of the Singer work he had seen.

The white guy frowned. "It's OK. Will you sell us this one at the same price we paid for the other?"

"Ahh, gosh, no. This one is bigger; you can see that. And like I said, that one you bought got away from me. I should have charged you more for that one, but it's a done deal now." Hawkman looked toward Leaphorn. "That man over there has been around the block a few times. He told me beginner rugs are going for as much as these at the auction at Crownpoint. And this is a first-quality piece created by a well-regarded weaver, Alva Singer."

"Did you know her?"

"I did. Alva and her daughters, Suzanna and Starla, her spunky little sister."

The white man looked at Leaphorn. "Are you an expert on rugs?"

"Well, I've lived with them all my life. That's part of the Navajo way. What Mr. Hawkman said is true. That rug is worth twice the price of the one you just bought."

"Hmmm."

Leaphorn walked over to where Hawkman had spread out the rug and looked at it more closely. He hadn't exaggerated. The exquisitely fine work reflected the weaver's artistry and expertise. Her sense of design and use of color were first rate. "This is a beauty. This composition is unique in the way it presents our four sacred mountains. And look at how perfectly she wove these zigzag lines."

Leaphorn ran his hands over them. "These are what carry blessing from the mountaintops." He turned to the man. "I didn't get a good look at this one in the rug room. I'm glad the trader pulled it out for you."

Leaphorn spent more time studying it, then winked at Hawkman. "How much did you get for the other one?"

Hawkman told him.

"This rug is a treasure. What are you asking for it?"

Before Hawkman could answered, Leaphorn was already reaching for his wallet.

"Wait a minute." The white man looked at the tag. "I was here first. It's priced at fifty-five hundred dollars, but I'll give you six thousand."

Hawkman turned to Leaphorn. "I'm sorry, Joe, but he was here first, and that's better than the price on the tag. It's only fair to let him have it."

Leaphorn frowned. "Are you sure?"

"He's sure," the white man said. "A deal is a deal."

"OK. I get it. Good purchase, sir."

The bilagáana spoke to Leaphorn. "You live out here, don't you?"

"That's right. In Window Rock, capital of the Navajo Nation."

"That means you'll have lots of opportunities to buy rugs. Not us. We're on our way back to Omaha."

The man paid and put the rug in his trunk with the earlier purchase before he drove away.

Hawkman joined Leaphorn at the table. "Thanks for helping with the sale. I owe you."

"You can buy the next cup of coffee and sit with me a minute. I'm curious about you and your business."

Hawkman stood and got them both more coffee. "What do you want to know?" He handed Leaphorn his cup and sat down again.

"Everything. Tell me the story of this place and how you got here."

Leaphorn sipped his coffee while Hawkman considered his answer.

"It's complicated. I took over the business when my parents died. In a nutshell, with a store like this, you work hard, you don't make any money, but you make good friends. People like the Singer family, Alava, Suzanna, and Starla. If you're blessed, a day comes along like today, and you sell a couple of rugs and it gives you hope. You pay the light bill."

"Tell me more about Starla Singer."

"Why?"

"I heard how your voice changed when you said her name, and again when you mentioned her to that man who bought the rug."

Hawkman sighed. "She inherited her mother's great sense of design. She probably would have been as good at the loom, or even better, if she had kept at it. She far outshone Suzanna when it came to talent. But weaving takes focus, and Starla ran short of that. And her drinking didn't help, either."

"You told me the sister was in Window Rock, working for the government. Where's Starla?"

He shrugged. "No one hears from her. No one knows."

Leaphorn saw the grief in Hawkman's face and let the quiet at the table act as a balm. He'd learned that silence sometimes made revelations easier, especially if the topic was uncomfortable. But instead, Hawkman asked him a question.

"I'm curious about that woman you were with, the one who thinks she might have relatives around here. What do you know about the people who adopted her?"

"Not much. She told me they traveled a lot, raised her as an only child, and didn't have any family around them. They said they adopted her through a lawyer. That was before the Native Child Welfare Act, so nothing was in place to keep Native children in their tribal communities. Her adoptive father and mother are both dead. Stella said their deaths made her curious about her birth family, so she hired me."

"And all you had to go on was that photo?"

"Pretty much." That, Leaphorn thought, and instincts sharpened by years of dealing with Navajo families and with the non-Navajos he came in contact with, beginning with his student years at Arizona State. "Back then, a lot of adoptions were closed, so the records that Stella has access to don't name her biological parents."

"Not the mother or the father?"

Leaphorn nodded. "I noticed your reaction to her."

Hawkman stammered. "Well, sure. She's an attractive woman."

"I don't think that was all of it."

"Oh, the moment she walked in the door, she reminded me of Starla. I think she might have some clans in common with the Singer family. How did your client get here to Tonalea, of all places?"

"The photo. Her adopted mother saved it, and when I saw the Elephant Feet, I figured it somehow connected her to this part of the reservation."

"Smart. But of course it could just be a pretty picture her mother liked, maybe a memory of time in Navajo land."

Leaphorn pulled out his phone, turned it on, and called up the photograph. He put the phone on the table between them. "Stella's adoptive mother must have considered it to be important to hold on to it for forty years, despite all the moves. Your father took that picture, didn't he?"

Hawkman nodded. "How did you know?"

Leaphorn ignored the question. "What can you tell me about it?"

Hawkman hesitated. "I'll start at the beginning. My dad ran the trading post then—I just helped. He was a good amateur photographer, and he enjoyed working with the people around here. Good folks and skilled weavers. He'd take pictures of the landscape, and if anyone asked for a photo, he'd do that, too."

Hawkman studied the picture, then looked up and out toward the landscape. "I haven't seen this for a long, long time. It sure brings back memories."

The trader was probably in his sixties, Leaphorn thought. "You grew up out here, right?"

"I sure did. I couldn't wait to leave, isn't that what usually happens with us bilagáana? Anyway, after a year of college, I came back to work for a summer because my sister was going off to an intensive program to work on her master's degree. She'd helped Mom and Dad while I went to summer school the last time, so it seemed only right to be here."

"Was that the summer you met Starla?"

A spontaneous smile crossed Hawkman's face. "Sort of. I'd seen her before, when we were kids. She was a few years younger than me, still in high school, but dropped out after a year. Not much of a student. She just wanted to party. I'd flirt with her when she came into the store with her mother. She was as wild and original as I was traditional."

Hawkman looked at the photo on the phone again.

"That's her in the picture, isn't it?"

"Yes."

"Is there a baby in that blanket?"

"No." Hawkman confirmed it with a shake of his head.

"Are you sure?"

"I'm sure, because I was there the day Dad took the picture. Starla was the best model, so he asked her to pose. Dad used to like Starla before she got so crazy." Hawkman sighed. "You're stirring up memories I haven't thought about for a long time. Let's talk about something else. Tell me about your family."

"Not much to say. I've got lots of clan folks out there, but we aren't very close. My Emma and I never had children. I regret it sometimes. But when I see the sorrow that can come with parental love, well, I'm relieved that we were spared that."

Hawkman sighed. "I guess Stella Brown should be careful about what she's looking for."

Leaphorn nodded. "I mentioned that to her, and she said she's open to whatever comes. She feels rootless, untethered. Even as a successful adult, she told me she desperately wants to know who she really is and where she come from. Even if the news is bad."

"I got some of that bad news recently. My sister died."

"Oh. I'm sorry. Were you close to her?"

"Yes, as children. She was a few years older than I am. After we grew up, we drifted apart, and I didn't see her much. She married a guy, and they raised a kid. Unlike me, rooted here and never married, they moved all over the place because her husband was in the building trades. I thought after that guy retired, we'd get together more, but he got sick and passed away. After that, her own health went down. More than you needed to know, right?"

"No. I'd like to hear everything, and I'm going to be here a while." The pieces of the puzzle Stella Brown had asked him to assemble for her were falling into place.

Leaphorn stood. "I can use a sandwich. You want one?"

"Sure." Hawkman smiled. "You're a good listener."

They each selected something wrapped in plastic from the refrigerator with its big glass doors, and then they went out to the trading
post porch. They shared the wooden bench facing the road and ate.
Hawkman studied a view he must have seen thousands of times before
and seemed to enjoy his lunch. An occasional vehicle cruised by on
the paved highway that ran in front of the store

"You've figured this out, haven't you?"

"I understand some of it." Leaphorn rewrapped half the sandwich
and put it on his lap.

Hawkman nodded. "I thought so when you were so interested in
the rugs."

"That look in your eyes when you saw Stella. And she's got your
dimple in her chin."

"My sister had that, too."

"Did your sister know Starla?"

"No. They never met. Starla disappeared a few years after she
dropped out of high school. She played too hard to keep up with her
schoolwork. Starla called to tell me she was expecting a baby any day,
that she'd moved away from home when she got pregnant, and that she
hadn't had a drink since. But now the baby was due, and she was tired
of being fat and slow, and what harm would it do if we had some beers
and some fun? She said she wasn't sure who the dad was, but she hoped
it was me, because she liked me best."

He sighed. "Starla was my first real girlfriend, but she'd had some
experience already. That didn't matter. I told her I wanted to marry her,
take care of her, help her stop drinking. I told her I loved her and that
she'd be a good mom. She just laughed and said she didn't want the baby
because she was too young to be a shimá, a mother.

"She'd already promised her child to a guy who lived in Tuba City
who knew a lawyer who worked with white people who wanted kids
and help with expenses. She told me that as soon as she got out of the
hospital and gave the baby away, she and the guy from Tuba were going
to Durango on a bender. I told her Durango was a bad idea, but she just
laughed and hung up."

Hawkman shook his head. "I'm talking too much."

"No. Tell me more. How old was Starla?"

"She said eighteen when we met, and I believed her because I was only a year or two older. But I thought about it after she disappeared and I think she was younger, sixteen maybe, because of where she was in school."

"Was Starla a few classes behind you?"

Hawkman laughed. "We didn't go to school together. My parents sent me to boarding school. The Navajos couldn't understand that, after all the sad experiences they had sending their kids away. But my folks thought different."

Leaphorn considered the information. "Starla was too young to give up the baby without her parents' consent."

"I know. Her mother, her sister, would have kept that baby in the family and loved that child. They never knew she was expecting and kept hoping she'd come home." Hawkman's voice broke. "I loved that girl so much. I would have loved the baby, too."

Leaphorn sat with his own thoughts. If that baby was Stella, her adoption had been a gift as well as a handicap. She had been raised by a pair of caring parents, but she hadn't known her rich Navajo heritage and the love of her grandmothers and aunties who would have embraced her.

Hawkman's story continued to unwind. "Starla mentioned the name of the lawyer who wanted to place the baby. I called my sister; I knew she and her husband had been struggling to start a family. I told her I knew a Navajo girl who was about to give birth, and a lawyer could arrange a private adoption. I offered to give her the lawyer's name.

"Clara thought about it for just a minute or two and said yes. I paid the fee with money I'd saved from my part-time jobs. Later, I sent my sister the bracelet—it was one Alava's husband had made and pawned here—and the photo of that couple my dad took at Elephant Feet, so the baby would have some idea of the place that her birth mother had come from."

He choked up again. Leaphorn gave him time to gather his emotions.

"After the baby, my sister and her husband disappeared. I had very little contact with them. They loved that little girl, but they never talked about the adoption.

"And whenever I asked Alava and her relatives about Starla, well, they all changed the subject. I stopped asking and started praying for her. At least I knew her baby was in good hands."

"So as far as you know, Starla has not been in touch with her relatives in more than forty years?"

"That's right." Hawkman rubbed his chin as he thought. "You know, people act like this missing Native woman issue is something new, but it really isn't. It's been a problem for decades, but I hear it is worse now than it's ever been. I hate to say this, but I assume alcohol and a bunch of bad choices killed Starla."

Leaphorn's mind turned to the calls he had dealt with in his years in active law enforcement and how many of the crimes he'd worked, from family violence to vehicle crashes, involved alcohol. Easily accessible booze was a tragic curse delivered along with the gifts that came from interaction with mainstream America. Bootleggers and trips to border towns worked to counteract the Navajo Nation's prohibition of alcohol sales.

"I'm puzzled. Why did you suggest that I talk to Janey Singer? It sounds like she won't have a clue about Starla or her baby."

"Janey's good people. She knows a lot about a lot of things. She understands the importance of roots and that a lost bird looking to find where she belongs deserves to be listened to. That's why."

Leaphorn nodded. "When I met her, I got the impression that she has a good heart."

"Whatever Janey tells Stella will be wrapped in love. It may not be the answer she thought she wanted, but it ought to help ease her spirit."

For the next hour, Hawkman focused on repricing the inventory in his rug room, and Leaphorn worked on his case notes. He was almost done with Stella's report when her rental car pulled up and parked in front of the old trading post.

23

Bernie tried to continue the conversation with Agent Johnson as Chee drove the truck toward Mama's house. But before she even looked at the bars indicating that phone service was fading, she realized the call was about to die. She knew the area's quirks too well.

"I'm heading into the land of no cell towers. If we need to discuss anything else, call me back in a while. I've told you all I have for now."

"Thanks, Manuelito." Johnson ended the call.

Mrs. Darkwater's dog, Bidziil, stood near the Darkwater house and barked when they pulled up. The barking grew even more fierce when Chee parked their truck. Chee, who had the day off, grabbed the bag with his tools, fresh batteries, and a replacement smoke alarm he'd purchased just in case.

"I know you don't like dogs, but this is Bidziil, the dog who saved a life. He'll remember you, but if you'd like me to go in there with you, I will."

She swallowed her fear. "That's OK. Get to work at Mama's place."

Chee went into Mama's house. Bernie opened the passenger door and climbed out slowly. "Hey there," she said to the barking dog. "I come in peace." But Bidziil kept up his racket while Bernie knocked on Mrs. Darkwater's door.

"Yá'át'ééh. It's Bernie."

"I'm working at the stove. Come on in."

Bernie stepped through the front door with relief. The house smelled like onions and hamburger meat. "Stay for lunch, honey. I'm making it now."

"Thanks. Is Mama OK?"

Mrs. Darkwater motioned toward the living room with her chin. "She in there with the TV."

Bernie heard the blare of canned laughter and then music and the honeyed voice of an advertising announcer. She followed the sound to a sofa where her mother sat with her eyes closed.

Bernie sat next to Mama and reached for her hand. Mama opened her eyes and closed them again.

"I was worried about you, Mama. I heard what happened last night."

"What happened?"

"Well, the smoke alarm started blaring, and then Mrs. Darkwater invited you to spend the night with her until Chee could come and help this morning."

Mama opened her eyes again. Bernie looked at her soft old face and felt a wave of love mixed with sadness. She settled in next to her quietly through the commercial and the next segment of the show. If Mama didn't want to talk, she would relax and enjoy the gift of being in her presence.

Mrs. Darkwater came into the room. "Your mom's lunch is ready. I've got enough for you, too."

Bernie shifted on the couch, and her mother startled.

"Lunchtime, Mama. I'll help you to the table."

"You eat it." Mama patted her hand. "You look too thin. Where's your sister? She should eat, too."

Bernie glanced at Mrs. Darkwater.

"That one must be over at your house." Mrs. Darkwater's voice had an edge to it. "I haven't seen her this morning. Her or her boyfriend."

Bernie slipped her hand under Mama's arm to help her up, noticing that she felt light but seemed steady on her feet as they walked to the kitchen. Mrs. Darkwater had concocted a hamburger stew. She dished all of them a small bowl full and put a warm tortilla on each plate.

Bernie inquired about Mrs. Darkwater's son and grandson and was pleased to learn that all was well with them. As she ate, she kept thinking about Darleen, wondering if Chee was talking to her sister with his counselor hat on, and what had triggered her to start drinking again.

Mama had a few bites, then put her spoon down, dipped a section of the tortilla in the warm broth, and chewed that. She took a cookie from the plate Mrs. Darkwater had set out and put it carefully in the pocket of her sweater. One of the changes Bernie had observed with Mama was that it took her a long time to eat, as though she had lost focus on the meal.

"I need to see how my husband is doing at Mama's house. Thanks for the food. Ahéhéé."

"Daughter, I want to go home now."

"Let's talk about that when you finish your soup."

Mrs. Darkwater nodded in agreement. "If that works for you, I can check on her later. Just let me know."

"Thanks."

Mama lifted her spoon for another bite, and Bernie headed out the front door.

Bidziil barked again, as though he had never seen her before. She took a calming breath and told herself the dog was just doing his job. He kept it up until Mrs. Darkwater yelled at him to be quiet.

She found Chee in the living room working on Mama's wood stove, the main source of heat for the house. She stood next to him for a moment. "How's it going?"

"I think that camping heater was the problem. It's out of fuel now. I put it behind the house. I started a fire in this old thing, and it seems to be drawing perfectly well. I'll be done in a few minutes."

"Have you seen my sister?"

Chee shook his head. "I knocked on the door to her bedroom to find out if she was in there and if she was OK. She snarled at me."

"I didn't see Slim's car. Is he here?"

"Not unless he's in there with your sister."

Bernie walked down the hall and rapped on the door. "Sister, you OK?"

Darleen didn't answer.

"Sister? What's going on? Sister?"

"I feel terrible. Leave me alone."

Bernie opened the door.

Darleen was sprawled on the bed with a pillow covering her eyes. There was a tower of beer cans on the floor.

"What happened yesterday that made the alarms go off in the house?"

"I'll tell you later. I need to sleep."

"It's Monday morning. Don't you need to get going to class?" Bernie had encouraged her sister to sign up for a nursing program, and she and Chee agreed to help pay for it. Darleen had been enthusiastic about participating.

Her sister pushed the pillow away and rose onto her elbows. "What time is it?"

Bernie told her.

Darleen cursed and moved herself to sitting. "Maybe I'll feel better if I take a shower."

"When did you start drinking again?"

Darleen laughed. "You mean, when did I start getting drunk again? None of your business."

Bernie stayed calm. "It is my business because you and I have to keep Mama safe. If you can't do your job . . ."

"Oh, shut up. Mama's fine. Mrs. D complained about me, didn't she?"

"No, but it looks like she should have. We need to talk."

"That's right. You give me a lecture, and I promise to be a good little sister."

"No. No more lectures. We just need to solve the Mama problem."

"How 'bout this? Maybe she should live with you and Cheeseburger for a while."

"Maybe." Bernie watched as Darleen stood and staggered into the bathroom.

In a few moments she heard the water running. And then Darleen was singing.

She found Chee standing on a chair in Mama's living room, examining the way the stovepipe met the hole in the ceiling and tunneled on through the roof and outside.

"Hey," she said. "That doesn't look very safe."

"I think this is OK. On our next visit, if I have some extra time, I'll check the seal, but at least the pipe looks good."

Bernie laughed. "No, I meant you standing on that wobbly chair."

Chee climbed down. "I replaced all the batteries in the smoke alarms. I can't remember the last time I did that."

"I think Darleen put in the old ones. We always used to do that in the spring when we went on daylight savings time."

"Did you talk to her?"

"Sort of. She's still pretty drunk. She suggested that Mama come live with us."

"That's not a bad idea." Chee used a shirtsleeve to wipe his footprints off the seat of the chair that had served as his ladder and pushed it back against the kitchen table. "Darleen must be on overload, taking care of Mama, going to school, and having a boyfriend all at the same time. But it wouldn't be any easier for you, would it?"

"No. But it might be my turn."

"Our turn." Chee's voice had a softness to it. "Ready to go?"

She nodded. "What's going on with you at work? I haven't heard much."

"It's interesting, actually. You know, there are so many challenges out there, funding for new technology, training, benefits to make the job competitive. And then the whole issue of hiring. That can be a sticky subject." He smiled at her. "I'm happier doing this than I thought I would be."

"I'm glad. When you didn't mention much, I thought there could be a problem."

Chee looked at her a long moment. "Well, there was a problem. I felt guilty about getting a promotion when I hadn't been looking for one, while you got passed over for the job you really would have liked."

"I see. I was worried that you were disappointed in me because I'm still just a regular cop."

"I was disappointed in the chief for not giving you what you deserved. I didn't say anything because I didn't want to make you feel any worse." He walked close and put his arms around her. "I love you to the moon and back, and my only disappointment is that we have so little time together."

Darleen had left her phone on the coffee table, and it began to ring. Bernie looked at the call, and Chee released his hug so she could answer.

"Hey, Slim, it's Bernie. Darleen's in the shower."

"Hey. How is she?"

"Still pretty high."

"Is Chee there with you, too?"

"Yes. He's looking at the stove."

"I did some research on carbon monoxide and wood stoves. He might find it interesting."

"Hold on." Bernie handed the phone to her husband. "Slim wants to talk to you."

She walked toward the bathroom. Darleen had turned the water off and cracked the door open in the steamy little room. She was combing her wet hair, which had grown out and reverted to its natural glossy black, although a bit of green and blue dye lingered.

"Your boyfriend is on the phone."

"I'll call him from the car. I don't wanna be late for class."

"How are you feeling?'

"OK. Tired. I've got a major headache, and my stomach is turning somersaults."

Bernie stood in the doorway, thinking of what to say next, and coming up short.

"Aren't you going to tell me I deserve to feel bad?"

"No, little sister. You deserve to live the best life you can."

Darleen set the comb down and put her hands on her face, cupping her eyes with her palms. "I know I screwed up, but I'm overwhelmed."

"What do you mean?"

"Mama, school, cooking, cleaning, homework, finding time to be with Slim, taking Mama to the doctor, dealing with Mrs. D. I don't have time to draw anymore, or to talk to my girlfriends." She was talking louder now. "It's frustrating. I think a beer or two will help me relax, help me have fun."

"Does it?"

"Sort of, but two aren't quite enough, and next thing I know I'm in trouble." Darleen exhaled deeply. "I really need your help with Mama, Sister. I can't do this anymore."

Darleen was crying now, but she kept talking. "I don't remember what happened last night, except that everyone got mad at me. Is Mama OK?"

"Yes, but . . ."

"But what? What aren't you telling me?"

"Mama was not injured or anything, but we both know she's not OK."

"I'm doing my best. I just can't do any more."

Bernie felt sorrow replace her anger. "Sister, I'm sorry I wasn't more help. You and I and Chee have to figure this out, come up with something that works better. I should have paid more attention to you, to Mama, to the whole situation."

Darleen wiped her eyes. "You've been busy, and you had your own problems to deal with. I'm sorry I let you down. I really tried not to fail with Mama."

Bernie took a breath. "I think your drinking is part of the problem."

"That's not it. You still don't get it." Darleen's voice had a tinge of anger as well as sorrow. "I have a problem with having too much on my plate, and with you and the Cheeseburger not doing your share."

Bernie didn't want to argue. "I hear you. Right now, I don't know how to fix things."

"Me either. I have to get to class." Darleen reached for her hair dryer and turned it on, ending the conversation.

BERNIE SAW CHEE WATCHING AS she walked toward him.

"I'm ready to go," she said. "Are you?"

"I'm done," he said. "What happened with Darleen?"

"I'll tell you later. We have a lot to figure out."

They found Mama and Mrs. Darkwater sitting together watching a morning show on network TV. The hosts were examining different kinds of shampoos, and Mama seemed enthralled. Bernie stood beside her, careful not to block the screen.

"We're leaving now, Mama. Enjoy your day."

"Study hard." Her mother gave her a sweet smile. "I know you'll get an A." She didn't mention wanting to go home.

"I'll call you about you-know-who and you-know-what," Mrs. Darkwater said.

Bernie came to Darleen's defense. "My sister has a lot on her plate, you know? She's doing the best she can. I heard that you have to go in for surgery. I hope it's nothing serious."

Mrs. Darkwater wrinkled her brow. "We can talk about that later, but remember that I won't be able to help with your mother for a while. You guys have to work this out yourselves." She turned to Chee. "Did you look at those alarms?"

"Yes. I changed the batteries. Both of them will be OK now. Slim and I talked about the stove."

"Good thing it's getting warmer now. She won't need many more fires."

AS THEY DROVE HOME, CHEE got a call from the captain, telling him he was needed at the substation.

Bernie went for a run, hoping the cool air and the sensation of her muscles, bones, joints, tendons, heart, and lungs working hard would counteract her gloom. Darleen's return to drinking and her sister's justified anger troubled her. The pressing problem of Mama's situation, combined with Mrs. Darkwater's pending surgery, the Eagle Roost explosion, and the dead person at the school, dampened her spirits.

The puzzle of the damage to the school and the body in the car would be tackled by the experts, she told herself. Mama's decline had been a long time in development, and at the moment, she was at a loss for how to solve the problem. As she jogged, she gave herself some space to figure things out, one issue at a time.

24

Stella Brown trotted toward the trading post, her face bright and her eyes alive with joy. The bell on the door clanged when she opened it. Leaphorn saw her scan the room and find him at the table. He stood and motioned to her to join him.

Hawkman called from the rug room, "I'll be there in a minute."

"No rush. It's Stella Brown. I'm here to pick up Mr. Leaphorn."

"Sit and catch your breath."

The trader emerged from the rug room and came to the table. "Leaphorn filled me in on the reason for your visit, and I'm curious, too."

"I don't know where to start."

The trading post owner leaned against a vacant chair. "Start with a cold drink. I'll get you something. What would you like?"

"How about a lemonade?"

He came back with three chilled bottles, grinning at them as he set the bottles down. Leaphorn noticed the dimple in his chin matched Stella's.

Stella took a sip. "Here's the essence of what I learned. Janey told me about a young woman named Starla who was a weaver here and disappeared. She talked a lot about the Singer women and their weaving and about what people said had happened to Starla. But she said no one really knows. Some people thought she might have left because she was pregnant, but Janey told me that the baby would have been welcomed into the family. No one knows what happened to the baby, if there even was a baby. Janey wasn't sure about that."

Stella's story came out in a flood of words. "Janey Singer told me that she had met Starla a few times. She admitted that she didn't know her well, but told me she had a bubbly personality. She told me that I have the same thick hair as Starla. She said that if I wanted to consider myself a Singer, that was fine by her."

She took a long drink from the bottle.

"Of course, lots of Navajos have hair like mine, but it was nice of her to say that. It made me feel good. I showed her the photo, and she looked at it a long time and said it reminded her of pictures the trading post owner used to take."

Stella glanced at the display of cameras overhead and then turned to Hawkman. "Maybe with one of those. Do you remember anything like that?"

"I do. My dad was a photographer. He took pictures out there all the time. He sold one once in a while to Arizona Highways. The one your mother saved for you is definitely one of his."

"Wow."

"Did your mother tell you that you were adopted?"

"Yes. Her exact words were: "My brother helped your father and me find the perfect baby, and that was you, Little Sunshine.""

Hawkman said, "Really? Clarita said that?"

Stella gave him a puzzled look. "My mother's name was Rita."

He fell silent, studying the water bottle, then he looked Stella in the eyes. "Your mother was my sister, Clarita Hawkman. She married a man named Stanford Bakerson." Hawkman put his hand on top of hers. "Stella, I'm so sorry I never met you. We have a lot to talk about."

Stella bristled and pulled her hand back into her lap. "Wait. My last name is Brown, not Bakerson."

Leaphorn said, "I don't know this for sure yet, but I believe your parents changed their names after you came into their lives. That would explain part of why it's been so difficult to find information about your adoption."

Stella took a breath. "John Hawkman . . . so you're my uncle Jackie?"

He nodded. "Jackie is what Clarita always called me."

"Why didn't you ever come to visit us?"

"Your family was always moving. And your father and I didn't get along."

She nodded. "Dad had conservative views about everything. Lots of people didn't get along with him. It was hard on Mom."

"Do you remember that your mother went away by herself for a couple weeks each summer?"

"That's right. I always wanted to go with her, but I was never allowed to. How do you know?"

"She came here, to the trading post and our parents' home. Besides being with our mother and father, Clara—that's what we called our Clarita—spent time with me, too. I'd moved back here permanently to help with the business. That must have been when you were about five. Clara loved to show me pictures of you."

Leaphorn saw Stella's skepticism begin to melt away.

"I remember that Mom always seemed conflicted about leaving Dad and me. She used to say, "Next time you can come with me." And then Dad got a new construction job in New England, and she didn't make the trip that summer. Then she told me that my grandmother had died.

"We moved again and again. Dad was working all over the place. Carson City, Lincoln, Los Lunas, Shawnee, Billings. It was wild. Even if you'd wanted to come and see us, we weren't anywhere long enough for you to make plans. Did you really want to?"

"Yes. Absolutely yes." Hawkman searched for the words and found them and told her almost everything.

Leaphorn listened, admiring the man for speaking calmly about what had happened, without judgment of Starla or himself.

Finally, Hawkman summarized. "The woman I believe was your biological mother was beautiful and talented. I asked her to marry me before we found out she was pregnant, but she said no and it broke my heart. Then she left, and I only saw her again once, the week before her baby was born, when I gave her a present for the child. I am sure that you are Starla's baby, and my niece, and perhaps my daughter. I never expected to see you after my sister died."

"Wait," Stella said. "You're my father, I mean, my birth father?"

Hawkman looked pained. "Well, I could be. I really don't know for sure. At the very least, I'm your uncle. I wanted to be in your life more than I was, but that was up to your parents. I'd like to make amends, if you'll let me."

Stella took a deep breath as the news washed over her.

Leaphorn said, "I've been thinking about all of this. I believe your mother Clarita knew that your biological mother had lived in this area. I think she wanted to protect you, herself, and her brother from nosy questions. She and Stan probably worried that the Singer family might have realized who you were and tried to bring you back to the Navajo Nation. As you know, that was before the ICWA. That law says Navajo children should grow up with their relatives on the Navajo Nation, so they don't lose their culture."

Stella said, "Now that I know the story, I guess I actually did grow up with relatives. People always said I had my mother's dimple. It's the one you have on your chin, too, Mr. Hawkman."

Hawkman softly put his finger on her dimple and grinned. "If you ever decide to do a DNA test, you'll know for sure, but I welcome you as the child of my sister no matter who your father was. I was young when I helped my sister with the adoption. I didn't understand how that deprived you of knowing your Navajo family. I'm sorry for that."

"I guess I really am Navajo, or at least half. That's something to celebrate." Stella wiped a tear from the corner of her eye. "I have a small silver and turquoise bracelet. My mother said I was wearing it when they first met me. Do you know anything about that?"

Hawkman stared at her. "Do you happen to have a picture of it?"

"Better than that." She removed the small piece of jewelry from her purse and set it on the table.

"It's a baby bracelet." Hawkman reached for it and then pulled his hand back. "May I take a closer look?"

She nodded, and the trader picked it up. He looked at it for several minutes, and then gently set it down. "Where did you get this?"

"It was in a box my mother, your sister, left me after she died. Is it a clue to my Navajo roots?"

He gave her a smile. "It's a sign that Clarita wanted you to know that you came from here." Hawkman picked it up again, moved his hand back and forth with its weight, and handed the bracelet back to his niece. "I gave this to Starla for her baby the last time I saw her."

"So it is another way her spirit tells us that you and I are connected, Mr. Hawkman."

"That's right, Ms. Brown. My sister raised you well. We have a lot to talk about."

Leaphorn hated to intrude, but he knew they had a long drive back, and after the trauma of yesterday, he wanted to be with Louisa. "I'm sorry to interrupt, but I need to get going. Stella and I have a long trip ahead of us, and then I have another client to deal with."

Stella nodded. "I understand. Just another minute or two?" She put her hand on top of Hawkman's. "Janey told me your father may have taken that photo I have, the one with the Elephant Feet buttes. Is that true?"

"Yes. He used one of the cameras up there." He shifted his gaze to the top shelf, where the old photography equipment gathered cobwebs.

"She said she thought the people involved were just models, and that there wasn't really a baby in that woman's arms."

"That's right. Starla was the model. The Navajo guy who was supposed to be the other model didn't show up, so the man in the picture with her is me. That's why the hat is so low. Dad didn't want people to know he'd used a non-Native, his own son."

"So I have a picture of my biological mom and my uncle as a young man? That's wonderful."

Hawkman chuckled.

"I'd like to stay in touch, Mr. Hawkman. Would it be OK if I called you sometime?"

"I'd like that." He brushed away a tear with the back of his hand. "I miss my sister, and I'm sure you miss your mother. We have a lot to talk about. A lot to figure out. I look forward to the day when you'll at least call me Uncle Jackie."

Their drive back seemed quicker than the trip that morning. Stella asked about what she had seen on TV at Eagle Roost.

"I thought school bombings were an urban problem, not something that I'd find out here. Do you have any inside information?"

Leaphorn told her what he knew about the situation.

"A very smart Navajo officer is dealing with that, working with the FBI."

25

When Bernie got home from her run, she checked her phone for messages before jumping in the shower. As she held it, it vibrated with a call from an unknown caller. On a hunch, she answered.

"Hey, it's Nadia again. We're providing snacks for my brother's basketball team today, and we could seriously use the cooler. And, well, I need to tell you something else, too."

Bernie appreciated the young woman's tact. She'd meant to leave it with Principal Morgan and had totally forgotten.

"Can you come and get it?"

"Not unless I can get a friend to give me a ride after school. Want me to call you back?"

"Tell you what. This is my fault. I'm working the late shift so I'll drop it off within the hour. Where should I bring it?"

"What if my mom and I meet you at school?" She told Bernie the time. "We will be there with the snacks for the team. We'll park in front of the gym."

"OK. I'll be driving a gray Tercel."

"Not the police car?" Nadia sounded disappointed.

"No, I'll be in my uniform, but I won't be on duty until after I see you."

Bernie was ready to end the call, and then she remembered. "Was there something else you wanted to talk about?"

"I don't if this is important, but I was taking my little brother Ely to basketball practice on Friday morning, you know before anything happened, and I saw Principal Morgan driving the car that you found in the garage."

She offered Nadia some encouragement. "That's interesting. Are you sure?"

"Yes."

"I want to hear the whole story."

"OK. It was the first day of morning practice, so Ely got the time wrong." She heard the girl sigh. "He's just a kid, you know? We were at school a whole hour too early. I parked by the gym and told my brother he could go back to sleep—I was going for a run, and then I'd wake him in time for practice."

Nadia talked so fast Bernie could tell the girl was nervous. "I went down toward the track. That's behind the special ed building, you know, that just blew up. As I ran by the building, I noticed a car parked outside. I thought that was funny, you know, odd, because I had never seen anyone parked there. I figured maybe the car was out of gas or something and got left by the building because it wouldn't start.

"I did my run, and when I was heading back to the gym, I saw that the garage door was open, and the principal was driving the car I saw into the garage. I had to stop with a stitch in my side, and so I watched Principal Morgan. He got out of the car, wearing one of those things that mechanics or janitors wear, you know, with a zipper in front. He looked funny in it because he's always dressed up at school. I thought it was weird, you know?"

Nadia stopped talking.

Bernie gave her a moment. "You did a good job remembering details. Then what happened?"

"I don't know. Principal Morgan closed the garage door, and he was still inside there. My side stopped hurting, so I ran back to our van and, you know, it was about time for practice to start and a bunch of other cars were there and Coach Duran was there, and my brother Ely was awake, so he went in to practice and I sat there and did my homework while I waited for him."

"Go back a little. Tell me about the thing the principal was wearing again."

"OK. It was white. One of those one-piece outfits like you see on hazmat crews on TV, you know, like when the alien is in the lab and the scientists don't want any weird germs." She stopped. "I got it. Like a jumpsuit. No, wait. They call those things coveralls."

"Thanks. That might be important. I'm glad you told me."

"I'll see you when you bring the cooler, OK?"

Bernie had a thought. "Are you sure the school is open?"

"Yeah. Coach's wife called everyone on the team and said the game was on. It's still a mess down there, but they put up a chain-link fence to keep people away from the special ed building."

Bernie considered this development. Perhaps the explosion investigators had found something that led them to conclude that an accident, not a bomb, caused the damage. She showered quickly, put on her uniform, and drove to the substation. Sandra had rescued the cooler from the trunk of her unit.

"I hope you don't mind that I dumped out the water. Everything was still nice and cool. You'll need to get some ice." She smiled. "Or you can leave the fruit and drinks here for us. There are a couple of sandwiches, too."

"Keep all that. It came from the fire department volunteers. Put it in the break room so the team can enjoy it."

Sandra grinned. "I thought that's what you'd say, so I already did."

Bernie took the cooler to her Tercel, put it in the hatch, and was about to drive off when her phone buzzed. The caller was Agent Sage Johnson. She got to the point quickly.

"Bernie, I need a favor. If you're going toward Eagle Roost today, could you pick up something from the school for me? I need the plans for the building that got damaged as part of the investigation. Fisher can get them at your office later. He has business in Shiprock today."

Bernie thought about it; she was heading to the school on her own time, so she didn't need anyone's permission to help Johnson. "Where will the plans be?"

"Principal Morgan should have them."

Bernie mentioned what Nadia had said about the car in the garage.

"Interesting," Johnson said. "We'll add that to the list of things to follow up."

Bernie called Morgan from her car and she explained that the FBI needed the plans for the special ed building, and that she would come to pick them up.

"All that information is in my office at school. I would have gotten it earlier, but that jerk Fisher wouldn't let me in the building or even in my own office, even though it's in a separate building. He and Johnson had their team do a search for explosives on the whole campus. What a waste of time."

"Why do you say that?"

"Bowlegs isn't smart enough to have figured out how to blow up anything, although he might have done something to cause an accident." Morgan took a breath. "And of course the FBI bomb techs didn't find anything. We're trying to more forward now."

"I'm about half an hour away. Meet me at the school, and I can take the plans."

"How about in the parking lot at the community library? The school will be full of parents now that the campus is open again. Everyone wants to eyeball the damage. And everyone seems to have questions for me about the explosion. It's hard to avoid them without seeming rude."

Principal Morgan was waiting as promised when she pulled up. He didn't recognize her old Tercel, so she rolled down the window.

He walked around to the driver's window and leaned toward her.

"I'm sorry, but I've got bad news for you. I just remembered that those plans aren't in my office. Beth, my assistant, was reviewing them, so they were in her work space. And that was in the special ed building. I'm afraid they're either burned or soaked."

"There must be a copy of them somewhere."

Morgan looked blank.

"The architect or the engineering firm that worked on the building ought to have the plans. Call Agent Johnson and explain it to her and give her the name and address of the architects."

Morgan sounded irritated. "This is just busy work."

Bernie didn't want to argue. "Talk to Johnson. When I was there I heard that there could be an issue with the construction that contributed to the damage. He noticed several things that might not be up to code."

"He's wrong about that. The building passed the county inspection."

"Agent Fisher is the man you need to get in touch with. He's leading the investigation. Tell him your concerns."

Morgan shoved his hands in his pockets. "I can't deal with that now." He rattled off a long to-do list. "And I have to figure out a temporary home for the special education programs."

"And music, too?" She studied the man's face.

"Music has been canceled ever since Mrs. Bowlegs quit."

Bernie remembered the body in the car, and what Nadia had said about the principal and the flowers. "What was your relationship to Beth Bowlegs?"

"Relationship? What do you mean?"

Bernie waited.

Principal Morgan stood a bit straighter. "Mrs. Bowlegs worked for the school district, and I was her supervisor. The relationship was boss to employee, the same as my relationship with her husband."

"Really?"

He took a breath. "Oh, I get it. Someone mentioned the flowers. I do that each Valentine's Day for all the new employees to let them know they are appreciated. This year, Beth was the only new one."

"I thought she'd started here as a teacher's aide, worked her way up to being your assistant."

"I—I meant, new to the position." He stammered.

"What work did she do for you?"

"The school applied for a bunch of grants, and she helped us keep it all straight. Some of the money we requested was to improve the heating in the new building. The teachers and students complained about being cold in the winter." He shrugged. "There was so much to do, and Beth took on the extra work. She seemed to enjoy it."

"You're saying she accepted a new job with more responsibility but kept doing everything else, too?"

"Yes." Morgan paused. "She told me she had some bills to pay off and needed the money."

"That's one busy woman. You must have given her a nice raise."

"Well, no. I did what I could but the budget is tight."

Bernie let him talk.

"Beth is good with numbers, you know? Competent, maybe even nitpicky to a fault. I think that's probably why her husband . . . he couldn't keep up, and her success stirred his resentment." The principal looked to her for agreement.

"It sounds like you think he killed her."

"It's always the husband, isn't it?"

Bernie kept her expression neutral. "Was Cecil Bowlegs jealous of you?"

"Of me?" Morgan chuckled. "Not that I noticed. He certainly had no reason to be." Morgan made a clicking noise. "If he was jealous, it was of her success. She had so much going for her, and that man was dragging them both down with his debts. I told you about that, right?"

She nodded, wanting Morgan to keep talking before she brought up the car.

"The question I always wanted to ask was, why didn't she divorce him? Bethany came to work in tears some mornings, and I knew they weren't getting along. She deserved better than a man with a gambling problem."

"Maybe she took marriage seriously, you know, the for-better-or-worse part. Maybe she thought her support would help him with that problem. Too bad we can't ask her any of that."

"You're right. I thought that about my ex, too." He leaned against his silver sedan. "I never suggested divorce to Bethany, but I wish I had for her own good. If that jerk didn't want to be with her, why not move out, or get a divorce? Why kill her?"

"What makes you think she's dead and not just missing?"

Morgan looked surprised. "I overheard that FBI agent say something to a state trooper about a tattoo on the body they found in that car. A bird. Bethany had a tattoo on her wrist. Bad news travels."

Bernie saw a chance to ask her question. "Someone mentioned that they'd seen you drive that car, Bethany's car, into the garage."

"No, that's not right. Cecil must have done it." Morgan studied his shoes a moment. "After Beth hadn't come back to work, it wasn't right for that car to be gathering dust. And there's a big problem out here with packrats. You know that they love to nest under the hood, eat the wiring. I thought that it should have been in the garage. But I didn't drive it in there. Cecil had a key to the car and to the garage. I didn't see him move it, but he must have. It was fine by me."

Odd, Bernie thought, that a missing woman would leave without her car. Odd that Natalie would have misidentified the principal. It didn't make sense. "Let's get back to the plans the FBI folks asked me to pick up. Why would Beth have had them?"

"She wanted to keep all the paper files for grant applications close to her desk so she could access them when needed. In her mind that included the construction plans for the building because she thought she'd need them for the heating system replacement work."

"I'm surprised that you didn't have backup files on your computer."

"I should have." Morgan rubbed his chin. "Now that I think of it, I may have a paper copy of the initial plans for the special education building somewhere, because that was before Beth went to work for me. If that would be helpful, I'll hunt for them."

"Fisher needs them. So yes, find them so I can take them back to Shiprock."

"If you'd do that, it would save me a trip and another unpleasant encounter with him. I'll see what I can do."

"I'll help."

Morgan said, "I'll meet you outside the admin building. We'll park there. It won't take long; either the plans will be where I think, or they aren't anywhere."

Whenever someone said "Don't worry," Bernie worried. Something was off about Morgan's relationship with Bethany Bowlegs. "Wait for me there, and we'll go in together."

As she drove to the gymnasium, she saw the fence around the

destroyed special education building and remembered the garage. She knew the car had been removed, and the dead woman taken to the Office of the Medical Investigator, or OMI, in Albuquerque for an autopsy. She tried not to think of the chindi and how angry that spirit must be after such a terrible death.

She parked and stood next to the car to make it easier for Nadia to find her. Hearing someone honking, she turned and saw the girl behind the wheel of a pickup. Nadia stopped in the row behind Bernie's car and climbed out, followed by a younger boy and a middle-aged woman who had to be Nadia's mother. Bernie put the cooler in the truck bed and then introduced herself to Nadia's mom in the correct Diné fashion, using her clans.

The woman did the same. The two children looked puzzled.

"My kids need to learn some Navajo." The mom switched to English. Ely will be taking a class next year, and Nadia knows a little, but she's shy with it."

Nadia said, "I think Navajo is hard to learn."

"It is. But it's worth it. It's the language of our hearts." Bernie switched to something more mundane. "I meant to return your cooler earlier. I hope you weren't inconvenienced. Nadia helped us so much with the investigation by delivering lunch and water to the officers. Everyone appreciated it."

The mother moved her head slightly in acknowledgment. "What do you know about the explosion?"

"Not much yet. The FBI is in charge now."

"Tell them to look at that janitor."

"Why?"

"The buildings aren't clean. They say he's lazy, and that's why his wife left him. They say that he had things in his closet in the building that could blow up. I heard they found someone dead because of the explosion. Is that right?"

Bernie noticed Ely shifting from foot to foot and bent down to talk to him, which also allowed her to avoid answering the question. "Do you need to go into practice?"

He nodded shyly. "I can't be late, or the coach gets mad." His soft, sweet voice reminded Bernie of the days when her sister was small and sweet.

Bernie turned to the mother and Nadia. "I have to go, but Nadia has my phone number, if you think of something that might help in the investigation."

"It's none of my business," Nadia's mother said. She and Ely walked toward the gym, but Nadia lagged behind. She handed Bernie a piece of light-green lined paper.

"This is what Mrs. Bowlegs gave me the last time I saw her. I wonder if it could be a clue."

The folded paper was blank on the outside. Bernie opened it and read: "Be careful who you love. Love can steal your voice."

She handed it back to Nadia. "Can you take a photo of that with your phone and send it to me?"

The girl nodded. "You think it's important?"

"I don't know. It's cryptic."

She saw Nadia's confused look. "Cryptic means confusing. Like a puzzle or something."

Nadia nodded. "There's something else I forgot to tell you. Principal Morgan yelled at Mrs. Bowlegs."

"Why did he yell?"

"I don't know. I couldn't understand what he said. I was outside, just waiting to go in for my lesson, and I heard him."

"What happened next?"

Nadia frowned, as though she didn't understand the question for a moment. "She yelled back. She said, 'That's not my problem.' And, well, the principal came out of the building, and I went in for my lesson."

"What about Mrs. Bowlegs?"

"Well, she seemed kinda mad or upset after that." Nadia glanced toward the ruined classroom. "That was the last time I got to sing with her."

Bernie parked outside the admin building. Morgan's sleek new car wasn't there. She decided to give the principal another five minutes before she left for Shiprock, and the time was almost up when he pulled in next to her, looking frazzled.

"I'm sorry I'm late. I had to take a call from the insurance adjuster. He needs the plans, too. I hope we can find them. I can't remember where they are, or even if they are here and not with Beth. I should have kept them safe. If I could have anticipated all this, I would have done a better job."

"I still have a few minutes before I have to get back to Shiprock. Let's go."

She saw him hesitate. "I have to warn you," he said. "My office is a disaster."

"Let's go." She said it with more force this time.

He frowned. "I hope it's not a waste of your time. Come on."

Morgan paused for a quick second to say hello to three little boys who were straggling in for basketball practice. A man who was with them gave Bernie's uniform a questioning look, then turned to the principal.

"Mr. Morgan, how much longer will this be going on? You know all this commotion isn't good for the kids. My boys are having bad dreams."

"I'm sad to hear that, and I wish I could tell you when we will get back to normal, Mr. Yazzie. But all I can say at this point is that the state police, Navajo law enforcement, and the FBI are working with us to figure out what happened. We were lucky no one was in the building when it exploded."

"How long before we get some answers? People are nervous. We're concerned about the safety of our children."

"I realize that," Morgan said. "The investigators have thoroughly searched all the other buildings. They say they are safe, and that's why we're able to reopen. Everyone has been working to find out what caused the explosion."

He turned to Bernie. "This is Officer Manuelito, with the Navajo Police. She's helping with the investigation. Bernie, this is Mike Yazzie. He volunteers as a coach here."

The large, roundish man looked at Bernie again. Bernie nodded and said, "Yá'át'ééh." Mr. Yazzie nodded back. "Yá'át'ééh."

Bernie frowned. "Excuse us, sir." It felt awkward to move on, but they had to. She began walking away.

"Wait." Yazzie raised his voice. "One more thing. I heard that Cecil

Bowlegs is gone. He's the one who always brought out the track-and-field equipment for the practices. If he doesn't show up, you better get someone to do his job." And with that, he ambled away.

Bernie and the principal walked down the hall of the administration building, one of the oldest structures on campus, past a colorful display of student artwork celebrating the imminent arrival of spring. A case held trophies for basketball and volleyball, and medals Eagle Roost students had earned for a variety of sports over the years. It pleased her to see a trophy for winning the *Navajo Times* annual spelling bee, and some certificates for academic achievement.

"My office is this way." Morgan unlocked the door, reached in to turn on the overhead lights, and motioned Bernie to go in ahead of him.

Bernie paused. "You first."

She'd expected disorganization, but this room looked like it had been through several dust devils. Every surface was piled with boxes, files, loose papers, notebooks, and more. She saw a coffee cup, a roll of stickers and a harmonica on the large desk in the center of the room. Dusty sealed cardboard boxes sat on the floor, stacked against the side of an old filing cabinet. The office resembled a large, unkempt storage locker. No wonder Morgan had hesitated to search for the plans in here.

"You don't see many old steel file cabinets like that anymore." Bernie counted at least five of them, each with five drawers.

"That's right. I inherited them, the paperwork inside them, and a bunch of problems from the past administrations."

"Problems like what?"

"Oh, a whole spectrum of them. Things like old buildings with poor insulation and insufficient heat for our cold winters. Vintage plumbing that clogs. Inadequate computer network wiring or no wiring at all. Slow internet. A history of insufficient funding for supplies, books, and computers for the students. A few staff people who should have been asked to resign long ago."

His last comment made her angry but she kept her opinion to herself.

"I'm going to start looking," Morgan said. "If we don't find something in the next few minutes, I'll leave it to the FBI."

"What's in those sealed boxes?"

Morgan stood straighter. "Old personnel files from ten years ago, invoices, students' suspension reports, stuff like that. I don't have the time to sort through and shred or digitize them, or the money to pay someone to do it, so there they sit." He shook his head. "There's a sense of resignation in the community, you know? The idea that what we've always had is the best we deserve. That is the hardest part, along with real resistance to change. When I took this job, I hoped to make the situation better."

His dismissive attitude stretched her patience to its edge. "You're wrong about that. Every parent I know wants the very best for their children. The Navajo Nation has a long history of working hard to educate our children."

"Sure, every place has interested parents, but they seem to be the minority here."

"Maybe you just don't know how to reach out to them."

"You're probably right about that, but I can't deal with that issue now." He glanced at the disaster of an office. "I'll start going through those shelves over there. Do what you think is best. I'm out of ideas."

Bernie opened a closet door and found more old filing cabinets. A basket filled with long rolls of paper sat in the corner. Hope flickered for a moment until she realized all the tubes held paper calendars for classroom walls.

"A lot of the buildings here are old," Bernie said. "But the one that blew up looked new. That seems odd."

"It was new; that's the mystery of it. Do the FBI investigators suspect an issue with the construction?"

"You need to ask Agent Johnson about that."

"If I were investigating this, of course I'd wonder why that building caught fire so quickly."

"We all wonder that," Bernie said. "That's why they want the plans."

"I'm looking." Morgan, a tall man, searched on top of several shelves, pulled off boxes and plastic containers, opened them, and left them on the floor as he continued the quest.

Bernie opened another closet door and saw an assortment of boxes.

Up against the back wall she spotted a tall container with about two dozen long cardboard tubes inside. Recognizing them as the kind architects and draftsmen used to store plans before almost everything could be reduced to a flash drive, she felt a flash of encouragement.

Some of the tubes were marked with numbers on the outside. She opened the first and extracted the contents with difficulty. They were plans, but for a playground. She noticed that the numbers on the sheets—day, month, and year—matched the numbers she'd seen on the tube.

"When was the special education center built?"

Morgan looked up from his mess. "Well, I started as principal here about three years ago, and construction began in June the next year when the grant money finally came in. Try that for starters."

Bernie did the math and came up with a date. She shuffled through the container, disregarding all the tubes that substantially predated the construction or didn't relate to the special education building. That left only the four which lacked labels and dates.

Morgan's cell phone rang. She recognized the ringtone, a version of the Beatles' "Blackbird." He stood and walked into the hallway, leaving the office door open, so she could overhear his end of the conversation.

Morgan sounded angry. "I can't believe this, and no, I'm not making a payment. Didn't you hear what happened Saturday? The building you worked on blew up. I'm suspending payments until we know what caused the damage."

Silence, and then he said, "Don't threaten me. Someone made a mistake, and until the investigation into the explosion is settled, no money is leaving the school account."

Morgan was putting his phone in his back pocket when he reentered the room.

"I heard some yelling," Bernie said. "Everything OK?"

He looked surprised at the question. "Actually, no. A problem with a bill from a contractor who worked on the special ed building."

He went back to work for a few minutes. "Bernie, I think this is hopeless. Are you almost done?"

"Not yet."

"Everything I see here is inappropriate. What we want must have been in her office." He stood. "Enough of this."

"I might have something. Help me spread out these sheets of paper." She looked for a flat surface more suitable than the floor. "Clear off some room on that desktop for them."

He shuffled boxes to make space, and she brought the first set of plans and laid them flat. They were the drawings for a pavement plan for the parking lot.

She had three sets to go. The second blank tube had landscaping designs for the new special ed site.

Close, she thought. She pulled the next set from its box while Morgan replaced the unneeded plans and labeled the tubes.

"Hey, this looks like what we want."

Morgan studied the sheets for a moment. "I can't believe you found them in this mess. Take them with you and let the FBI see if there was a construction issue."

"What about the other tubes? I want—" Her phone vibrated, interrupting. It was Sandra from the substation.

"The captain wants you to come in as early as you can. That rookie Officer Black made a mistake. The boss is in a very bad mood."

"Can I talk to him?"

"No. He went for a walk to cool down a little."

"How about Black?"

"He's gone, too."

"Is Chee around?"

"Bingo." Sandra transferred the call.

Chee got on the line. "Are you on your way in? We're swamped." He sighed. "We're always swamped, but more so today than usual. Roper's baby is sick and he didn't show up and forgot to call in. Roper is trying but . . . Hold on. The captain just walked in, and I know he wants to talk to you. Good luck."

She barely had time to wonder why he had said that, when Captain Adakai came on the phone.

"Manuelito, where are you?"

She told him.

"Eagle Roost? I thought you'd be done with that case by now. You need to follow up on that dog attack. Black just blew it off."

She gave him an abbreviated version of the situation. "I'll be there as soon as I can."

"I don't like you being an errand girl for the feds. They have their own agents, and we're short of people."

"Yes, sir." She ended the call and turned to Morgan.

"I need to leave. Besides the good plans we found, I'm taking the other tubes, the one's we didn't open, just in case." She knew that major projects often had several sets of complex drawings. And she realized from Adakai's comments that she probably wouldn't be back to Eagle Roost again.

Morgan motioned to the unopened tubes. "Leave them so I can review them. I'll let you know if there's anything crucial to the explosion in there. I'm sure you have more important things to do."

Bernie shook her head. "I'm taking them now."

"Oh, come on. Give yourself a break."

"Is there something here you don't want me to see?"

"No, not at all. It's just that you could be wasting your time."

Ignoring him, she sat at his desk and jotted down a statement saying what she was taking with her. She signed it, took a photo of it, and took photos of the tubes. "This is as official as I can make it."

Sticking the tubes with the plans and the two unopened cardboard cylinders under her arm, she left Morgan looking at her chain-of-custody note and began the drive back toward the Shiprock substation.

26

Leaphorn was pleased to find Louisa back at work on her research notes when he got home from his trip with Stella. She looked up and smiled at him.

"They let me talk to Kory over the phone. He sounds better, calmer. He apologized for what happened and told me he's starting a new medication that already seems to be working."

"That's good."

"Lin is at the hospital with him. She sounded better. Encouraged by Kory's progress and by the fact that the drugs seem to be helping his mood." Louisa rose from the table and went to the stove. "I made some soup. How about a bowl? It's cold out there."

"I'd love some." The cold, he assumed, was a result of her interior weather: the evening was warmer than usual, as though spring had finally arrived, at least for a few hours.

From his own experience, Leaphorn knew that the trauma Louisa had experienced would release its poison slowly, building the way a physical illness did, at first with mild discomfort, then more serious pain. He hoped that with support, understanding, and loving care, the shock and heartbreak of being threatened by her own son would begin to fade away.

She stirred the soup, and spoke with her back to him. "I'm embarrassed about what happened with Kory. You told me to be careful, that you sensed that something was wrong with him." Her voice cracked.

He waited for her to finish.

"I should have listened to you, Joe." She turned and took two bowls from the cabinet. "I thought I knew the man because he was my son, but too much time had gone by." She began to ladle soup into them.

"Louisa?"

"What?"

"Your son's mental illness is sad, but it isn't your fault. You have nothing to be embarrassed about. You're one of the best people I know. Give yourself more credit."

From the way she looked at him, he knew she wasn't convinced.

"What happens to Kory now?"

He shrugged.

"Well, here's what I think," she said. "They say a person has to hit bottom before they can get better. I hope that's what happened out there. When I talked to him at the hospital, he said he was going to get treatment."

"For the cancer?"

"Yes. And for his mental illness."

Leaphorn nodded. "He'll have to face criminal charges."

"My sweet, lost son told me he realized that he was lucky that Lin and I both still loved him. He said the chemo made him so sick that he stopped taking his other meds. And maybe the pressure of knowing he was going to be a dad pushed him over the edge, into depressive madness."

Her tears had started, but her voice stayed strong.

"And Kory said that someday, when and if he's glad he's alive, he might thank you for saving his life. You know what I said?"

Leaphorn waited.

"I told him he should thank you now. You and Largo could have killed him."

Louisa wrapped her arms around him for a moment, then she went to the stove. She put the soup on the table in front of him and another bowl for herself, and they sat down to eat.

Leaphorn sampled a spoonful. "Thank you. This is good. I haven't eaten much today."

"What happened with your client when you went to Tonalea?"

He gave her an overview and, when she asked, filled in the enhancing details, pleased that she was interested.

"If I were Stella, I'd do a DNA test." Louisa smiled at him. "But each person has to make their own decision on that."

Leaphorn put his spoon down. "I understand her resistance. And John Hawkman is willing and eager to be in her life, if she wants him there, test or no test."

They had cleared the table and started some coffee when Leaphorn's cell phone rang.

"I bet that's Largo," she said. "Checking up on you after your adventures."

But Louisa would have lost the bet. The caller was Bernadette Manuelito, and she had surprising information for him about the explosion at Eagle Roost and about Bethany Bowlegs.

27

There's nothing like a little time alone in a vehicle to clear your head, Bernie thought. She called the station and asked for a background check on Principal Charles Morgan.

"The captain has a new rule about that. You'll have to talk to him. Sorry."

Sandra transferred her back to the captain.

"Ask the feds to do that. The explosion and the body, all that happened at a Navajo school, sure, but they deal with school attacks. This is their case."

"Sir, they may not be focused on Morgan as much as they could be. The explosion has taken a backseat to the murder."

"You sound surprised at that."

Before she could explain herself, Adakai said, "Wrap things up and get back here. But don't hang up. Chee wants to talk to you. Make sure it's business."

She took a calming breath, and then her husband's strong voice came over the phone.

"I just wanted to check in. Are you doing all right?"

"Grumpy. I asked the captain for a background check on the Eagle Roost principal and got a lecture and some patronizing. Let's talk later."

"Sure. Leaphorn might have an update for you on the Cecil Bowlegs piece of the school explosion situation. Who did you need to check?"

She told him. "I think Morgan may have had something to do with the explosion or with Mrs. Bowlegs' death—if that's who was in the car. Or both. Maybe he and the custodian collaborated on the explosion. Maybe he was in love with Bethany. Maybe it's just coincidence that he was the last one seen walking away from that car where the body was found."

"You know what the lieutenant thinks about coincidence."

"If I lived here in Eagle Roost, I'd have a better handle on this because I'd know more about the suspects." And then she remembered Officer Stanley and the fire chief. Bernie felt a rush of excitement. "I'm going to lose my signal shortly. Will you call Leaphorn and ask about Cecil Bowlegs and Principal Morgan?"

"Glad to. Between us, the medical investigator may need Bowlegs to identify the body."

The idea made her cringe. "See you soon."

"Be safe out there."

"You bet. As always."

She left a quick message for the fire chief to call her. When she stopped at the convenience store on the way out of town, she noticed Officer Stanley's unit there. He was washing his windshield.

She told him about Morgan, and his suspicions about Cecil Bowlegs. "What's your take on all this?"

"I like Morgan, but he's changed over the past months," Stanley said. "Morgan knew that Eagle Roost was a poorly funded Navajo school, right, when he took the job. He understood what it paid, knew the budget. He seemed to get it, you know, to understand that the school might not be great, but it's ours. He has solid plans to improve things, but as some parents see it, things don't really need improving. He's an outsider, and he was doing his best to fit in. But then he bought that show-off car and started to seem more worried, less focused."

"Maybe he was anxious about the car payments."

Stanley shrugged. "Maybe family stuff. He never talked about his parents or if he had a wife and kids. A little off, huh?" He rolled his eyes toward the blue sky for a moment and watched a cloud float with the wind. "You know how it is when you have a rock in your shoe and you can't stop to dump it out? Well, that's how his spirit seems now. It's like something troubles him and he can't get rid of it."

Stanley replaced the squeegee in the bucket of soapy water. "I feel bad for Morgan about the explosion. That building was his baby, you know—he planned it, worked with the contractors. It was supposed to be bigger, with more bells and whistles, but he explained that the suppliers told him and Bethany that prices for everything had gone through the roof. And now it's rubble. Did you notice the walkway to it?"

"No."

"It's beautiful. He asked the art teachers to have every child make something that could be embedded in it. He wants the best for our families. His main fault is that he tends to dream too big." Stanley started to open the door to his unit, then turned back to her. "You want my view of Bowlegs?"

"Please."

"He's one of those guys who complains about everything. And I hear he likes to spend a lot of time in the casinos. It's no wonder Beth left him, if she actually did. I never understood what she saw in him. I mean, she was smart, had a lot of talent as a singer. And she was pretty, too."

Bernie noticed that he referred to the woman in the past tense.

"But to get to the heart of it, Cecil loved his wife. He was proud of her success. And he didn't drink, you know, and that sometimes gives people courage to act badly. When he and RP came in to report her missing, he was genuinely upset."

"Anything else about Bowlegs?"

Stanley shook his head. "I shouldn't have said what I did about him and Bethany. I've been married long enough to know that couples find their own ways of being together."

"How long have they been married?" The radio in Stanley's unit blared, calling his name and interrupting his answer.

"I'm not sure about the married part, but he and that woman had been together maybe five years. She'd leave to sing somewhere, and come back, and leave again until she got those two jobs at the school, music and working in administration. That settled her down for a while until she went missing."

"How do you know all this about the Bowlegs?"

"Oh, it could be because the missing woman is my wife's best friend."

BERNIE HEADED NORTH ON A road she knew well through landscape that felt like home. This arid, beautiful place was her nest, a nest where she hoped she and Chee someday would welcome a child. She passed a small herd of lean horses foraging on the early spring weeds that had sprouted on the mesa. She remembered how Mama always put out water for the wild horses, and in exchange they left their arrow hoofprints to keep her family safe.

When she had a strong signal, she called the FBI office. Agent Johnson answered on the third ring. The agent sounded cordial, friendlier than usual.

"Hey Bernie. I'm sorry we haven't had a chance to talk. The Eagle Roost investigation has me swamped. I'm glad you were there. I appreciated your help. They finished collecting evidence at the explosion site. Now comes the challenge of making sense of it."

"Any news on the body?"

"No. The partial prints don't match anything on file—but there were no prints on file for Bethany Benally Bowlegs, the vehicle owner."

Bernie knew that it was standard procedure for teachers to be fingerprinted. But a part-time music instructor like Bethany, who also happened to be an office worker, might be exempt. Judging from the disorganization of Morgan's paperwork, it could be that her prints had never been taken, or never recorded.

Johnson's tone changed from official to more curious. "What does your instinct tell you about the principal?"

"He's a complex character. He's nervous, and he wants to blame the custodian, Cecil Bowlegs, for the explosion without any evidence. He already assumes that the body is Bethany, Cecil's missing wife. But on the other hand, he acts genuinely concerned about the school and its teachers and students. I'd like to know more about him." Bernie changed topics "Any hits yet on the source of the explosion?"

"Not much. Talk about complex. Our investigation has ruled out most kinds of explosives and found nothing like an explosive device. They also determined that it wasn't a problem with the water heater. Sometimes those heaters can leak, get too hot, and the pressure makes them blow up. The investigators took a look at the wiring and the way the gas lines enter and leave the building, but I haven't heard yet. . ." She paused, waiting for Bernie's questions, but Bernie let her talk.

"So if that's not it, that leaves either a weird, unusual accident, or an intentional explosion made to look like an accident. If you hear anything, or have any bright thoughts on this, please let me know."

"I will. Bernie checked the time. "I ought to go."

"Great. I'll send Fisher to pick up the plans you found."

Bernie waited to see if Johnson had more to add. She didn't, so they said their goodbyes.

As she drove, Bernie thought about the dead woman and the way the body had been treated. Why shove it in a car in a locked garage? Why was that beautiful, neatly folded Navajo blanket on the seat next to the body? If the killer was also responsible for the building explosion, had the blast been planned to hide the murder? But that didn't make sense. No matter how powerful the explosion, human remains would still have been detected in the car's wreckage.

She wanted to understand the why of the murder and the decision to put the body in the car. The crime's where and how seemed evident: OMI had confirmed the head wound. Fisher speculated, based on his initial reading of the evidence, that the killer had murdered her somewhere outside of the garage. If she had been killed in the music classroom the fire and explosion could have obliterated the clues. The blast would have made it almost impossible to collect evidence of the murder. The car showed no evidence of foul play.

The question of motivation circled her mind like a hungry predator. If the dead person was Beth Bowlegs, what had the woman done to anger or threaten someone so intensely that it led to murder? No one

Bernie had spoken to bad-mouthed Beth. From what she'd heard, even her husband, who everyone agreed wasn't on the up and up, loved her.

Her thoughts swirled. She fretted over the details of the explosion, reviewing the same barren territory over and over without a conclusion.

Bernie parked at the station and put the tubes with the plans in the evidence room for safekeeping. Then she got some coffee, hoping caffeine would revive her fading energy.

Sandra walked into the break room.

"You look terrible, honey. What's going on?"

"Oh, a long drive to the edge of frustration, that's all. I'm OK."

"Good thing. I hate to say it, but the captain wants to see you ASAP."

She expected the captain to be grumpy because she hadn't come in early as he'd requested. But instead Adakai looked at her calmly when she rapped on the doorsill, invited her in, and asked her to close the door.

"Manuelito, give me detailed notes about what happened out there with the FBI and the state police. I'm concerned that our officers aren't being treated with the professionalism we deserve. Especially our female officers."

"I will, sir. But that wasn't my experience today at Eagle Roost."

The captain leaned forward in his seat. "Years ago, I noticed how disrespectful some of the officers who work with other agencies were to our Native cops and to women in uniform. That's getting better, but it has to stop, and the only way to do it is to call them out on it."

"Sir, in my experience, most men and women in law enforcement have dealt with me fairly. And those who had an issue with me are bad news on many levels. Nothing specific at Eagle Roost raised my hackles."

"Good." He nodded once. "Do the report anyway."

She waited for him to dismiss her, but he had something else on his mind.

"Agent Johnson called and asked if you could work with her on the case interviews." Adakai shook his head. "I think they should do their own work instead of poaching our people to help. They have more resources than we do by far."

Bernie couldn't disagree. "Did she say if this was about the explosion or about the dead person?"

"I didn't ask. Does it matter?"

"Yes sir." Because the captain was new to Shiprock, he didn't know her history with Johnson, so Bernie filled him in. She told him that she'd worked with Agent Johnson before as a translator and cultural consultant when the people who needed to be interviewed spoke more Navajo than English or, for personal reasons, would rather tell their story to a woman who looked more like them.

He listened, frowning. "I don't think that's the case here. It didn't sound like Johnson only wanted your language skills. It seems like she's trying to recruit you. Talk to her, see what she needs, and tell her I'll make the final call. That's how this has to be, because you're a Navajo cop. Your job is here.

"I understand. I think it's good that the FBI wants to collaborate with us now. I feel welcomed."

He gave her an unreadable look. "Don't say yes to anything else she wants you to do before you clear it with me."

"Yes sir."

"And I want you to help get Officer Black up to speed here. The rookie is finishing a car theft at the trading post. Chee went with him to do some introductions."

"What trading post?"

He told her. "And there's been another attack out there where those sheep died. The woman who called it in asked for you specifically and sang your praises. Head out there when you've finished the report and talked to the FBI. Take the rookie with you if he's back in time for you to ride together."

"Sir, I have good notes about the bombing incident, but the report you're asking for will be long and complicated, because we were all there for hours. The woman with those sheep just moved to the area, and her mother is bedridden. That call also will involve a lot of my time. And you told me to call the FBI and deal with the agent's request. I'm not sure how to get this all done."

The captain surprised her, "What do you think should come first?"

"Calling the FBI. We've seen too many murdered women out here. Officer Black can get in touch with the lady about the dog pack attacks. I can use the recording app on my phone and talk through my notes about the explosion while the details are fresh in my mind. Then I can write it up later."

She could see him thinking as she spoke.

"The report for me can wait a day or two. Do what you have to and then meet Black at the place where the sheep were killed. That's all, Manuelito. Get to work."

Her phone buzzed just as she left the captain's office. Of course, it was her sister, and Darleen was talking faster than usual.

28

As usual, Darleen got right to the point. "Hey, Sister, I've got a problem. Can you help me out?"

"What's going on?"

"I'm at school. I need a ride."

"What happened to your car?"

"It's out of gas. And I'm broke."

"I can't do it. I'm at work with about two days of backlog paperwork and phone calls." Bernie waited for her sister to beg for a loan, or press her for the ride, but Darleen surprised her.

"OK. I understand."

"Why don't you call Slim?"

"He broke up with me."

"When?"

"A few minutes ago. I called him for help first, and he got all mad."

Bernie felt her heart grow heavier. Of all the men Darleen had dated, Slim was special. Bernie knew they had been talking marriage.

"I'm so sorry."

"I've been calling friends for half an hour, and I can't get anyone to help me."

Bernie looked around the station. Officer Bigman, her clan brother, was about to leave for the day.

"Sister, if I figure out a way to help you, you have to promise me something in return."

"What?"

"AA. Starting tomorrow."

"Oh, that's just—" Darleen cut off the words in midflow. "OK."

"Do you have a gas can in your car?"

"A what?"

"Never mind. I'll call you in a few minutes."

"I'll be here."

Bernie explained the situation to Bigman, who had just finished his shift. When he agreed to the favor, she gave him money for gas for Darleen's car. They went out together to her Tercel to get her container for gasoline.

"Thanks for doing this. I really appreciate it. I know Darleen will, too." Bernie gave him Darleen's phone number. "She's stranded up at Diné College."

"Tsaile? Up there?"

"No. Here in Shiprock."

"She's taking classes?"

Bernie nodded. "She wants to work in health care, maybe with older people, so she enrolled in a beginning nursing program."

"I like Darleen. She has a good heart." He let the notion hang for a few moments. "She will do well in health care. Now with sisters and daughters and even grandmas working, the world needs more people with training like your sister is getting. And she still does her drawings, right?"

"She has not been drawing as much lately."

Bigman thought about it. "That's a shame. She's a good artist. I would love a sketch of the baby. I'll ask her if she'd be interested in that."

Bernie called Darleen and told her of the plan. "You're fortunate that he was available to help you."

"I know. I'm doing my assignment while I wait for him."

Bernie thought about how to ask what came next, and no easy words occurred to her, so she spoke from the heart. "I'm worried about Mama. We have to find a solution to this. Mrs. Darkwater is a lifesaver, but we need a better plan. Chee told me Mrs. D has to go to the hospital for surgery."

"I know. She's telling everyone."

Bernie said, "Sister, I worry about you, too."

"Oh, I'm OK. I just hit a rough patch last night."

"No. I don't think that's it." Bernie knew she had to say what came next, but she dreaded it. "You're a woman who has an illness called alcoholism. You need to treat it."

"Wait. I'm not an adláanii. I just get carried away sometimes. That's all. I can stop drinking whenever I want."

"I know you believe that, but I don't think it's true. You've tried it, remember? Until you get your life together, I have to make a better plan for Mama. This isn't about me or about us or about who's right and who's wrong. It's about your addiction to alcohol. Your drinking is trashing your life, but I am not going to let it endanger Mama or me."

"You don't get it, do you?" Darleen started to yell. "I can stop drinking whenever I want to, but I don't want to. It helps me relax, keeps me sane. Why are you so mean to me?"

Bernie felt her chest tighten with anger. "I'm not being mean. I'm just telling you the truth. No one can stop you from ruining your own life, but I won't let you put our mother in danger anymore. I really love you, but . . ."

Darleen spit out an expletive and hung up.

Bernie stared at her phone, feeling her heart pound. She took some deep breaths to calm herself and push away the hurt and the anger. Then Sandra buzzed her.

"Agent Fisher is here. He says you have something for him."

"Tell him I'll be there in a few minutes." Bernie rolled her neck a few times to release the tension, and then went to the evidence room for the plans.

Agent Fisher frowned when he saw her, but she realized that was his normal look.

She handed him the tubes. "Morgan told me that the updated plans you want were destroyed in the explosion. One of these I'm giving you is an original of the special ed and music building. I didn't have a chance to open the two that are still taped. I found nothing else of relevance, but I had to get to work here. I didn't have time for a complete search."

Fisher signed out the plans without a comment or a thank-you.

Bernie went back to her desk and called Joe Leaphorn. They had been playing phone tag, and he might be able to give her some good advice.

He answered and sounded so extraordinarily happy that she hated to ask her question. But she had to.

"I'm wondering if you've heard from Cecil Bowlegs?"

"Yes, Cecil Bowlegs and his friend RP are on their way to Shiprock."

She hardly knew what to say, but managed to blurt out, "Really?"

Leaphorn chuckled. "Lots of moving parts. I'll tell you the whole story later."

"Yes sir."

"Who's the new captain there?"

She told him.

"How's he doing?"

"No one can really replace Captain Largo. I miss him."

"That's a hard job."

"Have you seen Largo lately, sir?"

"Yes. He's doing fine, and I'll tell you about that later, too. For now, the FBI needs to know what Cecil and RP have to say. Can you and the captain set up a meeting in about an hour or so that includes the FBI agent responsible for this case? Chee should be there, too."

The request surprised her. "I can't, sir. I've got to go out on a call as soon as I finish this paperwork."

"Officer, I'm calling Adakai now and telling him you have to be there. Then you can talk to Johnson at the FBI. See you in about an hour." Leaphorn paused. "That is, unless your other call is murder, too."

"Well, it is, but the victims were sheep. You know how I feel about those dibé."

"I do, but they have to wait. This is more important than dead sheep."

LEAPHORN AND HIS PASSENGERS REACHED the Shiprock substation a bit sooner than promised. All three of them seemed cheerful, something unusual in people arriving at a police station.

After Captain Adakai introduced himself in the traditional way, Leaphorn did the same. He knew Agent Johnson, who was participating over the phone. And of course Bernie was there, and the newly promoted Lieutenant Jim Chee. Leaphorn introduced Cecil Bowlegs and his friend, R. P. Benally, noting that RP was a clan brother of Bethany Benally Bowlegs.

They all sat down in the conference room, and Adakai spoke first.

"Lieutenant, why don't you start?"

Leaphorn nodded to Cecil. "I think we should begin with what happened this morning, the fresh news."

Cecil grinned. "We got a call this morning from Bethany. She's OK. Not missing. Not dead."

Shocked silence filled the room.

Cecil looked at Leaphorn. "That's what I came here to tell everyone, right?"

"That's right. Go ahead, Cecil. Tell everyone what you told me. Give them the details."

"Beth said she drove to Tucson to get her head on straight, and today she's coming home. She's gonna give me another try. It's a miracle. I can't . . ." His voice choked with emotion, and he put his head in his hands.

RP looked eager to speak, so Leaphorn brought him in. "Tell everyone here about the phone call you got from Bethany."

"I couldn't believe it. The phone showed 'Unknown Caller,' but the number had an Arizona prefix, 520. I thought it might be Olivia, Bethany's sister from Tucson, and that she had a new number or something. But it was Beth. She called me because she needed to talk to Cecil, but he lost his phone, so she couldn't call him.

"I thought I recognized her voice right away, but well, I guess I'm naturally suspicious. So I said, let's do a video call, and then I could tell that it was really her. She sounded good, you know, and looked good, too. She said she was fine, but she was concerned about Cecil because they'd been out of touch. And she said she was worried about Olivia, too."

RP stopped again. Bernie prompted him. "Go on. Why was she worried?"

"Well, that was because Olivia was supposed to have come back to Tucson a couple days ago. But she didn't get there. No call or nothing." RP shook his head. "So the first thing I did was give Beth a lecture. I told her if she was worried about Olivia, well, what about Cecil and me and Big Rex and the guys in the band and people at school, you know? I told her she should hop in the car and come home.

"Beth said she didn't have her car. Olivia borrowed it, because they knew Olivia's old clunker wouldn't make it to Eagle Roost. Olivia probably needs a new transmission, you know. I know about vehicles and last time I was in Tucson, well, that car . . .".

Bernie sensed that RP's narrative was headed for a side road. Agent Johnson, not governed by Navajo politeness, interrupted. "Did Beth say why her sister was coming to Eagle Roost?"

"Yes, ma'am, she did. Their shimásání, their grandma, was a good weaver, and Beth had a rug, the last one that lady made. That sweet lady died a few years ago. So Olivia wanted the rug, and Beth said her sister could have it. But Beth wasn't ready to return to New Mexico, and Olivia had some days off, so she came to get it." RP looked at his hands. "That's all I've got."

Agent Johnson came in again. "I'm not clear on that. Tell us again why Olivia drove to Eagle Roost in Bethany Bowlegs's car."

"Because that's where Beth had the rug. She had taken it to her office, and Olivia was worried that it would become school property because Beth had quit her job and left it behind. That rug was a family treasure, since their grandma wouldn't be making any more." RP shook his head. "All that was before anyone knew the building was going to blow up."

"Ahhh. I'm beginning to understand," Johnson said.

"Beth told me she was OK with Olivia making the trip, you know, because her sister is a talker and without her, Beth could get a few days of quiet time. But Olivia never came back, and then Beth heard that the building where the rug was blew up."

Leaphorn, like a good narrator, added his perspective. "I'd figure Olivia's disappearance was an issue for the Tucson police. Except that she was driving the car that was discovered in the garage at Eagle Roost School. The car with the body inside it."

Cecil and RP's expressions suddenly changed.

Agent Johnson said, "I need to have a long talk with Bethany Bowlegs. Do you know when her bus is supposed to arrive?"

"It's due in Gallup in about two hours," Leaphorn said. "I'm headed back that way, so I'll take her husband to the station so he can be there."

Bowlegs nodded in agreement.

"We need to question Mr. Bowlegs and his wife separately about the explosion, so, Lieutenant Leaphorn, I'm counting on you to make sure he's safe and available."

"Wait. I already talked to the State Police. Why—"

Johnson talked over him. "Make sure we know his whereabouts." Her tone left no room for argument.

"Ma'am, I'll tell you whatever I can. I'm so sorry about the explosion, but I didn't have anything to do with it. I'd never store no bad chemicals or anything like that in the building. I love those kids."

Leaphorn said, "I consider Bowleg's safety my responsibility. You can count on me."

"I expect to have our preliminary report on the explosion in the next few days, but it looks like it wasn't a bomb or arson. Lots of questions to answer about the entire situation." Johnson waited a beat. "I have a few issues I need to mention to Mr. Leaphorn and Navajo law enforcement. Unless they have more to add, the two civilians can leave now."

Chee, who had been quietly absorbing the information, said, "Captain, I'm not involved in this case. Would you like me to stay?"

"You don't need to, Lieutenant Chee. Would you escort Bowlegs and RP out of the meeting?"

Chee stood. "Come with me, you guys. Let's go to the break room and have some coffee."

Cecil smiled. "Coffee? About time."

Leaphorn waited until they had left the room. "I'm not really part of the explosion investigation, only the missing person segment that involved Mrs. Bowlegs."

"I realize that, but you might have an idea or two for us. Please remain on the call with me a few more minutes, Lieutenant." Johnson was still on the speakerphone, but her presence took charge of the room. "Manuelito, are you still there?"

"I am."

"Bernie, those plans Fisher picked up from you were helpful. You were smart to bring the unopened tubes. The plans inside them had more details for the construction of the special education facility." Johnson cleared her throat. "We spoke to the contractor who had been the successful bidder on the special education building. His plans met code, but he said Morgan delayed the start of the project because he told them the money hadn't arrived in time. The delay meant the original contractor couldn't accept the job, so the school then found someone else who would take on the work, a construction firm from Gallup." The agent mentioned the company's name.

Leaphorn jumped in. "That company is out of business now. They declared bankruptcy after settling a bunch of lawsuits for shoddy workmanship. I heard about it because the case was in tribal court in Window Rock. The CEO went to jail."

"I remember something else about them, too," Bernie said. "A rumor about kickbacks for contracts. I'm not sure the company was ever charged with that, but stories were rampant."

Johnson said, "I've been calling Principal Morgan for the last two hours. No response as of yet, but I left messages at school and on his cell phone. He came to Eagle Roost from Gallup, right?"

"That's correct," Bernie said.

Leaphorn asked, "Did you or one of your agents talk to Morgan about the construction when they were investigating the explosion?"

"Agent Fisher did. Morgan told him he couldn't remember the names of all the companies who had done the work. He said his assistant, Bethany Bowlegs, had handled those details." Johnson paused. "As you all may know by now, the dead woman in the car died from a skull fracture, but it also looks like someone was planning to set the car and the body on fire."

Bernie remembered the red gasoline containers she'd seen in the shed.

"The name of the contractor is not something a principal would forget," Leaphorn said. "Even if a person doesn't have a brain for complex projects like that, the contractor and his subs are always asking questions and wanting the person who pays the bills to authorize changes. You're hearing that name multiple times a week."

"I agree that Morgan was either really distracted, forgetful, or lied to us about the construction," Johnson said. "The investigators are looking at the quality of the build to see if substandard work or defective parts led to or compounded the destruction. What went up at Eagle Roost doesn't jive with what was approved."

Adakai glanced at the clock. "Anything else from anyone? Time to wrap things up before the bus with Bethany Bowlegs comes in."

"Just a quick question," Bernie said. "One of Mrs. Bowlegs's students is also a volunteer with the Eagle Roost fire department. She's worried. Can I tell her Mrs. Bowlegs is alive?"

Agent Johnson jumped in. "Yes. That's fine. Captain Adakai?"

"Yeah?"

"I might need Manuelito's help again. I hope you'll cooperate."

Adakai frowned at the speakerphone. "We'll see what we can do."

Johnson chuckled. "That sounds like a firm maybe, right?"

"Our main responsibility is to our Navajo constituents here, but we'll help if we can. In the meantime, Bernie needs to check on a pack of rogue dogs."

Leaphorn pushed his chair away from the table. "Agent Johnson, I don't have anything else to add. The captain and Manuelito have my phone number if you need my help."

Johnson's voice had a smile in it as she thanked them. "That's all I have for now."

BERNIE HEADED FOR THE BREAK room when the meeting ended. Time for coffee before she went to see Celeste and her mother about the latest attack on the sheep. The school explosion and the body in the car now clearly belonged to Agent Johnson and the FBI.

Leaphorn was at a round table in the break room with Bowlegs, RP, and Chee. Chee glanced up when Bernie opened the door and motioned to her with a nod of his head. "I've got to get back to my desk, but step into the hall with me for a minute."

She did as Chee asked. He gave her a quick, warm hug, even though it was inappropriate at work, before he spoke. "Tell me what happened with Darleen and the car emergency."

Bernie explained. "Then Sister and I had a discussion that led to her asking—no, begging—for more help with Mama. She's at the end of her rope. And with Mrs. Darkwater going in for surgery, the situation is daunting. I don't know what to do."

"Keep your chin up, beautiful. We'll figure this out for your mother."

"What if she needs to live with us?"

Chee smiled at her. "You know, we'll have to find a way to create more room when the day comes that we start a family. If Mama needs a place with us, we can make it work."

Bernie thought about sharing their one-bedroom home with Mama and even a baby, then pushed the chaos to the back of her brain. "I like the *we* in what you said. Thanks."

She took a step away. "Did you learn anything about Principal Morgan with that background check?"

"Yes, but I don't know that it will be of help. He was Teacher of the Month several years in a row when he worked in Gallup. Served there for two years as principal before coming to Eagle Roost. Before he got to Gallup he was involved in a contentious divorce with charges of domestic violence on both sides, charges that were later dropped. He filed for bankruptcy right after he got the Eagle Roost job."

"And now he's driving an expensive car."

"Curious, isn't it?"

BERNIE RETURNED TO THE BREAK room and carried her coffee to their table to sit with her mentor and the two men with him. Lieutenant Leaphorn looked tired, she thought. Looked his age. Looked like he was ready to go home. Who could blame him, after putting up with Cecil Bowlegs?

Bowlegs sat next to RP. They both looked worried.

"There's nothing we can do now," RP said. "The body is at the morgue. We'll know soon enough. That FBI woman might even ask you to identify her."

"It has to be Olivia. But who'd want to kill that fine woman?"

RP shrugged.

Cecil raised his voice. "Who would want to kill her? I mean, she doesn't even know anybody in Eagle Roost except me, you, and Beth. The FBI better figure this out. And did you hear what that agent said about the explosion? If those guys who are after me didn't do it to scare me into paying up, I bet that jerk of a principal will try to pin this on me."

"Now calm down," RP said. "Don't let Morgan get to you."

"Easy for you to say. That man called me stupid more than once and blamed me for what happened. Come on! Why would I want to blow up the place where I work?" He clinched his hand into a fist. "That guy is a two-faced son of a gun. He pretends he's your best friend, and then he screws you."

Bernie asked the question that had been plaguing her. "Cecil, why do you think the building blew up?"

Bowlegs shrugged. "All I know is that I was lucky I went outside after I lit my cigarette to call Mr. Leaphorn. If I'd been in there, well, I wouldn't be sitting here now."

"You've been on the run ever since that explosion," Leaphorn said. "That makes you look suspicious. Why did you do that?"

Cecil shrugged. "We've been over this before, Joe."

"I want Bernie to hear it. More people than just the principal believe you had something to do with the explosion. They think you ran because you were the man who caused the blast. Even if, like we just heard, it wasn't a bomb, it was your job to keep things running, to keep the building safe, right?"

"Yeah, I know." Cecil Bowlegs studied his hands a moment. "I left because I was scared, OK? I owed a bunch of money to some guys who didn't trust me for it because I'd been late with a few of the payments—well, most of the payments—and they didn't like that. I thought they had taken Beth, you know, kidnapped her to get me to pay up. But the thing is, I didn't have the money. That's another reason I ran. I knew of a good poker game in Gallup."

Bernie put her coffee down. "Who was after you?"

He hesitated. "A guy Beth knows."

"What's his name?"

"The King. Let me get the story out first, OK?"

"Go on."

"Beth talked to this guy she knew about loaning us some cash so we could handle the rent and her car payment. She was makin' good money, more after she started that bookkeeping gig with Morgan. So she coulda paid it back."

Bernie said, "If she could have, why didn't she?"

Cecil shrugged.

Leaphorn said, "My assumption has been that Beth disappeared either because of something Cecil did, or because she wanted to sing and got tired of her staid life as a teacher and bookkeeper. The debt could have something to do with it. Because Cecil doesn't want to talk about it, we can ask Beth, can't we?"

"Good idea." RP finished his coffee. "Let's go to the bus station. I'm getting antsy."

"Hold on. It was my gambling. That's why I got that loan." Cecil sounded embarrassed. "I thought I could make us rich with what was left of that money from the loan shark, but I made some bad bets. No way we could repay it. So when the building blew, I figured the man I owed wanted to kill me because he was so angry about the money. Either that, or he thought those goons could scare me into paying up."

"Who loaned you the money?" Bernie asked the question again.

Cecil stared at the ceiling for a moment. "The King. Like I said. It was Big Rex, the leader of the band where Beth liked to sing."

BERNIE AND ROPER BLACK MADE the half-hour drive from Shiprock to T'iis Nazbas, also known as Teec Nos Pos, the closest place for gas to the ranch where the dogs had killed the sheep. Even though Black was still getting the hang of things, they drove in separate units in case another call came in for Bernie.

"I appreciate you coming with me." Black washed the windshield of his unit as he spoke. "I'm finding my way out here, but it can be a challenge."

"You have a good sense of direction, and if you get lost, just see it as a chance to make additional contacts with people in the area. That's what I did as a rookie." She remembered those days with some embarrassment, but she didn't share that. "Did you find out where the dogs involved in that attack came from?"

"No. But I had a couple good conversations with folks involved in spay-and-neuter operations out here. They gave me a schedule for their traveling clinic, and I can spread the word." He put the squeegee back in the water bin and then pulled it out again, walked to Bernie's unit, and started to work on her windshield.

"Finding out when the vet van will be here is great initiative, Roper. You'll do fine out here."

"I hope so. I'm not sure the captain likes me."

"Just keep responding to the calls and treating people with respect. That's what matters. Do the job the best you can." Bernie watched as he washed the road dust off the windshield. "How did you do with Celeste?"

"Fine, I guess. She lost two sheep in the second attack, the one that was wounded and the oldest one in the flock. I told her I was sorry about the sheep that died. She wants to try to trap those dogs, you know? Not just shoot them. I've got a trap for her in the trunk of the unit. I told the folks at the shelter that she might need them to come out and get the animals."

They headed off to Celeste's place, Bernie leading the way. She had a clear cell signal, so she called Nadia's number.

"Officer Manuelito? Wow. I never got a call from a police officer."

"Hi Nadia. I have some good news for you. Mrs. Bowlegs is OK. She's coming back to New Mexico."

"Really?"

"Really!"

"Oh, that's so great. When will she be at school?" Nadia sounded far away.

"I don't know exactly. She's on the bus and gets into Gallup later today."

"Awesome. I'm so happy."

Bernie could hear vehicle noise in the background of Nadia's chatter. "Nadia, I'm glad your phone is on speaker, but if you're driving, we should talk later." She knew beginning drivers were prone to distraction.

"It's OK, Principal Morgan is driving. We're going to Ely's spelling bee."

"Principal Morgan? Why are you in his car?"

"Not just me. Ely too. Ely is the best speller in grades one, two, and three. He even did better than the third graders."

Ely said, "I spelled *ambushing*. Wanna hear me do it now?"

"Not right now." Bernie took a breath. "Principal Morgan, can you hear me?"

"Yes." Morgan's voice was flat. "I heard what you said about Beth. Are you sure about that?"

Bernie avoided the question, chiding herself for talking too much. "Why do you have the children with you?"

"Their mother got called to work at the hospital, so she asked me if I would take Ely to the semifinal spelling bee. I always go to represent our school anyway and cheer for the kids. Nadia wanted to be there for her brother, so she came with us. You know, Bernie, it's nice to get away from campus, to have time to see something different, time to look at your life. Think fresh thoughts."

"What are you thinking?" She paused a split second. "You sound discouraged."

It was as if Morgan expected her to ask. "So a guy like me works hard to get ahead, and then an idiot janitor makes a mistake and years of work get blown away. It's difficult to take. That pushy woman from the FBI keeps calling. I've done the best job I could, given Eagle Roost my all. That school meant everything to me. Everything. You know that, right?"

Before she could answer, he changed the subject. "Do you like spelling bees?"

"Sure." She'd never been to one, but she needed to see where Morgan was headed. "What's not to love about a bunch of smart kids?"

"Come and join us. Ely and the girl representing the older Eagle Roost kids could use a cheering section."

"When does it start?"

He told her. "These contests are usually over quickly."

Nadia said, "Please come."

The school was on her way to the sheep lady assignment, and Bernie knew she could let Roper handle the call until she arrived. Both Morgan's tone and the fact that he was responsible for the two children set off warning bells.

"I'll stop by. It's on my way."

She ended the call, then reached Roper on the radio. "I'll be there when I can, but begin the interview with Celeste, OK?"

"Of course. Do what you need to."

Bernie hung up and sped toward the school for the contest. She saw quite a few cars in the lot outside the gymnasium and parked next to Morgan's fancy Lexus. Inside, one of the booster clubs had set up tables for selling drinks, popcorn, and cookies. A platform with three chairs stood in the middle of the gym floor, and a microphone perched on a metal pole in front of the judges. Two women and a man with his long hair in braids waited at the table for the contest to begin. The man chatted with the woman in the center seat, while the other glanced through some papers in front of her. From the judges' body language, Bernie assumed the spelling champions from each school would start to approach the microphone soon.

Ely was sitting with the other spelling contenders, and he waved shyly to Bernie. He and the taller girl next to him wore matching yellow T-shirts that read EAGLE ROOST SPELLING CHAMPS. Bernie was glad she was in her uniform; it made it easier for Ely to spot her. Some of the children looked sweaty. Some, like Nadia's brother, fidgeted. Some sat as still as death. The air near them smelled of nervousness.

Bernie was uneasy, too. She'd said too much on the phone before she realized Morgan could hear her. She knew he was hiding something, and she believed it had to do with Beth. She glanced up at the bleachers, where the seats were filled at about a third of capacity. A good crowd for a spelling contest. A bit of motion caught her eye, and she saw Nadia and the principal motioning to her to join them. Morgan wore a sleek sport coat, a well-tailored dress shirt, and a tie—his principal's uniform—and Nadia wore a cream-colored sweater.

Bernie climbed up the bleachers to them and sat next to Nadia.

Morgan started talking right away. "I'm glad you could join us, Officer. Something's come up, and I have to leave." He turned his focus to Nadia. "Officer Manuelito will be here with you. I know Ely will do just fine."

Nadia looked at the judges sitting at their table. "Where do you have to go? Can't you even wait until my brother gets his first word?"

"I'm sorry, sweetie, but I just remembered I have to get to Gallup. I have to do something important there this afternoon. I know Ely will do well. Please tell him I'm sorry I can't stay."

Bernie tried to keep the anxiety out of her voice. "Wait a minute. Don't leave yet. You said you wanted to talk to me. That's the reason I'm here."

"I do want to tell you something."

Morgan reached in his pocket, pulled out his wallet, and gave Nadia some money. "Young lady, would you please go down to the concession table and get me a bottle of water?"

"What about Officer Manuelito?" Nadia glanced at her. "She might want a drink or something."

Bernie thought about it. "I'd love a Coke, but water is fine."

Morgan grinned at Nadia. "Get something for yourself, too, and a cookie for Ely."

As soon as the girl left, he gave Bernie a sad smile. "I submitted my letter of resignation as principal last night. That's what I wanted to tell you. You helped me realize that I'm not the right person for the job. The kids and their families need someone who knows how to handle a terrible budget, how to hire the best people in a remote area, how to understand the community better than I can. And more. That isn't me."

Bernie decided the role of concerned acquaintance offered more possibilities for insight than police interrogator. "What are you going to do?"

"Clean up my mess and start over again."

"What mess?"

He exhaled, pursing his lips. "It's complicated. Some old business that bothers me."

"Tell me."

He stared at his knees. "I can't."

"There's no one alive who hasn't made a mountain of mistakes. We all have to figure out how to live with our failures, to shake off the disappointment and try to do better next time." Bernie thought she sounded like her own mother. "What prompted you to resign?"

"I realized it's time for me to move on. Like I said, a chance to start over."

"Why leave now? Because of the explosion?"

He rose. "Thank you so much for coming, Bernie. I couldn't leave the children here alone. Tell Nadia to keep the change. Take care of them."

"No." Bernie stood, too. "I'm not a babysitter. Wait. Tell me what you know about the body."

But Morgan skirted to the right, where the bleachers were empty, and trotted down. She started after him but a family group moved in to block her way. She noticed Nadia climbing up toward where they had been sitting, the girl's hands filled with her purchases, her eyes focused on the steps. At that moment, the judge seated in the center reached for her microphone and the building filled with colossal, ear-piercing feedback.

"Welcome to the Chuska Mountains spelling bee championship. Before we get started, I'd like everyone here to please rise for the Pledge of Allegiance."

Nadia stopped, put the cookies and drinks she held on the stairs, and placed her palm over her heart.

Bernie brushed the girl's shoulder and spoke in her ear. "Go back to your seat when you can, and I'll be there soon." Then she raced down the bleachers, avoiding people who frowned at her when she passed, and ran into the parking lot. The delay had only cost her minutes, but Principal Morgan's car was gone.

Bernie pulled out her phone and dialed Captain Adakai. She'd have to follow up with Morgan after she settled the children safely.

Bernie quickly explained the situation, then added some background. "Sir you might not know that an eyewitness saw Morgan drive Bethany's car into the garage where the body was discovered. He just resigned from a job he loved, and he's talking about new beginnings. To me, that means he's either going on the run, or plans to drive to the bus station."

Captain Adakai said, "Let me see if I've got this straight. Instead of doing your job, you are at the Chuska Mountains spelling bee because Morgan asked you to join him, and you were concerned about the kids. You think Morgan killed a woman and plans to go on the run but first might do something dangerous at the Gallup bus station."

"Yes, sir. That's pretty much it."

"Go do your assignment. Get back to Black. I'll let Agent Johnson know."

"Captain, I can't leave here until I've made sure the children are safe. Black can handle the dog problem."

Before the captain could object, she continued.

"Morgan doesn't seem like a violent man, but I have a clear sense that the situation has pushed him to the edge. I want to see this to the end."

The phone was quiet and she could practically hear the captain thinking about what to say, whether to change his mind or send her to the sheep case. He might even order her into the station, write her up, send her home.

As she waited, she saw Ely stand, walk bravely to the microphone, and spell his first word, *shed*. Bernie clapped for him as she waited for Adakai's response.

"Lieutenant Leaphorn is working with the Gallup police on Beth as a missing person." The captain's voice was devoid of emotion. "We'll call them and suggest that they have officers present when Beth's bus comes in, just in case. Call Leaphorn and tell him what you learned about Morgan. You have a sheep case to deal with, and I don't want Roper Black handling it on his own."

"I'll call Leaphorn. Then, sir, I have to take the rest of the day off for personal reasons."

"Oh, right." She heard the sarcasm. "Manuelito, we need to have a long chat tomorrow about your attitude. I can't—"

She interrupted. "I heard you say all right. Thanks sir. But you're breaking up."

"Officer, get back here. I didn't—"

She interrupted. "Sir? Sir? Sorry, but I've lost you. If you can hear me, I'll make sure the students are OK and then . . ." She left the sentence dangling and pressed the button to end the call.

With Nadia's help, she found the mother of the other child from Eagle Roost. The woman readily agreed to give Nadia and Ely a ride home when Ely finished.

Bernie headed for Gallup, regretting Morgan's head start. She had a soft spot in her heart for sheep, but they'd have to wait.

29

Bethany Benally Bowlegs hadn't realized that the trip from Tucson to Gallup by bus took forever.

Phoenix.

Glendale.

Flagstaff would be the next stop. And then, eventually, Gallup.

Earlier on the trip she looked out the Greyhound window and saw the green highway signs for the exit to Grand Canyon National Park.

After this came Holbrook, the second-to-last stop. Then, finally, she'd be home in New Mexico.

The bus was scheduled to arrive in Gallup a little after dark. She hoped her clan brother would meet her there. And, even more strongly, she hoped Cecil would be with him. She wondered if they both could understand why she had made such a huge mistake and forgive her.

Riding the bus was not her favorite mode of transportation, but it was better than staying by herself at her sister's place in Tucson. Especially now that she'd figured out what she had to do. It had taken her longer than she'd expected to come to terms with her mistakes. It might have taken even longer if Olivia had not given her a taste of her own medicine.

Olivia knew that Beth was a free spirit at heart, so her sister, her very best friend in the world, didn't seem surprised when Beth asked if she could stay with her awhile to get her head together.

"Sure. How long do you think awhile will be? A day? A year? A lifetime?"

Beth laughed. "I don't know. You can kick me out when you get sick of me."

"No. Even if I wanted to send you home, I have to be nice to you until you give me that diyogí." Olivia winked at her.

"Oh, I will. Our grandmother gave us that rug to share."

"Yes. The one you and Bowlegs still have. The one you keep promising to bring next time you come to Tucson. I'm still waiting."

"Point taken. I'll put it in the car. I'll be there tomorrow."

"Just you and the rug?"

"Yes. Legs is part of the problem."

Olivia laughed. "That man can be a walking headache. It's a good thing he's cute."

"Bowlegs thinks you're cute, too."

"You're his true love, and you know it. He just likes to flirt with me because I look like you."

Beth could recall the times they'd been mistaken for each other. She was only a year older than Olivia, and the physical resemblance was undeniable. They reinforced it by getting matching tattoos when Olivia turned eighteen.

"It will be great to be with you. Is this your school's spring break or something?"

"No. I quit that job."

"Seriously?"

"Seriously. Outta there."

"I don't get it. You loved teaching music. You just got a promotion or something. What's up?"

Beth sucked in a breath. "I had to leave. I'm in huge trouble."

"What happened?"

"It's complicated. We'll talk later, OK? We'll talk when I bring the rug."

But in her rush to leave Eagle Roost, she left the rug behind in her office, where she'd used it to hide the classroom's uneven flooring. She apologized for forgetting, and Olivia forgave her, but Beth could tell she had disappointed her sister. And keeping it at Olivia's place would be smart. In addition to winning the blue ribbon at Santa Fe's prestigious Indian Market, the rug had been featured in several magazine stories about Navajo weaving. A collector had offered them $20,000 for it. But of course it was not for sale.

After dinner and conversation, Olivia went to bed. That was when Beth went back to her car and removed the gym bag with the cash she'd withdrawn from her secret stash. She brought the bag into her sister's house and slipped it into the guest room closet without Olivia noticing or asking questions.

Now, the bag with the twenties Big Rex had demanded was at her feet on the bus. He told her he was sending a couple of his employees to pick it up at the station. No worries, he said. Just pay the debt, and all would be well.

The sisters' time together in Tucson rolled along quickly. Olivia went to her job at the library, and Beth walked, read, shopped for groceries, cooked for them, cleaned the house, and spent a lot of time worrying about her situation. In the evenings, she and Olivia talked about growing up on the Navajo reservation, about their old friends from those days. In honor of the meals their dear shimásání made, one night Beth fixed mutton stew.

After Bethany had been in Tucson a week, her sister surprised her by mentioning that she knew a hataałii through her work with cultural awareness at the library. "He's coming this weekend to see his daughter at the University of Arizona. What if I invited him to come and talk to us?"

When the healer had arrived, they talked about Beth's disappointment in her husband, her big mistake, and her deep fear. Then he prayed and sang over her and smudged her with the fragrant smoke from a sage stick. After that her head started to clear. Thanks to time and the hataałii's healing prayers, she began to grow strong enough to consider returning home and telling the truth. She had to explain her bad decisions and try to make things right with the people she'd hurt.

She told Olivia of her plan. Her sister gave her a long hug and then made a request.

"Before you go, I'd like to borrow your car for a quick road trip. I don't have to work Monday, and I can take Friday as a personal day." Beth knew Olivia's vehicle needed serious attention. It was safe enough for errands in Tucson, but neither of them would trust it on the highway.

"Of course you can take my car. Want some company?"

"As much as I love you, no. I'm craving some quiet private time."

Beth understood. She'd lived alone before she met Cecil, and sharing a space with someone had been a big transition. Olivia had been a gracious host, so Beth filled the car with gas and even took it to the Mr. Mister car wash before her sister headed off.

Olivia started her road trip, destination undetermined, early Friday with a bright smile and a travel mug of coffee. When she called from Sedona, she said she'd be back no later than Monday evening, in time to get to her job on Tuesday. "That is, unless I decide to become a woman of the road."

Beth laughed. Her sister was fun, but not wild. "If you go feral, what about my car? I'll need it back, you know."

"No worries. I'm planning to sleep in Tucson Tuesday." Olivia chuckled. "I may turn into a wild woman, but never a car thief."

And after that conversation from Sedona, radio silence. Beth called and texted and got no response. The Tuesday Olivia was supposed to return came and went. Her boss from the library stopped at the apartment to see if Olivia was ill, and Beth had no answer. She itched to drive home to Eagle Roost, but was carless until Olivia showed up.

Then, early on Sunday, she learned that her school had been the site of an explosion. No children were hurt, thank goodness, but the incident added an exclamation point to her resolve to return to New Mexico. Deeply distrustful of Olivia's car, she used her computer to buy a ticket on the bus to Gallup—the closest station to Eagle Roost. When the time came, she gathered her luggage, locked the apartment, called for a ride, and took the first steps to reclaiming her life.

She hadn't been on a bus for a long time, and her ignorance led to discomfort. In her old life as a teacher and bookkeeper and the principal's right-hand helper, she moved around a lot during the day. The students and the new assignment from Morgan kept her busy. She wasn't used to sitting for hours, and her body rebelled.

She quickly realized that she should have brought a pillow for her neck. She wished she had a bottle of water and some snacks in her carry-on. She had a lot to talk about when she reunited with Cecil and RP, and she wanted to be at her best.

She liked her window seat, except that the young woman next to her was even more restless that she was. Twitchy, constantly fiddling with her phone, crossing and uncrossing her legs, rummaging through her purse. Beth had told herself she was keeping quiet on the trip, but the woman irritated her to the point of distraction. How could she focus on getting her head on straight with this annoying cricket next her?

She stared at the young woman, and finally the woman turned to her. "Hey, you're Songbird Begay, right?"

"It's Benally, but yeah. That's me."

"I heard you and that band in Gallup. You guys are awesome. I love your voice. Is the band still out there?"

Beth noticed that the woman had a tongue stud. "Yeah, but I took a break from them."

"You were the best part. What happened?"

"Oh, life got in the way."

The girl nodded. "It had to do with money, right?"

It did, but Beth didn't want to talk about it. "Do you sing?"

The girl laughed. "Badly. Not at all like you. No one would want to hear me, but I love to listen to music. I left my headphones at my boyfriend's place, and I'm jonesing without my tunes."

Beth said she would feel unsettled, too, without music in her life. "I teach music, and I know almost everyone can learn basic singing. Just having a solid foundation, getting a feel for what makes music work, gives a person confidence. You might not be a star, but you could learn to carry a tune."

As she spoke, Beth realized the same was true of most things. Cecil for instance, dabbled in a lot of things without mastering any of them, but he had confidence in his janitorial work at the Eagle Roost School. The report she'd heard about the explosion said the cause was "under investigation." Her husband had his flaws, but she couldn't imagine him doing something that would create such destruction.

The bus began to slow and then took an exit off Interstate 40 east into Flagstaff. The girl leaned forward to look out the window and watch as the community came into view, then settled back into her seat. "When we stop in Flagstaff, I'll buy some headphones. And some cigarettes. This trip has been a killer."

"Do you get another bus here?"

"No, I'm from Flag. I'm going back to my parents' place. They own the Emerald. You heard of it?"

"Yeah." The club had a reputation as a good venue for bands.

"The Hop Toads ought to play there. Dad brings in lots of groups, and they get an audience. He pays, too. You wouldn't just be singing for tips."

"Sounds good."

"So, Songbird, let's put my name in your phone in case you wanna come up here to do a show."

Everyone stepped off at Flagstaff for a half-hour break. Before she went inside, Beth tried calling Cecil again. When that didn't work, she called RP and left a voicemail telling him that she was OK and where she was and asking him to let Cecil know she was on her way home. She told them when the bus would arrive, and that she hoped someone could pick her up. She couldn't blame her husband for ignoring her. Cecil had called her dozens of times since she'd left home, and she'd ignored him, not even listening to his messages.

Beth walked around the Flagstaff station a while, bought some chips and a cup of sweet French vanilla coffee, and reclaimed her window seat when the bus doors opened. Her spirits had lifted, and she felt more optimistic than she had in months.

As the bus began to move, she considered the fact that even though Cecil would never stop gambling, his luck improved periodically. What if he had won enough so she could pay back the rest of the missing money? She doubted that Morgan would rat her out. After all, he'd accepted what she offered to buy his silence.

The landscape between Flagstaff and Holbrook sprawled before her through the bus window, expansive and full of possibilities. On the horizon she saw the sacred mountains of the Navajo Nation in the distance. It felt good to be going home.

This time the seat next to her was occupied by an elderly man. She could tell he was an Indian of some kind even before he told her he was originally from Zuni and had been in California to see his brother. They chatted a bit, then he said he needed to sleep and asked her to wake him when they got to Holbrook.

She'd almost dozed off when she felt her phone ring. It was RP.

"Hello out there." She spoke softly so as not to awaken her seatmate.

"Oh Beth. Baby! We thought you must be dead."

"What? Gosh, no. I'm sorry I didn't stay in touch. I had a lot to think about, but I've got it figured out. Can you or Cecil meet me in Gallup?" She told him where the bus would stop. "Why did you think I was dead?"

RP said, "Well, there was this, ah, this situation at your school, but I'll tell you about that when you get to Gallup. We're there now, and we'll see you when the bus comes in."

She switched her phone to music and put on her headphones. But too many of the tunes on her playlist were songs that the band had covered. She could have kicked herself for making that arrangement with Rex. When he decided to collect the debt, she should have stood her ground, said no, let him kick her out of the band if it came to that. But the Songbird liked the gigs and the energy of the dark clubs. She had needed the contrast between her staid life as a teacher and bookkeeper and the rush of being onstage with a microphone, and dressed in lace and leather.

She found an audiobook instead of music, but it wasn't engrossing enough to engage the brain cells that tended to worry. She envied her seatmate sleeping calmly as the bus rolled east toward the Painted Desert, and then Gallup.

30

The call from Chee helped Joe Leaphorn connect the dots—the missing Bethany, the school explosion, the body in the car. He called Detective Short and explained.

"What time is the bus due?"

Leaphorn told her.

"OK then. We'll give that area some extra surveillance. You know, I'm only doing this because you are who you are. If you weren't Joe Leaphorn, things might be different."

"I understand. The officers who alerted us to this situation get things right." He knew it was better to be overprepared for a crisis than not ready. "And there's the other threat, the men who tried to intimidate Bowlegs."

"Bowlegs was halfway credible about that when I interviewed him. We'll handle it."

Traffic on Interstate 40 had been light, and a gentle spring breeze stirred up a few stray plastic bags that drifted along the shoulder. Now, as the afternoon wore on, the wind had started to gust, and the air had begun to cloud with blowing dirt. His truck needed a new tailgate after the incident with Kory, but it still ran fine and he felt more confident in it than Louisa's car.

Leaphorn pulled into the station parking lot with his passengers about twenty minutes before the bus was due. The place where the bus stopped wasn't a station like they showed on TV with a big sign outside, a ticket office, seating, restrooms, maybe a snack bar. No, this was a little all-purpose market and gas station just off Interstate 40 on old Route 66 on the west side of town. He saw only a pack of semis parked here, three passenger cars and no buses. He parked away from the store entrance and turned off the engine.

RP, who sat next to the door, undid his seat belt. "I'm gonna see if they've got coffee inside. You guys want some?"

Cecil nodded. "Milk in mine."

"No thanks," Leaphorn said. "Check to see if the bus is on time while you're in there."

"No problem."

When RP got out of the truck, Leaphorn noticed that the air smelled of dust. Spring brought wind that, they said, blew away the winter cold. It was his fourth favorite season. Spring always made him restless, and Leaphorn felt edgy now.

After RP left, Leaphorn turned to Cecil. "What's bothering you? Cheer up."

"What do you mean?"

"Your wife is alive, and she's going to be here in a few minutes. I thought you'd be happy about that. And the FBI now believes the explosion at Eagle Roost wasn't a bomb. You don't have to worry about being accused of setting off explosives there."

"I am happy."

"You don't look happy." Leaphorn studied him a minute. "Something's on your mind. You're afraid of something. If you talk to me, maybe I can help. You called me, remember?"

Cecil took a few moments to loosen his seat belt. "Well, there's lots of stuff goin' on, you know? The explosion. Beth coming home. The body in her car that's not her after all. The fact that her Ford is toast, and we'll have to get another car now."

First savor the joy of homecoming, Leaphorn thought. There'll be plenty of time for pain.

Cecil spoke more quickly. "And, oh yeah. Someone tried to kill me last night, tracking me down here, a long way from Eagle Roost."

"Tell me about that again. What did the men in that big SUV say?"

"Somethin' like, 'Get in the car, you jerk.' They didn't even ask me about the money. I think the money dude is so furious he just wants my legs broke or whatever." Bowlegs rubbed the bridge of his nose. "I figure he's the same guy who made the school blow. He'd know how to make it look like an accident, you know? Like I screwed up on my job."

"Big Rex, right?"

Bowlegs nodded.

"Why didn't you tell me this sooner?"

"It's over, man. Done with. As dead as a doughnut." Bowlegs stared out the window.

Leaphorn looked out, too, watching for RP as he pieced a scenario together.

"Describe the black car."

Cecil talked about the SUV with a mechanic's sense of detail. Leaphorn could picture it.

RP came back with coffee and a cold drink for himself. He handed the coffee to his friend through the open window. "They said the bus is running a few minutes late."

Leaphorn had parked in the rear of the lot, away from other vehicles, out of habit. Ever since getting ambushed outside a hotel years ago, he'd grown wary of anyone parking next to his truck. He'd recovered physically, but other scars were deeper and perhaps permanent. However, the implicit threat in Cecil's story about the Escalade meant that he needed to keep an eye on the road in front of the bus station. If the men who tried to kill Bowlegs were as smart as he thought they might be, they would be back, anticipating that Cecil Bowlegs might take the next bus out of town.

And he remembered Bernie's concern about the school principal who seemed to be coming unhinged, and how he might pose a threat to Bethany Bowlegs and her husband. "I'm going to move the truck so I can keep an eye on the road while we wait for the bus," he said. "I want to make sure you're safe if that SUV shows up."

"I'm tired of being afraid," Cecil said. "And I'm tired of sitting here." He reached for the door handle.

"Stay in the truck," Leaphorn snapped.

Cecil's glare was like black ice. "Leaphorn, let's get this straight. I paid you to find my wife. That's all. She's not missing anymore. We're done, and you're not my bodyguard."

"Actually, you haven't paid me anything yet. If you don't want my help, fine, but I told Agent Johnson I'd make sure you stayed safe until she could talk to you about the explosion, remember? And you agreed to cooperate."

A silver Lexus sedan—sleek, elegant, and out of place—turned into the lot. The car backed into a vacant parking spot near the station entrance, close to the area where Leaphorn expected the bus driver to unload his passengers.

Cecil started to open the truck door, but RP called to him from outside. "Cecil, stay put. The guys who tried to kill you could be on their way. You want to die before the bus gets here? How dumb are you?"

Cecil pushed the door open anyway, slamming it against RP's arm, causing the large drink he was holding to fly out of his hands, drenching the front of his shirt in the process. Cecil charged out of the truck, heading toward the front of the store, but stopped when he saw RP's shirt.

He turned back toward his friend. "Sorry."

"You idiot." RP's voice was full of anger as he wiped his damp hands on his pant legs. "Look what you did. I'm a mess, and Beth is almost here."

"You're the dumb one, dude. Why didn't you get out of my way? I need to stand there by the store so Beth will see me when the bus pulls in."

"Cecil, get back here and wait until we see the bus coming in," Leaphorn said. "There's plenty of time, and—"

"Stop telling me what to do," Cecil yelled, adding some swear words. "I'm tired of taking orders from everybody."

RP grabbed for his friend's arm. "You're gonna get yourself killed."

Cecil squirmed free and threw a punch that didn't connect.

Leaphorn ran toward the confrontation, wishing he was thirty years younger. Cecil had his hands on RP's shoulders and was screaming at his friend. "If you had given me that loan, none of this mess would have happened."

"You already owe me more money than I'll ever see. You're the reason she ran off. What kind of a man makes his wife pay his poker debts? I offered to loan her the money, and she told me no, she'd figure out another way. The name for you, buddy, is loser." RP was yelling now, too. "This is all your fault, Bowlegs!"

"Hey." Leaphorn kept his voice calm, even though he had to speak loudly to be heard over the howling wind. "Cool it, both of you. Calm down and—"

"RP, you're a stinkin' liar." Cecil added some choice swear words.

"You've got it all wrong, buddy. You need to sit down with your wife."

Cecil shoved RP's chest. RP took a step back and held up his hands in surrender. Cecil shoved him again.

Leaphorn moved toward Cecil. "Bowlegs, calm down."

Automatically drawn to the sound of his voice, Cecil turned toward Leaphorn, swung, and struck the older man in the jaw. The unexpected blow nearly sent Leaphorn to the ground. Shocked, RP pulled Cecil away from Leaphorn, who had his hand on his injured face. "Come on, buddy. Relax, OK?"

"Shut up, bro. I told you I'm sick to death of people telling me what to do." Cecil broke free and looked up. A black SUV was turning into the parking lot, headed toward the gas pumps. A thin, nervous-looking man in a black jacket climbed out.

"Oh God." Cecil seemed to grow smaller as he spoke. "That's them. That's Ramon. Earbuds must be with him. They are here for Beth. They probably want to kill her, too, kill us both." And then Cecil headed for the store at a dead run.

Leaphorn saw a Navajo police unit drive up and park next to his truck. He watched Officer Bernadette Manuelito climb out and jog toward them.

"Sir? Your lip is bleeding."

"I'm OK."

He took the tissue she offered, and blotted away the blood. He realized that his face hurt, and he had a pounding headache. "Manuelito, I'm surprised to see you here."

She raised her eyebrows. "What happened to you, sir?"

"Cecil was having a tantrum. Caught me off guard, but I'm fine."

"You need a better class of clientele."

Leaphorn chuckled. "That's what Louisa tells me. Cecil says that SUV over there is the one that the men who grabbed him were driving. He called the driver Ramon and says he thinks they work for Big Rex. That's the name of the bandleader. Give me a minute." Leaphorn made a quick call to Detective Short, then went back to Bernie.

"What brings you here, Manuelito?"

"Well, partly intuition. A man lied to me, but it took me a while to figure out why. Then I got a text from Agent Johnson with some new developments that concerned the autopsy on the body." She turned to the store where the fancy silver car was parked then back toward Leaphorn. "Have you seen the person who drove that Lexus?"

"I saw the car pull up, but no one's gotten out, as far as I know." Leaphorn moved his chin. Bernie looked in that direction and saw the bus, still just a spot in the distance, approaching from the west. They watched it approach, wondering what Beth Bowlegs would have to say about her reappearance.

Leaphorn noticed the change in Bernie's posture as a well-dressed man left the Lexus and stood in the cool April air, also watching the bus advance toward the station.

"Who is that?"

"It's Charles Morgan," she said. "He's the principal at Eagle Roost. Or he was. I'm worried he means to harm Beth."

Leaphorn noticed the fellow with the Escalade at the gas pump looking west, too. That man stood straighter, as though at the sight of the bus, his batteries had been recharged.

Leaphorn realized his own energy was flagging. He was ready to go home. He needed to wash the blood off his face and clean up as best as he could before facing Louisa. She had enough on her mind with her son and Lin. No need to worry about him. He went inside the convenience store to buy a small box of bandages and get a cup of ice to help with the cleanup. And swelling. He had plenty of time before the bus got there, and two police officers were already on site.

Inside, he saw RP looking at the colorful display of candy. "Beth loves chocolate, and I bet she's hungry. I'm going to get her some treats."

"Where's Cecil?"

RP shook his head. "Hiding somewhere inside here. He freaked out over the black Escalade at the gas pump."

Leaphorn went into the restroom, where he did the best he could with soap, water, and the bandages to conceal the damage to his face. He washed his face and smoothed his hair. He saw shoes he recognized beneath the door in one of the stalls.

"Cecil?

"Is the bus here?"

"Not yet. Another few minutes. You can tell when the male passengers rush in to use the facilities."

"Right."

"I called the Gallup police about that SUV. They will have someone here shortly."

"That's fine, but I'm staying in this stall until you or RP come to tell me it's safe out there."

Leaphorn left the restroom. He could see the bus approaching the store's street-facing windows. It stopped at a traffic light. He prided himself on his ability to judge speed and distance, and estimated that it would pull up in about two minutes.

The well-dressed man and Bernie were talking. Then the man stepped away from her, pulled out his phone, and typed something. He stared at the phone a moment, then slipped it into a slim leather case on his belt.

Leaphorn left the store and approached them. Before he could ask about the man, Bernie's phone buzzed, and she looked at the screen and then at him. "It's Agent Johnson, Lieutenant. She and I have been playing phone tag. I need to take this."

She walked toward her unit, phone at her ear. Leaphorn turned to the man. "I never had a chance to introduce myself. Principal Morgan, I'm a private investigator, Joe Leaphorn. I was helping Cecil find his wife.

We were worried that she might have been the body in that car that was discovered after the explosion. I'm not surprised to see you here."

Morgan kept his eyes on the bus. "I met Officer Manuelito when she was investigating the school explosion. She mentioned that Mrs. Bowlegs was coming home. Beth worked for me, so I came to welcome her back. The station, if you can call it that, was on my way, and I don't have to be back at school this afternoon."

After decades in law enforcement, Leaphorn could tell when someone like Morgan was lying to him, or giving him only part of the truth. "You're here for another reason, too, aren't you?"

Morgan stared straight ahead.

"It's cool out here, but I see that you're sweating. I'm wondering why you seem nervous."

"I have to talk to Beth about something important, something she doesn't want to hear."

"What's that?"

"Oh, it's complicated. It's about an arrangement we had that I have to get out of."

The breeze had come up again, blowing sand across the road. Leaphorn saw paper food wrappers trapped in the wire fence, dancing in the wind like banners. And now, on old Highway 66, he saw the Gallup black-and-white moving toward the bus stop.

"A deal, huh? What kind of arrangement?"

Morgan dodged the question. "Mr. Leaphorn, you seem tense, too. Why is that?"

"I'm not a fan of spring wind. I find it unsettling."

"What brought you here?"

Leaphorn thought of the most concise answer. "I want to see the woman who disappeared get home safely."

The bus slowed down as it neared the turn for the parking lot, and rolled to a stop. It sat for a few minutes, and then the driver opened the door. Morgan walked toward the bus, and Leaphorn did the same. From the corner of his eye, he noticed that the black SUV was moving toward the parked bus and the front of the store.

After a few moments, the passengers began to climb down the steps and walk toward the building. A slim Navajo woman was in the middle of the group. Leaphorn moved toward her. "Bethany Benally Bowlegs?"

"Yes. Who are—" She looked over his shoulder and spotted Morgan. Leaphorn saw her expression change from neutral to something between surprise and disgust.

"I'm Lieutenant Joe Leaphorn. . ."

And then Bernie was there. "I'm Officer Bernadette Manuelito. Bethany Bowlegs, you are under arrest for embezzlement from Eagle Roost School."

"What? No. I can explain. The money's right here. I just borrowed it." She indicated a bag she'd dropped at her feet. "I was bringing it back. I swear."

Leaphorn unzipped the container. He saw more money than he'd even seen outside of a bank vault. He zipped the bag shut.

"This is all a terrible mistake. Cecil?" Beth's voice had some energy. "Where's my Cecil?"

"He's OK. He's in the building." Leaphorn noticed that RP was also missing.

"Officer Manuelito, just call Big Rex. He can explain everything. He told me to do the right thing."

Bernie pulled the woman out of the bus line and handcuffed her quickly. The Gallup police arrived and helped keep the scene calm. Leaphorn gave them the bag of money, Beth's purse, and everything she'd had on the bus, as possible evidence. Then he went back near the bus to wait for Cecil.

Principal Morgan stood watching, too, and Leaphorn saw a Gallup officer walk toward him.

She asked Morgan his name, and then Leaphorn heard her say, "You need to come with me, sir. We need to talk to you about Olivia Benally."

"Who?"

The officer repeated the name. Morgan looked baffled, but Leaphorn understood.

"She's the woman you killed," Leaphorn said. "The one you assumed was Beth. The person you thought had damaged your school."

The officer's voice was tinged with impatience. "Mr. Morgan? Let's go." She recited the Miranda rights and turned on her body cam recorder.

Morgan looked sick and miserable. He turned to Leaphorn. "It was dark. They were the same height, the same build, same hair, so much alike. I saw Beth's car and a woman who looked like Beth in Beth's office. She kept screaming when she saw me, something about how she'd left her purse on the desk to carry the rug to the car. I was reaching for her to calm her down, but I tripped over that bad board and lost my balance. I fell on her and pushed her into the wall, and she hit her head hard and then bashed it again when she fell to the floor. I never meant to kill anyone. I'd undo everything right now if I could."

"Really?" Leaphorn's voice was full of skepticism. "But you used the money Beth gave you to buy that expensive new car."

"I can explain. I didn't buy that car. Beth did. She registered it in my name and paid for it with a check from the school construction fund, forging my signature She was damaging our beautiful school, stealing money that should have gone to improvements for the kids. I'd asked her to stop and threatened to call the police, but she told me her husband would be hurt if she didn't pay off his debts. So Beth bought the car to shut me up. I told her I didn't want it."

The officer with Morgan stood stone-faced. "Let's go." Morgan nodded and accompanied her without a struggle. Bernie had already taken Bethany Benally Bowlegs to her patrol car to drive her to jail.

Leaphorn watched both police cars cruise away, and, shortly after that, the black SUV. He saw RP standing in front of the store with the bag of candy and walked over to him. He explained the situation.

RP shook his head. "I can't believe all this. I'll tell Cecil."

"I'll explain it to him while we're on our way to the police station in Gallup. They'll keep him there as a material witness, a guy whose life was threatened and a person of interest in the school explosion."

JIM CHEE WAS NEAR THE end of this shift when the black Escalade sped past his unit. Traffic was light, but traveling ninety miles an hour on the road marked for seventy-five made driving interesting.

He turned on his light bar. He saw the brake lights flash on the vehicle in front of him and the turn signal come on. Chee slowed and followed the car onto the shoulder, got the license plate number and called it in, then drove around and stopped in back of it. He called for backup, but learned that the closest officer was fifteen minutes out. Not bad for this vast coverage area, but in the meantime, he was on his own.

He approached the car on the driver's side. When the driver rolled down his window, Chee noticed that the front-seat passenger with the white audio receiver in his ear was fidgeting, tapping his fingertips on his pant legs.

Chee said good evening, told the men his name and that he had pulled them over for speeding, and asked to see his driver's license and proof of insurance and registration.

The driver didn't move to comply or raise a protest. He just sat.

The passenger removed his earbuds, opened the console, and handed Chee two of the three items. Then he tapped the driver's shoulder. "Hey, Ramon. You in there?"

No response.

Chee spoke more loudly. "Sir, I need your driver's license. Now."

Ramon finally extracted his wallet and gave the license to Chee.

Chee went back to his unit, got the report on the license plate, and checked on his backup. Ten minutes out. While he waited, he sensed an opportunity.

He went back to the car.

"Gentlemen, this car strongly resembles a vehicle that has been involved in a kidnapping and assault."

The driver stiffened in the seat. The passenger said nothing.

"Let's talk a minute, just the three of us, before the report comes in to confirm that." Chee turned on his recorder. "I think you guys have heard of someone named Cecil Bowlegs."

The driver laughed. "Oh boy. That's one crazy canary."

"Shut up, Ramon."

"Well, Mr. Bowlegs got a good description of the two men who tried to kidnap him, and they look a lot like you guys. But if you tell me who pays you, I might be able to make some of this go away, you know? Free up the little fish in exchange for the whale."

Ramon ran his hands through his hair. "You're lying about that Bowlegs guy, right? It was dark, man. He couldn't have seen much."

"You're an idiot," Earbuds said.

Ramon said, "This cop didn't read us our rights or nothing, man. This won't stick."

Chee said, "This car is registered to Alvin Rexworth. That's not you, is it, Ramon? Or your buddy here."

"Not us. No way. That's the boss."

"You guys were just doing a job, right? And you didn't actually hurt Cecil, and you wouldn't even have been there if it hadn't been for the boss, right?"

"You got it, man." Earbuds exhaled with relief. "The boss just wanted us to scare that joker into paying what he owed. We wouldn't have hurt him too bad."

Chee knew that they would face charges for kidnapping and aggravated assault or perhaps attempted murder. No need to get into that now, he thought. He waited to hear what they had to say.

Chee saw the lights of another patrol car headed toward him. "That's real helpful. Do you know where your boss is?"

"Yeah. The band has a gig in Gallup." Earbuds told him the name of the club. "Big Rex will be there."

31

A week later, Leaphorn met Bernie and Chee at their house for a Sunday lunch. He came without Louisa because she had gone to California with Lin to help plan for prenatal care and the future, with or without Kory. He was still hospitalized but would face charges most likely including kidnapping and attempted murder once he was released. Leaphorn wanted the man to be punished for what he had done to Louisa, but also hoped for her sake that Kory's cancer and mental illness would mitigate his sentence.

The spring wind was calm that afternoon, the day warm enough to be outside. They sat on the deck and watched the San Juan River flow past, high with runoff from mountain snow. Every time he visited their place, Leaphorn noticed the improvements Chee had made. Being a husband seemed to have improved his handyman skills. Or maybe Bernie's clan brother Bigman helped. Whatever the case, the change in their little house was for the better.

"I like what you've done here." Leaphorn indicated the new deck railing with a jut of his chin.

"Thanks. It was nice to get a little pay hike when I got the promotion. Bernie did the staining." Chee stood. "I'm making coffee for us."

Chee went inside, and Leaphorn turned to Bernie. "I thought Darleen had all the skill with paintbrushes."

She chuckled. "Not much skill involved in painting a railing. It felt good to do a job like that, but I don't have any of Sister's talent."

"How's Darleen doing these days?"

Bernie sighed. "Better now. She and I and Chee and Slim worked out a plan that gives my sister more time to focus on school and getting her life back."

"Tell me about that."

"Well, Darleen's cry for help and Mrs. Darkwater's surgery made me realize that I needed to step up. Mrs. D has been our angel, but we need a better solution. So, it's in the works."

Bernie stopped, and Leaphorn noticed her fidgeting. The topic made her uncomfortable, but it was important. He pushed.

"What's the plan?"

"Well, one of my sister's nursing instructors also works part-time as an aide for elderly people. She lives fairly close to Mama and has time four afternoons a week to come to help. And, best of all, Mama likes her. Chee and I are paying for most of her hours, but Slim is helping too."

"Slim. That's Darleen's boyfriend?"

"Fiancé." Bernie smiled. "That's another big change. They told us they plan to get married."

And, Leaphorn thought, another reason Bernie had accepted more responsibility.

They listened to the soothing rush of water, and then Chee came back with fragrant mugs of coffee.

Bernie took a sip. "Mama will be spending the weekends with me and Chee, or mostly with Chee if I have to work."

Leaphorn nodded. "Good thing that old taboo against mothers-in-law having contact with their daughter's husband is mostly gone now."

Bernie shifted in her seat. "Mama's house. That's the other issue—we want Mama to come and live with us full time. She's resisting, but now that Roper Black is on staff, I might have a more regular schedule."

Leaphorn nodded. "Getting back to your mother. You'd have to make some changes here if she moved in. Add on a bedroom, for starters."

Chee nodded. "That. Or find a bigger house. But I love this place." He looked out toward the river. "Tell us about that case you asked for my help on. You know, the photo of the couple at Elephant Feet."

"A happy ending. The woman found some relatives who are willing to accept her as part of their lives. To take in a lost bird." Leaphorn put his mug down. "My client met someone from the family that had woven the blanket in her photo. Thanks for your help in tracking down the photographer. That let me tie up some loose threads."

"Speaking of weaving, what ever happened with Beth Bowlegs?" Bernie asked. "How sad that her grandmother's gift led to such a tragedy."

"From what I hear, the prosecutors may go easy on Bethany Bowlegs because most of the money she'd taken from the school fund was in the gym bag. But she will have to face charges for embezzlement and the way she extorted Morgan to buy his silence. Those are felonies."

Bernie nodded. "Complicated and sad. And Morgan will face some consequences, too."

"Yeah. After the courts deal with her, Bethany has offered to do some fundraising concerts with the Hop Toads to raise money for music programs and special education. She met someone on the bus to Gallup who is a fan and offered to organize a show in Flagstaff."

"The Hop Toads? I thought that was Rexworth's band." Chee rubbed his chin. "Is that guy out on bail for what happened to Cecil?"

Leaphorn nodded. "We're waiting to see what the DA or the US attorney general have to say about all that. Cecil told me he was happy to be alive and didn't want to think about any of that stuff, but it's not up to him."

"If you talk to him again," Bernie said, "tell him he's not a suspect in the school explosion. That should make him happy, too. Agent Johnson said a poorly installed gas line caused the blast, but they don't know where the spark came from to set it off."

Leaphorn remembered Cecil Bowlegs mentioning that he'd lit a cigarette before he made the call that set things in motion.

"The investigation found that damage was compounded by other flaws in the construction. The school's insurance company is fighting the claim, but the bottom line is that most of the cost for rebuilding something better will be covered."

"I'll tell Cecil. He has a new job at the hospital that pays enough so

Beth can focus on singing and teaching once she's a free woman again. Cecil said he'd called one of those phone numbers from a safe gambling commercial on TV. He's trying to stop."

Chee shook his head. "I hope that works out. Gambling addictions are tough."

Leaphorn said, "Have you heard when Principal Morgan's trial will be?"

"No, there's a plea deal in the works, because Olivia's death was an accident."

Bernie and Chee had both noticed that Leaphorn seemed somehow changed, more thoughtful, perhaps. They asked about it.

"That experience with Kory, almost losing Louisa, well, it gave me a lot to think about. When Largo and I were out there looking for them, acting like two patrol cops, Largo said, 'We're too old for this stuff, Joe. It could kill us.'" Leaphorn straightened in the chair. "I think he's right."

"What?" Bernie couldn't hide her surprise. "I don't think of you as old."

"Mature, maybe. And grumpy sometimes, but we're all used to that." Chee said it with a smile. "We need you around here."

Leaphorn watched the river for a moment longer, noticing the emerging green along the banks prompted by the warmer days of late April and the moisture winter had left. "I'm not planning on checking out any time soon, but I know the road I've been on is longer than what lies ahead for me. If I'm going to make a change, there's no time to waste. The detective work that Cecil Bowlegs needed was hard on me, physically and mentally. I'm ready to do something different, take some time off and spend it with Louisa."

Chee shook his head. "That's sounds fine, but you're the guy who told me, once a cop, always a cop."

"That's right. Always a cop in spirit, but what if the body isn't willing? You should have seen Largo and me after he pushed my truck off the tracks and we jumped out to make sure Louisa was safe. We were huffing and puffing like . . . like senior citizens. But we got it done. We finally walked in beauty."

"What comes next?" Bernie asked. "I bet you've got something in mind."

Leaphorn didn't respond right away. Finally he said, "Well, I had a call from some people who are making a movie out here that features Navajo cops as the heroes. They're looking for a guy with law enforcement experience, preferably a former Navajo police officer, who can be a consultant, you know, make sure they get the cop stuff right. I told them I was just the man for the job."

ACKNOWLEDGMENTS

First of all, a big thank-you to all the readers, librarians, and booksellers who have helped me keep the beloved Leaphorn, Chee, and Manuelito series alive. I have special gratitude to those fans of Bernadette Manuelito who share my satisfaction in seeing a woman law enforcement officer working side by side with the classic male characters Tony Hillerman created more than fifty years ago. It continues to be my honor and pleasure to write the series my father began, now twenty-eight volumes deep and still attracting new fans.

Although I usually set my stories in real places, the community of Eagle Roost and its school are made up. I also used my license as a novelist to move and redesigned Gallup's commercial bus station and to breathe fresh life into the historic Red Lake Trading Post. And, yes, I understand that most people with mental illness aren't violent and suicidal, and I know that cancer isn't necessarily a death sentence.

While the storyline in this book is fiction, some of the incidents and places I mention are real.

The idea for *Lost Birds*, my ninth book about these characters, was born from the possibility that the US Supreme Court might overturn the Indian Child Welfare Act (ICWA). In its decision in June 2023, the court let the law stand, to the relief of Indigenous communities throughout the United States.

Congress designed the law to protect Indian children against the possible removal from their tribal communities. Before the ICWA, up to a third of Native children in need of adoption or foster care were placed in non-Native homes or sent to boarding schools. One of the goals of these placements was to ensure that the children assimilated into main-stream culture. Congress created the ICWA and passed it with little opposition in 1978 in response to the tribes protesting the removal of these children. They argued strongly that the practice erased the child's tribal heritage. The ICWA sets standards and requirements designed to keep Indian children with their extended tribal families.

When the US Supreme Court announced its 7–2 decision upholding the decades-old law, Native American nations, including the Navajo, celebrated the reaffirmation of their sovereignty against threats from state governments.

Another true element in this book is the plague of stray dogs on Navajo land and in towns that border the Navajo Nation's boundaries. By some estimates the reservation, about the size of West Virginia, has more than 250,000 stray dogs. Dog bites and injuries to people, sheep, and other livestock are an ongoing problem. According to the Navajo Nation Animal Control, each year there are roughly 3,000 cases of dog attacks which required the person to be treated at a clinic or hospital. The reservation has few veterinarians and only four animal shelters to deal with this abundance of loose dogs. Things are looking up, however, with a growing number of mobile clinics to make spaying and neutering as well as vaccinations easier for rural residents in remote places.

Navajo storm pattern rugs are real, too, a beautiful style often found on the western side of the reservation. As you'd expect from the name, the designs are partly inspired by rainstorms. The classic Storm Pattern weaving always contains a central house, or hogan, which is connected to the four sacred mountains with lightning bolts. Highly stylized water insects at the top and bottom of the tapestry provide protection to the home.

Travelers encounter the geologic formation known as Elephant Feet on drive along Arizona highway 160, about a mile and half north of the Red Lake Trading Post. The buttes warrant a stop and a photograph.

Speaking of trading, reader Patrick Dee traded a generous donation to Albuquerque's Tenderlove Community Center for the opportunity to see the name of his wife, Debi Jo Dee, in this book. Thanks for your generosity.

I have many, many people to thank for their help with this novel. Thanks to Dave Furman for his advice on railroad safety and to Sherri Saint and David Greenberg for help with proper law enforcement procedures. Greenberg, and his wife Gail Greenberg, graciously read an early draft of this book and helped me fix what ailed it. I also deeply appreciated the advice of my other fine beta readers: Lucy Moore, Wendy Graham, Benita Budd and certainly Dave Tedlock. Dave's extended encouragement, sharp brain, and intuitive appreciation of what makes a good mystery helped me to finish this novel and move to the next book.

These books would not exist without the help of my wonderful team at HarperCollins Publishers: executive editor Sarah Stein, her assistant David Howe, freelance copyeditor Miranda Ottewell, Senior Director of Publicity Rachel Elinsky, Associate Director of Marketing Tom Hopke, Editorial Production Manager Nikki Baldauf, and the other editors, designers, and creative talent at HarperCollins.

I am deeply grateful to attorney Deborah Peacock for all her help on contract that made *Lost Birds* possible and to Andrew Werling of the Peacock Law Firm for his thoughtful and important assistance with manuscript preparation.

Thanks to my friend Margaret Coel for encouraging me to continue this wonderful series. Coel's book *The Lost Bird*, focuses on the issue of Arapahoe children adopted out of their tribal communities. I highly recommend her well-crafted mysteries.

And last, but not least, thanks to my father, Tony Hillerman for creating the character of Joe Leaphorn, the detective who runs the show here, in his first novel, *The Blessing Way*. It was great to write a book that put Leaphorn front and center again.

GLOSSARY

amásání	paternal grandmother
ahéhéé	thank you
adláanii	drunkard
awéé'	child (gender-neutral)
bidziil	strong one
bilagáana	white person
dibé	sheep
Diné	the People (the Navajo word for the Navajo people)
diyogí	rug
Hajíínéí	Navajo origin story
hatááłii	medicine man, healer
ho'aahidziniih	he/she stays with me
Kinłitsosinil	Church Rock, New Mexico, a Navajo community five miles east of Gallup on historic Route 66
né'éshjaa'	owl
shideezhí	younger sister
shima	mother
shimásání	maternal grandmother
t'aachil	April
T'iis Nazbas	Teec Nos Pos ("Circle of Cottonwood Trees"), a settlement about thirty miles northwest of Shiprock, New Mexico
yá'át'ééh	hello

ABOUT THE AUTHOR

ANNE HILLERMAN began her career as a journalist and writer of non-fiction books. This is her ninth novel featuring Bernadette Manuelito and the twenty-sixth in the Leaphorn, Chee & Manuelito series begun by her late father, Tony Hillerman. She lives in Santa Fe, New Mexico, and Tucson, Arizona.